ONCE UPON A NIGHTMARE

Once Upon
A Nightmare

A NOVEL

BY

NAT GOODALE

Bowditch Press

Editors: Rosemary Ahern, Deke Castleman and Jen Blood.

Cover design: Damonza.com

Publisher: Bowditch Press
Seven Hundred Acre Island
Lincolnville, Maine 04849
USA
Printed in the USA
First Edition: 2014
ISBN 978–0–9898406–1–3
Fiction Crime Thriller

To my mother, who has always encouraged me to write.

*"Now let me dare to open wide
the gate past which men's steps have ever
flinching trod."*

— *Goethe*

PART I

CHAPTER 1

Miami Herald, February 26, 1989

President George Bush designates William Bennett as the Director of National Drug Policy. Mr. Bennett says he will quit smoking today.

Miami Herald, March 26, 1989

The Bureau of Alcohol, Tobacco and Firearms says the twelve-day-old ban on imported semi-automatic assault rifles is being widened.

COMMUTER FLIGHT 1632 was going to cost him his life. The whimpering woman several rows to the rear seemed to agree. The Beech 99, a twin-engine prop job bound for Rockland, Maine, had been in the dark clouds since leaving Boston. The mid-afternoon light was a dusky gloom.

They left late, rising into the low overcast and blowing snow. A March low-pressure system was disrupting the entire eastern seaboard, bringing turbulence and reduced visibility. Airports below minimums were closing one after the other.

The turbulence had gone from moderate to severe as they made their descent toward the Rockland airport. Each time the commuter plane took a lurch, Jesse's seatbelt brought a cutting pain.

He felt little, helpless, and close to panic. Eyes closed, he was a child, gleefully wading into the surf, mesmerized by the battering of the curling foam, fascinated by the pull of the receding water. Then the bigger wave slammed into him, sending him rolling and tumbling underwater, end over end. The weight of the water held him against the bottom, his head and back scraping sand. No control. No air ever again. Full of feelings of the end. It was the same now.

The plane rocked back and forth. They hit an air pocket and lost several hundred feet. A man behind Jesse let out a bellow, then went into a mumbling prayer.

Jesse opened his eyes. He focused on the cockpit. In the intimate setting of the Beech 99, there was no divider between pilots and passengers. As was his usual custom, Jesse had chosen the front-row seat, so he could admire the work of fellow pilots.

There wasn't much to admire on this flight. The crew had trouble holding headings and maintaining altitude from the start. The pilot and copilot were tired and sloppy and they were not flying well. They were chasing the airplane, and it was running away with them.

The copilot attempted twice to clip the Rockland approach plate in front of the pilot before finally succeeding. At least they wouldn't be distracted by sights out the windshield, a blank gray screen.

The plane descended slowly through the rough air. It yawed violently to starboard. Something fell to the floor with a thud. The engine sounds slewed asymmetrically.

Jesse had flown into Rockland enough times in bad weather to know the drill. They'd fly down to 1,300 feet, maintaining a certain heading that would intercept the final-approach course, the Localizer 3. Once established on the approach, they'd maintain 1,300 feet until crossing the Spruce Head Non-Directional Beacon. After the needle swung from front to back, they'd descend to the minimum altitude of 440 feet. The pilots would keep the localizer needle centered as they came down to the runway. The plane would break out of the overcast before reaching 440 feet and land uneventfully.

Jesse knew they were receiving radar vectors from Brunswick control, so he had no idea what heading they should be on. But whatever it was, it wasn't being consistently held.

The rules of the instrument approach are based on honesty and self-preservation. Once established on the final-approach course and aligned with the runway, you need to keep the needle close to centered. If you get too far afield, your correction time is limited and that doesn't account for the trees and other obstructions swaying in the gusty north winds. So you never *ever* go lower than the minimum descent altitude. At and above it, you have a small margin for error.

The pilot throttled back and said something to the controller. He started a shallow left turn. The copilot watched the instruments and was ready to call out the appropriate altitudes.

The plane descended out of 2,000 feet.

Jesse placed them south of Rockland, out over the ocean.

The pilot concentrated on the artificial horizon indicator, which is driven by gyros and not subject to the violent tossing and turnings of inclement weather. His hand on the control wheel was in constant motion, countering the effects of the wind. He pulled back on the wheel as the plane reached 1,300 feet and kept turning to a course of 079 degrees.

Jesse leaned full forward in his seat, straining on his seatbelt. His life was in the hands of these two tired pilots, who now looked too young to be flying an airplane.

Jesse checked the panel to be sure everything was set for the approach. The Non-Directional Beacon frequency was set. Their speed was fine. The pilots had dialed in the Rockland Unicom frequency, but the localizer was still set at the Navy Brunswick frequency of 115.2. The copilot also looked, then reached and set 110.7 into the number-one Nav. Jesse knew then that these guys were far behind the plane.

The pilot's head was frozen straight ahead, probably fixated on the one instrument that gave the most information, the artificial horizon. The plane jerked to the right. They were at 1,200 feet and not yet established on course. The pilot abruptly pulled up and gained altitude. His heading was off by twenty degrees.

The localizer needle came alive and the pilot slowly turned left to 030 degrees. He anticipated the strong left quartering headwind and compensated to the left, but too soon. The needle wasn't centering. He came right ten degrees and waited for the needle to react. The copilot was also fixated on the localizer needle. The NDB needle swung aft and went unnoticed.

As the localizer needle began to react, the pilot noticed the NDB. He brought back the throttles and called for the copilot to lower the gear and the flaps. The grinding sounds of flaps and the clunk of lowered gear were all but lost in the thrashing.

The localizer needle swung through center and headed way left. They were too high. The plane slowed and started to descend too rapidly. The pilot turned left, but the needle didn't react.

At 500 feet, the copilot looked longingly out the

windshield for the airport. He found only thick cloud and snow.

The altimeter spun through 440 feet. The localizer needle was still way off. They were right of course and below their minimum descent altitude. The copilot noticed the altitude, reached out with a bouncing arm to tap the instrument with his finger. He looked at the pilot, who nodded and slowed the descent but still went lower.

Jesse knew the approach was irretrievable. The premonitions were finally coming true.

Without regard for pilot etiquette or convention, he leaned against his seatbelt and shouted, "Missed approach! Divert to Bangor! Missed approach! Divert to Bangor!"

It was an eerie moment, a pause in time. But then the pilot firewalled the throttles and pulled back on the yoke. The plane wallowed, then rose. Once a positive rate of climb was established, he called for flaps and gear up.

The pilots changed to the Bangor frequencies and got out the approach plate. Jesse slumped back in his seat. He could feel the pain where the seatbelt had been digging into his waist.

With responsibility lifted and the trance broken, the pilots concentrated well and landed in Bangor without incident. The plane taxied up to the ramp and the pilots shut down the engines. In the resulting silence, everyone sat still, feeling the wind buffet the small plane. Then a spontaneous combustion of applause and nervous voices filled the fuselage.

The copilot slowly got out of his seat and, after smiling weakly at Jesse, opened the air stair door. Passengers, filled with manic chatter, filed past Jesse.

Alone in the plane now, the crew and Jesse looked uneasily at one another. Jesse said, "Nice landing."

There was an awkward moment.

The pilot said, "Thanks."

Jesse gathered his coat, lifted his briefcase and descended the stairs to hard ground. He felt in his pocket for his pack of Drum tobacco.

CHAPTER 2

THE WIND CAUGHT his overcoat and whipped it open. Jesse put his head down and with his free hand pulled the coat back together, then hunched his way to the terminal.

The Downeast Airlines counter churned with a cluster of discharging energy. A businessman was yelling at the woman behind the desk about loss of life and legal action. The others surrounded the scene, as if expecting violence.

Jesse approached and the crowd parted to let him through. The businessman looked put out, but seemed reluctant to get into it with him.

Jesse set his briefcase on the floor and leaned both arms on the counter. "I imagine you have a vehicle to get us to Rockland."

The Downeast agent visibly relaxed at the mild approach and said that a van would be available within the half hour to take them all to their final destination.

She added, "If any of you would like to make a call, you're welcome to use this phone. We apologize for any inconvenience, but the safety of the passengers is our main concern."

Jesse smiled, leaving the businessman deflated. A few passengers lined up to use the phone. The others dispersed to the bathrooms or to get baggage appearing at the carousel. Jesse slumped down in a red molded-plastic chair. He took the packet of Drum tobacco from the left pocket of his tweed jacket, sat back, and rolled a smoke. He lit the cigarette, careful not to let an ember burn a hole in his silk shirt. Drum was cheaper to buy, but more expensive to smoke. He leaned forward and brought the standing ashtray in closer.

He looked around. Bangor International was in the clutches of a traveler's nightmare—diverted or canceled flights, irate passengers, and relief hopelessly out of reach. The waiting area sported what appeared to be the aftermath of a wild party. Strewn amongst the worn and weary travelers were discarded cups and soda bottles, trash cans overflowing with rubbish, ashtrays smeared with cigarette butts—some still smoldering.

To his left, passengers streamed out of a far gate looking bewildered, as if they'd landed in a foreign country. Out the window he saw an Air France 747, probably Paris to New York, diverted to Bangor waiting for the weather to clear or the aircraft in holding patterns over JFK to land.

Speakers blared a call for the Rockland passengers. Jesse strolled out the automatic doors and under the concrete overhang. The rest of the group huddled together in a bunch, looking down the line of vans idling at the curb.

An old man with weathered face and hands came around the middle van. He wore matching khaki trousers and shirt and a red and black checkered hunting jacket. His khaki cap cocked at a dangerous angle. He seemed impervious to the wind and cold.

"Where's your destination at? If you're headed to Rockland, you best be getting on now." A toothpick bobbed up and down in the corner of his mouth. He opened the rear doors and stuffed baggage into the cargo area.

Jesse ducked and snaked his way to the back bench seat and settled with his briefcase on his lap. A smartly dressed dark-skinned Latin man in an elegant steel-gray overcoat sat beside him.

The angry businessman and two women took the next seat forward. A broad- shouldered, tall young man in a Bath Iron Works jacket, jeans and work boots rode up front. He cradled a blue gym bag on his lap.

The driver climbed in and turned rearward. "She may not look like much, but the heater will blast you folks back to Miami." He said it with sadistic relish, catching the eye of the man beside Jesse. "The going's slow, but you ain't gonna get there no sooner than me, so sit tight and enjoy the snow." He turned forward, clucked, put the column-mounted transmission in drive and pulled out, just nicking the van parked ahead. That amused him some more, and he clucked again.

The businessman broke the silence. He turned toward Jesse. His big round balding head shook as he seethed, jiggling his second chin, which flowed over the mismatched fabrics of his cheap patterned suit and stained windbreaker. "Can you believe this? They almost kill us on the plane, and then they stick us in this piece-of-shit van." The poor man was working the camaraderie angle. He looked around for approval, but got none.

Undeterred, he turned to Jesse and said, "Hey, fella, you seem to know something. Did we almost crash in Rockland or what? How about we stick Downeast with a fat class-action lawsuit? It's my specialty. They'd settle out of court and we'd all have a bunch of cash. What do you say?"

Jesse had debated bringing the incident to the attention of Downeast Airline's management. But he'd come to the conclusion that the pilots had learned their lesson. They'd scared themselves almost to death.

Jesse thought about his reply, knowing he'd get more satisfaction stuffing tennis balls down this guy's throat. He said civilly, "It sure was bumpy, but when we reached minimums, the pilot did a go-around and we came up to Bangor. Perhaps they should never have attempted the approach, but sometimes it's worth a try. They were probably just trying to accommodate our desire to land in Rockland."

Mr. Legal Action turned and looked unsure about the comment, perhaps wondering if he'd just been insulted.

Traveling out of Bangor on Route lA to Hampden, the roads were covered with a thin layer of snow and the snowplows were out. Being caught behind one, as they were now, would mean very slow going. Most of the coastal route to Rockland was two lane, with few places to pass. The driver seemed content to travel at thirty miles an hour.

The warmth and rocking of the van was womblike.

The older woman turned in her seat and addressed Jesse. "Young man, I want to thank you and I don't know why. I have a feeling you were instrumental in our salvation. I was very frightened, but I don't really know if we were in any danger. I don't know what you said to the pilots, but whatever it was, thank you." She smiled.

Her words were well-enunciated and spoken with a slight accent that sounded almost British. Her features were refined. She had high cheekbones and a Roman nose, sat ramrod straight, and exuded fine breeding and extensive financial backing.

Jesse didn't know how to respond, so he said, "You're welcome."

She turned back and whispered something to her daughter.

The flight already seemed so long ago. There'd been times flying when he'd scared himself. The urge to give into panic and let events take their course was always the ultimate danger. The line was thin and easily crossed.

A hand touched his right sleeve, soft as a caress. Jesse turned to face the Latino gentleman. He was full of grace and composure and spoke softly. "Unlike the woman there, I know what to thank you for. I did not hear your spoken words, but I recognized your command and their reaction to it. As you shouted at them, I was glancing out the window of the airplane. I thought then I saw the tops of trees, but now, upon reflection, I am certain of it. I am in your debt, for I believe you caused the pilots to take a safe path. I believe you saved all our lives."

In the dim light, Jesse sensed he was being assessed and the man's words made him uncomfortable.

Jesse said, "I don't know how close we were to the ground, but we were closer than we should have been. I suggested they come to Bangor. They did the rest."

The man, with a dismissive wave of his hand, said, "It was far more than that, but you may have your way. I would like to introduce myself. I am Sheldrick

Santee. I am Cuban by birth, American by naturalization and Floridian as I live in Miami. I am in the import-export business and have come to Maine to assess opportunities."

Jesse turned awkwardly and offered his hand. They shook. "My name is Jesse Langdon."

Mr. Santee waited in vain for more information, and when given none, asked, "You are a pilot? Do you have a plane? You see, I need to see your state and I have yet to arrange for one. Perhaps I could hire you to show me around?"

The man's perceptive, Jesse thought. The only thing he was good at was flying, where he was in true control of his fate. The discipline and focus required to fly safely in the clouds relaxed him and took him away from his life, such as it was, on the ground. So he belonged to the Civil Air Patrol and flew missions in search of lost hunters. He also flew an occasional mercy flight, taking a terminal patient to Boston for treatment. Mostly, though, he just flew.

Jesse said, "Yes, I'm a pilot and I do have a small airplane, but I imagine you'd like something larger and more comfortable. Anyway, I don't have a commercial rating and I'm not allowed to charge for flights."

"There are always other avenues. I am very adaptable, Mr. Langdon, and I am sure your plane would suit me. Do you have the time?"

Jesse felt smaller and younger than Mr. Santee,

though they appeared to be the same age—late thirties. He also felt a subtle pressure he didn't understand. "I'm not sure. If you could give me your card and a local phone number, I'll think on it and get back to you tomorrow."

"I am afraid I am always difficult to locate," Mr. Santee replied. "It would be more convenient for us both if I could call you tomorrow."

Jesse did a quick calculation and figured there was no harm in giving his phone number. Mr. Santee repeated it and turned away.

When the van finally pulled up to the small passenger terminal in Rockland, it was much colder, but the snow had stopped.

Jesse walked toward his car through the white neon light. Mr. Santee called after him. "We will speak tomorrow."

Jesse drove up coastal Route 1 to Belfast.

CHAPTER 3

J ESSE LAUNCHED OUT of bed the next morning. The coffee grinder-percolator was on a timer set for seven, and when it went off, it was alarming.

He was sleeping at his office. In the kitchenette, he climbed on the drain board with his feet in the sink and took his daily sponge bath.

His marriage to Emma had deteriorated gradually. There were money troubles. He had it and she didn't. They were comfortable by any standard, but far from bringing peace of mind, it had embedded tension and bitterness into their relationship. When her sister's husband went missing in the fall and Jesse had sympathized with his brother-in-law and then done nothing to find him, it was her final straw. He'd been living in the small corner office above Key Bank ever since.

Jesse poured strong black coffee and called home. Emma answered in her singsong voice, which quickly deadened when she realized who it was. She asked if he could come this morning to babysit while she played tennis. Yes.

The Saab kicked right over and he smiled. Even with 135,000 miles, the car felt and handled as solidly as new. In his drinking days, he'd never had the opportunity to test the longevity of Swedish engineering. His previous Saabs had all been driven off the road, into trees or telephone poles or ditches, before he could put 20,000 miles on them.

The plows had cleared the snow and salted the roads, but drivers were exercising too much caution. There was little occasion to pass and Jesse tried to be content with the slow pace, but he became more and more annoyed. He was racing inside and the world was conspiring to get in his way. By the time he got to his house on the hill, he was frazzled.

Ashley was six, Ike four. They rushed Jesse's legs and held on tight. Emma spoke to him as he patted his children's heads.

"I can pick them up at your office this afternoon after tennis and my therapy session. You'll have to take them to lunch. The food in the fridge is for a small gathering here this evening."

All four of them wanted Emma to be on her way. She left after nailing down the retrieval time.

"Okay, little ones, let's settle on the sofa and I'll read you some more of *The Old Man and The Sea*."

With a small head tucked under each arm, it was

hard to turn the pages, but they laughed a lot. He read them thirty pages, the old man being towed around the Caribbean.

Ike asked, "How big is the fish?" He was content to know it wasn't as big as the house.

Jesse put the book on the coffee table. "So, how about McDonald's for lunch?"

The children looked at each other. Ashley said, "Mummy doesn't like us to eat there."

"Well, she's not the one taking you to lunch. You want it or not?"

"Yeah!"

"Let's go."

He buckled them into the car seats left by Emma and they headed down the hill into town.

The kids wanted to do the drive-through and eat in the car. That, too, was a forbidden activity. Jesse enjoyed the banter and was shocked again at how quickly his children were growing up.

The three of them went through the storm door of the co-op and into the bustling Birkenstock crowd. Marie, their favorite clerk, looked up from ringing in a customer's organic okra, kefir, almonds, brown rice and granola. Jesse laid three quarters on the counter. They exchanged smiles.

"A large coffee, Jesse?"

He nodded.

She smiled at the children. "Make sure your father buys you a treat."

Shaggy clean people in peasant clothes clogged the narrow wood-floored aisles, stuffing hand baskets with natural products. They dipped and poured and filled their containers from canisters of raisins and dates, cauldrons of honey and maple syrup, bins of flour and cornmeal. They were living in right relation.

The coffeepots were in the nook next to tubs of hot soup, rolls of French bread and sweet pastries. From today's selection—French Roast, Amaretto, Chocolate Raspberry and assorted decafs —only one caught his eye. He poured an ink-black flow of Colombian Supreme into his paper cup. He stopped and paid Marie for the two yogurt push-ups that Ashley and Ike were unwrapping.

They crossed the street into a different world. The Bi-Right Market was a long rectangle of near-empty shelves of canned beans, canned peaches and potato chips. The thick smell of fish going bad assaulted him as they came through the heavy door. The store was as empty as the shelves, except for the red-faced owner behind the cash register and a heavily bearded companion sitting on top of a stack of newspapers on the window sill. They both looked worn down.

This was the retired Skidder crowd. Years of yarding out pulp logs and selling them at the mill had given way to afternoons of small talk about family and forests and evenings full of beer and coffee brandy.

Bernie's red face smiled up at Jesse. A man who smoked real Camels couldn't be all bad, even if he held a cup of coffee from that hippie store across the way.

Jesse felt more at home here, too. "Hey, Bernie, how about a pack of Camel regulars?"

Bernie slowly reached to the sparse rack of cigarettes behind him.

"Here you are, Jesse. Now that's a real smoke. You gonna be running for mayor? You'd get the votes."

"Probably not this time around, Bernie, but you never know."

"Well, anyway, good to see ya in here. Come again soon."

Jesse placed a five-dollar bill on the counter. Bernie took a wad of bills from his work-pant pocket and peeled off two dollars. From another pocket he counted eighty cents. He bunched the change and smokes and handed the roll to Jesse, saying, "Thank you right kindly, mister man."

"Always a pleasure, Bernie," Jesse replied, meaning it. He nodded at the man on the papers and they left the store, letting the quiet voices of the two resume whatever conversation had been interrupted.

Jesse hummed a country tune as they walked back up the street, hand in hand, to his office. He waved to a man in an old Ford pickup stopped at the only light in the county. The girl from the office supply store was coming out of the post office and they said hello. In this world, people were courteous, honest and empathetic. Jesse was conscious of walking across the veneer of life, the delicately refined and polished layer that covered what was. Like wandering the lush lawns of the cemetery beside the high school in the center of town with Ashley and Ike on their 'special days,' picking flowers off the graves.

He unlocked the stairway door and stamped his feet on the worn carpet. The approach to his sanctuary was seedy. The stair's carpet was worn and dirty, the hall lighting on the second floor dull and the atmosphere close and dank.

Jesse unlocked his office, settled the kids on the sofa, and got them paper towels to catch what was left of their frozen yogurt. They were in the middle of their second game of Old Maid when Emma came through the door.

She sniffed and made a face. "Smells like cigarettes. You shouldn't smoke around the children."

Ike came to the defense. "Papa wasn't smoking. He was playing with us."

"Well, it's time to go home."

The children's protestations were interrupted by the phone. Emma, by the desk, picked up the receiver. In her kewpie-doll phone voice, she said, "Hello." She listened for a moment then said, "Yes, he's right here."

She handed the phone to Jesse and said in a low voice, "He sounds scary."

Jesse took the receiver, said yes, and listened.

"Mr. Langdon, I understand you own an amphibious aircraft, a Lake. It would be perfect for my needs."

Emma was herding the kids out the door. They turned and waved goodbye. He waved back.

"I would like to pay you two-hundred dollars an hour to fly me over the state. I will be here for a week and I expect it will take over ten hours to do your countryside justice. I would suggest I pay in cash. We therefore eliminate any silly hindrances regarding your lack of a commercial rating. The weather will begin to cooperate tomorrow. I would like to be off first thing in the morning. Are you interested in my proposition?"

Jesse remembered Mr. Santee, and the self-assuredness and his commanding way of speaking. And all his weeks were free. "Yes, Mr. Santee. I had a chance to review my schedule. I'll need to rearrange some things, but I'd very much like to fly you around. Your terms are generous. We could meet at the airport tomorrow morning. Say around ten a.m.?"

Jesse listened, then said, "Yes, seven-thirty will be fine."

The bright afternoon light enveloped the large room, divided in half by the futon that faced the fireplace. The fireplace didn't work, but the sight of it made him think of old and proper sitting rooms, quiet, serious, contemplative and correct. His had been a patrician upbringing and the office reflected this. Attorney bookcases along the left wall held his books. A green leather chair faced the sofa on the other side.

His work area was to the right. Formica tables ran in a U shape along the walls. Piles of folders sat neatly on the middle desk. A desktop computer and two printers covered in plastic dominated the right table. The table on the left was empty.

When asked what he did, Jesse often replied that he was in the mail-management business. It seemed he spent his life opening his mail, addressing each concern and filing it away.

He wished he had a profession where he was paid for his contribution, respected for his expertise and praised for his performance. He found himself envious of others who'd worked their way up, while seeing the irony of their envy toward his footloose lifestyle.

Jesse sat down at his desk and rolled a smoke. Why had he started smoking again? Was he getting too pure and needed to be smudged? It was his dance with the devil. And why was he rolling his own when he had a new pack of Camels?

He felt useless. If he disappeared, life in Belfast would go on without him. The responsibilities would handle themselves. He glanced at the photograph of his vanished brother-in-law. The picture was taken at the beginning of the lobstering season, when Jesse was helping him set traps. Now he was gone without a trace and only the family suspected dark deeds. Without evidence, the police had brushed the whole thing off. "Happens every day. Husband runs off and gets a new life." Jesse tended to believe them.

The fact that Seefer had been away during the summer for mysterious intervals and was flush with cash seemed of no interest to the cops. Yes, he had troubles at home. What do you do with a domineering wife? Keep her? Or run away to something better?

Emma blamed Jesse for not being more involved, more forceful, more helpful. But what the hell was he supposed to do, not knowing anything about anything? Only the slightest threads of a spider-silk trail were left behind. There was idle talk, but nothing worth following up. Who would talk to him, anyway?

He ate at the diner across the street. The counterman wrote out his order without being told. Jesse always had a cheeseburger deluxe with a raw onion slice, fries and a nonalcoholic beer. He read the local paper while he ate. By the time he was back in the office, he'd forgotten all about dinner.

He sat on the sofa and rolled a smoke, then lay down and put his feet up. He lit the cigarette and contemplated the smoke curling up from the lit end, the light blue of a dawn sky. It rose with an anxious sense of purpose, straight, then curled into swirls and geometric patterns. He took a drag and blew a small smoke ring toward the ceiling. The smoke was lifeless gray. Somewhere inside him a transformation had taken place.

He was drifting away, flowing into the darkness, swirling in the dull gray smoke. He thought uneasily about Mr. Santee, the fading love for Emma and his sweetness for Ashley and Ike.

He stubbed out the butt in the ashtray and curled into a fetal position. He closed his eyes. Soon he dozed, semiconscious.

He is sitting in an aluminum skiff, drifting in the flat calm bay. He can see where he wants to be. It's just over there. The shore. He doesn't have the energy to start the outboard motor. He has to work up to a hard pull.

There is a loud bang. He sees a small rivet fly up from the bilge, out over the gunwale and into the water. Concentric rings spread from where the rivet pierces the water.

He looks down and sees a small waterspout between his feet. His boots are getting wet. He doesn't move, as if he can't. His socks are getting wet. The bay is coming up to get him.

The water rises slowly in the bottom of the boat. It creeps up the sides of his boots until it finally reaches the tops. The bilge is now full, and the water is consuming his legs, inch by inch.

He doesn't move his foot to cover the leak. He

doesn't stand or make any attempt to bail the skiff. He looks to the shore.

The water is now enveloping his calves. His jeans stick to his skin. The water is so cold it's numbing.

The skiff is getting heavier and sinking faster. A seatbelt is tight around him. His ass is wet now. He sits in the rising water.

He reaches out and touches the hard gray aluminum gunwale. It feels sturdy. As he sinks lower, the horizon is less defined.

He's becoming one with the sea. As he feels the coldness surround his waist, the water reaches the gunwale and flows into the skiff. A life jacket floats just beyond reach. If he releases the seatbelt, he can reach forward and snatch it. He does not.

He and the skiff sink. He takes a breath of fresh salty air, not a deep final breath, but a normal one. The water runs up his back and over his neck. His hair swirls around his face.

Where he once watched the shore, there is now flat calm sea.

He breathes in the cold water as he and the skiff sink to meet the rivet below.

Cold drool on his cheek startled him to consciousness. The wooden wall clock showed eight-thirty. Where had the day gone? He looked at his unopened mail. It could wait. It could wait forever.

CHAPTER 4

Miami Herald, April 2
The U.S. Attorney's office in Miami says it will reduce the number of criminal indictments by turning them over to the Dade County State Attorney's office.

JESSE WAS UP at dawn. In his bathrobe, he poured coffee at the kitchenette window. The weather was promising. The blustery winds had subsided and the skies were clear.

His dream of drowning left him feeling unbalanced and scared. But today had potential. The prospect of flight always aroused him. He could become lost in its intricacies and leave the earth behind.

He rolled a Drum and spun his chair over to the computer. The modem dialed DUAT, the free weather service for licensed pilots. He saved the local weather forecast to the hard drive, printed it out, then sat back and read through the strange groupings of letters that told him the high-pressure system over the Great Lakes was expected to dominate the region for the next several days. Light winds from the northwest, sunny skies and above-normal temperatures. It looked good for Mr. Santee.

He folded the forecast and slid it underneath the sectional chart on his clipboard. He put that next to the booklet of approach plates for the New England states and nestled both into the outside pocket of his flight bag. He added an additional headset. As an afterthought, he threw in three old charts that covered the state. Maybe Santee would like to refer to them.

Bright sunlight spread across the bay and onto the hills surrounding Belfast. The woods were brown and gray. The soft wood looked washed-out and weary. But the snow and ice would melt and the drab colors would give way to the shocking color of green, born new each spring as if never seen before.

The Dunkin Donuts parking lot was full of pickups. The smoker's fog bank hung heavy over the shoulders of the town's blue collars.

Coffee in hand, Jesse drove out to the airport. His individual hangar was at the end of eight, set in a line down the middle of the unused runway. He scanned the airport for traffic before driving down the taxiway. He realized that he hadn't given Santee directions. The man wouldn't need any.

He parked between the hangars, took out his

flight bag and locked the car. He patted his pocket to be sure he had tobacco. He turned the key to the door and stepped over the threshold.

Jesse never flew without some apprehension. He had no fear of the elements, really. Rather, he understood that a human being at the controls is his own worst enemy. Do right and you return safely to earth. Poor judgment was rewarded with disaster.

Jesse smiled at his airplane. The Lake Renegade was the only single-engine amphibious airplane in production. It married the mystery of flight with the magic of water. Being a flying boat, the engine sat on a pylon above and just aft of the cabin. The propeller pushed and the drag created by the nacelle reduced her airspeed. She was slow, but she sat six and had a range of 700 miles.

Moving through the preflight with careful attention and practiced ease, Jesse unlocked the pilot's gull-winged window and threw the electrical master switch. The hydraulic pump clicked on and ran up pressure in the system to the green on the gauge. Fuel at three-quarters in the main tank, full in the wing tanks. He switched off the master and climbed the port wing, checked the engine and hydraulic oil.

Around the left side, he caressed the leading edge of the wing.

The sponson tanks were full. The aileron, rudder and horizontal stabilizer hinges all had their pins and full movement. The landing struts had the proper inflation.

He took a small plastic tube and drained the fuel sumps on each tank, checking for water. None. Finally, he visually confirmed that each tank had the proper amount of fuel.

He unbolted the hangar doors and slid them to the side. Early morning freshness enveloped the plane. After he pulled her out, he slid underneath and unscrewed each hull drain to be sure there was no accumulated water in the bilge. Jesse did this out of habit. The Lake hadn't been in water since the fall, but good habits tended to save lives.

He closed the hangar and climbed into the plane. Getting into a Lake, with its winged windshield and doors, was like climbing into a bathtub. He settled into the seat, placed the flight bag on the rear seat, and checked that the paddle was secure. Two life jackets lay on the seat behind him. They would not, however, be landing in water. There was still too much ice on the lakes.

Jesse left the windshield open and ran through the prestart checklist. Master on, hydraulic pressure in the green, fuel okay. He reached overhead, advanced the mixture to full rich and cracked the throttle a touch. Primer for a count of six, head swiveling, attention to the outside, all clear. Jesse rubbed his hands together, then reached with his left for the key and with his right to the throttle overhead.

He turned the key. The engine kicked the propeller over once, twice; then, with a shudder, she caught and roared to life. The nose of the plane slouched a bit as the force of the propeller pushed against the toe brakes. Jesse retarded the throttle and set the engine at 1,000 rpms. A smooth hum washed over him as he let her warm up.

Jesse reached back into the flight bag, pulled out the charts and the extra headset and placed them on the passenger seat. He looked at his watch—7:20. He let the Lake warm up for five minutes, closed the windshield and taxied out to meet his client.

Santee stood on the edge of the tarmac with two brushed-aluminum cases, one in each hand. Jesse eased the plane up to the terminal building and swung her around to face the runway. He shut her down and got out. Santee remained still and looked with keen interest at the plane and the pilot. He put the cases down.

Jesse strolled up and offered his hand. "Good morning, Mr. Santee."

Santee's grip was firm and dry and he held Jesse's hand too long. Their eyes remained locked. Hoping to break the awkward silence, he gestured toward the plane with his free hand and said, "Well, here she is."

Santee was still looking into Jesse's eyes, still holding his hand.

"She is very beautiful. I have only seen pictures of this type of aircraft. I understand they are marvelous at what they do." Santee finally released Jesse's hand but stood, unmoving.

"Thank you. She really shines in the water."

"Perhaps another day, in the future, you can show me."

Santee moved to the passenger side. Jesse opened the windshield over the copilot's seat, took the two cases from Santee and laid them carefully beside his flight bag on the rear seat.

"Mr. Santee, I'm at your disposal. I imagine you want to see the coast first, so we could go northeast. We call it Downeast up here."

"I will tell you where we are going." He ran his hand along the leading edge of the starboard wing. "And you may call me plainly Santee."

There was nothing plain about the man. Jesse watched him walk slowly around the plane, doing a preflight check of his own. Santee was six feet tall, slender and graceful. He was dressed in Doberman colors: trousers of finely woven black wool that fell with a single sharp crease over polished black boots, black leather jacket with a chocolate mink collar, dark turtleneck and brown cashmere sweater. Supple, brown leather gloves moved the rudder back and forth to its stops.

Santee's attire made Jesse feel decidedly

underdressed in wrinkled bush-pilot, the-plane-doesn't-care jeans and worn plaid shirt, insulated canvas barn coat.

Santee's gaze rose smoothly from the hinges to Jesse's eyes. He said, "I always like to have a feel for what I'm getting into." His face slid into a charming smile that lit up his unblemished smooth brown skin, turning to glitter in an instant. His face had no lines or dents or evidence of the need to shave. His eyes continued to watch, dark and probing.

Jesse smiled and looked away first.

"I am sure you are a very good pilot, Mr. Langdon. Your plane is immaculately maintained. That says a lot about a person and his particular gifts. From that unfortunate commuter flight, I already know enough about you to entrust you at the controls. I am just a cautious man. Care has served me well."

Santee stooped catlike under the port wing, pushed both fuel sump drains and let some aviation gas pool on the pavement. He removed his right glove and touched the gasoline with his forefinger, which he brought to his nose.

After laying his jacket across the back of the rear seat, he climbed into the plane and settled into the copilot's seat. Jesse eased that portion of the hinged windshield over to Santee's outstretched hand, then walked around the nose and got in on his side.

Santee asked, "May I call you Jesse? It seems so much more friendly."

"By all means." Jesse adjusted the seat forward. "Where are we headed?"

In the closeness of the cramped cockpit, Santee explained quietly that he wanted to circle the northern half of the state. Given the winds and the amount of fuel the plane could carry, they should be back slightly after lunchtime, and that would be enough flying for the day. He wanted to fly at 3,000 feet and realized they'd have to climb a bit toward Greenville and beyond, but they could descend again over the plains and the coast of northern Maine. "From the slight smell of tobacco, I assume I can smoke. Where is the ashtray?" He pulled a silver cigarette case from underneath his sweater.

"I use a coffee can." Jesse leaned over to reach the can on the floor behind Santee's seat. "But like the airlines, I'd like you to honor the nonsmoking sign until it has been extinguished." He said it with a laugh to ease his tension.

Jesse busied himself with the restart procedures, thankful to be distracted from the man beside him. He engaged the starter and when the engine fired, he advanced the ceiling-mounted mixture control to full rich. Then he brought the adjacent throttle back to idle.

Jesse was both intimidated and intrigued. The air

crackled in the cockpit. Santee's eyes were closed, hands folded calm and patient in his lap. Santee smelled like a freshly watered greenhouse. Jesse donned his headset.

The plane began to roll. Jesse informed the local traffic of his intentions. He pressed the toe brakes and stopped the plane at the end of the runway, then ran up the engine to 1,200 rpms. The plane bucked against the counterforces. It wanted to be free of the ground. The rpms dropped when he turned the key and checked the magnetos.

Santee said," Very thorough."

Jesse advanced the throttle. The plane accelerated down the active runway and lifted off into the warming morning air. Earth fell away. The gear came up and the Lake flew directly over town and turned northward.

Jesse was light on the yolk. He brought back the propeller pitch and then the throttle as they leveled off exactly at 3,000 feet. He was comfortable in the air.

Jesse dialed in Bangor approach control and asked for flight following. Even though the controller said there was no immediate traffic, he scanned the sky from left to right. Three thousand feet and heading 360 degrees. They listened to a Delta flight contact Bangor for their initial approach. It was all so orderly, clear and precise. He was reoriented. The discipline and concentration he gave each flight amounted to his meditation. He'd once tried to explain it to Emma, to tell her of the peace he found up here. She'd laughed and called his flying a rich boy's pursuit. She told him not to romanticize it. It didn't matter. It was enough to hold it privately in his heart.

Santee motioned with his finger at the cigarette case. Jesse smiled and nodded.

Jesse watched Santee open the slim case and remove a remarkably rough-looking cigarette. It was filterless, made of unrefined white paper and smaller at the end with the red stripe. Santee lit the fat end with a golden lighter. An aroma of moist tobacco and cloves filled the cockpit. Santee caught Jesse staring and donned his headset. Jesse flicked the intercom switch.

"Years ago I fell in love with these Indonesian cigarettes. An associate sends me a resupply each week. They are delightful. Will you try one?"

Santee offered the open case across the cockpit and Jesse took one. He swiveled the microphone up and out of the way so Santee could put a flame to the end. Jesse inhaled the easy smoke with a sweet taste.

Santee sat back and watched Jesse's reaction. The cigarette was mild and strong at the same time. Jesse licked his lips and tasted cloves. It was delightful.

They both smoked and looked out at the countryside scrolling beneath them. This altitude was high enough for perspective on the land, while also low enough to appreciate the details of life below. Jesse kept heading north.

Santee finished his smoke first and stubbed it out in the can at his feet, then moved it over for Jesse.

Santee reached to the backseat for the larger of his two cases. He set it on his lap and popped the locks with manicured and polished thumbs. Nestled in the cut-out foam was the smallest Loran receiver Jesse had ever seen. Santee withdrew the instrument and a cable and set them at his feet.

He exchanged the empty case for the smaller one, which held a microcomputer. He plugged the two gadgets together with the cable and turned them on. The small computer screen came to life.

Moosehead Lake was a thin sliver of water on the horizon.

"I want you to fly west of the lake, then due north again to the Canadian border. We will follow the border east and south until it reaches the coast. Are you familiar enough with this territory to do that?"

"I can do that." The plane made a shallow bank to port and gained altitude.

Squaw Mountain needed some room. The quiet town of Greenville slid under the nose.

Santee stared at the shoreline of Moosehead Lake as if searching for or planning something. When they flew over a small cove with a single cabin at water's edge and a dead-end dirt road, he pushed a button on the keyboard. The coordinates registered and were saved to the hard disk. He repeated the procedure as they passed over locations farther north along the shore.

They crossed the northern tip of the lake and Jesse turned directly north. He understood what Santee was doing, but couldn't figure out why. He waited to ask Santee what was going on. For now, Santee didn't need any help.

They flew over timber country crisscrossed by private logging roads owned by the paper companies. The recreation industry, just now coming out of hibernation, was gearing up for the season. But they too seemed to dance to the paper conglomerates' tune. Timber was the major industry here in the north and it provided the livelihood for most of the residents scattered below.

Santee's lyrical voice came over the intercom and startled Jesse.

"You are a master of flight. It is rare indeed that I am in a small plane and feel so comfortable and safe. Were it not for the reference of the ground, I would not be able to tell if we were turning or changing altitude. I have been looking for a pilot like you. They are so hard to find."

Jesse sat up a little straighter.

"So what do you do with your life that brings such harmony to your flight?"

Jesse burst into a short mocking laugh. "It isn't my life that brings harmony to my flying. Quite the opposite. Flying for me is a refuge. It's where I feel at home. I hope at the end of each flight that I can bring some of it back with me. Mostly, I fail."

"What do you do that brings so little satisfaction?"

"I'm an investor. I invest in opportunities, growth areas, little companies with great potential." If only he had the talent and authority to make such plays. He let the canned speech roll. "It's financially rewarding, but I've become bored."

Jesse could sense Santee watching him closely. He fidgeted, as he felt waves of emotion cross like turbulence over his face.

Santee said, "You and I are in the same business. I too am an investor. I see opportunities and I reach for them. I see a need and I fill it. But I get great pleasure playing the game and counting the money."

Jesse nodded, not sure where the conversation was going.

"Your politics?" Santee probed.

"Confused, mostly, but leaning libertarian. I'm pro self-government, freedom and personal responsibility. Gun rights. Not happy about the erosions of constitutional freedoms."

"Life is what you make it," Santee said after a pause. "I learned that growing up outside of Havana. In the end, you can rely on no one but yourself. My family was poor then and is poor now. I realized that if I did not make some aggressive moves, I would never escape. I have made my way by being strong and quick. It is nobody's business to look after me. That is only my concern. The founders of your country had the correct vision—individual freedom and responsibility to oneself. You are right in your assessment of government intrusion into our affairs."

They flew over the endless forest without speaking. Santee was busy with his machinery and Jesse with thought. How could he put the pieces of his life together? But the puzzle seemed too big and monochrome and he wondered how many pieces were missing. He was his past, and he felt powerless to change. He wanted anonymity, to be known simply as Jesse Langdon, not the third, not the son of the harsh fighter-jock father and the blue-blood mother. The weight of his negativity became too much, so he returned his full attention to the airplane and discovered he'd allowed the Lake to descend and move off course.

He made the adjustments and focused on Santee, who was lost in his peculiar work. Jesse said, "If you like, you can show me the spot, so I can fly directly over it and you'd have perfect coordinates."

In a flash of fury, Santee turned venomous. "I do not make mistakes. You do not know the ramifications of my actions or my purpose. I hired you to fly, not to think."

Stung by the response, Jesse replied in anger, "Sir,

you are in my plane and at my pleasure. You hired me, but you do not own me. Helpfulness is not a sin."

Crackling arrogance rubbing against frustration filled the air with electricity. Santee returned to the computer screen.

Uncomfortable minutes passed before Santee held out a peace offering. Jesse removed a clove cigarette from the silver case. Soon the cabin was filled with aromatic smoke.

Santee sat back and spoke softly, hardly moving his lips, "You are right of course, Jesse. I understand now that your comment was one of thoughtfulness and assistance. I apologize for my outburst and beg your forgiveness."

Jesse removed a flake of tobacco from the tip of his tongue. He rolled it between his fingers and flicked it to the floor.

Jesse looked into Santee's face and saw a smile fill from the chin up, first with the subtle turning of the corners of the lips, and then into the eyes that now strangely sparkled with life. The gratuitous grin hollowed out the gracious words.

"No need to ask for my forgiveness. I spoke out of turn." He looked out the windshield and said, "The border is coming up, right there, beyond that field." He pointed.

Santee nodded and motioned with his hand for a slow turn to the right, saying, "If you would be so kind

as to fly on the Canadian side, I would be very pleased.
"

Jesse looked down. The land north and south was the same, yet the people on either side were controlled by different governments, dictated by different laws. And in the end, weren't they all the same? Just getting by, fighting through life to the next meal, yearning for a meaningful moment, buffeted by the natural forces of wind and snow. Spring came green with promise, then the short summer, swept under a killing fall frost and buried beneath the snows of winter.

Jesse squirmed in his seat. His ass was numb. He arched his back, took off the headset and rubbed his face.

Santee looked perfectly comfortable beside him, intent on the border below. He hadn't fooled with his computer since they'd flown into Canada. Jesse removed his nearly empty packet of tobacco from the left front pocket of his shirt, creased a paper, dropped a fingerful of tobacco into it, rolled it up and lit the end.

He consulted the chart on his lap then struggled to refold it.

The sky was cloudless and the air was smooth. The sun was bright now and Jesse put on his orange tinted Revos sunglasses. He felt safe behind the mirrored lenses.

The forest below was a carpet of greens, grays and browns. They flew the border east and then south as it bent. As they approached the coast just north of Eastport, Santee finally spoke.

"I have been thinking about what you said about the government. I have a different perspective, having seen the situation in Cuba, living under such control and domination. You sense correctly the direction your government is taking, but by relative standards, the United States is the freest, most accepting country in the world. It is the Communists that are to be fought. They are the disease that needs to be terminated. And rightly so, your government is very serious about that endeavor."

Jesse didn't want to talk politics. He changed the subject. "Would you like me to set her down in Machias so we could stretch our legs? It's a short walk to town, and there's a restaurant there that's long on local color and has the best pie in the state."

Santee looked at his thin gold watch. "No. I have some connections to make this afternoon. Please fly a bit off the coast. It will not be long now, before we are through."

"Whatever you say."

Santee became intent on the coastal bays and coves. His fingers flew across the keyboard as he watched steadily out his window.

Jesse sat back and from 3,000 feet admired how the sea greeted the land. The swells came ashore into the reaches and crashed upon the rocky coast. They flew over Mount Desert and Blue Hill. Penobscot Bay and Islesboro spread ahead of them.

They were a half hour out of Belfast when Santee said, "I have a proposition. I like to fly fish and I have been marking suitable spots, but I need further help. I would like to hire you for the remaining six days at 2,000 dollars a day. That price would include any flying you do for me. I will also pay expenses. All in cash. In addition to your flying skills, I will hire your knowledge of the state, and I will call upon you for your insight. At the end of the week, I will return to Florida."

Jesse was silent. He reached forward and set the unicom frequency for Belfast. A Cessna 210 announced left downwind for runway thirty-three. Jesse prepared the Lake for landing.

Santee turned off his Loran and detached the cable. He eased the computer screen down. He didn't seem bothered by Jesse's lack of response. He reached for the empty cases in the rear and methodically placed each component in its rightful slot.

They flew directly over the airport and dropped the gear. Flaps to ten degrees. The Lake dipped the port wing and descended into the pattern with a consistent reduction of power. It came over the threshold, flared gently, nose up, cushioned in ground effect, and lost all lift. The main wheels touched lightly on the tarmac, nose held high until it came gently to earth.

Jesse taxied up to the terminal building and swung

the plane so that the passenger door was closer to the parking lot. Santee said, "The choice is yours, Jesse. I need you. I am proposing nothing illegal. I will be here at seven-thirty tomorrow morning. If you are not, I will take that as your decision."

Santee pushed his windshield up and got out. He gathered his belongings and stood back from the plane like a splinter off a hemlock board and watched Jesse.

With catlike grace, he scooped the cases from the ground and headed to the parking lot.

Jesse blindly went through the motions of putting the plane away. He patted the nose and listened to the cooling engine tick and thanked her for the safe flight.

CHAPTER 5

JESSE WENT STRAIGHT to his office from the airport. He sat at his empty desk and rolled the last of his tobacco. He leaned back and blew a smoke ring into the accumulating haze.

He was fascinated by Santee's offer, drawn by the flying and the money and the mystery. This guy was no more a simple fly fisherman than Jesse was the Pope. And the fact that there was more beneath the surface felt like blood to a mosquito or a shark. Santee was reeling him in, sensing rightly what might appeal to Jesse. That fact alone argued against any further contact. On the other hand, what was the worst that could happen?

Jesse reached for his phone and turned off the ringer. He didn't want intrusions. He went to the bottle of Wild Turkey that sat beside a bottle of Scotch on the mantelpiece. He'd been sober for two-and-a-half years. He popped the cork and brought the neck to his nose. He closed his eyes and savored the sweetness and strength of the liquor. He inhaled the captivating quality alcohol had for him, the snake within that longed to turn around his torso and squeeze tighter and tighter as he exhaled, reducing by small portions his ability to breathe. He didn't need the snake. He took another sniff, then re-corked the bottle and set it back.

He took out the pack of Camels he'd bought at Bernie's when he'd had the kids, opened it and knocked out a group of cigarettes. Pinching the end of one with his fingers, he swept the other end to his mouth.

The processed tobacco had an abruptness that the Drum didn't. It was a small change of pace.

And then it came from nowhere, as it always did, unheralded and unwelcome, the waking counterpart of a sleeping nightmare he'd had since childhood—the nightmare he could never remember but for the sensations of smallness and danger at being crushed by immense unknown forces. These waking moments had the vivid feel of being swept backwards through the optic mechanism of binoculars into the smallness of the images.

Everything around him receded from his grasp. He was too far from the coffee. He was a speck of nothingness in the vast expanse of space between himself and the rest of the room.

Then it vanished, as suddenly as it had come, disappearing like a plane into a deep blue sky. Jesse sat looking at the dead cup of co-op coffee. Unsure, he reached out, testing reality. Saw the arm extending, a hand opening and wrapping the brown cup, the lack of heat in his palm.

He hunched his shoulders. The movement of his body was reassuring. He spoke for the sake of hearing the familiarity of his own voice. There seemed to be no pattern or trigger to the bizarre takeaway sensations of his dark daydream.

In the gathering darkness, he felt like a piece of furniture, an antique chair, beautiful in the swirls of the bird's-eye maple and delicate in the sweep of arm, but too tender to be of any real use. He was completely still, not letting go of the image. In the holding on, he wondered if he'd been twisted and turned, fondled and examined, eased into by Santee, testing the strength and structure of the wood before buying and taking home the chair.

Jesse had marijuana stashed in the gun cabinet at the house. He smoked it every now and again. It worked deliciousness into his body that made his limbs heavy and his mind acute. Even though there seemed to be a little hand erasing the thoughts as they went by, the thoughts themselves had a perspective and a truth that tweaked his concept of reality. It slowed him down just enough for him to appreciate the smallest details of life, the details that went unnoticed in the rush of living.

He did cocaine, too, for the exquisite rush, as if

life were a stalled traffic jam, bumper to bumper, an expressway leaving New York City in the steaming summer haze, the cars overheating with the tempers of their sweaty drivers, powerless to turn the tide, until a breath of fresh air comes wafting into the brain and the traffic opens ahead as if by magic, and he accelerated, running through the gears, faster and faster, cool wind tossing his hair, no one on the road ahead as he hit a hundred and laughed from the depths of his heart, feeling the car glued to the road so sharply drawn in color and form.

He used the drugs carefully, aware of the lessons that alcohol had taught. It was no one else's business, least of all the government's.

Jesse took his key to the roof door and went up. The stars were bright, and the Milky Way stretched strong and wide over his head from horizon to horizon. He breathed them in, for the navigational guidance, for the light that took so long to traverse the darkness and reach into his eyes. He opened arms wide and tilted his head back. Four words came to him as he embraced the heavens: spark, ember, smolder, die.

Why did Santee trust him? Was it the nature of his need? What was his need? Was there a longing hidden in the beckoning gesture, a yearning more instinctual than anyone could fathom? Or was it all a game, the sleight of hand, where is the kernel? And what the hell was he going to do? His grandmother would counsel sleep, clarity with the dawn.

Sometime in the middle of the night, Jesse came flashing out of sleep and sat up in damp sweat. He'd heard a loud crack, like skull hitting pond ice or a gun-shot. All was dead silent around him.

He got out of bed and splashed water on his face. His heart was pounding. The water washed away some, but not all, of the fear.

PART II

CHAPTER 6

Miami Herald, April 14
It was revealed by the State Department that
they were paying drug traffickers to supply
the contras.

HOW DO YOU pack for a life of crime? Jesse took out his formalwear and set it across the bed. The black cloth with the satin lapels, the strip down the trouser leg, the cummerbund. Too much? Definitely. He returned it to the closet and brought out a baggy brown feather-weight silk suit.

Other than the suit and a blue blazer, he opted for comfort. He packed two pairs of loose cotton khakis, several different-colored Brooks Brothers shirts, three lightweight Land's End chambray short sleeves, jeans and some white wool socks.

Santee had been gone a week. He'd left 13,000 dollars, the silver cigarette case and another offer, for bigger money longer term. Jesse was now taking advantage of an empty house. Emma and the children were shopping in Bangor, but they'd be back soon and he had to hurry.

He retrieved his paddock boots and the Nikes he'd wear on the flight. He pushed the boots down along the sides of the suitcase. He closed the bag and took a look into the closet for some last-minute thing. The closet looked barely touched. No gaps where he'd taken clothes. No initial sign he was running out.

He took his bag downstairs and set it on the leather chair in his home office. He flipped his Day Timer to the list: money, sunglasses, ammo, pens, flashlight, micro-recorder and some tapes, little Minox camera, pistols, film, breath mints and condoms.

He began extracting things from drawers and cabinets. They fit nicely in the bottom compartments of his leather satchel. He unlocked the gun case and took the holstered Beretta. He drew the gun and leaned back in his chair. What the hell was he doing? Too many gangster films. He was going to be flying an airplane, not shooting people. So why take the guns?

He took an Indonesian cigarette from the small silver case Santee had presented as a bonus. He'd learned to keep the flame on until it really caught fire. The clove smell filled the office. Perhaps Emma would catch the faint fragrance and take it as a slap in the face, leaving her momentarily bewildered.

He licked his lips and leaned back to the creak of the springs and the crack of the leather as his weight shifted. His grandmother, his father's mother, told him before she died to live his life always prepared. What on earth would she say now? Would she understand, or would she be appalled?

In the course of flying Santee across the state, they'd become close. They worked well together and developed an easy rapport and trust. Santee had seemed excited about Jesse and his ability to plan, and had complimented him often and rewarded him well.

His time with Santee seeking the "famous fishing spots" would have been laughable had the ruse not been covering such serious business. The mission had changed and the objective became obvious, but still Jesse made no comment until Santee suggested an exercise in logistic gymnastics, the "hypothetical" task of clandestine importation. The tacit cover story gave them both an almost plausible deniability and, after a time, Jesse's uneasiness faded.

They'd flown the state after studying the Gazetteer, the summer event schedules, road maps and topographical charts. They created approaches to small northern strips, noting on the Loran and the computer the initial approach fixes, the altitudes and the obstructions. They "imported" at lakeside campgrounds, coastal coves, near future county fairs with masses of humanity in their campers, tents and trailers. At Jesse's suggestion, they'd written a book based on chronological events, a chapter for a fair and date, details of the drop and the retrieval, exit roads, type of vehicle and methods for disappearing into the crowds. They made backup plans and contingency escapes. The final chapter was Greenville's float-plane fly-in, late September.

Santee said he liked books and dreamed that someone, someday, might want to write one about him.

Over the course of their time together, Jesse had become more forthcoming about his estrangement from Emma and his deteriorating home life, all of which had culminated with the disappearance of his brother-in-law. Santee had seemed intrigued and Jesse volunteered Seefer's name and the details surrounding the final hours.

The week had passed quickly.

Jesse remembered verbatim the conversation as they came in to land that final time. "I will not insult you by being vague," Santee said. "I want you to come to Florida for several months and implement this plan of ours. There are small risks of being caught, but the rewards are immense. I will pay you handsomely and then you can come home. You spoke of your brother-in-law several days ago. I have made inquiries and perhaps I can solve the mystery for you. You can bring the answers home with you."

Jesse couldn't have been less surprised by the offer,

though its attraction to him remained something of a mystery.

But now that it was spoken and open, his misgivings took on a prominent strength. He'd concentrated on the landing while the offer hung in the air.

He shut the plane down. "I need time to consider your request."

"I am leaving at nine tomorrow morning. I will call you at eight-thirty for your answer. If you decline, I will be disappointed, but our lives will go on." With that, he was gone.

Jesse had heard that decisions take ten seconds to make. The rest of the mental wrestling is pure justification. Jesse took a lot of time with the justification. Life in Maine had become an aimless drift and he was entirely out of tune. He was being pulled away for a reason, for the sake of distance. It would be sad and dangerous to go, but sadder and more dangerous to stay. In the end the prospect of solving Seefer's fate became the deciding factor. Who knew? It might be the beginning of reparations with Emma.

He was now committed to getting to Florida and joining Santee's team, in order to fine-tune the delivery of the marijuana and cocaine Santee imported. His grandmother was probably rolling in her grave.

The pistol was heavy and warm from the heat of his body. Be prepared. He holstered the gun and slid it into the inside pocket of the satchel. He took his week's pay from the desk—nicely banded hundred-dollar bills—and put it beside the pistol.

Jesse took the credit cards from his wallet and put them in the drawer. He rechecked the list. His mind had been made up days ago, but it was now down to walking out the door. With the two bags gripped surely in his hands, he looked across the desk in a final check. He set them down and reached into a cubbyhole. He wrapped his fingers around a silver chain on which Ike had strung a small white periwinkle shell that looked like a real heart with two valves. He put it over his head and around his neck and tucked it in his shirt. A framed photograph of Ashley and Ike caught his eye. They were leaning in, foreheads touching. Their sweet smiles made his heart jump. How could he run out on them? But he knew he needed to get away from his married life, and this adventure was temporary, after all. He slid the photo alongside his pistol.

He loaded the car, then returned to the house to write a note.

> *I have to go away for a little while. It's personal business. I've made arrangements. Call John Settlemire in New York. I love you all. I will be back.*
>
> *love,*
>
> *Papa*

He read it over, then added, *Jesse*.

Jesse stuck it in an envelope, addressed it to Emma and would drop it at the post office on his way out of town. He didn't look back, but drove straight out the drive and down the hill toward Belfast.

He pulled the flight bag out from under the desk. Approach plates for the East Coast. He spread the en route charts on the empty table and marked his route with a yellow highlighter. A scenic flight across New York State, central Pennsylvania, over Virginia, the Carolina Mountains and into Atlanta for the night. He highlighted tomorrow's flight, out to Savannah and down the eastern shore to Miami.

He logged into flight service. The computer printed out the actual weather for the flight route, and the forecast for later in the day and tomorrow. He requested a general briefing for the East Coast, purposefully not discussing specific destinations. He didn't know if Emma would try to find him, but he didn't want to give her the chance. The printer spewed out reams of unnecessary data, all of which he packed into the bag.

The gods were with him. He'd planned to leave today, but was flexible because he needed clear weather. An Instrument Flight Plan was too easy to trace. The whole coast was Visual Flight Rule weather, severe clear in spots, partly cloudy with high ceilings in others, and forecast to remain that way through Tuesday.

He referred to the list on his desk. He'd taken care

of all the financial details. It had taken much longer than he'd imagined. With the monthly bills he'd paid on Friday, he had included instructions to send the subsequent statements to his home address. He'd written letters to his accountant, his stockbrokers and the trust officer at the bank. They were instructed to work with Emma in any capacity she saw fit.

Distributions would be wired into their joint account. She'd have plenty of money.

Several days before, he'd called John Settlemire, his attorney in New York. There wasn't any way to avoid it. The conversation had started with the usual banter.

"John? Jesse here."

"*Jefe! Qué pasa, hombre?*" John said in a thick bandito accent.

"Well, Mr. Maximum Attorney, I'm planning a trip and I need to arrange some details."

"What's up?"

"This is somewhat personal, John, and what I say is confidential." There was only concentrated silence on the other end. Jesse could picture his rumpled lawyer leaning forward over a desk piled high with stacks of yellow legal pads. "I'm going away for several months, I think. I haven't told Emma or the kids, nor will I, nor will you. I'll leave a note. You can expect a call from Emma after I leave. I'm not telling anyone where I'm going. I have to get away and be by myself and figure out what I want. Emma and I aren't doing so good."

Jesse had been twisting a straw around his finger as he ran all this by John, conscious of how it might sound, and worried that his attorney would try to talk him out of this foolishness.

"I'm mailing you a power of attorney. You probably won't need it, but you might, especially if I'm gone for five or six months and you have to attend to tax or stock details."

In the pause that followed he could almost hear John arrange his words, as if delivering a closing argument. *Gentlemen and ladies of the jury, we have before us a certifiably insane young man.*

But his actual words surprised Jesse. John said, "This sounds like more than run-of-the-mill soul searching. Are you sure you want to do something so drastic? There are easier ways to work things out between you and Emma. Are you in the deep end, Jesse?"

"What do you mean?"

"Are you already in trouble?" John Settlemire was an extremely bright lawyer, frayed on the edges, but with a razor-sharp intelligence. "As your attorney and friend, I advise you to lay it out for me." His voice was full of genuine worry and it made Jesse question this part of Santee's instructions.

"No, I'm not in trouble, John. I'm just getting away to think. Really."

"I don't believe it, but if I try pushing my clients

and friends around, well then, there won't be any more dinner parties." He paused and when Jesse didn't respond, he said, "Okay, okay, I can do that. You've taken care of the bank and the money end, right? Emma will be all set? She'll probably be happy to see your moping face gone. Can she and I elope with all the cash?"

"Be my guest, and God be with you," Jesse laughed.

They settled into the legal details of notary publics, wills, the estate, which Jesse would do by next-day air at the post office.

John did extract a promise, wormed from Jesse in classic Settlemire style. "I know you're not telling me something. It's not a bimbo, I believe you, but there's something. You don't put my kids through gilded kindergarten paying for stupid advice. I want you to call me at the office or at home, anytime day or night within two days either side of the end of the month. That gives you four days and a lot of flexibility. You're a wealthy man and you have responsibilities to your family. I don't want to lose you. My God, my kids would have to go to public school! What I mean, fella, is that if you get into trouble and need help, I can marshal all kinds of people. Consider it insurance."

Jesse agreed, first to get John off his back, but then because it really did make sense. And he didn't doubt for a minute that if John wanted to find him, he could.

They agreed that if no call came, the search would begin with foul play suspected. John seemed to get lost in the gangster aspects of it all and Jesse wondered why he hadn't called John about his brother-in-law. "Hey, you aiming for a dictatorship in Panama? Haiti? I could be a *bueno* attorney general. You could give me my own province!"

The conversation ended with laughter.

Jesse packed up his Compaq laptop. He took the multi-pocket fishing vest from the hanger behind the door, put it on over his black cotton sweater, and left the office with bulging flight bag and the computer.

He filled his mind with the things still to get, pushing out a tugging loneliness and grief that felt hollow in his core. He removed the plane from the hangar and loaded things within reach. He backed in the Saab, grabbed the Walther from the glove compartment and locked everything up tight.

Jim, the line man at the airport, asked him where he was headed as he topped off all the tanks. "Just west and south," Jesse said.

Once airborne, he chanced a glance at his house on the hill, sitting in the greening pasture. It represented all his confusions, frustrations and failures, but also his anchors and the love he held for his children.

He loved to fly alone. The solitude lacked loneliness and offered only serenity. He watched the waters ebb and flow along the rocky coast.

Some lobstermen were setting their traps in early for the season. Sailboats bobbed on moorings in Casco Bay off Handy's Marina north of Portland.

He'd stay well above or beyond the high-traffic areas of the major airports, so he wouldn't have to contact control towers with his tail number, fading into the sky without trace or trail. Later, if needed, he'd give control towers a number off a West Coast Lake he'd gotten from an article in *Flying* magazine. But for now, he headed well west of Boston, toward Poughkeepsie, New York.

He'd flown this route many times. Beauty lay inland in the hills and valleys off the coastal plain. Spring was running rampant as he flew steadily south out of New York and into Pennsylvania. The ground below went from the grungy green and browns of Maine to grow steadily more alive, the endless carpet rolling into life.

He refueled in Lancaster and paid cash. He stretched and took off his sweater. As he climbed away, he looked down on farmers plowing the fertile soil of Amish country.

The Shenandoah Valley stretched along his route. He stopped in Roanoke, Virginia, for more fuel and a walk-around. He emptied the coffee can that on longer flights became his urinal.

Jesse flew over western North Carolina and his favorite sight, Asheville, set deep in the Appalachians.

The land rose sharply in rocky shifts from the coastal lowlands to meet thick forest and small patches of hilly cropland. A waterfall blew out of a mountain crevice.

The weather held steady and he didn't have to talk to anyone except the towers where he landed. He flew into Charlie Brown Airport north of Atlanta and took a courtesy van to the Holiday Inn down the road. He prepaid his bill in cash and was lost in the room, alone, and with the phone so close. Ike and Ashley's voices called to him, only a line away if he'd just make the call.

He fell asleep with the television on, a distraction from thoughts of the turmoil in his house and the confusion and questions that must be turning it upside down.

CHAPTER 7

ATLANTA TO MIAMI. He was at the airport early the next morning, dressed in a T-shirt. It always took a surprisingly long time to get out of Georgia. Florida all looked the same, flat and uninteresting. He passed Kissimmee, where the Lake Company had its major dealership and an instructor had taken him through the intricacies of flying this peculiar airplane.

For old time's sake, he picked a canal to his right and swooped down, fighter style, leveled out at the last moment and did a touch-and-go. He climbed and turned and came again and landed with a swish and a tug at the fuselage. He step-taxied, then pulled up abruptly and banked left and went skimming over the trees that lined the canal. He climbed back up to altitude and resumed his flight.

He contacted Miami Approach. With Fort Lauderdale Executive and Miami International, the flow of planes, both big and small, made for a confusing and frenzied approach and transition through the area.

"Lake 4974V, Miami Approach. Say Destination."

"Miami Approach, Lake 74V. Tamiami Airport."

"Lake 74V, understand Tamiami. Fly heading 180, descend and maintain 2,000 feet, radar vectors to runway nine left. Expect a visual approach."

"Right 180, 2,000, radar vectors nine left, visual. Roger. 74V."

They handed him off to the tower and he turned final at 2:45 in the afternoon, fifteen minutes before he was to be picked up.

Tamiami Airport consisted of parallel east-west runways bracketing a dozen aviation concerns spread across generous acreage. The effect was open and rambling.

He greased the Lake on the numbers and contacted Ground Control as he turned right on the first turnout.

"Tamiami Ground, Lake 74V, clear the active. Looking for InterRegional Aviation. Unfamiliar with the airport."

The Lake idled smoothly at a standstill as he awaited clearance and instructions.

"Lake 74V, Ground, good afternoon. Welcome to Tamiami. Cleared taxiway Alpha on your left. Taxi down near the threshold of 27, turn right. The hangar is the big one on the right. Watch for Robinson traffic in hovering taxi opposite direction Alpha. Please stay to the right."

"Ground, Lake 74V, Alpha left to end, then right, roger the Robinson. Thanks a lot. Good day to you, sir."

Jesse popped his windshield open and taxied to the left, careful to keep well away from the small helicopter coming steadily down the left side at about ten feet off the ground. The warm breeze tussled his hair. The outside temperature gauge read eighty-five degrees, the air smelled like the sea and the swampy humidity felt healthy in his lungs.

InterRegional Aviation's hangar was huge and dwarfed the little T hangars on either side. The big doors slid sideways along parallel tracks in the concrete into side-by-side sections.

A slender man dressed in crisp white coveralls appeared from the center of the hangar. He beckoned the Lake. Jesse taxied into the hangar, careful of his wingtips. The man's arms swept slowly inward and crossed to an X when the plane was within two feet of his chest. Jesse shut down. The gift of silence filled his ears. The doors behind him closed with an electric whir.

He set the headset on the yoke, pulled himself to standing and stretched with hands on hips. The attendant offered a smile and friendly handshake after chocking the front tire.

"Good afternoon, Mr. Langdon. My name is Sam Wilbur. I take care of Mr. Santee's planes. Welcome to Miami." His grip was firm, his blue eyes pleasant and open. He was about twenty-five years old, with sandy hair and a lithe build.

Jesse stepped down and looked around. "Hi, Sam. Call me Jesse. I've never gotten used to the mister part." The floor was polished, gray-painted concrete that reflected the overhead lights and the other plane, a squat and shiny Mitsubishi MU-2.

"I'd like very much to call you Jesse, sir, but I'm under orders to refer to everyone as Mr. or Ms." He said it with a lightness that spoke much about the warmth in this young man.

"You sure do have quite a shop here. Looks like you could skate across the floor." The back wall was mostly Plexiglas, which looked in on an avionics department, several office spaces, and to the far left, a passenger and pilot's lounge. It was all immaculately maintained.

Sam smiled at the compliment. "Thank you. Mr. Santee is very particular. He wants everything just right. I got a call from the driver, who'll pick you up. He said he'll be about fifteen minutes late. His being late gives me a chance to go over anything you want done to your plane. She sure is a beauty."

Jesse patted his airplane and thought she looked a

bit shabby in these surroundings. Oil dripped from the engine cowl and ran down the side of the pylon. The engine's exhaust had left a greasy film across the tail.

"You can make yourself comfortable in the lounge. There's coffee and soda in the refrigerator. The bathrooms are at the back."

"Thank you, Sam."

Jesse opened the door to the lounge and walked across thick carpet, passing leather furniture and a coffee table with organized flying magazines and sparkling ashtrays.

When he came out of the bathroom, relieved and refreshed from a splash in the face, Sam was sitting on the leather sofa along the back wall facing out toward the hangar. He stood when Jesse entered.

He poured himself rich black coffee from the stainless steel pot. He sat down beside Sam, saying, "Please. Sit." The coffee was strong and full bodied. He set it on the table and took out his Drum, leaning back into the enveloping folds of black leather.

Sam reached for the clipboard in front of him. "I've been instructed to wash and wax your plane, fuel it up and top off the oil and hydraulic fluid. I've never worked on a Lake, but we had all the maintenance books mailed in, so we're fully prepared to do anything you might want done."

Jesse was impressed. "She's had her annual inspection and she's running fine. You might look at the seal along the windshield. Last time I was in the clouds, it leaked along the top edge. I use synthetic Mobil AV1 oil. Have you got some of that?"

"That won't be a problem. We can get some." Sam noted it on his list. As he wrote, he asked, "Will you be here long?"

Sam's eyes went wide and he tensed, as if he'd just committed some grave error.

Jesse was struck by the change in his body language.

After a pause, Sam said, "I shouldn't have asked you that." His voice was full of apology and what sounded like fright. "I'm somewhat new here and still getting used to the rules. Mr. Santee is very clear about not asking questions that don't relate specifically to the work on the planes. You won't tell him, will you, if he asks?"

Jesse leaned toward him and said, "No, of course not. Santee runs a tight ship here, does he?"

"Very tight, sir, yes, very tight." Sam returned to an easier manner, the relief visible. "Thank you very much. Okay, I think I have it." Back to business. "Wash, wax, fuel, oil and the windshield."

They heard the muffled sound of the automatic door opener. The lounge was soundproofed. Jesse followed Sam's gaze. Sam was uncomfortable again. "That will be your driver."

Jesse watched a dark-maroon BMW 735ii come

into the hangar from the right, pass behind the MU-2 and swing around easily to the Lake. A man came out of the driver's door and looked intently into the lounge at the two of them standing still. Jesse took a gulp of coffee and stubbed out his smoke.

Sam introduced Jesse to Mr. Pasque. He was short, thick and thoroughly disagreeable. He had terrible taste in clothes and no discernible charm. He wore a steel-colored suit with a green shirt opened to the waist revealing a smooth hairless chest underneath several gaudy gold chains. He took Jesse's hand reluctantly with the limpness of someone who despises human contact. He didn't look Jesse in the eye. He hurried to the rear of the car with a mumble of something unintelligible and opened the trunk.

Sam helped Jesse get his things from the plane and place them in the trunk as Mr. Pasque looked on. They arranged the bags and the computer around an odd rectangular box, carpeted with a different shade of rug.

The driver slammed the trunk shut and opened the rear door for Jesse.

Sam seemed relieved to have his hangar back.

The car sped smoothly into the afternoon sunshine. Jesse leaned forward from the deep backseat and said, "Nice weather."

The man said nothing, but reached down to a small panel underneath the dash and pushed a button. A sheet of glass grew out of the back of the front seat, forcing Jesse to remove his arm, and closed snug into its grooved track. Despite the rebuff, Jesse felt more comfortable. Finding his brand of nonalcoholic beer in the small refrigerator, he settled back and stretched his legs and watched tomato fields pass the window as the brew cooled his throat.

They traveled the speed limit up the Turnpike and took the Dolphin Expressway east. Palm trees lined the wide avenues and shrubs flowered in the median. A pastel world of aquamarine bays and blue skies.

They crossed the Intracoastal Waterway and turned left. Jesse lowered the window and the car flooded with soft sea air. He rolled a smoke.

He caught Pasque's eye in the rearview mirror and they locked glares. Jesse smiled and was surprised to see the eyes in the mirror crack at the edges. Broken ice, test passed, perhaps.

They drove north along a quiet neighborhood street, large houses on the left with close-cropped lawns and glimpses of flat blue water reflecting the skyline of Miami.

They slowed and turned left across a bridge to a gate where the guard recognized the car and waved them through. They passed several mansions on the island, then stopped at closed solid-wood doors embedded in ten-foot concrete walls rimmed with broken glass and tightly strung wire. Jesse leaned forward for a better look as the driver spoke into a box and a camera lens. The light faded to shadow as a cloud passed before the sun.

The wooden doors swung open. A crushed-gravel drive swept to a courtyard wrapped by an apricot house backed by Biscayne Bay. The walls encased a huge expanse of lush lawn and flowering plants. A fountain pumped water straight into the air, making rainbows in the mist.

The car crunched through the gate. On the right, a man in a dark suit holding a sawed-off shotgun leaned against the doorjamb of a small guard house. Pasque drove toward the house, circled right around the fountain and stopped in front of the opening front door. Doors and gates always seemed to open and close in anticipation of their arrival.

A more friendly Pasque helped Jesse with his bags. He introduced the woman who had bustled through the front door as Carla. She looked about fifty and round in her tight eggshell-colored uniform dress and matching shoes.

"Mr. Santee wants me to welcome you to La Primavera, Mr. Langdon." She had a shy smile and a faint Spanish accent. "I have instructions to make you feel at home. Mr. Santee will be away on business for a few days, but he has left you some information in the sitting area of your room. May I show you?" Her voice was quiet and he had to lean in to hear her as he watched Pasque drive toward a bank of garage doors.

"Thank you, that would be very kind, Carla." He started to gather his luggage. Carla waved her hand and said she would arrange for the bags to be delivered to his room. Jesse left all but his satchel on the semicircular marble steps.

He followed her into an expansive hall. His sneakers squeaked loudly with each step on the polished black and white tiles. He gawked at the ceiling three floors up and its chandelier of twinkling crystal. A side table on the left blossomed with a riot of flowers. He whistled. Carla smiled. They climbed the sweeping staircase.

At the landing on the second floor, they went down a short but wide hall to a closed door.

"This is our nicest room, Mr. Langdon. Mr. Santee thinks very highly of you. I trust this will be comfortable?"

She swung the door open to a dazzle of thick yellow afternoon sunlight streaming through five-foot windows that looked across the water to Miami.

To his left, the room dwarfed a queen-sized canopy bed. To the right, a sitting area with comfy chairs and butler table ringed a fireplace. Pastel rugs separated the shining spaces of hardwood floor. "Yes." He smiled. "This will be fine."

Carla threw open the leaded windows and let in a salty breeze. The lacy curtains blew around her and she laughed.

"We didn't have time to prepare a dinner of your choosing, so we have planned a meal of roast lamb for seven-thirty. I hope that is all right. You will be dining alone, I'm afraid. Your belongings will be sent up shortly. Can I get you something to drink, perhaps?"

"No, Carla, everything is fine." He fell back heavily into a chair, feeling suddenly overwhelmed and tired. "Actually, could you bring me a small pot of black coffee?" She nodded and padded away silently.

Jesse stood again and went to the window. The horizon held in deep relief the jagged line of Miami high-rises beneath the falling sun, hidden now behind a bank of dark clouds that promised rain. To the south, the connecting bridge curved gracefully over the waterway. Farther north, some boat traffic hardly moved in the distance. The bay was slate gray and calm but for a little ripple of breeze stirring waves.

A large Bertram Sportfisherman and a go-fast Scarab were tied to the dock. The walls around the property extended to the pier. Curved staircases swept down from the small lawn below the window to an Olympic-sized swimming pool that dominated the backyard, a bath house on the left.

Carla came through the door, struggling with his luggage. "Let me help you with that," Jesse said.

"Not allowed. I will be back with your coffee."

Carla returned and set a tray of coffee on the table in front of the fireplace. He sat again and poured the dark coffee into a delicate black octagonal cup on a matching saucer.

A thick manila folder sat on the tray. It had his name written in bold black marker across the front.

Jesse retrieved his Drum from the vest pocket and returned to the chair. He went through the ritual of rolling, lighting and inhaling deeply. He took a sip of coffee and opened the folder.

Jesse,

I am sorry to be called away as you arrive. I trust you have been well tended to and that your flight was uneventful.

Please make yourself at home. The only rule is that the third floor is off limits. Other than that, you may investigate the grounds, swim in the pool, and order your meals from Carla.

In the drawer in the desk between the windows you will find a set of car keys. The car is in the garage. The Scarab is at your disposal.

I have taken the liberty to arrange for your multiengine training and rating. You are to be at the InterRegional Aviation hangar at 8:30 Thursday morning. You will meet Edgar Fischer. He is a very thorough man, but I'm sure you will do well.

Following that he will qualify you in the MU-2. I trust I have not presumed too much.

You will find the balance of this package helpful and informative.

With best wishes,

Santee

P.S. A man called Emmett Flagler will arrive before I return. He might be somewhat disagreeable. Try not to take it personally.

Jesse sat back. How did Santee know he was comfortable enough on the water to operate the Scarab? He'd never told Santee he was missing the multi-rating. Flagler?

He thought about the third-floor rule and remembered Sam. He'd test no rules.

Underneath the letter was a road map of Miami and the surrounding area. Beneath that was a marine chart of the immediate coast and its waters.

He set these aside and stared at what lay underneath. On official stationery was a complete history of his driving record—fines, drunk driving charges, even parking violations. Then a credit report—lines of credit, mortgages and margin accounts. School records from kindergarten through Yale, with grades and comments, class standing, results of psychological tests.

Medical history, copies of his birth certificate, driver's and pilot's licenses, and finally an accurate profile of his likes, talents and interests.

As if falling downstairs, Jesse rushed on.

On the next-to-last folder was his brother-in-law's name: Seefer Rollerson. Inside was a single-spaced page without letterhead that contained some information he already knew and some details he was just learning.

Seefer Rollerson, also known as "Reefer." Born and raised in Rockland, Maine. Son of divorced, alcoholic, abusive parents. Underachiever in school and truant after the eighth grade. Did not graduate.

Became involved in local motorcycle gang with history of petty crime and suspected of deeper felonies. Fished for lobster out of Rockland. Though a hard worker, the cost of the boat seemed to be beyond Seefer's means. Named his boat "Reefer."

Married in 1986 to Sylvia Lancaster (sister of Emma Lancaster, now Langdon). No children.

Last seen boarding a Downeast airplane in Rockland bound for Boston on September 13, 1988.

Reports indicate that during the summer of 1988 he spent impressive amounts of cash although the fishing season was mediocre. Also reports of marital discord.

Police files indicate no evidence of foul play, and the missing-persons case is inactive.

Of note: information was difficult to obtain and some of it is questionable. Those close to the subject were reluctant to speak and grew hostile. He has a loyal and hard group of friends and family.

His name has surfaced in South Florida. Cursory investigation reveals involvement in the purchase and operation of fast boats.

Whereabouts unknown at this time.

At the end was the Maine book, the compilation of the work Jesse had done previously with Santee.

He slowly closed the folder and reached for the coffee now grown cold in the cup. His cigarette had gone out in the ashtray. He relit it and sat back.

Santee had a long reach into confidential personal information and he was obviously connected in ways that Jesse could not imagine.

Jesse's relationship with Reefer had been based on recreational drugs and mutual sympathy regarding their wives. They had grown up on different sides of the tracks and on the surface had little in common. But their time together was unusually easy, taken on the surface without need to address the deeper parts of themselves, including their pasts. They shared a sense of humor, which came in handy.

Jesse had suspected that Reefer was involved in the low-key drug trade in Maine, but until now believed that his brother-in-law had fled his marriage.

He went to the window. It was six-thirty. The sun was falling behind the city's buildings, now coming to life with evening lights. Their reflection came wiggling toward him across the channel.

He unpacked, hanging the clothes carefully on the wooden hangers in the closet, laying out his toiletries beside the marble sink in the bathroom. The bathtub was six feet long and deep. Polished metal pipes on the wall heated towels. There was a standalone marble shower, big enough for two with three jets on each side.

The desk between the windows was an antique. He sat down and brought his satchel into his lap. He slid the drawer out to put his things away.

True to Santee's letter, there was a set of car keys with a BMW medallion. Next to them was a stack of crisp hundred-dollar bills. It looked like 10,000. Beside the money was a silver ashtray with a half-dozen thick joints, beside those two packs of Garam cigarettes. On the right edge was a crystal salt server like his grandmother's. The base and top lid were silver. A little golden spoon protruded through the lid's groove.

Jesse eased the lid open and looked down at the small bowl, filled with cocaine. A spoonful to one nostril, deep and quick inhale. Another sharp inhale with the head tilted back, finger over the nose to keep the coke from falling. A spoonful for the other nostril, to be fair. Same thing, head back, quick snort, fingers pinching the nose shut. Now a tremendous sigh, sitting back and letting the powder come rushing. Good stuff! His teeth were starting to feel numb. He dipped a finger, rubbed his gums and tasted the medicinal sharpness.

He sat for a moment and looked around the room, just to get the sense of space. Then he opened his satchel and took out the contents. He slipped the magazines from both pistols and loaded them. The Walther took six .380 rounds straight down the center. He decided not to chamber a round. The Beretta clip took sixteen 9mm rounds that leaned right then left. He fondled the pistols, then slammed the magazines home.

Jesse loaded a spare magazine for each gun and put the pistols back in their holsters and into a side drawer. The thought of the ability, but not the intention, had a calming effect. He set the picture of his children beside the desk lamp. He felt better.

He was grubby from the day's travels and it was getting on toward supper. He took a very hot shower, playing with the jets. He shaved and washed his hair. The towels were soft and fluffy. He rubbed himself vigorously and felt crisp, clean and alive.

It was only seven when he was ready to go downstairs. He considered another toot, but didn't want to lose his appetite before testing Carla's cooking.

He didn't know which way to turn at the bottom of the stairs. He'd come in from the right, so he went left and quickly smelled lamb.

Doors to his right were open, and he walked into

the dimly lit room. At the far end, floor-to-ceiling windows framed the perfect view of Miami at night. The sight, so dazzling and bright with life, stopped him. A vast and empty dining table dominated the room. In the far back corner a small round table glowed with candles. A bottle of wine breathed in front of an elegant place setting.

He took the bottle and read the label. It was nonalcoholic. He brought the neck to his lips and took a swig. It was dry. He set the bottle back on its silver coaster.

A door with a brass push plate led to the kitchen. He listened carefully before he pushed it open, not wanting to meet someone coming the other way. It opened to a brightly lit pantry, painted white and immaculate. He went through another swinging door and found a huge kitchen with institutional cooking equipment. The stove was an enormous black gas monster with white enamel knobs across the front.

Two stout women looked up in surprise and stopped their conversation, then smiled in unison. They were seated at a large white table on the right underneath two dark windows. Carla stood up quickly and said, "Mr. Langdon. How nice of you to come back here. We rarely see guests in the kitchen." She seemed to consider what she had said. "This is Mrs. Sanchez, our chef."

Mrs. Sanchez got to her feet with some effort,

came toward Jesse, and shook a meaningful hand, eye to eye. She looked tired. "*Mucho gusto*, Senor Langdon. Your supper will be ready shortly."

"How do you do, Mrs. Sanchez? I'm glad to meet you. I hope I'm not barging in on your territory. I just thought I'd look around before supper. It sure smells good. Lamb is my favorite."

"Thank you, Senor."

Jesse took in the walk-in freezer and refrigerator, an expansive butcher-block working space and large metal pots hanging on steel hooks. "It looks like you could prepare food for an army, Senora."

"Sometimes we do, sometimes we do." Mrs. Sanchez sighed. "Mr. Santee likes to entertain. Of course, I have lots of help. But tonight I cook for one, a lamb-leg roast with potatoes and steamed broccoli, spinach salad and flan." Though her tone was apologetic, Jesse could see pride in her eyes. She was intent on his reaction.

There was no need to fake a polite response. Regardless of the appetite-squashing effects of the cocaine, Jesse hadn't eaten since breakfast, and he was famished. Just the smell of the roasting lamb made his mouth fill with saliva. "Senora, it sounds just wonderful. I'm too hungry to describe. My grandmother was fond of the expression, 'Eat hearty and give the house a good name.' I've tried to follow her advice all my life." Jesse smiled and patted his stomach.

"Your grandmother was a wise woman. There is little I enjoy more than cooking for a man who enjoys his food."

"Do you have any nonalcoholic beer?"

"Certainly, Mr. Langdon," Carla said. "Come. A man too hungry for words needs to eat." Carla led him out of the kitchen and sat him at the table. She returned with a brown bottle of Kalibur and a frosted glass. "I think you have made a good impression on Mrs. Sanchez."

"Thank you, Carla." Jesse took the tall tapered glass and poured the beer to halfway, letting it foam to the top. "Where is everyone? I kind of expected a house so large to be full of people."

"When Mr. Santee goes away, the staff is kept to a minimum." Carla leaned back on the counter and seemed more relaxed. "He manages everything very carefully. There are enough of us to keep the house in order, and the gardener is here every day, and of course the security men."

"What happens when Mr. Santee returns?"

"Then calm is shattered. He is very generous and fair. But he is particular. We all learn to do things his way. Perhaps I say too much." It was clear that she'd taken Jesse into her confidence, then realized that she'd done so without knowing who he was or what he was doing here.

"I know what you mean," Jesse said. "I made the

mistake of correcting him once. Just offering a suggestion, really. He was not pleased."

Despite Jesse's reassuring tone, Carla looked uncomfortable with Santee as a topic, and she pardoned herself and returned to the kitchen.

It wasn't long before both Carla and Mrs. Sanchez came in bearing platters and covered dishes, which they placed in front of him, then stood back to watch his reaction. He expressed his delight and they went back to the kitchen, reminding him to use the little golden bell beside the wine bottle to call them if he needed anything else.

He ate everything on his plate and had seconds, to be polite. The flan melted in an explosion of taste as soon as it hit his tongue. He rang the bell and asked Carla if he could have some coffee out by the pool. She said of course and told him to leave all the dishes at the table. She had an admonishing tone, though playful, because she had caught him beginning to clear.

He went out to the pool and lit a smoke, letting the meal settle into just the right spot. Carla emerged with the coffee. He thanked her and asked her to send his regards to Mrs. Sanchez. Before leaving him alone in the cool night air, Carla consulted about tomorrow's breakfast.

After downing two cups, Jesse couldn't sit still. He skirted the pool that looked inviting, but his interest was really in the boats.

He stood in front of the Bertram and admired her lines. The windows were tinted black and gave the whole vessel a menacing character. He decided not to go snooping aboard this evening. Along the rail was her name in gold leaf—Kingpin. The name suited her. The Scarab was on the left. Her bow was tied to the back corner cleat and her stern was held back by a pulley line attached to the seawall. She gently rocked in the swells of the channel.

Jesse had grown up around boats. His family had a summer place on the Chesapeake and he'd learned to sail before he turned ten. They'd had a twenty-five-foot run-about outboard, but his real experience came from his summer job at the local boatyard. He worked his way up from rookie and gofer to gas boy and eventually ran all the hauling and launching activities.

Here was a boat that could take flight off a single swell and knock your kidneys down to your socks. Jesse pulled the bow line and brought the Scarab closer to the float. He stepped on board and felt his weight taken calmly by the boat. The deck was long and smooth. He walked along the middle, sea legs taking the sway and toss, then jumped over the tiny windshield into the cockpit. He sat in the pilot's seat and pulled out the joint. As he smoked, he toyed with the idea of taking her out. But this stuff wasn't the rotgut homegrown he was accustomed to. He had to sit and gather the energy and spirit to unglue from the seat. He was in no hurry.

The city lights swam like sparkled snakes into his head. He was transfixed.

Finally, it was time to head back to his room. There, he was overcome by the drugged feeling. He shed his clothes, leaving them in a pile beside the bed, and slipped under the covers. The linen sheets were cool and the blanket just heavy enough.

He rolled over, hugged one of the two feather pillows and fell asleep as a relaxed spectator to racing thoughts.

CHAPTER 8

JESSE WOKE FROM a sound sleep to bright sunshine in an unfamiliar room. He raised his arm to look at his watch—a little after seven-thirty. He threw off the covers and swung his feet to the rug on the floor.

Mornings came easily to Jesse. When he opened his eyes, he was fully awake and raring to take on the day. Often the feeling of inertia that could stifle his motivation took several hours to work its lethargy. But this morning was to be full of adventure and exploration.

He pulled on a bathing suit and walked to the window to confirm that the scenes of last night weren't a dream. The Bertram and the Scarab floated calmly at the dock. The pool glistened invitingly. He padded silently in bare feet through the now-familiar dining room with a warm bath towel around his neck. Poolside, he flung the towel on a chair and dove into the deep end.

The water was colder than he expected and he was shocked, but pleased; no sense in swimming in bath water. It enveloped him and washed away any remnants of sleep. He let the momentum of the dive carry him deep, then lifted his outstretched form slowly to the surface, rolled onto his back and took in an invigorating breath of clean morning air.

He swam to the shallow end and dipped his head back in the water. Laps. Twenty would be good to start, but he came up breathless after five. The pool was very long. He did another five before the heaviness of his limbs stopped him.

There was no one around. The house looked massively empty, like a museum before the gates opened to the early crowd. He made sure he was dry enough not to leave water prints through the house before returning to his room. He wrung out his trunks and put them and the towel over the heat pipe to dry. His clothes were even more wrinkled this morning, but he put them on anyway.

Carla came whistling into the bedroom as he emerged from the bathroom. She said in a bright voice, "Good morning, Mr. Langdon. Did you sleep well?"

"Like a log, Carla. And the pool really shocked me into the life of the living. That's the way to start a day!"

She set the coffee tray down on the butler table and slipped away whistling. She seemed relaxed this morning and her mood was contagious. Jesse sat down, put his bare feet across the table and sipped the hot coffee. There was a feeling of being at home, like he was meant to be here. That nebulous sensation developed into a full-fledged deja vu. He had been here before and a sense of familiarity wrapped him in knowingness. He waited for a boat's horn in the distance, and it came. He rolled a smoke and lit it. His body delighted in the nicotine. He had two full days to play with the boat, to explore the grounds, to cruise the streets and see the sights. He felt terrific.

Breakfast was chilled slices of papaya, mango and banana. The light meal made him feel charged with healthy high-octane fuel. He was ready to see how the house was laid out, what secrets the grounds held, and what the BMW looked like.

He carried his empty plates back to the kitchen, so he could wish Mrs. Sanchez good morning and thank her for the fruit. She seemed pleased with the compliments, but said, "You are a nice young man, Senor. Thank you for bringing the dishes back to me, but when Mr. Santee is home, he will not look with favor. It is a word to the wise, Senor. You will only bring trouble for yourself and for us if you lend us your assistance. We are the help and that is our job."

"Thank you for the advice, Mrs. Sanchez. I'm not used to living like this and I really don't know Mr. Santee that well. I've just been hired for the summer to do a specific job." Jesse bowed a little and felt awkward. "You have been very kind."

Carla rose to follow him to the pantry. She touched his arm lightly and he turned. She wore an expression of concern and conspiratorial secrecy. "Mr. Langdon, you seem to be a very courteous gentleman. I am stepping beyond my bounds, and I will do this only once, because we are alone." She looked to the corners of the room as if checking for a listening ear, then turned on a radio in the corner and continued. "Forgive me for saying so, but you seem out of place here. Perhaps when Mr. Santee returns, you will feel it too. I do not know the nature of your business, and I am taking a risk in speaking like this. I only say, be careful with his crowd. They are very rough and determined, and I sense danger for you." She let go of his arm and backed away. She smiled and her eyes met his, and then she did something that did more than any words could to make her point. She reached her hand to his face and gently touched his cheek, a grandmother's gesture of concern and care. She smiled weakly and returned to the kitchen, leaving him standing alone in the pantry.

Could he pack his things, retrieve his plane and fly home, admit it had all been a terrible mistake? He probably should, but then he thought of returning to Belfast and facing Emma. The prospect was anything but appealing. He'd made up his mind to get away for a little while. He would be careful, and take it a step at a time.

The mystery of Santee, all the little hints and comments, deepened his need to stay and experience this man. That kind of logic could be dangerous, but it had been good so far.

He returned to his room. The bed was already made and the coffee service gone. He left the drugs alone and went to explore the house.

The second floor was mostly bedrooms with attached baths. There were four large ones and a small one tucked away in a nook at the front of the house. His room was the largest and most posh, until he came to a door at the opposite end of the hall.

He turned the knob and opened the door to a room twice the size of his own. It too looked out on the channel and city, but the decor was completely different. The walls were a shiny dark-brown silk. The ceiling was black, except for the round mirror over the circular bed in the middle of the room. The bedspread was of the same shiny material as the walls. The wall-to-wall carpet was deep black. Polished aluminum furniture gathered around the fireplace with a huge block of clear Plexiglas as a table in the middle.

A wooden cabinet curved along the head of the bed. Sliding doors were open to a dazzling display of screens, monitors, telephones, dials and knobs.

Jesse felt like a voyeur, stumbling on a show about

to start that he wanted no part of. Without stepping onto the carpet, he slowly eased the door shut. It was as if he'd interrupted something and when the door clicked loudly shut, he felt he'd been given away. He checked over his shoulder. No one.

He walked back along the hall and admired the Flemish landscapes hung between the bedroom doors. There were freshly cut flowers in a colorful bouquet on a table. Beside the table was a door he hadn't opened. He turned the knob and found an inner steel door with an electronic combination lock.

The downstairs was dominated by three rooms that faced the bay. In the dining room was a fireplace over which hung an old-fashioned and formal portrait of an elegant woman with a long and vulnerable neck. She sat straight with her head turned slightly toward the artist. She had a hint of a smile, though it had little warmth. Jesse imagined this was Santee's mother.

Next to the dining room, through a door on the pool side of the house, was a large living room with three separate furniture groupings, down sofas, wing-backed chairs and antique tables. At the far end, a Steinway grand piano gleamed.

The floor creaked as Jesse walked across to the next room and opened double doors to an expansive space filled with books along all three walls and an intimacy that defied the size of the room. Jesse remembered Santee saying that he liked books. To his left was a large antique desk with green blotter and standing lamp. In the far right corner was a small spiral staircase that wound tightly up to a second-story walk-around ringing the room. The ceiling was a full two floors tall. Intricate, black wrought-iron railing protected the second-story ledge. The room smelled of leather. It was quiet except for the ticking of the grandfather clock in the corner. Jesse checked his watch and found the clock to be precisely correct. He would spend the evening here, browsing through the leather-bound volumes.

He gave a cursory glance to the rest of the first floor, and didn't venture down either of the wings. Off the hall by the library he found a solid door that opened to carpeted stairs leading down to the basement.

At the bottom of the stairs, the carpet continued down a hall to the left. There were numerous closed doors on either side. He turned on the overhead fluorescent lights and started opening doors. The first revealed a well-stocked workout room. In the center were various Nautilus machines that looked like torture devices.

All the walls were mirrored and it gave the room a *Twilight Zone* atmosphere. There were too many of himselves. Along the back was a line of free weights arranged by size, several weight benches, and a wall-mounted desk under a wall phone and several TV monitors. Speakers were suspended in each of the four ceiling corners.

Jesse went through a door on his left and found himself in a small but well-arranged locker room. There was a cedar sauna off the showers.

The next was a massage room with two waist-high tables and a wall of stacked towels and bottles of oils.

The last door before the stairs was unlocked. Jesse walked into a totally dark space. He felt for the light and as he let go of the door, it closed by itself with a soft swish. For a moment, he imagined himself mummifying in this dungeon room. Then he found the switch and his eyes traveled to the far back wall of the narrow rectangular space and five round targets.

A shooting range. Each target was attached to a wire that ran along the ceiling beneath the recessed lights and ended at the elbow-height bench, running perpendicularly from wall to wall. On the opposite wall, ammunition was arranged by caliber. Five sets of green ear protectors hung on pegs. To the right was a glass-fronted cabinet. Jesse looked in at twenty or so different handguns, machine pistols, automatic shotguns and a separate section for black cylinders that must be silencers. Three high-powered rifles with scopes hung above the cabinet on pegs.

He left the room, returned to the first floor and walked out the front doors. The four large garage doors took up the entire lower floor of the south wing. To the right he found a regular door. He fingered the keys in his pocket and felt like he was on *Let's Make A Deal*.

"And behind door number three is your brand new *car*!"

The bays were two car-lengths deep. The first was empty and looked like it was a service area for the kitchen. A twenty-two-foot Boston Whaler Avenger on a twin-axle trailer was hooked to a coal-black Range Rover with a delicate red stripe running the length of her. He walked around the stern and admired twin 200-horsepower Evinrude outboard engines.

His vehicle was in the next bay. It was a late '70s cherry-red, mint-condition BMW 2002. He opened the driver's door, settled into black leather upholstery and checked out a mobile phone, tape deck-radio, and a radar detector, internally wired. The sun roof opened manually. The car smelled old and fresh at the same time. There was not a speck of dust on anything. He tore himself from the 2002 to peek under the cover of the car to the rear and found a metallic silver Dino Ferrari.

The 735ii was parked in the last bay in front of a huge, dirty green and dented Pontiac station wagon of indeterminable age. It looked out of place amongst all the shiny cars.

Jesse exited the garage and stopped at the kennels tucked beside the garage along the perimeter wall. Three outside pens behind a ten-foot mesh-link fence fronted three doghouses with sinister black openings. The middle pen seemed empty, but the other two were definitely occupied. Jesse stepped back as a large Doberman came silently from each door. Their taut bodies slinked up to the fence and they stood motionless, staring. They didn't bark, they didn't pant, they didn't move an inch. They just stood there and watched him move back a step, slowly so as not to encourage them to break through the steel and rip him to bloody shreds.

He didn't turn his back on their penetrating gaze until he was back on the gravel driveway. He looked nervously around and caught the eyes of a guard at the gate. He was watching, smiling without humor.

Jesse retreated to the house and the safety of his room.

He needed to drive at a cleansing speed down an open road, windows down and sunroof open wide. He took his dark glasses and Daytimer from the desk drawer, ripped a blank page out, spooned some coke into the crease and folded the edges around to form a triangle, then again to secure the dope into a small rectangle. He stuck it in his shirt pocket. Before putting the silver dish away, he took a couple of toots. As an afterthought, he stuck the half-joint into the empty credit card pocket of the wallet. He patted his pockets to make sure he wasn't forgetting anything. He remembered to get the street map out of the folder stashed in a side drawer. Just opening the folder made him nervous. He'd deal with the implications later.

The dash clock in the 2002 said eleven-thirty. He found the garage door control on his sun visor. As he turned right toward the gate, he had the dreadful thought that the man wouldn't let him out. The gates swung open as he drove up. The guard nodded as he went by.

The short-throw stick was smooth as he shifted to third and drove easily away from La Primavera. It felt good to get out and be in motion. He slowed down when he realized he was already twenty miles an hour over the speed limit. No need to rush. He adjusted the mirrors.

He took the 36th Street Bridge to Miami. The day was bright. He put on his sunglasses and felt more protected. He found 99.9 on the radio, Kiss Country, and had to turn it way up because of the wind rushing through the windows. It seemed strange that in a land so foreign to Maine, the same songs were playing through all the speakers. He made good time getting to Route 41 that crossed southern Florida and ended in Tampa.

The drive got boring and he looked for a little road that would be more fun. He took a left and went south, away from the strip malls of fast-food joints and tacky liquor stores. He drove along large deserted lots of sand and scrub. He sped along the road as it turned west, then south again. He could feel the suspension take the small bumps, the tie rods and rack-and-pinion steering hold the curves, and the radial tires grip the pavement. The scenery whipped by and the sound of a wicked fast Outlaws song seemed to melt with him into the seat. He hung his left elbow out the window and tapped the frantic beat against the steering wheel with his other hand, head bopping and nodding to the rhythm.

Jesse heard a siren. He sat up with a start and looked in the rearview mirror. He let his foot off the accelerator and found a sandy spot in a dent in the overgrowth and pulled in after dutifully using the turn indicator. He turned the radio off.

In the side mirror he watched a fat hatless man in uniform struggle out of the cruiser. It was a local cop.

Jesse looked up expectantly as his window became totally filled with the massive form. The belly rolled out like a wave from the belt that divided the fat, like trying to cinch in a weather balloon around the middle. With effort, the man leaned down and stuck his fleshy jowls forward.

"Nice car, young fella." His voice was surprisingly melodious and soothing. His smile parted flesh and kind gray eyes twinkled. Jesse smiled helplessly back and said, "Thank you, sir."

The policeman stood up straight and Jesse had to lean out the window to look at his face. He put hands on wide hips and said pleasantly, "I sure would appreciate it if you all'd let me see your license and registration."

"Yes, sir." Jesse fumbled through the glove box praying the registration was there. It wasn't.

Starting to panic, he found it in the pocket in the passenger's visor. He reached across and took the Daytimer from the side seat and opened it to remove his license. The joint was just visible and, as smoothly as he could, he placed his thumb over it and removed the plastic card. As he handed the papers up to the cop, he patted his shirt pocket.

The man stood there and examined the information. "A company car and an out- a-state driver. You down here on vacation?"

"Yes, sir. I was just out for a drive. It got too boring at the beach."

"Well, young fella, you sure been windin' this here car through the countryside. You ain't even goin' slow enough to appreciate this here fine scenery." He paused so that Jesse could take a look around at the swamp on the right and a picturesque horse farm on the left. "Now, I'm paid to protect these here folks of mine, and you haulin' ass down this road ain't making me look very good."

"Sorry, sir. I must not have been paying any attention."

"You got that right, boy. That there's ma point. This here is fine country, full of fine people."

"I didn't mean any disrespect, sir."

He listened to that and considered for a moment.

"I'm just going to warn you this time, and nothing formal either. But I want you to consider what I'm a going to say." He paused for effect. "Slow down, think on it a bit and admire this here pretty countryside. You can get into a heap of trouble barreling down the road like that. You slow down and put that fancy mind to work, and you'll be fine."

Jesse sat in a mild daze, astonished at his good fortune. Maybe he was truly on a roll, where nothing could touch him.

The man returned the license and registration and said, "Y'all have a nice safe afternoon." With that he strolled back to his car, which sighed under his weight. He pulled a U-turn and headed back the way he'd come.

"You lucky son of a bitch," Jesse said out loud. He sat back and took a deep breath. Slowly, he pulled out of the sandy spot and headed forward, looking for a place to turn around. He'd had enough of country driving.

He drove the speed limit back into Miami, but instead of going directly home, he drove over the causeway and headed to the beach. It was after lunchtime, but he wasn't hungry. He turned north toward Fort Lauderdale and looked to his right at the waves curling onto the white sands. Small cumulus clouds dotted the horizon.

He got some double takes from nearly naked

tanned girls strolling the boardwalk. Must be the vintage car. He drove another mile and pulled into a parking lot. He took off the Nikes and his socks, gathered smokes, money and the half-joint, and locked the car.

He felt conspicuous walking along the wet sand in street clothes. He rolled trousers and sleeves to knee and elbow and let the water swirl around his ankles. He lit the joint and smoked it from his cupped hand.

From behind his mirrored glasses, he admired the female talent lying on towels stretched smoothly across the hot sand. They glistened with oil and seemed totally out of reach. He flung the unfinished joint into the water after three tokes and felt frivolously wasteful.

He walked up the scorching sand that gave under his bare feet and left him with the impression that he was getting nowhere. The sidewalk was cooler. He crossed the street to a narrow beach store and took a Diet Coke from the glass-fronted cooler. He took it to the counter and pulled the only money he had from his pocket, a crisp hundred-dollar bill.

The teenaged blond girl behind the counter looked at him funny. "Don't you got something smaller?"

Jesse shrugged his shoulders, afraid to say something stupid. He managed to say no.

She made change with a disgruntled sigh, making the point that he was putting her out. As he was leaving, she said to his back, "You sure don't look like no dealer I ever seen."

He walked slowly back toward his car, browsing in the store windows, sipping the Coke. He stopped at a cutlery store and his eye caught a stainless folding contraption that had all sorts of tools compressed into a chunk of steel. The man in the store made him leave the soda outside, but didn't give him any more trouble. He bought the Leatherman and put it on his belt.

He eventually ran out of ways to delay his return to La Primavera. The ride back was uneventful and he felt foolish talking to the camera at the gate. "Mr. Langdon, returning," he said in his most authoritative voice. He thought he sounded like an underage teenager trying to buy liquor at the state store.

After a minute, he thought they hadn't heard. He was just about to embarrass himself by pleading when the gates swung away. They'd been toying with him. Fuck them.

He returned to his room and changed into his bathing suit. Carla found him poolside. "Can I get you anything, Mr. Langdon?"

"Could I have some lemonade without sugar?"

"Of course, Mr. Langdon." She seemed to have removed herself from their earlier intimacy and resumed the remote politeness of servility.

For the rest of the afternoon, he flipped from side to side and watched his skin turn pink. He took occasional cooling dips in the pool.

CHAPTER 9

JESSE WOKE TO another glorious day. Florida seemed endless in its flatness and succession of sunny days.

An erection led him to the bathroom. Jesse followed and had trouble fitting himself on the toilet. Lenny Bruce's suggestion of the over-the-shoulder technique made Jesse smile through the marijuana hangover and the slight headache. No drugs today.

His skin was tight and tender. He got confirmation in the mirror. He was sunburned with white stripes between the rolls of fat.

Four aspirins might do the trick. The medicine cabinet was well stocked. He cupped his hand and filled his mouth with water to wash down the melting aspirin. He looked at himself in the mirror.

Fleshy burned face, thinning hair, high forehead, prominent cheekbones, good nose and strong jaw. Bloodshot brown eyes. Drunk driving scars carved across his eyebrows. All in all, an admirable structure that needed some tending.

Shaving was not a pleasure this morning, but he got the whiskers off. He went down to breakfast in bathing suit and T-shirt.

Carla brought food to the pool while he was doing laps. The ten he could manage were no easier the second day, and he was glad to have it over when he sat down to black coffee. He ate the fruit, but left the muffin and butter. He lathered on sunblock he'd taken from the medicine cabinet.

He eased back on the chaise, jittery, and positioned himself so he could just reach his coffee. He closed his eyes and tried not to think.

Carla came out to get the dishes and he asked her if she knew when Mr. Santee was coming back.

"Yes, sir, he is supposed to come home tomorrow around noon." She stood in the sunlight and he couldn't look up at her. "And Mr. Flagler is due in today." With that she hustled away with the tray of plates.

Antsy, he got up and took his things back into the house. He felt like flying, maybe to Key West for lunch.

The drive to the airport took twice as long as it should have because he wasn't paying attention and got lost. He found the airport by mistake, then had trouble getting to the InterRegional hangar. He parked outside and went through the side door. Sam came walking swiftly up and shook his hand. "Good morning, Mr. Langdon. Most of the work has been finished on your plane. All that's left is to mount the fuel pods. That's why the bottom of the wings are apart." He motioned with his arm toward the plane. Jesse's eyes followed. Fuel pods?

They walked over. Jesse said, "I thought I'd take her down to Key West for the afternoon. Guess not." They stood together facing the Lake. All sorts of tools and wing pieces were sitting beside the port landing gear. "What's this about fuel pods?"

"I assumed you wanted it done." Sam sounded defensive and stuck both hands into his coverall pockets. "Mr. Santee called the afternoon you arrived and read me a list of stuff to do to your plane. You know, the curtains, the reliever tube and the fuel pods. I have the avionics box all wired to go. It works great. It's got a handle and everything." He sounded proud. Jesse didn't have the heart to ask what the hell was going on.

He looked at the windshield and saw that new glazing had been applied to the seam. His gaze went deeper into the cabin. The rearmost seats had been removed and there were flowered curtains across the windows.

"Mind if I see the avionics box?" Jesse was the uncomfortable one now.

Sam said, "Hey, yeah, I'll go get it." Then he turned and ran to the avionics shop.

He returned lugging a suitcase-sized plywood box. He set it down on the glassy floor and Jesse stooped beside him to see. The box was well made; the little door fit perfectly and swung on hidden hinges. Sam was obviously delighted. "You open this here, like this. And whalla! An autopilot and Loran and even a cassette deck." Sam continued enthusiastically, "See, you set it on the passenger seat, it even straps down in case of turbulence, then take these cables out the back, like this, and hook it into the jacks I've installed just under the panel. It all works great in here, but of course you need to take her up and test it in the air. By then the paint will be dry."

"Paint?"

Sam was uncomfortable again. "Mr. Santee told me you wanted new numbers. We put them on yesterday. They came out real good too."

Jesse stood up slowly. His knees popped. Sam followed him around the wing tip. Sure enough, his plane was no longer N4974V, but N6311U. The old numbers had been sanded off, a new base perfectly matching the fuselage sprayed on, and the new numbers painted. He went up close and looked at the aluminum FAA registration plate underneath the horizontal stabilizer. It had been changed to match the new numbers.

All he could think to say was, "Handsome labor."

Sam couldn't have been more pleased with the compliment. "Thank you, sir. Thank you. The new fuel pods will give you a full twelve hours of endurance. That's the reason for the reliever tube. You can just piss in it and it gets dumped out into the slipstream. The pods will be mounted under the wings and can be controlled by your other fuel-management toggles. It's slick. I'll be finished by tomorrow."

Jesse put on his sunglasses. "I'm supposed to meet some instructor here tomorrow morning for dual training. After that we could test the avionics."

"That'll be great. I'll make sure I'm free."

Jesse drove away slowly and considered the liberties Santee had taken with his plane. He hadn't thought about having to turn his plane into a long-hauler, but if he was going to run drugs, it made sense. The autopilot would be nice. But the logic didn't allay his violated feeling. Aimless driving didn't help, so he headed back to La Primavera and took the Scarab for a spin.

The other boaters looked with envy as he eased past them. He passed under two causeways, idled by Miami Beach Marine, and headed to the open sea beyond Fisher Island.

He'd never felt such speed and grace on the water. As she hurtled faster and faster the thrill increased into a light fear.

He spent the better part of the next hour cruising the channel up past La Primavera and then back again. He got so many jealous looks he became practiced at the nonchalant, just-a-small-toy wave.

As he was hooking her up, he heard footfalls on the incline.

Jesse looked up. A barbed-wire man was leaning on the rail, staring down at him. He was wearing worn black cowboy boots, faded jeans slung low on thin hips, a wide belt with stitched curls and an old thin multicolored cotton shirt. The short sleeves were rolled up as high as they would go. His arms were brown. His face was creased and dented, gaunt and tan. Mid-forties, the Marlboro man gone to seed.

He was carrying a tall green bottle of what looked like champagne. He ripped off the foil, unwound the wire and popped the cork, which flew past Jesse's head. Foam gushed from the neck and poured onto the incline. The man tilted back and guzzled from the bottle. "Fucking spic piss water. Who the fuck are you?"

"Jesse Langdon."

The man stared at him. His dull gray eyes were alive with menace. "Oh, that lame-ass white-boy preppy that's 'spose to know stuff but looks like he don't know shit." His voice had sharp gravel in it.

"Had a hard day?"

The man took two quick steps down the incline toward him, his eyes going from menace to malignancy.

But he stopped, as if Santee had suddenly materialized between them.

Jesse stood very still and unclenched his fists. Flagler reached to his breast pocket and took out a pack of Pall Malls and a Bic lighter. With his lips he drew out a cigarette and lit it with the lighter turned up to flame thrower. He never took his eyes from Jesse. "A fucking natural-fiber drug runner? You gotta be shitting me." He spat the words out.

"That's right. Shitting you. My favorite turd." He thought it, but said instead, "You must be Flagler."

Flagler made smoking look like a bad habit, dirty and mean, something to kill you. He didn't like being appraised. He stood there defiant, with legs spread. "How the fuck you know that?"

"Mr. Santee mentioned that you'd be stopping by."

Flagler mimicked Jesse. "Oh? Mr. Santee said I'd be stopping by, did he?" He took another swill of champagne.

Jesse didn't have to put up with this shit. He lit his own cigarette as Flagler watched him. The flame shook too much, whether from fear or anger, he couldn't tell.

"You a real little Santee, smoking those candy-ass slant-eye cigarettes."

"And you're a real piece of gear, Flagler."

For a moment, Flagler looked confused about whether or not it was an insult. In the end, it didn't

113

matter one way or the other. He moved in toward Jesse, fists flexing. Jesse got ready to kick him in the crotch. Either Carla had been watching from the house or she had perfect timing. She hurried down to the dock, calling out with forced pleasantness, "Hello, Mr. Emmett! Good to have you back."

Flagler stopped and looked at her, then back at Jesse, deciding.

Carla continued brightly, "Mr. Santee will be back tomorrow and is very anxious to hear your news. Mr. Langdon is staying in *the front room*." She looked meaningfully at Flagler, who was processing the information. "Will you be sleeping in your room over the garage tonight? I'll make sure it's in order."

Flagler took out another smoke and put the flame thrower to it. Something meaningful about the front room established Jesse's place in the pecking order, and she'd made that plain to both of them. Again, it seemed as if Santee had stepped between them. But Jesse knew he'd have to watch his back from now on.

"This shit ain't fit to drink." He hurled the bottle toward the end of the dock where it exploded in glass and foam. "I'm gonna go out and get shitfaced with some real men." He shot a glance at Jesse as he strode up to the house.

Neither Carla nor Jesse moved. It was as if they were waiting for the disturbing energy of the man to dissipate, let the evil flow away of its own accord.

Jesse spoke. "Is he always like that?"

"Sometimes better, sometimes worse. He is very mean and will strike quick, like a switchblade knife. It is best to stay out of his reach, Mr. Langdon." The confiding tone was back. Carla turned toward the house, then turned back and said, "I think his news for Mr. Santee is not good."

CHAPTER 10

FLIGHT INSTRUCTION ALWAYS dumped a big pit in the stomach. Practicing stalls, when the plane just falls away, will do that to you every time. Jesse fought the urge to turn around.

He parked the car beside the hangar and was relieved to see that the Lake was put back together. They said their hellos, Sam chipper and busy with the MU-2, then Jesse left him alone to do his work. He took his bag to the lounge and got a cup of coffee. He tuned in his handheld radio to the Ground's frequency and wondered if he would hear his instructor taxi over.

After a half hour, he heard a Seneca request permission to taxi to the InterRegional hangar and he got up and walked out to watch.

A Piper Seneca III came down the taxiway and turned in. The pilot spun the plane around so that it was heading out. He let the turbos cool down before cutting the fuel supply. If you shock-cooled them by cutting them off too soon, invariably you were looking at a premature engine overhaul. The pilot waved. Friendly enough. He looked the part, floppy cowboy hat and the requisite aviator sunglasses.

The plane was clean and looked new. She was white on the top half, red on the bottom, with four distinctive black stripes dividing the colors, a sleek nose and raked windshield. The engines looked huge, hung out on the low wing. Jesse was tingly with excitement at moving up the aviation ladder.

After five minutes, the pilot shut down the engines and climbed out with a briefcase. Any picture of the dashing cowboy instructor was ruined as he came around the nose of the plane. He was tall, thin, and walked hunched, leaning forward like he might topple over when he stopped. He had on a blue synthetic western shirt with pearl snaps, his undershirt visible beneath. His jeans were worn high and he had on a brand new pair of shining white Reeboks that didn't go with anything else he was wearing. Mid-sixties.

The handshake was a firm two pumps and release. "Edgar Fischer. And you're Jesse Langdon. Like to be called Jesse?" He took off the glasses and looked at Jesse with sympathetic watchful brown eyes.

"Yes, sir."

"Jesse, call me Ed. Now follow me into the lounge and let's talk a spell."

They each got coffee and settled around the corner

of the table. Ed opened his briefcase and handed Jesse some books. "These are the engine and airframe logs for the Seneca. Thought you'd like to review them. You can give me your log book and license."

Jesse handed over his papers. Ed took off his hat and leaned back to examine the log book. He had a full head of thick gray hair parted on the left and oiled down so that the comb tracks were visible. It was cut short enough so none came over the ears. He had the tan of a Floridian and the face of a boxer. His eyes were alert as they scanned the entries. "You can tell a whole lot about a person by looking at his log book. This here one is neat, has some details, and looks pretty complete. You cheat any?"

"No. I've never needed to. I do mostly cross-country business flying and have no real need to amass hours. I'm not aiming for a commuter job and I've got enough hours to satisfy my insurance."

Ed nodded and looked over the license. He looked out into the hangar. "That your Lake?"

"Yep. She's slow, but fun in the water."

"Used to own one a long time ago, but got tired of not being able to get stuff in. Traded up to a straight float 206. What a plane! Could load her full of people and gear and still get her off with two canoes tied to the struts. Took some distance, I'll grant you that, but she'd rock up on one pontoon and be off the water after a spell." He returned his attention to the license. "Santee said you needed a multi-ticket and MU-2 time. You probably want to be able to fly them in the soup, so we'll do some hood work toward the end and tack on the multi-instrument. Sound good to you?"

"Yes, fine."

"That Mitsubishi, she's an orange when you fly her single-pilot."

"Orange?"

"We'll get to that. You proficient with a handgun?"

"Excuse me?"

"It's about frame of mind. There's lots similar between a pistol and a twin, kinda require a similar attitude." He leaned forward to the edge of the sofa, rested his weight on elbows on knees, got serious. "You gonna answer my question?"

"I'm familiar with firearms. I can shoot and hit the target."

"That all? Listen, here's an example. You come out of your favorite restaurant with your honey, walking arm in arm, humming a tune, under the streetlights. You're comfy and got that deep bourbon glow in your belly. She's leaning in real close. You ain't alert, mind somewhere else. That's condition white.

"You walk to the car in the dark parking lot. You hear a rustle. You're relaxed, but alert. Your head swivels around, like you're lookin' for traffic in the New York Traffic Control Area but can't find it. You're ready. That's yellow. You with me so far?"

Jesse was spellbound and nodded.

"Okay, so now you catch a glimpse of two guys coming out from behind a car. They're big and one of 'em's got a shiny knife. They ain't too close, but they are coming. Something's about to happen, a mess that needs a good resolution. You've figured that out and you're on your toes. That's orange.

"Now comes condition red. You reach back behind your coat, draw out your handgun, bring her up, aim two handed and say something like, 'Hold it right there.' They can tell by your voice you know what you're talking about, mean business. If they run off, that's great, but if one makes a quick move for his gun, you shoot him first, then the other guy." Ed leaned back now. "Between yellow and red shouldn't take you more than about five seconds."

He paused for effect, then said, "If you ain't in yellow when you walk out to that plane, we're in trouble. Think of a twin as a loaded gun that can't wait for you to relax so it can kill you."

Jesse was impressed.

Ed, eyes boring into Jesse, said, "You're thinkin' this'll be fun. It won't. I'm from the old school where we push hard, but in the end you gonna end up knowing how to fly that twin without killin' yourself or anyone else. That is if you can stand me. Others might run you right through the program, but I'm gonna show you how to fly, and especially how to think. In the end, you'll have the satisfaction that comes with knowin' what you're doin'.

"I'm gonna talk through some of the preliminary stuff here in the lounge, then we'll take a hop. Nothing too demanding today, just to get a feel. Tomorrow, we go at it hard, then polish her up on Saturday. If you got any talent, you should be ready for the check ride on Sunday. I'll tack on some of that instrument stuff, and maybe some short-field, rough fieldwork at the end. You need to take a piss?"

"How'd you know that?"

"You don't look like the kind that gets fidgeting and holding his legs together 'cause you want to dance." Ed smiled.

Jesse headed for the bathroom, then returned. Once settled again, Ed continued. "Any turd can fly a twin. Not too many can handle an engine-out doing eighty-five knots and dirty after liftoff in the Seneca. In my airplane out there, and it is *my* airplane, so we ain't gonna fuck it up, you lift off at seventy-nine knots. You want to build up the speed to ninety-two knots. That's the blue line speed. How are you with your V speeds?"

"Like V for velocity? I've kind of forgotten most of it."

"I like you already—no bullshit and you can admit you don't know nothin'. The blue line is the best rate of climb on one engine. Happens to be the same speed for best rate on both engines. They call it Vyse. Anyway, then you clean her up, flaps and gear, and head for the sky. You gonna want enough altitude. You're on your way to happy trails.

"Now let's say you take the runway and you're bopping along under eighty-five knots just as pretty as can be, and you sense some trouble, just off the runway. Abort, pull the power and land into the trees straight ahead. 'Course if there's a field you go for that. Above eighty-five knots, then you got to be real good, kinda like swallowing your chaw, brown juice dribblin' down your chin, and you still get the girl." He slapped his knees and stood up laughing. Jesse realized that the sides of his scalp hurt from grinning so much. Ed said, "Let's go cheat death."

Ed took the checklist from the cockpit and led Jesse through a thorough preflight, noting all the peculiarities that distinguish a twin from a single. That done, Jesse mounted the starboard wing and maneuvered into the left seat. Ed followed. Jesse removed the paperwork from the see-through pouch beside his leg. It contained the airworthiness certificate, registration and radio permit. Ed handed him the operator's manual, which included the weight and balance graphs and worksheets.

"You take this home tonight and study up on the plane. I got a spare one. I'm gonna baby you today, set you up for the kill." He chuckled, and Jesse set sweaty palms on the control wheel and studied the panel and instrument placement. "I'll coax you through the start, work the radio and help with the air work if you need it. Tomorrow you do it all yourself, so pay attention."

They went through the hot-start procedures, mixture off until the engine caught, then full rich. The maneuverability of the Seneca was similar to a twin-screw power boat and he fiddled with asymmetric thrust as he turned out onto the taxiway.

After the run-up and clearance, they took the runway and held, looking down the long centerline. Ed said, "Gun to your head, boy. Remember, yellow."

Jesse advanced the throttles evenly, felt the turbos kick in, and held direction with the pedals. He cocked the yoke into the gentle crosswind, checked the engine gauges, listened, and watched the airspeed approach seventy-nine. Ed's hands weren't far from the wheel and he was all attention. At precisely seventy-nine knots, Jesse applied slight back pressure and the twin rose smoothly into the air, one wing dipping to the wind. They accelerated and climbed above the runway and at ninety-two knots, he raised the gear and flaps and held airspeed as they climbed out. Ed motioned with his hand to fly toward the Everglades.

For the next hour, Ed demonstrated how the plane could kill you if you made the wrong decisions with an engine out. Ed directed and Jesse flew. Ed brought back the power on one engine to zero thrust while Jesse held a steady ninety-two knots. The plane climbed at

200 feet per minute. At eighty-five kts, she climbed at only 100 fpm. Jesse was told to increase the airspeed to 100 kts and they lost climb all together. At ninety-two knots again, Jesse dropped the gear and any climb. With only the flaps out, the plane descended. With both gear and flaps down and the dead propeller wind-milling, the Seneca descended at 1,000 fpm.

"Vmc," or "velocity manure's coming" as Ed defined it, is when you don't have enough airspeed to control the plane on one engine. Vmc was sixty-six knots. Ed had Jesse slow the clean plane, then go to full power. Then Ed pulled the power on one engine and Jesse maintained altitude as the airspeed decayed. Before any stall buffet or loss of directional control, the warning horn went off and Jesse eased the yoke forward and gained airspeed.

By now Jesse was a little more comfortable in the plane. His palms weren't sweating so badly, but his shirt was wet and he squirmed in his seat to ready himself for the next assault.

Ed was all business and continued with the last of the morning's work. He demonstrated the need to bank the plane into the good engine and keep the skid indicator deflected. He explained that if you try to keep the wings level you push the Vmc way up, even as high as Vyse. "By then, you're not only shitting elephants, but the ground's just a-spinning in the windshield and the manure's coming fast. You gonna be dead."

They headed back to Tamiami and Jesse spent the last of his energy on the landing. He was rewarded by a smooth touchdown and easy rollout. They taxied back to the hangar in silence. Jesse and Ed sat in the cockpit while the turbos spooled down and cooled. Ed made the entry into Jesse's log book while humming Jerry Jeff's "Redneck Mother."

Jesse collapsed into the sofa beside Ed, who said, "You're pretty smooth on the controls, boy. Shouldn't be any trouble for you, till I pull some of my tricks. Then we really see if you can keep your head."

He chuckled with devious anticipation. They reviewed the demonstrations and Ed stressed again the important parts. "I want you to stop at a bookstore and pick up *Cooper on Handguns*, by Colonel Jeff Cooper. He's the guy behind all that color-condition stuff. You'll see the parallels to flight. I also want you to know that operations manual real good. You gonna need it." He smiled. They set a time for tomorrow morning and Ed whistled himself out the door.

Jesse sat still and let the feelings sink in. He'd done well. But there was a small spot of dread deep inside. He had no idea what Ed had in store, and he knew that any confidence he might feel was a mistake.

He pulled out of his reverie and went to talk to Sam. A Lear jet was parked in the middle of the hangar between the MU-2 and Jesse's plane.

Sam and two other guys in the same coveralls were

washing the Lear. Jesse walked over. He'd not met the two new men, but they were hard at it, so he talked to Sam.

"This Santee's?"

Sam looked up from his soapy bucket. "Yeah. Quite a bird, huh? He got in just after you took off with Mr. Fischer, then headed to the house. She always comes back real dusty from Mexico. This is going to keep me and the other guys busy the rest of the afternoon. So I'm not going to get to your avionics box today. That okay?"

"Hell, Sam, I'm not the boss. He is. There's no rush anyway. I'll have my hands full with Ed for the next several days."

"Sounds good to me. See ya tomorrow."

Jesse got his flight bag from the lounge and headed into town. He found a big mall and went to the bookstore. They had Cooper's book, the handgun shooter's bible.

Jesse drove back to La Primavera apprehensive about the coming scene, but glad in a way that things were on the move and he wouldn't be alone in the big house anymore.

Turning in at the gate, he knew things were different. The placed looked like it was on red alert. The gates opened easily, but two guards with sawed-off shotguns stopped him before he could drive on. The gates swung shut behind him and locked with a definitive clunk.

The guards wore their shiny suits and stuck their heads into each window and checked the car, then had him get out and open the trunk. They seemed a bit disappointed he wasn't hiding a DEA agent in the glove compartment and grunted for him to continue toward the garage.

He backed in beside the 735ii and took his bag to the front door. A guard opened it without a fuss. When the door closed behind him, he stood quietly in the entrance and listened to house noises.

From the dining room came sounds of the big table being cleared of lunch dishes and voices he didn't recognize talking in Spanish.

From the other end of the hall, to his right, he heard an angry shout and the sound of a door slamming. He thought he heard some other voices down toward the library, but wasn't sure. Now that the door was shut, he couldn't hear anything.

He stood there, undecided. Not wanting to interrupt an important meeting and not eager to intrude on an unpleasant scene, he finally stole quietly up to his room. Upstairs, maids he hadn't seen before scurried from room to room with piles of folded linen held tightly to their breasts. One looked at him curiously, then continued into one of the guest bedrooms. In his room, he found a note on the desk tucked under the leather corner of the green blotter:

Jesse,

Come down to the library when you get in, meet some of the team. We will be going over some material you will find informative.

Ed is quite an instructor, I am told.

Santee

Jesse read the note twice. So this was it. The ball would get rolling here, now, today. Jesse quelled second thoughts and concerns about consequences. Instead of thinking, he pulled out the drawer and removed the coke. He took a spoonful up each nostril, shook a little and sucked it in again, head back. He went to the mirror in the bathroom to make sure he wasn't advertising, let his gums go numb and changed his shirt.

CHAPTER 11

J ESSE'S TENTATIVE KNOCK silenced the conversation on the other side of the library door. "*Pase!*" someone called.

Three men sat around the desk. From behind it, Santee flashed a smile. "Jesse, welcome to La Primavera."

He came around the desk with outstretched hand. "I want you all to welcome Mr. Jesse Langdon the Third." Santee pulled Jesse into the room and presented him to the three other men.

"This is Coley Blades, head of security." Blades' hand was rough and claw-like. He held the grip. Under an appraising gaze, Jesse got the impression that anytime Blades felt like it, he'd be dead meat. Blades released the hand.

Jesse turned to the next man, tall, handsome and relaxed. "And this is Biano Martinez. Biano had a warm welcoming smile and a limp Latin handshake.

"And I hear you have already met Mr. Flagler." Santee's arm froze as he pointed to the chair where Flagler sat, subdued though vaguely menacing, even in Santee's presence. He wore yesterday's clothes, and they were dirtier and wrinkled.

Santee spun a fireplace chair toward the action and pointed Jesse to it. He sat carefully. Santee returned to the desk.

Santee swallowed coffee, leaned back in the creaking chair and studied his black linen trousers, smoothing an invisible imperfection. He removed a small vial of cocaine from the side pocket of his suede vest, examining Flagler. "The first order of business involves Jesse's quest to find his brother-in-law. His name is Seefer Rollerson, also known as Reefer. He would be forty-five years old, six-two, 200 pounds, heavily bearded. He knows boats and how to take care of himself. Put the word out. When you find anything, come directly to me."

Santee exchanged a glance with Flagler, then turned the vial upside down and twisted it. He brought it to his nose and inhaled. "Flagler, now we can speak of your business."

Flagler sat back, rubbed the stubble on his chin and seemed to think about how to put it. "It's like this, Mr. Santee. I got a feeling the fucking feds have made the farm. It ain't nothin certain, just a feeling, but I don't like the vibes I'm getting around town, you know? The looks." He judged that he had said enough.

Santee smiled and leaned forward for some more coffee. He looked kindly upon Flagler. "Well then, what is the worry? You say you have no knowledge. We continue as planned."

He reached into the drawer and took out six big hollow-point bullets and lined them in a row. He pulled out a large revolver and leaned back, caressing the engraved and inlaid pearl handle, all curled figures and snakes and demons and twisting vines. He pointed the hollow end at Flagler.

Flagler tried not to pay attention and cleared his throat. "I ain't got no knowledge, but this feeling I got's strong. But fuck, it ain't my fault." He took a single Pall Mall from his breast pocket and lit it. He leaned back and crossed his legs. He took a deep drag and re-crossed his legs. "It's this way. We set it up. Me, cousin of mine, his girl. Bought the place, bulldozed the strip, filled the place with cows. Looks jus' like a fucking ranch. Don't really know about this feeling."

Santee pulled the hammer out two clicks, popped the cylinder and loaded the pistol, taking his time. "Are you telling me, Emmett, that these hick farmers in Louisiana have made this ranch as a smuggling operation? Called in the DEA?" He said it sweetly, softly. He spun the loaded cylinder.

Flagler didn't respond.

"Damn it, answer me!" Santee slammed his palm on the desk, spilling coffee. Flagler jumped in his seat. A blush came onto Santee's olive face. His expression contorted. He sat back and calmly unloaded the gun.

"Hell, I don't know." Flagler waved his beer bottle. "I ain't tellin you that, I just got this feeling." He took the last swallow of beer and wiped his sleeve across the sheen on his face.

Blades and Martinez seemed at complete repose. From their calm expressions, Jesse thought the two men could be listening to Santee and Flagler discussing the nature of roses.

Santee loaded and unloaded the pistol with confusing dexterity. Was it loaded? He pointed the gun at Flagler's head, cocked the hammer, and pulled the trigger. The gun clicked and Flagler nearly jumped out of his seat.

Santee reclined and said sympathetically, "Flagler, Flagler, what are we to do? You do not know if the operation is compromised or not. Can you answer this question? Can anything be traced?"

Rivulets of sweat ran down Flagler's cheeks. He wiped them away. "Goddamn it all to hell, of course not! Everything got paid with cash." His voice quavered. He got up and went to the bar, presenting a bullfighter's small and confident back, still hoping to convince the bull. He took a shot glass off the shelf and a bottle of rum, holding it by the neck.

Flagler sat down, poured the little glass full and downed it in a gulp.

Santee rose, turned to the window and stood, looking at Miami.

Jesse pulled on a cuticle on his left thumb and it began to bleed.

Santee turned. "For your benefit, Jesse, Mr. Flagler will fill you in."

Flagler squirmed and looked at Jesse with hatred.

Flagler spit it out. "Me and my cousins set up this cattle ranch in Louisiana as a drop point. Got all the critters in place. The landing strip is all carved out. Nice big place, real private. But now I'm getting a feeling is all."

Santee looked over at Jesse and said, "Jesse, you did well in Maine. Admittedly, this is different, but what are your thoughts?"

Biano leaned forward. Blades didn't move, but Jesse could feel his keen awareness. He fought for focus amid a swirling mess of unconnected thoughts. His face felt flushed and hot. "You say you paid for everything with cash."

"Of course I paid with cash. I ain't no fool."

"I mean lots of it? Did you pay the asking price for everything?"

"Yes." Flagler looked more comfortable now, but wasn't sure where this was headed.

"In Maine, locals always try to feel out a person

from away. They ask ridiculous prices to see how you'll react. You or your cousin know about the cattle business?"

"Well, no, not much. You put up fence, they eat the grass. What's there to know? We ain't in the fucking cattle business. It's just a fucking front."

Jesse didn't look up from his hands folded tightly in his lap. "But it's got to *look* like a cattle business and not a front. Anyone blowing into a small town waving wads of cash and paying full price is going to look suspicious. The local ranchers will want to see what the new operator is like, that type of thing."

Jesse had control of the room and decided to risk his further opinions. "Better might be to set up a rich gentleman farmer, justify the flying in and out. He comes and goes, plays a lot. He doesn't know much. Uses some credit, does some banking, makes sense to the locals. Maybe even a fancy horse farm, something like that. Of course, it would cost more, and you'd need papers."

Jesse looked at Santee, then finished. "You end up with both an investment and good cover."

Flagler stared at the fireplace. Santee was fooling with the pistol again.

Jesse looked at Biano. He was the youngest man in the room, but the most regal. It was the bold features, the noble bearing of Aztec royalty. His face was smooth and dark, a straight nose coming down to a very full but carefully trimmed black mustache. The lower lip was prominent, the chin square. Dark eyes, full brows. A gentleness to the face that seemed out of place in this room. He wore shined boots and tailored jeans. His starched white short-sleeved shirt with epaulets was open to show a thick gold chain. The watch was gold and enormous.

Jesse looked to Blades and found himself being observed in return. Blades smiled, wiping away the severity in his face. He looked a little older than Jesse, maybe forty, but had no facial hair. He wore canvas desert boots, black baggy cotton pants, maybe a drawstring, light blue silk shirt, some hair coming over the second button. He was stretching his fingers. No jewelry, no watch. He wore the confidence of someone who had been highly trained.

Blades looked in Santee's direction. As Jesse's head swiveled, the room exploded. He felt the concussion in his chest and testicles. Santee was still aiming the smoking Colt at Flagler.

Flagler sat trembling but not bleeding. Behind his head several books had been blown to bits of confetti, which floated around Flagler and drifted to the floor.

Through ringing ears, Jesse heard Santee say, "Go shut it down, Flagler. Clear it out. No fuckups. Now!"

Flagler dashed from the room. The rest of them sat still, nobody willing to break the spell.

Santee spoke. "I hope a lesson has been learned."

He took another hit from the vial, didn't offer it around.

The pistol had vanished. Except for the blasted books, it could have been a dream.

When Santee spoke again, it was with softness. Jesse strained to hear him over the echo of the gunshot pounding in his head. "We need a tighter ship, gentlemen. We have come far, but my horizon is very broad and we have only just begun. I have lofty plans."

The comment left no room for response. Santee stood up. "We have work to do. Coley, you and I have an appointment. I will be ready in ten minutes. Biano and Jesse, I leave you to your own devices."

Santee left and Biano Martinez came over. "Nice work with Santee. But don't count Flagler out. He likes backs, and he's quiet."

Jesse said thank you, then, "If you don't mind, may I ask what you do?"

Biano frowned, then let go a deep laugh. Blades chuckled from the corner and watched patiently.

Biano slapped Jesse on the shoulder. "No, I don't mind. Well, let's see. I am the chief pilot for this strange group of outlaws." He spent a moment considering. "And I suppose I attend to odds and ends. Speaking of which, I need to be off for the evening too. My mother is expecting a visit, and if you think Santee can be tough, wait till you meet Mama." He laughed, shook Jesse's hand again, this time firmly, and left.

Blades came up quietly, moving deliberately. He took Jesse's elbow and looked carefully into his eyes. "It's a pleasure to meet you, Jesse. Santee speaks highly of your flying skills."

"Good to meet you too, Mr. Blades."

"Call me Coley." He gripped Jesse's hand. Coley's felt like oak.

Jesse had the strange sensation that something about Coley was more than met the eye.

"You handled that spot nicely. I haven't seen a blush like that in years." He let go of Jesse's hand. "As Santee said, I have an appointment." He left.

Jesse sank into his chair and breathed deeply. He looked longingly at the rum and the shot glass. He ran fingers through his hair. Not today. He consciously relaxed his shoulders. He set his head back, closed his eyes and felt queasy. A swim, he thought. He needed to cleanse himself of the afternoon's encounter.

He did fourteen laps before his body gave up. He went to his room and fell asleep naked on the bed.

A light rap on the door woke him. He looked at his watch and it was already seven-thirty. The windows were dark. He got a robe and opened the door to Carla with a dinner tray. She came in and set it on the table before the fireplace.

He ate slowly for a change, cold beef slices, steamed spinach leaves, a Kaliber in a tall frosted glass. He couldn't make sense of his day, so full of contrary emotions that they became a palette of multicolored paints turning brown, then gray. He took coffee and tobacco to the desk.

For an hour, he tried to concentrate on the Seneca's operation manual. He went over the same material again and again. It was no use. Then he remembered the gym in the basement and thought physical activity might bring back his concentration.

He was struggling with leg lifts when Coley came in. Jesse was about to count six, but instead said sixty. "Oh fuck, 6,000." All the day's tension came gushing out as he laughed at himself and his pretensions. His legs collapsed on the floor.

"Six thousand, huh?" Coley sat on the bench, pulled out a bucket of dried beans and dangled his hands. The middle knuckles were grotesquely enlarged and had little white spots on them. Coley considered his hands and stretched them. While watching Jesse, Coley drove a hand into the beans, clenched his fingers and brought out a fistful.

Jesse looked away and got awkwardly to his feet.

"You want to know about my hands?"

Jesse forced himself to walk over and sit beside Coley on the bench. The man made him nervous. "Yeah, okay."

Coley spread them, palms down. "I call them knife hands. See how rigid they are? Go ahead, touch them, try to bend the fingers." He brought all the fingers together. Jesse grasped the fingertips and tried to bend them back. The intimacy was unnerving.

Coley smiled and said, "Do you know anything about taking care of yourself?"

"Beg your pardon?"

"These hands take care of me." Coley thrust his other hand into the bucket. He let beans slide through his fingers. He spread them palm down again. "The white spots on these knuckles are calcium deposits. They come from repetitive contact with a hard object. I use any solid wall, but you can use anything. After a while, the pain subsides and you end up with knuckles that can disable a man. I can also use these hands straight out." He made quick jabbing motions. "Hit the throat, a kidney, maybe under the ribcage. It does a number." He admired his hands. "You notice I stretch them a lot. Unless I do that, they stiffen up and become useless. If I treat them right, though, they take good care of me."

"Interesting," Jesse said, then busied himself with the free weights and stoically did repetition after repetition. Coley joined him. They both sat on the bench. Jesse wiped his wet face with a soft white towel. He was fighting for air. Coley hadn't broken a sweat.

Coley looked over and smiled. "Time to shoot. Go get your guns."

Jesse returned with his two pistols and found Coley at the shooting bench in front of a broken-down

Browning 9mm pistol that looked like it had been through a war or two. He slid the pieces back together, *click click*, pulled the slide, and checked the mechanism. Without looking up, he asked Jesse to get ammunition. Jesse placed four boxes of 9mm and a box of .380s on the counter.

Coley checked the three guns. "All guns are always loaded." He removed the magazines.

"You should be able to break down and reassemble this gun in the dark. Your life may depend on it. Fix the problem quickly before the other guys kill you. You can practice that on your own."

While Coley loaded his magazine, he continued. "Lucky McDaniels taught me to shoot in Virginia. Little teeny guy, but boy could he shoot." Coley spoke with reverence. "When he was little he'd go to the westerns, see gun fanning, shooting bottles off fences. Nobody told him that it was make believe. He'd go home, set bottles up and blast them off the fence.

"He was a natural. He taught me to point, both eyes open, said shooting was nothing more than the ability to point your finger. Said aiming was bullshit. He could hit anything with a pistol, rifle, or shotgun, and this is from the shoulder or the hip. I've never been able to shoot like him."

Coley removed two hearing protectors from the pegs and donned one. "The last thing is, if you ever want to hear again, you might want to put this on."

Coley took the Browning in a two-handed grip and emptied fifteen shots at the target. He set down the smoking gun, removed his head gear, and pushed a button that brought the target skimming back along the wire.

"This is vicinity shooting." Coley took thumbs and first fingers of both hands and made a circle around the middle of the target. All but one bullet had fallen in the circle. "Lucky would laugh and say he wouldn't want to be standing there." Coley reloaded his pistol. "Your turn." He clipped on a fresh target and returned it to the wall. Jesse slid the magazine into the Beretta. He racked the slide and chambered a round, released the safety, and took aim with one eye and one hand, aligning the sights and leaving the target an unfocused blur. He squeezed off fifteen shots, slow and evenly paced.

Coley brought the target back. "Nice shooting." Twelve bullets had hit the paper, six of them in the inner two circles. "You might want to try using two hands—push with the right, pull with the left. It keeps the recoil to a minimum. Try pointing with both eyes open. If you ever have to shoot in the dark, the practice will come in handy." Coley handed him the hearing protector. Jesse tried the new approach, but it felt unnatural and he did worse.

Coley kept up the encouragement. "It takes practice." He motioned for Jesse to take the left target. "Practice with the Beretta. The Walther is a phone booth gun, meaning it's only accurate at really close range. Take it slow and work from one comfortable position. When you get the hang of it, try another position. In the end, you'll be shooting from the hip and hitting close to where you want."

Coley shot off fifteen rounds from the hip. All the bullets hit the target, eight of them in the circle.

Jesse changed the targets less frequently than Coley. He wasn't as hard on them. Between boxes of cartridges, he looked over and watched Coley remove a cleaning kit from underneath the counter and break down the Browning.

Coley motioned for him to remove the protector. "Always clean your gun. It's like the hands. You treat it well and it will return the favor."

Jesse set the Beretta to the side to cool and took up the Walther. It was harder, light in his hand, none of the balance. His performance was dismal, but he fired off fifty rounds. When he was finished, Coley was gone.

He broke and cleaned the pistols. It was after midnight. He worked methodically in the aroma of gun solvent until the barrels gleamed. By the time he was done, it was closer to one a.m. He straightened the counter, tossed his targets in the wastebasket and replaced them with fresh ones. He swept up the brass casings and threw them away. When everything was in order, he opened the door and turned out the light.

He dragged himself through the quiet house and

up the stairs. He loaded the pistols, stowed them in the holsters and put them in the drawer.

The photograph of Reefer and him on the stern of the lobster boat, surrounded by traps, caught his eye. The mystery kept coming at him from odd angles. Santee's mention of him to the team seemed gratuitous, and the look to Flagler strange. What transpired after overwhelmed the subtle exchange. Looking at his guns and his brother-in-law, he wondered if they were destined to come together.

CHAPTER 12

H E CENTERED THE plane and applied the power, cocking the yoke so the wing would dip into the crosswind. It was twenty knots and thirty degrees off the nose to port. Gusty crosswinds weren't his favorite.

The turbos kicked in and the Seneca bumped and slewed down the runway. Jesse worked the foot pedals to keep her on the centerline. The airspeed indicator came alive and climbed toward seventy-nine knots. The plane got light on its feet. In the headset, Ed said calmly, "Watch the port wing."

Jesse looked left. There was a distinct drop in noise. Jesse spun back to the gauges—starboard rpms dropping, airspeed decaying.

Jesse felt sluggish. As he brought both power levers back to idle, the plane lost its float and settled firmly on the runway. He took the last taxiway off the runway. Ed said, "You going to mention anything to the controllers?"

Jesse pushed the talk button on the control wheel and said, "Tamiami Tower, Seneca ..." He looked frantically for the call sign and found it on the panel. "... 8478T aborted takeoff. Request taxi back to the active."

"8478T, tower, please contact ground frequency for clearance."

"Sorry, sir, I guess I'm a little confused." One mistake. More to come?

"8478T, Tower. You flying with Fischer?" There was sympathy in his voice.

"Yes sir, 8478T."

"Well, y'all have a nice day." The tower controller chuckled before he let go his transmission button.

With the proper clearance, Jesse got back to the run-up area, set the brakes, and wiped his palms on his jeans.

"You were too slow on that reaction, Jesse. Remember, you're in condition yellow and you need to be ready to jump to red and resolve anything that might come up. We were running out of runway. But what the hey, we made the last taxiway."

Jesse thought, small consolation. Tower gave them permission to depart and they climbed uneventfully to 3,000 feet, then flew off to the practice area. Ed had Jesse slow the airplane, drop the gear and flaps, and go to full throttle while maintaining liftoff speed. Ed reset the altimeter to zero.

The morning blurred into the thrashing of turbulence punctuated with gunfire commands barked by Ed—"React! Bank it! Which engine? Feather! Reaction! Clean it up! Bank it, goddamn it! React!"

Jesse felt assaulted and battered, and always behind the airplane.

By the time Ed was hungry, suggesting they break for lunch, Jesse was lost in exasperation and felt sick. Ed pointed toward the airport and handed Jesse a hood. "Might as well shoot an approach. Here, put this over your head, contact Miami Approach and request an ILS to Tamiami."

Sadist! To buy time, Jesse turned away from the airport and fished out the approach plate. He set the autopilot and studied the ILS chart. Sufficiently informed, he contacted approach and made the request.

"78T, squawk 2725, fly heading zero eight zero, maintain 2,000." Jesse fell into the familiar and felt confidence return. He settled in his seat and repeated back the instructions. With the hood down, his world was reduced to the instrument panel and the approach plate on his lap.

It took a moment to get the scan going, confirmation and reconfirmation of position and altitude. He disengaged the autopilot. Now, would Ed pull some funny stuff?

Even with the wind, Jesse flew the plane smoothly and kept both glide slope needles centered or showing slightly high. At minimums, he looked up from under the hood to find the runway straight ahead and close. Always a miracle. He brought the power back and let the Seneca settle nicely on the windward tire—a good approach and smooth landing. Though it didn't erase the morning's trauma, he felt a bit better about his prospects.

Ed jumped off the wing and rubbed his tummy. "Nothing like a little flying to get the juices flowing. Let's go slop down some grease."

At Burger King, Ed put away two double Whoppers with cheese, large fries and an enormous vanilla shake. He went back for small fries and an apple pie. Conversation was out of the question with Ed shoveling and Jesse witnessing with awe. "Do you always eat this much?"

With a mouthful of food, Ed said, "Oh, you students worry the calories right off. You'd be amazed how dense some of you can be. I had a guy pull both mixtures back and kill the engines. I had to make a landing on the road. He ain't flyin' now, and we're all safer for it." He smiled and wiped sauce from his lower lip.

Jesse poked at his hamburger.

"Off we go for some afternoon delight." Ed slid from the booth and Jesse rushed to catch up.

Once in the hangar, Ed pointed toward a storage

room door. "You'll find some sandbags. I want you to fully load the plane with aft center of gravity. We'll top off the tanks before takeoff. Compute the weight and balance. Each of them bags weighs eighty pounds." Ed strolled off toward the Lear and engaged the boys in shop talk.

The starboard prop rotated two times, the engine caught with a shudder. They both looked left and watched the port engine do the same. Ed smiled and said, "Well, so far so good."

The afternoon was no less relentless than the morning. Jesse struggled with the controls and reacted sluggishly.

"Enough of that," Ed said. "Get the airplane dirty and at blue line with full throttle."

Jesse slowed the plane, dropped flaps and the gear, then advanced the throttles.

"Now picture this. Full load, trees on either side, and we're takin' off." He pulled the port engine and let the prop windmill.

Jesse was ready. He stomped on the right rudder to maintain the heading, gave the good engine full power, and raised the gear and flaps. He confirmed the bad engine and feathered the prop. He should have been climbing slightly, but the airspeed and altitude were decaying.

Ed said in the headset, "Now looky here." Ed reached for the starboard throttle and pulled power back a bit on the good engine. The speed stabilized at the blue line and the descent was arrested. Jesse wrestled the plane to equilibrium and they started to climb. "Okay, let's start again and do it over."

The afternoon rounded out with instrument holding patterns, localizer approaches, high-angle descents to short-field landings. They practiced rough-field take-offs and landings and finished with standard instrument work and a final ILS to minimums.

Back at the hangar, Jesse collapsed on the sofa, damp with sweat. Ed kindly brought him some coffee. Jesse lit a Garam and exhaled with a groan. He was all too aware of his failings as a multiengine pilot.

Ed sat down easily beside Jesse and flung a loose arm over the back of the sofa. His face crinkled. Stark-white hairless shin showed between burnt-orange pants and bright red socks. "Well, fella, wasn't that fun? What did you think—about your performance, I mean?" His tone was playful and serene.

Jesse wanted to hate this guy, his torturer, but smiled weakly. "I was slow to react and for most of the time I was behind the airplane. Maybe I should just stick to singles and not bother."

"Oh, don't be so hard on yourself. You did okay. I seen a whole lot worse. You got a mouthful and dribbled some out." Ed nudged Jesse in the ribs with a sharp elbow, threw his head back and laughed. "You sit on all we did today. Tomorrow we'll review some.

It'll be a piece of cake compared to today. Then let's see how you feel and I'll tell you what I think. What I'll say now is that you've got the makings. You fly a real smooth plane."

Ed strolled out of the lounge humming and disappeared. Jesse heard the twin start up and wondered about the sand bags.

Jesse drained the coffee and stubbed out the smoke. In the car, when he went to depress the clutch, his whole leg got the jitters and his foot did an uncontrollable dance on the pedal. He slipped in a Jackson Browne tape and drove slowly home.

Everyone was gathered by the pool in the waning hours of the afternoon, sitting in a semicircle at the round table, facing the city. Light chatter came on the wind as Jesse came out of the living room and looked down on the friendly get-together. Santee sat in the middle, Biano to his left, Coley to his right. Santee was laughing at something Biano had said.

The morning's breeze had slackened and the late yellow sun sparkled off the pool, accentuating the bright colors of the umbrella shading the table.

Jesse descended the circular steps to the pool level. Biano noticed him first and motioned to the empty chair facing the house. Jesse fell into it and sloughed back, arms dangling over the side.

Santee leaned forward. "Old Ed got you down?" He shared a smile with Biano, then looked at Jesse.

Biano took an hors d'oeuvre, held it in midair, and said, "Ed's been known to eat good pilots alive. How do you like it?"

Jesse sat up straighter. "Ed's a human torture chamber. I didn't know which way was up. He wouldn't say how I did."

Biano plopped smoked salmon into his mouth, chewed and swallowed. "When you take the check ride, you'll be ready. You'll be as safe as any twin pilot ever off the tarmac. I know." He sipped champagne from a crystal glass. Jesse was suddenly thirsty and hungry.

An ice bucket with a green bottleneck peeking out of a draped white cloth stood between Santee and Coley. Smoke rose from a Garam cigarette in the crystal ashtray in front of Santee. Several unlit joints lay along the edge. A covered sugar bowl of cocaine and golden spoons lying in carved niches rounded out the display.

Santee, dressed in his silky browns and blacks, waved an inviting hand toward the table. "Help yourself, Jesse. You have earned it today." His emerald ring the size of a McNugget. Golden chains glittered around his neck. He looked very pleased with himself.

Jesse spread gooey cheese and caviar on toast tips. Crumbs fell in his lap.

Biano said, "You are not going to find a better instructor than Ed. I haven't seen anyone fly like he can. He puts on a plane like we put on trousers."

"Speaking of trousers, Biano," Santee flicked a

hand at Jesse. "Can't you get this man some normal clothes? Take him shopping, dress him up."

Biano said sure. He and Jesse made a date for Sunday lunch, buy some clothes, celebrate the check ride.

Santee helped himself to some cocaine, then slid the bowl to Jesse. As the back of Jesse's teeth went numb, Santee took the bottle from the ice and filled the glasses all around, finishing with his own. "End of the bottle means good luck." He let the last drops punctuate his remark, then tossed the empty bottle into the pool. Jesse noticed that no one thought it unusual.

Santee turned to Coley. "Coley, tell us about last night." Santee fidgeted in his chair, turned to Jesse. "You shoulda seen this, Jesse. Am I right, Coley? The guy was beautiful. Go on, tell how you put it to those two assholes."

Jesse had never seen Santee so animated. He was surprised to hear his speech slip into street slang.

"Well, you told the buyers they had to come alone, no bodyguards or anybody else. After I checked the room out, I noticed these two guys sitting in a car a couple doors down. I made them right away as the buyer's guys."

Santee interrupted. "Jesse, here comes the good part." He whipped up a little shadow boxing. "Wish I coulda seen it. Holy mother of Christ. Musta been great! Go on, go on." He rolled his wrist.

"So you and the buyer leave the room and get in your cars. Pasque drives you away. I slip out the back window, come around behind their car. They don't know shit, window open, waiting for me to come out of the room. I jab the passenger-seat asshole with a set of fingers, here," Coley touched his neck just below the skull, "and he's out cold, slumping forward."

Santee came out of his seat, puffing on a new Garam to keep it lit. "I love this next part!"

"Well, obviously the driver is aware of what's happening, looks over and down the business end of the old Browning and he gets all pale."

Just then, Carla arrived with a new bottle of Dom Perignon, poured a small amount into a fresh glass, and stood back as Santee took a sample. Everyone was quiet.

Santee swept his hand downward, jarring the bottle from Carla's grasp. It burst splintered glass and foam. Santee turned crimson. Carla was white and frozen.

Santee shouted, "It's too goddamn warm, goddamn you, *puta*! Bring another *cold* one *now*! Or get your fucking cunt back to Cuba! And get Jesse here something to drink!"

At the mention of his name, Jesse felt like a gawker at a multicar smash-up. A pointed shard must have pierced Carla's toe. Blood flowed over her white sandal onto the pool deck, diluted by the frothy champagne.

Apparently, she was too scared to notice. She cowered away, leaving little blood spots with every other step. Santee could not notice. He'd turned his attention to the others and laughed lightly, "Fucking help, what can you do?"

Biano and Jesse laughed nervously, but Coley's silence ended the story. Just as well, as Santee seemed to descend into depths, unaware of anything around him.

Carla was back quickly with another bottle and three sweating Kalibers in a silver bucket. She was wearing white shoes and walked with a little hitch in her gait. She set the tray on the table.

Santee returned from his trance to go through the tasting ritual again, as if nothing had happened. This time, he approved.

Carla produced a small brush and dustpan from her apron pocket and swept up the broken glass.

Out of instinct, Jesse rose to help, but caught a stern eye from Coley and sat back down. Carla finished and made a noble retreat.

Santee rose and stood over the table, took two nosefuls of coke, leaned back and vibrated. "I gotta move." He rubbed his hands together. "Let's forget about dinner here and go have us some fun. What do you say?" He swept a glance at his audience. "We head down to that new hotspot disco and get drunk, tag some pussy, maybe ruffle Pasque's greasy hair. How about it?"

A change of scenery sounded good to Jesse, but he begged off as the tired and hard-worked pilot. Biano said it was a good idea and Coley shrugged as if he was still on duty.

Santee said something over his shoulder to Jesse about tomorrow's flight with Ed, but Jesse couldn't make it out. Santee laughed, slapped each of his companions on the back and walked away, an arm around each.

The big dining table was set for four. Carla carried in a tray of food and set it on the warming table. Without rancor, Carla said, "It appears you will be dining alone this evening, Mr. Langdon. You may sit at the head and I will serve you."

She brought sliced Virginia ham, sweet potatoes, Spanish rice and freshly tossed salad. He leaned in as she stood at his left, and with the silver serving fork and spoon, extracted generous portions of each, feeling guilty that there was so much food and only him to eat it.

Before she left him alone, he said, "I'm sorry about what happened at the pool. I feel badly that I did nothing to help you."

Carla stopped at a chair and turned, hands resting lightly on the polished wooden back. "It could have been much worse, Mr. Langdon. It has been. It was my fault. The bottle was not cold enough. As for you helping me, you made the right decision. Helping me would have made matters worse for me and for you. You need to look after yourself. But I thank you for saying it." There was sadness in her voice, and she walked more heavily to the pantry.

CHAPTER 13

TIME TO IMPROVE the outlook—marching powder, the breakfast of champions. He slid open the drawer and found only the slightest bit left. He scooped the sides with the tiny spoon and got a single nostril full. He wet his finger, swept the bowl clean and rubbed his gums. How to replenish his supply?

At the airport, Ed was jovial and dressed in a neon-blue jumpsuit. The incongruous cowboy hat sat raked to one side on his head. In the air, yesterday's rigor paid off and Jesse felt confident again. Ed was full of compliments—until it was time to finish with unusual attitudes.

Jesse donned the hood and closed his eyes, feet on the floor, hands on thighs. Ed twisted the plane into power-off climbs approaching a stall, accelerated dives and sixty-degree banks.

"She's yours."

Jesse oriented and recovered, oriented and recovered.

"Nice flying today, Jesse. Stay under the hood. We'll shoot a localizer. I'll play controller. 'Fly heading 170, vectors to final-approach course, descend and maintain 2,300 feet.'"

Jesse repeated the instructions and complied.

"Turn left 030, descend to 1,500 feet."

"Left 030, down to 1.5." Jesse banked left and pulled the power, rounded out on heading and applied power as he approached his assigned altitude.

"Left 330, maintain 1,500 until established, cleared for Localizer 27 approach."

The localizer needle centered. He pulled the power, lowered flaps and gear and began his descent. He felt the effects of the increased drag from the flaps, but the gear motor didn't sound. He looked over for the familiar landing gear lights, but didn't see them. With attention diverted, he drifted left of course. He corrected and reached for the manual gear-extension lever.

The plane slewed to the left. Jesse knew what that meant. Port engine out. He stomped on the right rudder pedal and advanced the throttle on the starboard engine.

He was left of course and had trouble turning right with all that power. As he reached to pull back the starboard throttle, a huge flame erupted in his face. He could see Ed's hairy hand holding a Zippo lighter.

Ed yelled, "Cabin fire! Cabin fire!"

"Get that fucking thing out of my face, Ed! What the hell are you doing? We're too close to the ground!"

Ed continued to wail, "Fire! Fire! Fire!" Sweat dripped from Jesse's face. He managed to get the starboard throttle back and was sort of on course, but way too high. The airspeed was decaying rapidly. He pushed the nose over and feathered the port prop.

He craned his neck to see the instruments blocked by the fucking lighter. Now he was coming down too fast and was approaching his minimum descent altitude. Then he remembered the gear.

He reached down and yanked the lever. The gear fell into the slipstream and clicked in place. The increased drag increased the descent rate. Jesse applied power to the good engine. Localizer needle was close to center. He was almost at minimums. Full right rudder not enough to hold heading.

He looked through the flame at the timer and knew he should be over the runway.

He threw the hood off and looked for the runway. But they were high above the flat Florida landscape. The stall warning blared. With all that altitude, Jesse pushed the nose over and stabilized the Seneca.

Ed clicked the lighter shut and burned his fingertip. Served him right. Ed let the lighter fall on the floor between his feet and laughed. "Gotcha there, buddy boy. Had you sweating bullets, didn't I?"

Jesse sputtered a string of swear words, then immediately turned his attention back to the plane and brought the port engine back to life.

He called Tower and got clearance for a visual approach. Resetting the altimeter to the correct height, he left the flaps and gear out and spiraled slowly down to enter the pattern and land.

No words were exchanged until he parked the plane beside the hangar and shut down the engines and removed his headset.

"Now Jesse, before you get off that horse and come gunning for me, I got somethin' to say."

Jesse swallowed, forced himself to listen.

Ed was satisfied with that and continued. "You may think all that was a might unnecessary, maybe even cruel. But they ain't nothing crueler than a fire in the cabin, a shitty engine, and turbulence in the clouds as you get down close to the ground. Do things just right or else you...are...dead. There ain't no second chances, ain't no go-rounds." Ed let that sink in.

Jesse listened.

"It wouldn't have been real if you thought you had all that altitude to play with, so I monkeyed the altimeter. And the little fire was a nice distraction, don't you think?" He paused, then, "Last thing, before you attack me, is if we'd been on a real approach, you were set up just right and we'd be sitting here just the same as right now. Nice job flying. I'm ready to sign your log book."

Jesse was truly rattled. Ed looked sympathetic and uncomfortable. He reached over and patted Jesse's shoulder. He said, "It'll be all right."

Jesse sat up and blew his nose on his shirt tail.

Ed said, "I've had all kind of reactions to that stunt, but never that one."

Ed took off, leaving Jesse standing in the prop-wash. The feeling of being tumbled in a clothes dryer dissipated and gave way to a burst of confidence. He had handled the dire situations. But then he wondered if it was just false bravado. Was this exercise to fend off panic when things went sour just preparation for things to come?

He told himself again that this was all just tempo-rary, a summer vacation, and a chance to get his feet back on the ground. He'd be returning to his children. And he just might find Reefer. Who knew?

A sweep of fright passed through him and made him shudder.

With an open afternoon ahead, Jesse had time to do a little snooping. He parked downtown across from the *Miami Herald* and found the microfilm archive on the second floor.

If Reefer had become involved with smuggling dope in boats, any untimely end might be mentioned in a local article. The timeframe was the last six months. Jesse took reels from late September until the present.

It was tedious and he had to guard against the

urge to stop at interesting but irrelevant stories. On the other hand, all the articles about drugs in Florida pertained in some way to his new life.

He spent three hours and learned that much of the smuggling involved the use of fast boats coming in from the Bahamas late in the weekend, covered by and lost in the confusing multitude of returning local fishermen and vacationers. The authorities estimated that only the smallest fraction of drugs were intercepted. But specific stories about successful drug busts with displays of contraband, cash and weapons, held no information about Reefer. Nor did the articles about gun battles over turf that brought violent ends to many of the drug runners. Jesse looked carefully at the grainy pictures.

By the end, his eyes were tired and his ass hurt.

CHAPTER 14

THE CHECK RIDE was anticlimactic. Behind black aviator glasses, the flight examiner wasted neither words nor smiles. Jesse flew well, hit all the approaches and was smooth on the engine-out drills. With little comment, the examiner took Jesse's license and gave him a slip of paper with his multiengine ticket.

Jesse was home by ten-thirty.

Biano tossed keys at Jesse. "The Ferrari. You drive." It started with a hum and a rumble. "Try to keep it under a hundred." They headed for Miami.

Though the Cuban restaurant was modest, delicious smells assaulted them as they came through the door. Jesse stopped at a front table beside the window. Biano shook his head and motioned toward the back of the darkened room. "Always sit with your back to the wall, so you can see anyone approach. You need to start thinking like that."

Biano introduced Jesse to the waiter. They bantered in Spanish, laughed, then got down to the serious business of food. Juan brought back two Kalibers and set them on coasters.

Biano took a long pull on his beer.

Jesse lit a smoke. "How did you end up with Santee?"

"I grew up in Sinaloa, northern Mexico. My parents were well-off and that brought connections. I went to good schools and was accepted into the Mexican Air Force. We flew a lot with you Americans. My father was murdered while I was in the military."

Biano played with his beer bottle and the moisture it left on the table. "It took time to avenge his death. Then I had to flee. My mother and I came to Miami and I was put together with Santee. For a long time, I couldn't return to Mexico, but eventually the friends of my father's murderers were replaced. Now I travel freely." It was Biano's turn to grill Jesse. "Please take no offense, but what are you doing here?"

Jesse thought a moment. "I was having trouble at home, with my wife and my life. Santee needed a pilot and offered me a job. It's not forever. I needed some perspective."

Biano squinted at Jesse and was about to say something when the waiter brought the food. Between bites of beans and shredded meat, Jesse said, "Santee mentioned something about the pilot I'm replacing. What happened to him?"

Biano's fork stopped in midair. "Santee suspected he was running something on the side and sent him to Mexico to bring a load north. He never returned. Let's just say that nobody knows what happened. It is best left alone. End of story."

Biano stopped to consider something, then went on. "This business about your brother-in-law should also be left alone. I have no specific knowledge, but... If I were you, I would let it die."

Jesse wanted to pursue the topic, but after what he'd just been told, knew this wasn't the time. After sweet black coffee they went shopping.

In a blur of cash and heavy tipping, Biano wrapped Jesse in silk, linen and soft leather. Shirts, trousers and quiet shoes. Jesse was now outfitted for stealth.

They also bought a Breitling watch and four heavy gold necklaces. Biano insisted Jesse wear them all.

A three-figure haircut rounded out his new look. He spent a long time getting dressed for dinner. He kept checking himself in the mirror, trying to recognize himself. He looked sharp. The haircut almost seemed natural. He folded the sleeves of the burgundy silk shirt to just below the elbows and opened the collar to show a single golden chain. He wore the cream silk trousers with an alligator belt. The thin flesh-colored socks were almost too much, but they allowed him to luxuriate in the softness of the calf-skin loafers.

He hesitated before opening the library door. He wanted to turn back and get into his old clothes, he felt so foreign to himself. He took a deep breath and plunged ahead.

Conversation stopped.

"Who is this? Where is the preppy pilot?" Santee looked him over, then turned to Biano. "Nice work, Biano, You have created a drug lord. I feel underdressed."

Carla saved the day by announcing dinner.

Supper conversation was trivial and socially pleasant. Only Coley didn't participate in the banter. It seemed to Jesse he was working his memory like he worked his hands, hammering details into his concrete brain. But why? Perhaps he was simply always on yellow alert.

Over coffee Santee announced, "We will discuss the Maine sector. The booklet is in front of you. We start in July. Upon that success, we continue the northern operation."

They each leafed through the operations book and considered the big picture.

Santee said, "Jesse's contribution to the plan was substantial. It is why he is here."

"Jesse, Flagler and Claire will comprise the Maine

team. Biano will contribute when available and Coley in an emergency. Are there any questions?"

Jesse almost raised his hand. He looked at the others. Claire?

Coley was immobile.

Biano set an empty shot glass on the table and said, "Are you sure Flagler makes sense?"

Santee grew rigid. He stared at Biano. "Flagler will do what I tell him. And Jesse will be there to make sure."

Biano nodded and that subject was finished.

"Who's Claire?" Jesse asked.

Santee smiled, but his stare was flat. "Claire is my treasure. You and she will masquerade as a tourist couple, a nice cover." He continued staring, then said, "Maine represents the final sector. From there, we have easy access to New York. This greatly expands our distribution. The implications are enormous. Added to the rest, we will have the potential to strengthen my plans for Guyana. There will be no mistakes." He swept his gaze across each of them, gathered up the books and pads, and adjourned the meeting.

PART III

CHAPTER 15

"COME IN, JESSE. Pull up a chair. We will go over the Maine operation." Santee hunched over the operations book, vulture protecting carrion. "You are important to me, Jesse. Fate has brought us together."

"Fate? Like coming down a new river, waterfall around the bend?"

Santee looked up from the desk, squinted in the cigarette smoke. "We are better planners than that, I think."

"I should be back in Maine."

"Trust in fate, Jesse, even if it is not clear. The answers will come in time."

"You aren't scared of the waterfall?"

"Afraid? I am never afraid. I was born for the river. I have it dammed at the top and I control the flow. We are a team and this is meant to be."

Jesse sat uneasily, an actor on an unfamiliar stage. "As you would say, *vaya con Dios*."

Santee laughed. "Yes, that is correct. Now we get down to details."

For the next hour they planned. A thousand pounds of cocaine flown through the Windward Passage and up the eastern seaboard to Oxbow, Maine. Jesse calculated fuel burn, weight and balance, travel times, schedule.

"You have a head for this, my friend. But do you have the heart?"

"Does it require heart?"

"That makes it complete. When the head and the heart are together, the feet know exactly what to do."

"Time will tell, Santee. It seemed simpler back in Maine."

"Yes, because it was not so close then. It is close now. This load will bring us twenty-five million dollars. It is a king's ransom."

The sharp taps of high-heeled shoes came down the hallway and to the door, deliberate and sure.

"That will be Claire."

Santee opened the door and Jesse stood.

She walked straight in, short black dress and tanned skin. She looked at Jesse, then turned to Santee. He held her close. She looked into his eyes and kissed him. They turned to Jesse.

"Claire Seekins, may I introduce you to the newest

and brightest member of the team. Jesse Langdon." He let her go.

"Pleased to meet you, Jesse." Her auburn hair was gathered on top, a long vulnerable neck. Her eyes were direct, clear and effervescent blue. They seemed to say, *Dive in, the water is warm.*

Jesse took her offered hand, long strong fingers. "The pleasure is mine." They looked into each other, connection in the gaze.

From behind, Santee wrapped her in his arms. His chin rested on her shoulder, his ear on her neck, his cold face on Jesse.

Jesse watched Claire break into a warm open smile, bright teeth and sparkling eyes. Santee kissed her neck and let her go. "We are just finishing here. Please, sit down, Claire."

Jesse watched her sit. She was long and firm and fully packed. She made a spinning descent into the soft pillows on the sofa, kicked off her shoes and gathered her feet beneath her.

"Where were we? Yes, the twenty-five million." Santee settled behind the desk. "This is your trip, Jesse." Santee glanced at Claire. "And Claire will keep you honest." She took a smoke from the case on the table and lit up.

"I will pay you one percent of the load. Prove yourself, and the pay doubles, triples. How does that sound?"

"Sounds fair to me. Good pay, chance for advancement."

"It's settled then. I will fill Claire in on the details. For now, Claire and I must make up for lost time." He took her by the hand and led her from the room. With the light from Claire gone, the room seemed suddenly dull.

The next morning, Jesse was in no mood for company and headed straight for the pool. He dove in. The water was cool. He swam hard, fifteen laps. He squinted as he arranged the pool furniture to take advantage of the sun. He lay down, closed his eyes, thought of Claire.

He wanted to look into those eyes, listen to her talk and feel that connection again. This was a dangerous fantasy, he knew.

Jesse drifted off and his daydreaming produced an image of himself baked by the sun in the center of an amphitheater. A sense of urgency came through the calls from the stands. Then, appearing before him was a more tanned and competent version of himself. He was armed with a sword and looked intent on combat. Jesse looked down and saw that he too was dressed in fighting regalia, but had no desire to engage his mirror image.

He wondered if he could even move. He looked toward the massive crowd and to his alarm, all the men, women and children looked like him, too. Then they began receding from his vision, falling away like jettisoned sections of some spacecraft, drifting farther and farther, becoming smaller and smaller.

He looked toward his adversary, and he too was diminishing. But now Jesse was sure that it was he who was transforming. He was shrinking in size and power, about to be overwhelmed by immense forces that had left their previous form and taken on a mantle of malevolent energy, pulsing and threatening to squash the insignificance that he now represented.

This was all too familiar, this waking nightmare. He rolled over into a fetal position. The poolside table, right in front of him, seemed miles away and beyond his reach. The loss of contact with what he knew and understood, the onset of the unknown and immense, made him feel infinitesimal and without power.

Jesse lay there staring at the table and the pool beyond. He examined the feelings brought by this dreamlike state. He felt like an observer from afar, and was now more fascinated than afraid.

His vision refocused on the steps leading down from the house, where bare tanned legs stepped lightly down, moving slowly. She wore a sleeveless, white cotton dress, flowing folds of lace floating above her knees. She smiled.

Jesse sensed a return to the reality of warm white concrete. Conscious of his awkward position, he uncurled his body and lifted his head to rest in the cup of his hand. His elbow dug into the soft plastic strapping of the lounge chair.

"Hi there."

"Hello, Claire."

She pulled a white chair around and sat opposite Jesse. "Shell, I call him that, wants you on the dock at three." She gathered the folds of her dress and pushed them down between her legs. "He said he and some of his men are, and I quote, 'doing some serious fishing this afternoon.'"

Jesse sat up. "That would be fine. Santee's plans are my plans."

"We're all in that category, Jesse."

His name coming off her lips, he liked that. Without thinking he asked, "How old are you, Claire?" As soon as he said it, he blushed.

She had an enchanting smile. "Old as dirt, and only twenty-eight." She stood and raised both arms to gather and re-knot her hair.

She turned to go. Jesse said, "Thank you for the message."

Claire looked over her shoulder. "No problem."

Jesse watched her go up the stairs and vanish into the house.

On the dot of three, Santee, with Coley and Flagler, filed down the incline. Flagler's white sneakers looked stupid and Jesse grinned. "Nice footwear, Emmett."

"Fuck you."

Santee boarded the Bertram and paused on the ladder to the fly bridge. "Cut the crap and get ready to cast off." Flagler went below.

Each engine roared to life, throaty gurgle spewing from the wet exhaust. From the float, Jesse uncleated the bowline and flung it aboard. Coley let the stern go. Jesse shoved her off the dock and hopped aboard.

Santee steered the Bertram toward Miami, looking grim.

Coley and Jesse gathered in the fenders. Above the noise of the accelerating engines, Jesse asked Coley, "How come we're headed this way? Aren't we going fishing?"

"I think we have another guest coming aboard."

Jesse held the rail as the big boat rose out of the water. The wake was impressive. The sun gleamed off the stainless steel and white fiberglass. Light wind and warm air. Glad to be out on the water, Jesse took a deep breath.

Santee called his name. Jesse climbed up and sat on the cushion beside his boss. "Are you comfortable taking the helm?"

"I've handled boats this size before."

"Good." Santee slapped him on the back. "Take her over to that pier at the end of 71st Street." He pointed.

Jesse picked out the spot. Santee looked at his

face for confirmation. Jesse nodded. No dock, wind and current working against him. But who said no to Santee?

"We will be taking on a friend of mine and I want to greet him personally. She is all yours." Santee disappeared down the ladder.

Jesse turned his concentration to the pier. A large man stood waving. Jesse waved back.

The breeze was coming in straight and the current wanted to pin the boat to the pilings. Jesse spun her gently to port, swung the stern so he could back her down toward the pier.

Jesse faced the stern and the pier, hands reaching behind, working the throttles.

The wind and current were drifting her in a little too fast. He goosed her ahead with both engines. The boat rocked up and down, wake from a passing yacht coming ashore.

The stern swung toward the ladder. A little forward on starboard, a touch of reverse on port, back a bit on the starboard, not too much. Guy coming down the ladder. Good.

The Bertram's stern drifted back and rolled up to meet the foot of the boarding passenger. He stepped aboard, no more complicated than stepping off his porch.

Jesse slid each transmission into forward. Water

swirled at each corner of the stern, propellers thrusting water against the pier. Jesse gave her more gas.

"Nice finesse, Jesse." Santee stood on the after-deck with his guest. He pointed toward the MacArthur Causeway, indicating the way to open water.

The newcomer wasn't dressed for fishing and looked uncomfortable. His street shoes were polished, his trousers pressed. He was middle-aged and had a nice gut, slicked-back hair, the wet look. His face showed concern. His pop-eyes swept across Jesse and settled on Santee.

Jesse tuned the radio to marine weather forecast for southern Florida and the immediate coast. Light offshore breeze, ten to fifteen knots, diminishing this evening, waters becoming calm. Swells two to four feet. Clear skies tonight and tomorrow.

Jesse kept the Bertram's speed in check until they broke into open water. The bow plowed into each swell and sent a shower of white spray across the dark blue water.

Santee came up from below with a chart. He pointed to a spot west of Bimini, but still in the deep waters of the Florida Passage. He fiddled with the Loran, entered the coordinates written in pencil on the chart, and pushed the course-to button. A bar graph came onto the screen with a number below—105 degrees. He spun the wheel to the right, the compass came around to 105, and he steadied on course.

"You run her. I need to visit with Enrique. There is not much time. When you arrive at the coordinates, head due north, cut her back to slow. Continue north until we are done. Do you understand?"

"Yes, sir."

Jesse swayed with the boat, alone on the bridge. From this high off the water, he could admire the sea, the sheer of the bow, how she took each swell, plowing and shedding water.

They made good time going east. The Bertram was seaworthy and fast. Only a few other boats dotted the horizon.

Except for the sliver to the east, the Bimini islands, they were in open ocean. Jesse throttled back and turned north, uneasy so far from land.

Fishing sounds drifted up—rods and reels and laughter and beer cans popping. Jesse checked the course and looked down on the commotion, tops of heads. Flagler and Coley were on either side, planting the great rods into holders. Santee's friend sat in the fighting chair bolted to the deck.

Coley opened the bait well and withdrew a live fish. He forced it on the cutting board with his gnarly hand. Flagler handed him an enormous hook from the line on the nearest rod. Coley hooked it through the upper lip, giving it a little tug to make sure it was secure. The fish was not pleased.

Coley leaned over the side and let the fish swim,

though not for freedom. He was hooked, his fate to be dragged through the ocean as an offering to larger fish, his every movement sending signals of vulnerability to marauding predators.

To catch a marlin, one needed a sacrifice. Still, Jesse felt sorry for the fish. He adjusted the course slightly. The swells came broadside and the sun was hot. With little forward motion and no breeze, he could smell exhaust fumes.

Santee was talking loudly. Jesse looked down. Santee leaned against the stern, gesturing with his arms. His friend paid close attention, his hair shiny in the sunlight, combed back over a bald spot. The man kept nodding.

Flagler and Coley approached from behind, one on each side. Coley held his Browning beside his leg. Flagler carried a roll of duct tape.

Santee kept on speaking, not missing a beat, like a conductor waving his hands, captivating his guest.

Flagler and Coley pounced at the same time, gun to temple and forearms taped to the chair. There was no fight. Enrique looked up into Santee's eyes, perfectly still.

Jesse was mesmerized by the spectacle. Flagler and Coley retreated to the shade of the cabin, leaving only Santee visible beside Enrique on the stern.

Santee went to the reel and released the line. He waited, then satisfied for no apparent reason, locked the drag lever down. The line went taut, then quivered as the bait fish wiggled and fought.

Santee looked up at Jesse with a mirthless smile. Enrique turned in his chair and lifted his eyes. His expression was watery and accepting. There was a strange element of fear in each face. The boat pitched gently. Santee took the line and held it in his open hand.

Jesse tightened his grip on the railing as a larger swell tossed the boat. He looked on with a sense of morbid fascination and dread as Santee spoke softly to the man, then with a smooth circular sweep, Santee looped the line around Enrique's neck. He leaned back on the transom and surveyed the waves.

Line on skin twitched, fish and man linked, the fate of each dependent upon the hunger of the larger fish. Sweat trickled down Enrique's neck.

Enrique's shoulders shook, but his voice was strong and carried, as if appealing to the others. "Mr. Santee, it is true that I killed the DEA agent without your approval. He was responsible for the loss of the load, playing both sides. The whole operation was compromised, regardless of his death. I made an example of him."

Santee seemed to reflect on this for a moment. Jesse looked from Enrique and tried to follow the transparent line into the sea, the depths that held life and death. Jesse's eyes stung from the exhaust fumes and he felt sick. Santee was about to speak when a marlin crashed the live bait. Santee jumped back and the line sliced cleanly through Enrique's neck. The glistening hair, the head, lay for a moment on the neck, then toppled with a thud onto the white fiberglass. The body slumped forward, gushing arterial blood, as Enrique's head rolled to the corner of the deck.

Flagler and Coley dashed into view. Flagler chased the head as it rolled with the swells.

Santee shouted, "Look at the mess! The blood, it will never clean off. Goddamn you, throw him to the sharks, *now*!"

The reel played out, most of the line gone.

Coley cut the taped corpse loose, dragged it to the edge by the feet and heaved it over the stern. Flagler, wicked pale, grabbed the head by the hair and flung it after the body. The fish took the rest of the line and the reel fell silent.

"Get rid of this blood!"

Coley reached for the wash-down hose and slipped in the blood. He went down hard, but didn't make a sound.

The red on white was startling. Santee and Flagler leaned on opposite sides while Coley worked the pressure washer and turned the blood to pink, water washing out the scuppers.

The body bobbed eerily in the wake, then the water erupted into a shark feeding frenzy.

Jesse staggered to the leeward side of the flying bridge and vomited over the side. The open ocean spread wide and unfriendly. It had lost its shimmer.

Sometime later, someone shouted his name. Jesse looked over. Santee motioned for him to come. Reluctantly, Jesse flicked his smoke and climbed down.

But for the helm on the starboard side, the cabin was laid out much like a living room. Santee motioned for Jesse to take the wheel and head for home. He came around to 285 degrees and pushed the throttles ahead.

Flagler and Coley sat on the portside sofa. Jesse turned and looked in their eyes.

Flagler looked away. He was smoking nervously, tapping nonexistent ash into the porcelain ashtray he held on his lap. Coley returned Jesse's stare. He looked tired. The blood from handling Enrique and falling on the deck was almost dry on his clothes.

Santee stood at the mirror over the bar, preening and admiring himself. He combed his hair straight back, smiled, checked his teeth. He spoke softly. "What did we learn from that little episode?"

Silence settled over the familiar sounds of the boat making way.

Coley spoke first. "When you don't want to catch fish, they hit."

Santee looked at Coley in the mirror and squinted, determining whether Coley was making fun. Then his hard thin lips turned to a grin and he laughed. He took four glasses from the rack beside the mirror, half-filled each from a bottle of Chivas, handed them around.

Jesse had the urge to do laps in the glass.

Santee sat down in the easy chair and crossed his legs. "Perhaps we should always fish like that. It gives new meaning to live bait, heh, Flagler?" Santee was relaxed and in the mood for games.

From the stub of his cigarette, Flagler lit a fresh Pall Mall. "If you ask me, I think that neck trick, that head trick, whatever you want to call it, works damned slick. I thought the line would get hung up on the bones or something. Lotta blood, though." Ingratiating himself, not a bad plan, given the consequences of being on the wrong side.

Santee didn't seem impressed. He sipped his Scotch and said, "How about you, Jesse?"

The Scotch burned as it went down, then burst into a flowering glow, warmth emanating from his core. "Who saw this man board the boat? What do we do with his car, if he has one? Was it necessary to kill him? If things were really as fucked up as he said, then we are too disorganized. He was a brave man." Jesse sloshed down another gulp, caught in the embrace. Fuck it if he'd said too much. And fuck it if he had to stand up at the AA meeting as a newbie, take a white chip again.

Flagler bent over in a coughing fit.

Jesse said, "You know, Flagler, smoking's going to kill you."

Flagler recovered and said, "Minding someone else's business will kill you faster."

Coley leaned back. "That, and messing with someone tougher than you."

Flagler lit another smoke but remained silent.

Santee took out a packet of cocaine, slit the corner with a switchblade and dumped an ounce on the glass table. With his knife he carved out a rude line and snorted it with a silver straw. "The rest is for you. Business is done for the day. Call me when we are back at La Primavera." Santee took the Scotch bottle and went down the companionway to the staterooms below.

Jesse inhaled two fat lines, patted his pockets for smokes, then went up to the flying bridge and into the deepening dusk. He turned on the running lights.

The festive glow of Miami did nothing to bleach the desolation.

CHAPTER 16

THE NEXT MORNING, Jesse's appetite returned with a vengeance. He ate a ham, cheese and onion omelet, home fries, toast, sausage and black coffee. He tried to focus on the morning paper.

The war on drugs was going well. Good thing.

He leafed to the back pages, lit a smoke. An article caught his eye. The head of an emerald mine had been murdered along with seventeen male guests at a housewarming party forty-five miles west of Bogotá, Colombia. As the guests danced beside the pool, twenty-five uniformed men stormed the lavish ranch. They systematically killed all the men, including the cooks, musicians, host and his friends. They left the women to moan over the pooling blood and riddled bodies. The mine owner was widely suspected of involvement in drug trafficking.

Jesse became aware of his fingers being burned by

the remains of his cigarette. He fumbled it to the ashtray and watched the smoke die as he stubbed it out.

His gaze fell on the date on the paper, the end of April. He'd lost track of time. It was time to call John Settlemire.

Back in his room, he emptied the ashtray into the wastebasket. His drug supply had been replenished. Two eye openers and he put the coke away.

From an overturned baseball cap on the bedside table, he distributed a wad of cash, nail clippers, change, cigarettes and his lighter to the various pockets of his shorts and shirt. Wallet and car keys from the desk and he was good to go.

The measure of his acceptance and acknowledgment of his importance was clear in the smoothness of his passage through the well-armed gate of La Primavera. A guard he recognized twitched lips in a small smile and nodded his head.

He headed toward the beach, glancing here and there for a payphone. He didn't know if he was doing anything wrong, but after the display of the day before, paranoia had set in. He looked in the rearview mirror. Nothing unusual. Jesse walked to a seaside phone.

"Jesse, Jesse! *Mi general. Cómo estás?*" John was excited as always. His use of Spanish, so playful in earlier times, was hauntingly appropriate now.

"Hey John, I'm fine." Jesse looked out onto the

strip of sand and the sea beyond. He took a drag from his smoke. "Touching base, as we agreed."

"Well, all right, *hombre*. You're early, actually. You miss me? Getting centered? Found yourself yet? In right relation?" John let go a peel of laughter, making fun.

Jesse had to chuckle. "No, buddy, but I'm doing fine. How are Emma and the kids? What happened after I left?"

"Let me tell you, baby, the shit hit the fan. Emma came through the roof, pissed as bloody hell. I had to hold the phone way out to here she was screaming so loud. Thought I was in cahoots with you, like we were planning some elaborate scam. She called us all sorts of unflattering and names and said some shit about her brother-in-law. Never knew she could swear like that. I think better of her now. Ha! She's calmed down now that the money's coming in. I don't know what to make of it, but I've never seen her brighter, kinda like a weight's been lifted.

"Ike and Ashley miss you awful. We lied to them. Told them you were on important business, the bullshit business trip. You know the line. But they don't understand why you don't write or call. They want to know if you're going to bring them presents. Life goes on."

News from home pierced a hollow spot and found the mark. John gave Jesse time to gather himself.

"Tell them I'll bring presents, will you, John? And thanks for everything."

"Are you almost done, wherever you are? Coming home soon?"

"I think it'll take a little longer than I thought, but I'll be back. Listen, I've got to run. I'll call you next month."

Jesse walked across the street and bought a carton of Camel regulars. He was tired of the taste of cloves.

He knocked the top of a pack on the heel of his hand, removed the cellophane and silver paper, pulled out a cigarette and lit it with Santee's lighter. He looked at the lighter for a long time.

Time for a drink. At an oceanside bar, he ordered a double Wild Turkey on the rocks, paying with a hundred-dollar bill. The first sip made him shudder. The rest went down smoothly. Jesse felt fluid as he crossed the baked asphalt and got into the BMW.

On the small street close to La Primavera, Jesse drove up on sparrows feeding on the side of the road. They flew as he approached, some not fast enough. Several ended up in the wheel well, whipped into loose feathers and limp bodies. In the side mirror, he watched them fall. His heart sank. Fishing line through the neck, a car's tires. It happens just that fast.

CHAPTER 17

Miami Herald, April 27.

The editorial noted that if the massive resources being used by the government to fight drug smuggling were working, the supply would be down and the prices up. In fact, the prices were coming down as the purity went up. Something was not working.

"HELP YOURSELF TO some of our fine Colombian coffee, Jesse." Santee motioned with his hand toward the coffee service on the table by the sofa. He folded the paper and tilted back in his chair.

Jesse went to the bar, pouring a shot of Wild Turkey, then sat on the sofa and waited for Santee to speak.

"You are drinking again. Can you handle it? Your survival may depend on it."

Jesse sipped his drink. "Did it help Enrique?"

"Ask yourself how this tragedy could have been prevented. If Enrique had only paid attention, been more careful, he would not have lost his way."

"Lost his way? That's an interesting way to put it."

"You see, he took matters into his own hands. He overstepped his authority. How did he know whether what he was doing might be right or wrong? He didn't and couldn't see the big picture. It is sad, really, but I say you must know your place. He leaves behind a wife and two small children. I have arranged money for them. I do not abandon my people."

"You are such a fine man, Mr. Santee. If only the world had more like you."

Santee fastened his focus down hard and tight. Jesse was struck by the depth of power in the face, yet he held fast and returned the glare.

"Jesse, you speak bold words. Are you an ice walker? Are you not afraid of falling through, losing your direction, finding no air?"

"Mr. Santee, I'm from Maine. I'm accustomed to cold water. Yet I meant no offense, and if taken, I apologize."

Cat quick, Santee spread a grin across his face and laughed. "Well done, Jesse, well done. For the moment, we can warm the waters with some advice. You are naïve, but not stupid. Speaking from your heart will cost you dearly someday. For now, I accept that you feel for Enrique." He took a final drag off his cigarette and laid the burning tip in the ashtray. They both watched the smoke rise. "I believe destiny has brought us together. We have empires to build. But first you fly." Santee turned to the window. "Biano will pick you up in an hour. Good luck."

In the shower, hot water running down his body, sobering him up, Jesse wondered if life could be stranger. He breathed in the steam. His mind bounced from danger to friendship, death sentence to kinship. He was beginning to feel close to Santee, like loving a tightrope.

He sat on the front stoop and admired the driveway, the row of palms, the blue sky. The grass was being watered by the automatic sprinklers. Biano was coming up the drive in the station wagon.

Biano was delighted. "This is a surprise. I'll trade you for Flagler any day." He punched Jesse lightly on the arm.

Jesse laughed and said, "Where to?"

"Not so fast, Mr. Big Shot Natural-Fiber Prep-School Drug Smuggler. All in due time." He spun the wheel and spewed gravel. The guards struggled to get the gate open in time. Biano waved as he turned toward Tamiami, fiddled with the radio, and found raucous Cuban. "Had breakfast?"

"Just coffee."

Biano took some time, then said, "You don't look so good. I mean, you look good, you lost some weight,

but you don't look healthy. Mama would say too little sleep and not enough food. Of course, she means
Cuban. I know a real nice spot. Anyway, we've got to
wait till the stuff comes to the plane." Biano clucked
like a mother hen, proud of himself.

Poor Paco's Swanky Franks was an offbeat diner,
about half a star out of five. They took the only empty
booth. The late-morning sun baked through the picture window onto the table. An older waitress with a
teenager's body wiped away crumbs with a wet rag. She
sashayed as she said good morning and handed them
both menus. "Call me Linda." Only her face gave away
her age.

Jesse watched her back as she returned to the
counter, thin bra strap, nice ass.

"Look any deeper, she'll get pregnant." Biano
chuckled as he put the closed menu on the table. "You
are in Biano's hands now." He took Jesse's menu and
waved them at the waitress. Biano ordered two portions of poached eggs on black beans, hot salsa, and
black coffee for two.

"Doesn't he talk?"

She pointed the eraser at Jesse, who smiled and
said, "No need."

She put the pencil back in her hair. "Nice voice."

Layers of cigarette smoke hung like stratus clouds
along the booths toward the door, no houseplants,

health food or attitude here. Steady hum and a relaxed atmosphere. Jesse lit up his own contribution.

Biano said, "That smoking is slowly killing you."

"Who's in a hurry?"

Linda brought breakfast on two arms.

The aroma made him salivate. They wolfed in silence and sat back content.

"Wonderful to be alive today, hey, Jesse? You said your blessings and thanked God?"

"You think he listens?"

"Every day, every day."

Tamiami was busy, planes coming and going. Biano parked the station wagon inside the InterRegional hangar.

Sam wiped oily hands on a rag, shook with Biano and Jesse, then handed them clean rags from the workbench. "The Lear is loaded and ready for the preflight. I did the weight and balance calculations and left them in the cockpit. The fluids check out and the fuel is full. The crates are crazy heavy. I weighed them myself and then strapped them real good."

"Thank you, Sam. You ever learn to fly this bird, I'm out of a job." Biano smiled. Sam gushed and said no, not ever.

Jesse followed Biano onboard. The windows were covered with curtains. Four large crates with no markings were lashed in a row. Four big suitcases sat behind the crew seats.

Biano retrieved the paperwork, then walked Jesse through the preflight item by item. "I don't have to say this, but the plane was only as safe as the pilot."

Sam brought the tug up and pulled the plane into the sunshine. They donned their Ray Bans, strapped in, and Biano handed Jesse the Central America charts. He said, "Panama," then looked over the weight and balance calculations.

Biano looked left, then right. "Clear." He gave thumbs-up to Sam and started the port engine. He repeated the procedure for the starboard engine. Both spooled up and whined.

Jesse put on the headset, tuned to ATIS, and jotted particulars on his knee board.

Biano switched to Clearance Delivery and said, "Code Thirteen at InterRegional." There was no reply. Biano switched to a different frequency. A voice came on. "Yeah?" Biano looked over to Jesse's curious gaze. Jesse felt like he had missed the assignment. Biano said, "Icarus." There was a pause and the voice said, "Cleared." Biano looked over. "Easy as that."

"Are you going to fill me in? That wasn't standard."

"You'll get used to it."

Taxi to the active, run up, clearance to depart toward the south and they were airborne in a scream of thrust, climbing out over the translucent green waters of Biscayne Bay.

They left Miami airspace and Departure Control

had them squawk 1200. Biano dialed Panama City into the Loran, then handed the plane to Jesse. "Level off at 25,000 and keep the needle centered."

Jesse took the controls and shrugged to relax. He found the flight manual and reviewed the emergency procedures. Biano read a book.

Jesse checked the charts. Their flight path took them over Cuba, east of Havana.

"Don't worry," Biano said, looking at him. "More nonstandard stuff, I'm afraid." He went back to his book.

Jesse leveled at 25,000 feet, brought the power back and hand flew.

Cuba was on the horizon. Biano dialed in a new frequency and said, "Icarus."

There was a pause. A voice said, "Claro." Biano motioned straight ahead with his hand and said, "Recto, adelante."

Flight over water always brought a sense of doom. Jesse felt himself sinking into his waking nightmare. *The engine is running too hot, spewing oil. You're about to crash in the ocean and be eaten by sharks.* Jesse listened intently to the whine of the jet. He looked down to the clear waters. The sharks were hiding and waiting for a Langdon feast.

Biano read his book, unaware.

"What are you reading?"

"*One Hundred Years of Solitude.* Looking for

insight into the murderous ways of our business partners. Seems they like to kill each other for no apparent
reason." Biano put the book into the side pocket beside
his left knee.

They left Cuba behind and were approaching the
Caymans. After that, nothing but the open waters of
the Caribbean Sea. Jesse said, "Are you ever afraid of
losing an engine out here?"

"We have two engines. She'll fly on one. Partly, I
trust Sam and the maintenance crew. Otherwise, I trust
that when God wants me, he'll just take me."

Biano pulled a thermos and two Styrofoam cups
from his bag. He said, "You have to be careful when
you open these at this altitude. The pressure can blow
the whole thing and burn the shit out of you." He gently unscrewed the cap, poured two cups and handed
one to Jesse.

"You going to tell me what's in the suitcases and
the crates? And how about that stuff you said over the
radio?"

Biano turned his body and faced Jesse, looking
him over before answering. "I got a question of my
own. What is it with you and Santee? You guys seem
to go way back for knowing each other so short a time.
You're moving real fast without any footing."

The coffee was hot. Jesse blew on it, took a tiny
sip. He flew with his right hand. "I don't know the
answer. Santee thinks I can help him. I wake up and

feel so out of place, then the next minute it all seems to be just right. Can't remember feeling so confused." Jesse took another sip and shrugged.

"I'll tell you one thing, Jesse, this isn't a playground. You play for keeps or you're dead."

"How do you play for keeps?"

"Just mind your back and stay out of the way." Biano looked out the windshield. "Santee didn't say it was a secret, so, there is cash in the suitcases, millions I'd guess, and automatic weapons, grenades and stuff in the crates." He took a breath. "I say the words Santee tells me to say and there is never trouble. I don't know more than that, if you're planning to ask. I don't want to know. These people are big time and they've got big-time friends. I just go where he tells me, when he tells me. That's all."

Jesse was a little surprised, which surprised him. Of course this is what they were doing .How else did this stuff get around? Not on TWA.

"Who's getting the guns?"

Biano was incredulous. He let loose a nervous chuckle. "Didn't I just say these guys are the big show? I don't give a fuck *who* gets the guns, as long as they're not turned on me. They grease the way down and back, everything's cool, we're safe and rich. Who needs to know more than that? Tell me."

"You really don't know? Wouldn't it be smarter to

know, so you had leverage?" Jesse straightened in his seat.

Biano said, "I suppose you think we ought to land in the Caymans and open ourselves a little bank account?"

"It has crossed my mind. How smart can these guys be? How far can they reach?"

"*Hermano*, you're not listening to me. We have two choices. Only two. First is we fly the mission and collect our pay and live nice. Second is we pull the fast one and drink to our new life and end up dead the next fucking day. Nobody comes to the funeral, nobody even knows, but sure as fuck we do."

Jesse thought of Reefer and kept his mouth shut.

Biano greased the landing in Panama City, then followed a military jeep to a hangar at the far end of the airport.

Doors opened. Biano pulled the Lear through, then shut it down. The doors closed. A well-decorated army man in green fatigues greeted Biano at the air stair. Biano offloaded the suitcases, which went into the trunk of a Mercedes. A small fuel truck topped them off with Jet A. The doors opened, a tug pulled them out of the hangar, Biano fired up the Lear, they taxied to the runway and took off. The whole operation took less than ten minutes.

The mood lingered, heavy and serious, no smiles

or laughter. It clung to their clothes like stockyard stink. They flew silently, considering different angles.

Biano said, "You haven't seen anything yet. By the time we're back at La Primavera, you'll be scared shitless and full of respect."

"So, maybe I don't know it all. Yet." Jesse smiled to Biano and they both laughed.

The Lear flew out over the Pacific and headed south. Biano let the autopilot fly while he consulted the charts and the approach plates. The weather looked fine. The land to the east was mountainous and lush. The sun was heavy in the west, but night was still hours away.

They landed at a small airport outside of Manta, Ecuador, and it was a repeat scene, except with more people and heavier equipment. Inside a hangar, away from inquiring eyes, they shut down the Lear, opened the cargo door and were greeted by a forklift. They rolled each crate to the door. The forklift loaded the crates into a canvas-covered army truck. The men did their jobs, matter of fact, not much said. Biano talked to the man in charge.

Jesse didn't want to mix, so he stayed onboard. Earlier, it seemed pretty simple. But guns, military, and code words in broad daylight didn't fit into his picture. Life in Belfast was on another planet in a different era. The world quivered and wavered like heat off pavement.

While Jesse was lost in thought, Biano took the left seat and started the engines. Doors opened. They flew off into the Ecuadorian night, navigation lights blinking, and headed to Bogotá for the night. Biano was in a good mood, as if the hardest part was done. Jesse felt disoriented.

Bogotá was a blur in the dark. They got a room at the Hilton and Jesse was asleep as soon as his head hit the pillow.

The next morning over toast and coffee, Jesse yawned and said, "Dare I ask what's next?"

"We fly into cocaine country. I love to say that. Up in the mountains. They'll have cargo skids for the underbelly. The coke goes in that. Makes for the slickest unloading you'll ever see. No more army types from now on, which is fine with me. They make me edgy." Biano gave Jesse a big grin. "Remember, I'm ex-military."

They flew to a small strip carved into a mountain covered with coca plants. Biano got serious as he slowed the slippery Lear for a short-field landing. He bled off airspeed and held her just above a stall, talked through it, little throttle and yoke adjustments. Had there been numbers on the dirt runway, Biano would have hit them. He braked hard, but didn't use reverse thrust because of the surface. He stopped in plenty of time and seemed pleased with himself.

Everyone was in the best mood. Biano introduced

Jesse to a well-dressed crisp Colombian with freshly creamed jet-black wavy hair. He left to supervise the attachment of the cargo skids. A truck approached. Banana boxes with soccer-sized duct-taped balls filled the flat bed. Locals with broad smiles did the heavy work.

Biano explained, "Each contains a kilo of hundred-percent Colombian, and I'm not talking Juan Valdez."

The sun was warm, the sky blue and the mountains verdant. The air was crisp. And they were watching millions of dollars of cocaine being loaded in full daylight, 200 kilos fitting neatly into each skid.

Their departure was swift. After inspecting the skids and a cursory preflight, they took the strip. Biano spooled her up, then released the brakes. The Lear leapt forward. The foliage loomed larger and larger and filled the windshield.

Jesse braced himself in the seat, feet pushing against the firewall. At the last second, Biano rotated and they sailed over the trees. He leveled off, raised the gear, retracted the flaps and gained airspeed.

Mountains rose to the west. They climbed out over the town of Montería and headed for Jamaica. Everything happened quickly in the Lear.

The sky was severe clear. Biano gave the plane to Jesse.

A maximum-performance climb in a Lear has been

likened to an orgasm, for a man, anyway. Sensing Jesse's desire to max it out, Biano smiled and said, "Easy does it. No need to do anything foolish. Especially with this cargo."

"You're no fun at all." Jesse brought the nose down to maintain best-rate airspeed.

"Have fun navigating. Set the Loran for threading Jamaica and the Caymans. Then over Cuba, direct to the Everglades. We'll be home for dinner."

Before Biano could take his book from the side pocket, Jesse couldn't stop himself from asking, "Do you trust those guys or worry about coming back? Seems easy enough to jack the Lear and keep the cargo." Jesse concentrated on holding 26,500 feet.

"It's all honor among thieves. It's bad for business to shoot the buyers. The money holds it together. Bad can happen, sure. Someone gets greedy, or turned by a narc, or cheats. Piss the big guys off, death happens real fast. Or some stupid coked-up asshole thinks a bullet solves everything. I just keep the faith, do what I'm told, smile a lot. But you can never close your eyes. Coley ever talk to you about this shit? He doesn't want things to unravel. He talks a good line and I listen."

Biano squinted at Jesse, appraising. "You're not very alert or careful."

"Just a minute. I thought I was under your wing. I was counting on you, Biano."

"Big mistake. It's obvious you've never been in

uniform. Don't ever give someone the responsibility for your life. I don't know how or why you are here. You didn't come up through the ranks. You get tumbled up here, you're going to be dead real soon." Biano took a deep breath before continuing, "And if I've got to nursemaid you, I'm dead too. We're on the same team, sure. So we try to look out for each other. But in the end, you fend for yourself."

Jesse inhaled the Camel deep and it felt good, like a punch to the deep side. He could do this. "Okay, I get your point. I'll be more careful, watch my back, that sort of stuff."

Biano shook his head. "Mr. Big Shot now? Santee likes to play with people, but for all I know, you'll be running the show next week. Or he might tell me to push you out of a helicopter. You ought to think about that, is all I'm saying."

Biano said the magic word to Cuban air-traffic control and they sailed over the island.

Between mouthfuls of hotel box-lunch sandwiches, Jesse asked, "How big is this, really? What's Santee into?"

"Persistent little bastard, aren't you? That's a question for Santee, if you dare to ask him. I can tell you this. You got Flagler fucking up in Louisiana. You got flights coming in from Mexico full of coke, but some smoke too. Marijuana comes across the border in tanker trucks. Can you believe that? Tankers loaded to the gills with dope. Santee pays out a hundred grand a week in bribes. You got what we just did, guns and money down, coke back. I heard about opium and heroin coming from Turkey and Burma. Don't want to know much about that. Those Asians are mean mother-fuckers, worse than the Colombians."

Jesse looked through the windshield. "What's this password stuff? And all the army people?"

"My advice, stay out of that shit. Santee is crazy and he's got friends who've got friends in real high places. Official places. Too high for the likes of you and me."

"So Santee brings all this shit in." Jesse tossed wax paper into the scrap can. "Where does it go then? Who gets it?"

"Junkies get it! Mainliners and snorters and pot-heads and addicts. Santee's got people in the cities. They distribute to wholesalers that cut it up and sell it to retailers that cut it up and sell it on the streets and in the ghettoes and projects." He took a breath. "Why you want to know this stuff? Want Santee to shoot his fancy pistol at your head?"

Biano took a pad from his flight bag, typed some coordinates into the Loran, then selected a fre-quency off his notes and put it into a handheld radio. Biano took over and started a gradual descent toward the Keys, strung out on the horizon like pearls on a necklace.

"We fly an improvised approach. We drop the skids and head for home. Pull the lever between the seats when I tell you."

Biano took the Lear down to the water, coming in hot over the marshy glades. The sun was a big red ball low in the west. They circled and slowed with gear and flaps as if to land.

"You pull when I say to pull." Biano concentrated, looking from the dusk to the instrument panel and back.

Biano said, "Ready? Okay. Pull!"

Jesse pulled. The skids fell away and the Lear lifted free.

Biano circled to check the drop. "When the skids fall, a parachute deploys and slows them down. They land and our guys pick them up. Mission complete."

Out Biano's port window, Jesse could see air boats converging on the long marks made by the skids.

They climbed for the short flight to Tamiami. With a few well-placed words into the headset, Biano was handed from approach to Tower and set up for landing, which he greased.

"Nice flight." Biano smiled at Jesse and headed to the InterRegional hangar, whose big doors underneath large pools of light were opening to swallow the Lear. "Let's do it again someday."

La Primavera was quiet. Biano begged off for

supper with his mother and Carla said something about a note in the library.

Jesse went to the library and poured Wild Turkey.

A note on the desk read, *J.—Security detachment to Mexico. Back tomorrow afternoon. Claire needs escort to beach in morning. You will oblige. Trust trip went well. S.*

Jesse swirled the drink, took a big sip and shuddered.

CHAPTER 18

CLAIRE SAID SHE knew where they were going, so she drove the BMW. She handled the car well, fast, but staying just on the good side of safe. She leaned into turns, downshifted and spun around slower traffic. Warm midday air gushed through the windows.

She wore a short blue dress, now riding up her thighs, showing delicate golden hairs that glistened when the sun hit her legs.

They sped north along the seaside boulevard. She paid attention to the rearview mirror. She turned abruptly left on Surfside toward Indian Creek Country Club, but before she got there, turned left again and headed back toward the ocean on 88th.

Jesse watched Claire look in the mirror. He asked, "Are you worried about being followed?"

"You ought to know by now that Shell wants to know everything. And he gets what he wants."

"We're just going to the beach. What's the big deal?

Won't it look suspicious if we're being followed and you lose the tail?"

"Shell knows I hate that he doesn't trust me. He expects me to lose them and I usually do. Did you notice how glum the gate guys looked? They always catch hell."

Jesse was realizing that a deep competence lay beneath the surface beauty and girlish charm. He watched her with admiration and curiosity. And more. "Where are we going?"

"Just looking for an empty piece of beach. Fat chance, huh?" She pointed a finger at the dashboard, then around the car, made talking motions with her fingers, then pointed at her ear.

Jesse considered for a moment, then almost asked out loud that if Santee was that paranoid, in addition to a bug, why not a location transmitter? Did they know he called John Settlemire?

Claire pulled into a beach just south of Boca Raton. Even this late in the season, the beach was half full.

"You get changed over there in the men's room and I'll meet you down in the middle of all that humanity."

Jesse took his bag. "How will I find you?"

"I won't let you get lost." A bug wouldn't pick up the disarming smile. She felt in her bag to make sure of something, then swept the parking lot and beach with a watchful eye.

She was still in the little dress, arranging things on the blanket, when Jesse found her. "Very nice."

Satisfied that all was right, Claire crossed her arms, reached down and pulled her dress up over her head. Jesse took a breathless step backwards.

Claire laughed at the sight. "Have I embarrassed you? I didn't mean to."

A good time to lie down and get some sun on his back. Jesse was getting stiff. He shrugged off his T-shirt, hiked up his loose suit and lay down without responding. He felt like he was about sixteen years old.

Flimsy bikini, full breasts and flat tummy. Claire lay down on her belly, in close. Santee would be a deflating topic. "Did you consider a homing device on the car?"

"I pulled the transmitter from under the rear fender and put it on the station wagon." Claire rolled over and smiled up at the sun.

He was up on one elbow. She felt familiar and the silence was comfortable. Claire sat up and did her hair, elbows out to the sides, while hands lifted, bunched, twisted and tied. She was finer than fine.

She took a bottle of chilled white wine and a corkscrew from the wicker picnic basket and handed them to Jesse. Two jam jars followed. He half-filled each, Tom and Jerry for her, a dinosaur for him. She raised the glass and looked Jesse in the eye. "To successful adventuring." She clinked and they sipped.

Jesse took a Camel from his bag and lit three matches before it caught. He was downwind and the smoke blew away. He leaned back and looked around.

She asked, "What have you got going with Santee? He doesn't tell me much." A slight breeze caught some wisps of her hair and blew them in her face. She brushed them away and waited.

"Not much for small talk, huh?" He took another sip. "I don't really know the answer, Claire." He wondered how her name would sound whispered in her ear. "I'm nervous when dealing with Santee, even scared. It sounds silly. Reminds me of clearing ice off my tin roof in Maine. The pitch is easy enough to walk, but with my slick boots, I get to slipping toward the edge. The thrill is in the danger. I never did fall."

Claire looked interested and waited for more.

"He likes how I plan logistics, see the big picture. I get the feeling he likes me and doesn't know why. To be honest, it's the same with me, like we were meant to meet and do something together. I'll get done and we'll go our separate ways."

He poured more wine for them both. Claire seemed to be weighing a response, wondering how much to say. They looked out on the flat ocean. Two surfers took the small waves for short rides. Surf washing up on hot sand.

"Why do you think Santee's putting us together?" Jesse looked her over.

"He's got us here today and then we do the Maine run." She examined her cuticles. "It's a game to him, like he's God, dishing out spoils or punishment. I don't think he cares either way. He just wants to see what happens, then come smashing in, making us understand who's calling the life-and-death shots." She smiled sadly and shook her head. "Sometimes I think he cares for me, but mostly I feel like a trophy. It used to be fun. I'm very good at what I do, and Santee respects that. He might even be afraid of me, just a little."

Jesse tilted his head. What did she do so well?

"When I was a girl, I liked the bad boys best. It was exciting and different—run with the fast crowd, live on the edge. Now I seem to be speeding down a dead-end street. Hardly seems worth it anymore."

Claire looked out over the waters and took a gulp of wine. "God, I sound like I'm about fifty and all used up." She smiled and busied herself in the picnic basket.

Jesse wanted to touch her skin. Not a good career move.

Claire laid out hard-boiled eggs with salt and pepper mixed in the creases of wax paper, cold fried chicken with scotch bonnet dressing. They ate with their fingers, watching each other.

Rosy from the wine and full with food, Jesse asked Claire what she did so well.

"You don't want to know. I'm not trying to be mysterious, but we may be passing each other on this dead-end road, going in opposite directions. The less you know, the safer you are." She licked chicken grease from her fingers.

She looked deeply at Jesse. "You seem too innocent

to be involved with Santee. You're in this game pretty late. I've been in training since I was little. I can bob and weave, deke and dash. No offense, but you seem to be a bit slow on your feet."

"I can manage." Jesse blanched. "I'm learning and I'll be okay. I can help make this operation run smoothly. I can solve the problems Santee doesn't even see." Jesse took the second bottle of wine from the ice bucket and opened it, glad to be busy.

Claire let the moment sink in.

"I didn't mean to offend you." She reached over and touched Jesse's cheek. Her fingertips were light and tender. "It's just that when I hear you say this is a short-term part-time thing for you, I want to shake you. This is a career for them, a way of life and death and money and power. I don't know whether you're seeing the same thing, and I...well... " She trailed off and took her hand away.

"I'm sorry," Jesse said. "I appreciate your concern. But Santee and I are fine. Don't worry."

It was hot. A trickle of sweat ran down between Claire's breasts. She rolled over. Jesse felt proud to be on the beach with her.

The wine made them drowsy and they dozed on their stomachs amongst the beach crowd into the early afternoon.

***

The guards were alert and all business. Santee was

home. Jesse backed the car into the garage. Claire got out, retrieved the transmitter from the station wagon, returned it to the BMW and smiled.

They parted company at the head of the stairs. She winked.

A note on his desk said, *Library. 6 p.m. sharp.*

The library was full of agitation. Jesse was right on time and the last to arrive.

"Get yourself a drink, my friend." Santee paced and waved his arms. "Sit down and listen to this."

Claire smoothed her floral dress and looked uncomfortable sitting between Biano and Blades on the sofa. Flagler was slumped in the chair underneath the hole in the books. They caught eyes and locked.

"Jesus, get your drink," Santee said. "Stare each other down later."

Jesse went to the bar and put Wild Turkey in a small glass. He settled in the chair by the fireplace.

"In case you don't know, Coley flew Flagler and me down to Mexico to do a little business."

Coley flew? He looked at Blades, who shrugged and smiled.

Santee vibrated around the room. Jesse wished he'd sit down.

"Blades, tell it good, like it really was, all of it. What a scene!"

Eyes went to Coley. He drained his drink. "We took the MU-2 to Monterey yesterday morning. Santee needed to discuss the concept of respect with our competition."

Santee interrupted. "And by God, we did, didn't we, Coley? Didn't we?"

Coley started to continue, but Santee interrupted again. "I had Coley bring some supplies along, for the festivities." Santee laughed at his little joke. He paced to the window, now dark, and doubled back. "We got picked up by my *federales*, took us east to Guadalupe. It was fucking beautiful. They had no idea we were coming. You did a great job, Coley."

Flagler smiled at Jesse. Jesse finished his drink and lit a smoke. He wanted more bourbon, but was afraid to interrupt the show. Santee was in his manic phase again. Too much coke or, Jesse speculated, bloodlust.

Santee continued. "We left the *federales* on the hill and went down to the warehouse, real quiet. Coley took care of three sentries. Three! With his bare hands! Then he snuck around back with the satchel charges. Tell them, Coley."

Coley picked it up. "I set the C-4 so the radio signal would trip the relay and trigger the igniter—"

Santee interrupted again. "Three pounds in three charges! Tell them about the boom! Tell them!"

Coley let out a breath that sounded like a sigh. "I set them even along the wall, backed by junk so the force would come into the building. When it was all set, I came around front and joined Flagler and Santee in the dirt driveway, fifty yards from the front door."

Jesse felt his stomach start to turn over. Claire caught his eye.

Santee interrupted again. "We had our H&Ks hanging out of sight, standing there like the fucking Texas Rangers! We coulda just blown the whole thing sky high, but I wanted them to know who had come calling. I yelled for someone to come out, to get their attention."

Coley shook his head, like he couldn't believe it, then or now.

"When they saw us standing there in the open, I guess they got confused about the guards. Head guy says, 'What the fuck?' I tell this dipshit he's out of business. He fucking looks at me like who are we? The fucking army? He laughs at us and goes for his gun. Wrong fucking move, man. Coley punches the transmitter and *ka-fucking-boom*! Shoulda seen that bozo with the machine pistol, fucking flying through the air with his eyes real big!" Santee let out a sound, halfway between a laugh and a squeal. "I send Coley around back to pick off the stragglers. Building's burning, all that pot and coke, guys running out, we mow 'em down. Put on quite the show for those *federales*, huh, Coley?"

Santee didn't wait for a response. He was waving his arms again. "I go over to some guy and make him pay attention, fucking crybaby, tell him don't ever fuck with

Sheldrick Santee and he can spread the word. And he thinks I'm going to put a bullet in his brain." Santee and Flagler looked at each other.

"That's the way to deal with the fucking competition." Santee collapsed in his desk chair, out of breath.

The rest of the evening was strained. Jesse excused himself as soon as he could without giving offense and walked out the gate into the quiet neighborhood. The streets were deserted, the huge houses well lit, expensive cars in the driveways. He was cold in the warm evening air.

Most people, Jesse ruminated, believe their lifespan is generous. Sure, some of your choices might accelerate the end. For example, the guys in the warehouse must have had longer-range plans. This led Jesse to wonder if his own life expectancy might be measured in units smaller than generous, like months or weeks.

He reassessed his departure date, shortened his horizon, decided he would quit after the Maine run. That was his baby and he was responsible. Beyond that, why not walk with the money?

He found a note from Claire on his pillow. *God speed. C.* On the paper was a gold chain attached to a gold Saint Christopher locket that opened with nothing inside but the letter C.

Jesse nestled into his bed and fell asleep, one hand clutching the Saint Christopher.

PART IV

CHAPTER 19

Miami Herald

5/4 William Bennett announces a policy of consequences and confrontation and guarantees punishment for recreational drug users.

5/19 President Bush urges children to report drug use.

5/25 CIA Director William Webster will create an anti-narcotics unit to lend analytical and operational support.

5/30 Escalating violence in Peru is thwarting the U.S. War on Drugs. One DEA agent and five State Department contract employees are killed in a plane crash in Peru.

6/9 New aggressive measures are considered by U.S. government officials, including assassination of major international drug traffickers. The National Security Council is planning military operations against a number of high-value targets.

6/16 William Bennett says on *Larry King Live*

that he has no moral qualms about beheading
convicted drug dealers.

THE DREAM CAME again that night. He was
gigantic, aware of his size as he lay still and
slept. For all his mass, the blocks of color and sound
surrounding him were larger still, and they passed
without regard to his presence. He was at their mercy.
They had the power to crush him. He was in extreme
danger over which he had no control.

He woke up clammy in a tangle of sheets. He lay
confused and shivering in the darkness.

When he finally got up and drew the curtain, he
guessed it was midmorning. He walked to the desk
and untangled the two necklaces while looking in the
mirror. He clutched the Saint Christopher and smiled.
Jesse stood still and stared into his own eyes. Someone
else was looking back, someone deeper, different, more
serious. He sucked a line of blow up each nostril. From
the half-empty bottle of Wild Turkey he took a haul
and shuddered.

Today they'd go over the final details of the Maine
operation. Jesse took another pull of bourbon.

* * *

The level of trust had risen between him and Santee.
Santee had revealed more of his reach into the drug
business, and Jesse had naturally added levels of
logistics. This was paper planning and it was hard to

translate it into real events. When he did act, on rare occasions, it reminded him of his dream. He snorted or drank away the implications.

At six o'clock, Santee assembled the crew. Biano and Coley were on the sofa, Claire and Flagler in the two wingbacks by the fireplace. Claire wore a faded T-shirt and khaki shorts, but Jesse couldn't get away from seeing her near-naked in her swimsuit.

Santee carried his briefcase, nodded hellos, and took his chair at the desk. He told Jesse to speak.

Jesse leaned forward on his knees and starting laying out the plan. Tomorrow he and Biano would take the MU-2 to Medellín and load 1,000 pounds of ninety-five percent pure cocaine and thirty plastic ten-gallon pails filled with Jet A. Jesse handed Biano a diagram of the inflight refueling system.

He then walked over to Claire and handed her plane tickets. He said, "Coley will drive you and Flagler to the airport to catch tomorrow's eleven a.m. to Boston. You'll be met by a man in a chauffeur's uniform holding a cardboard sign with the name Billingham on it. He'll show you to a Ford pickup with dual rear wheels and a camper, then disappear. He knows nothing of you, your names, or our business."

Jesse returned to his seat, fetched more papers, and handed them to Claire. "These are maps of Maine, with refueling locations and a timetable. Don't deviate from this route or routine. We'll meet you at the airstrip at the end of the yellow-highlighted route.

"The camper will be carrying 300 gallons of jet fuel hidden in a special tank. The truck may be a little sluggish. Behind the seat you'll find an H&K machine pistol with five full magazines. Under the driver's side is an Uzi and five more magazines. There are loaded handguns in the side pockets with ammunition. They're all untraceable. If we have to use these, we've failed.

"The preliminary weather looks fine. A high-pressure area is moving east from the Great Lakes. It'll be clear for our rendezvous. That will be at three a.m. Tuesday morning, if all goes…according to plan."

Jesse looked at Flagler. "You'll take flares from the right side closet in the camper and place them at ten-yard intervals on either side of the runway. Don't light them until we fly over, then bust your ass, because by then we'll be coming around to land, low on fuel and in a bad mood. We'll try to make as little noise as possible, but the MU-2 has a certain signature.

"We need to accomplish the following in no more than ten minutes: Biano and I unload the cocaine, pails and tubing. Claire helps us load it into the camper. Flagler hooks the hose to the fueling port and uses the pump to transfer the fuel. The switch is on the right of the steering column. You engage it like any hydraulic pump driven off a truck engine. The fueling should take seven minutes.

"When the fuel is transferred, we place the cocaine in the space vacated by the Jet A. Flagler and Biano board the MU-2. Claire and I leave in the camper. We get a fifteen-minute head start, because of the noise the plane will make on departure. The plane flies low over Greenville airport, climbs, and files a flight plan to Lancaster, Pennsylvania. You'll then file for Tamiami and be home for supper on Tuesday.

"Claire and I drive to Hicksville on Long Island, where we deliver the coke to distributors only Claire knows about. We'll use the ten-digit code. We bring the cash back here, arriving no later than Sunday night. In an emergency, we can communicate by encrypted cellular phones. I remind you, there's no guarantee of security, so be careful what you say. Are there any questions?"

Flagler was ruffled. "How come I've got to drive up from Boston? I'd rather fly both ways."

It was a mistake, and everyone except Flagler knew it. Flagler wasn't in a position to question anything. As Santee was opening his mouth to pounce, Jesse said in a calm tone, "You'll be there to protect Miss Seekins. It's an important job, as she's the only one who knows where the stuff goes once we get to Long Island. You've closed up Louisiana, you've got the Mexican border trampoline working. Now we want you to get a feel for the north."

"What the hell is going on here, anyway? Who's

running this fucking show, you or Santee?" Flagler stared at Santee, unable to check his ego or his mouth.

Jesse came to the rescue again. Santee watched. "I was asked to relay the details of Mr. Santee's plans."

Biano pitched in. "Looks good to me. Nice job, Jesse. I'll go put some stuff together. See you first thing in the morning."

Flagler and Claire left to pack. Santee addressed Blades. "On the drive to the airport tomorrow, tell Flagler that he is to protect Claire and nothing else. He is *not* to think for himself, unless he wants to follow Enrique. Tell him that comes from me. If anything goes even a little off the plan and he has anything to do with it, tell him there is not a corner in this world small enough for him to hide. He might as well make funeral arrangements, hang out in front of the morgue and wait for me."

Santee turned to Jesse. "When this shipment comes off as planned, we make good on our expansion plans. The fucking country is a sieve. We are big time. Think more about how to integrate. I want more of the retail profits. I'm also considering getting into the paste.

"And Coley, we may need to beef up security. As we expand into manufacturing and distribution, we'll be stepping on some toes. I'll need you to smooth some higher-ups, and that's going to cost. We may have to scare the shit out of the lowlife, but I have a good feeling." Coley nodded.

Santee continued. "I would say we are on schedule, and when Maine comes through, we will have the imports coming in from the north going to New York, from here in Miami distributed locally, and from Mexico bound for Houston, Vegas and L.A.

"The Mexican trampoline is working well. We get the stuff close to the border and bring it across in tanker trucks. It costs about ten percent to bribe the border patrol and customs agents, and another ten percent for the lift across. We have several locations where we distribute it to U-Hauls that drive it to the cities." Santee paced and waved his arms.

"Except for Arkansas, which I will touch on later, it is getting riskier to fly into south Florida. We have been successful getting three-ton shipments onto cargo ships in Jamaica. The agents only search four percent of the containers, so the odds are in our favor. Even if they search, it is fifty-fifty they will not discover the shipment.

"You have seen the hollowed-out lumber from Honduras. The stuff comes into Lauderdale, thanks to all the confusion with the cruise ship tourists and the restaurant traffic. All great cover and loose security."

Jesse was bored and he yawned. Santee clapped his hands. "Wake up, Jesse, this is important."

"Even if they find the stuff, there is no link to us.

We have shipping agents, crew members and some of the security people on the take. If the DEA is hanging around, we will be notified. It means a lost shipment, but there will always be another one.

"In the next couple of weeks, we have more shipments of wood and bananas. I think we may be getting a little ahead of ourselves in terms of supply. Storing is as risky as smuggling. We may want to go to an on-demand inventory system. It will take flexibility, but it can be done.

"Our shipments of weapons to Ecuador has problems, as do the returning skid drops. Mena, Arkansas, is secure. It is out of the way and flights each way go full and protected. I have to say that it has worked so far, but I do not like it. We are relying on bought politicians and law enforcement for cover. There is bound to be a leak and that links to us. I think the risks are less if we go pure import, by ourselves.

"But for now, there is enough money to grease the whole way. We have informants in the DEA and ATF. We have several district attorneys and three judges. We are beginning to pump money into anti-legalization groups. On the laundry end, we have stopped shipping dollars out of the country. It is as hard as bringing the coke in, for Christ's sake.

"We have formed separate companies in each of the following centers: Miami, Houston, Los Angeles and New York. They are incorporated as bullion dealers.

As far as their records go, they are making big buys and sales with legal-looking cash transactions." Santee was proud of himself, strutting, and looked around the room for confirmation. Jesse nodded approval and smiled and thought he really should be paying better attention.

"We are instituting something new. We have drug dogs screen our money. If there is enough coke residue to get them excited, we literally wash the cash. It is more complicated than that, but you get the picture.

"We have accounts with regional banks. The money is deposited, then turned into cashier's checks that go to shell corporations. Finally, the money is wired offshore.

"I project by the end of the year we will clear over half a billion dollars, secure and untraceable, in twenty banks in ten countries.

"We could double our profit, but triple our exposure, if we go retail. The risks are great. For one, we do not have the networks to cut and distribute on the street. We will have a war trying to establish territory. Once the blood starts to flow, good citizens pressure the law. Let me remind you that our money will not spend so well from behind bars. I think we stick to importation and wholesale supply, and let the punks fight for the street corners. They are our best customers.

"We have several longer-term opportunities. We could run and process paste, but that means stepping on our major suppliers or reaching a formal agreement. We can expand our heroin and opium operations from Turkey and Burma. The most promising avenue is to increase demand for coke in Europe and export more there."

Santee was finished. He waited for reaction. It was an overwhelming picture, and no one had anything to add. He nodded for Coley to cover the security end.

Coley put down his coffee cup on the table without a sound. He smoothed his black cotton trousers.

"Our competition has been respectful. So far, there has been no more violence. I think our trip to Mexico had a sobering effect. I agree with you that further turf wars will be counterproductive.

"We have great loyalty from our employees. We pay the best, they know what we expect, and they understand that we'll take care of their legal bill and families if they're caught. I'm using Colombian nationals, almost exclusively, for the heavy work. That means the warehouses and counting houses. They're loyal and they know the price their families will pay back home if they aren't.

"The need-to-know rule has compartmentalized all the information. Only four of us have the whole picture. You, Jesse, Claire and me. Of course, Jesse, Claire and I are out of the highest loop. I do share some of the concerns about Arkansas. The politicians don't really need the money, tend to get spineless, and are messy to take out. They feel safe.

"We sweep for bugs all the time, so at least what we say here is secure. The phones are likely tapped and monitored constantly.

"Our reach into and around law enforcement is deep. We know when the AWACs go up and come down. We know of any secret action by the Justice Department. We have an informant in the Miami branch of the DEA.

"We have armed escorts for our shipments and deliveries. I still think it would be smart to have something like that for Jesse and Claire on the drive south.

"The counter-surveillance training is going well for the drivers and mules. I like the ten-digit system and I think it should be standard. We can be as close or as far away as we want, in case we smell something fishy." With that, Coley was finished.

Santee sat down, then got up and began pacing the room again. "I like how we are branching out. I like the new deliveries. I especially like making twice and three times the money. This gives me more to invest in the Guyana exit strategy. Leave Arkansas to me. We have the big umbrella and we will not get wet.

"If something goes wrong, we can teach a lesson with Los Palestinos. That way, we do not do the killing ourselves and this gives us a buffer. They shoot clean, kill quick and don't get caught, because no one talks.

Just like in the barrio in Medellín." He paused, then looked hard at both Jesse and Coley. "I got a guy who doesn't know me. He arranges the hits. I don't know if the Palestinos even know him, but the money flows and everyone is happy. Keeps everyone in line."

Blades usually ran the outside hit teams. Coley and Jesse got the message. Santee's sticky web contained a very lethal reach.

CHAPTER 20

J ESSE TOOK THE yoke of the MU-2 as Biano adjusted the navigational radios and cross-checked the approaches. On the run-up pad, Biano synchronized the two VORs.

Over the Straits of Florida Jesse asked Biano, head in technical manuals with charts strewn all over the cockpit, what the hell he was doing.

Biano looked up, surprised by the harsh tone. He said, "I'm making sure that we know where we are. You and Santee got us going into rinky-dink strips at night, middle of nowhere, low on fuel. If you don't mind, I'm making sure we can do this and get home in one piece."

"Christ, Biano, you think I'd fuck up something this important?"

"You might not mean to, but stranger things have happened. I told you. I don't put my life in anyone else's hands." Biano was right. Jesse turned his attention to the panel.

They flew out over the open water. Without looking up, Biano said, "You have found a home here, haven't you? You like doing this shit."

Jesse shifted in his seat. "Like the song says, 'I once was lost, but now I'm found.' During the day, it's like I'm doing good, making the operation run smoothly, more like a business. At night, before I go to sleep, I think about my children. When I wake up in the early morning and I didn't have enough to drink, then I am not so sure."

"You've done all that, Jesse. But Santee always wants more. He thinks we're going to move to Santeeland in Guyana and go legit. All I'm asking is if you have any idea where you're going?"

"Hell, Biano, you're the one with the charts." They both laughed.

"Maybe we could show Santee our escape-route charts?"

Biano howled.

"Maybe we could sell them to him."

When the laughter died down, Jesse was amazed they were still on course and at altitude.

Biano looked out his window to the blue-green sea and said, "You ever wonder why enough is never enough? How come Santee doesn't quit now and we all retire? Because it's never enough, not until someone falls hard.

"You and I are so small in all this. How rare are

pilots? Dime a dozen. We get squashed like bugs and nobody notices. Christ, you see the money involved. That means politicians, spooks, lawmen, attorneys. You got the DEA, the ATF, the DHS, whole Latin American governments. Everybody fighting over the money. I just don't want to get caught in the crossfire. It comes to that, I want the gun, and it's going to be a big fucking gun."

"Biano?" Jesse spoke softly, though it was maybe too late. "Is this plane bugged?"

Biano chuckled. "You think I've got a death wish?" He took a small transmitter from his pocket. "I drenched it in some soda before we took off. I'll say it malfunctioned. Happens all the time."

Jesse flew over Cuba and onto Medellín.

The MU-2 was ushered into a spacious hangar at the airport. The doors shut and armed guards stood inside each locked entrance. A small team of Colombians swarmed the plane, loading the coke and the pails of fuel.

Biano walked over to the side of the hangar with a Latin gentleman, engaged in conversation.

When he returned to the cockpit, Jesse asked about the man.

"That is Seve Rodrigues, middle son of one of the three Medellin families that processes the paste from the Hernandez family in Peru. I just gave him information about wire transfers to secure accounts. Seve graciously invited us to his ranch for the night, but I declined. We have a schedule to maintain."

Biano supervised the positioning of the refueling system, and rechecked the weight and balance figures. Fuel burn would be high at the lower altitude, but they should have an hour's reserve when they touched down in Maine, God willing and no strong headwinds.

They took off with no complications an hour and a half after arriving in Medellín.

Jesse took the first shift. He flew due north, east of Cartagena, out over the Caribbean Sea, and descended to fifty feet in the gathering dusk. They skimmed the waves and he fought a strong urge to gain safety in altitude. Keep the faith, he told himself, and maintained fifty feet.

Jesse flew across the Caribbean deck, skirting the western tip of Haiti. Along the Windward Passage, he wondered how alert Guantanamo was. He looked left, as if he could make out the tip of Cuba. He told himself he was low enough.

In four hours, when the main tanks were almost dry, they'd manually pump fuel from the containers. There was no way to have the engines feed directly from the pails. Jesse could smell the fuel, and immediately wanted a forbidden smoke. It was going to be a long night.

He dialed Nassau ATIS into the radio. He listened for the barometric pressure; any deviation would make their altimeter read wrong. There was little margin for error at fifty feet.

After Crooked Island, it got lonely in the Atlantic. Jesse couldn't shake the feeling of being lost, even with the Loran and all the gauges in the green. Jesse listened for an engine to sputter. Ocean flying turns pilots into neurotic, paranoid pessimists.

The time dragged. Jesse watched his watch, watched the fuel gauges, watched Biano sleep, watched the blackness. He remembered Ed Fischer and drew some reserve strength and confidence from him, his training style and his attitude.

He fiddled with the radio and finally confirmed that the pressure was rising. That brought limited peace of mind. He'd remind Biano to confirm with Bermuda. They'd be well to the west and very low, but with the powerful radio, they might pick up something.

They would fly through several shipping lanes. They were below bridge height of most freighters. The ships were well lit and as long as he didn't fall asleep, it wouldn't turn into a kamikaze mission.

Even with all the dancing demons in his head, being beyond the reach of the land-based U.S. Customs radar was well worth it. They could be detected in northern Maine, but that was a remote possibility. And it would take a dedicated snoopy asshole to stir up the law in time to make a difference.

The hour came to wake Biano. He dry-scrubbed his face and reached for the coffee thermos. "Wish the tops to those pails were on tighter. I can smell the fuel, and it's not doing anything good for my head."

Jesse mentioned the barometric pressure, then went aft to transfer fuel. It took twenty minutes to complete the job with the small hand pump. Jesse switched arms frequently.

He took a cold beer from the cooler. Biano looked over frowning, which Jesse saw in the dim cockpit light. He barked back, "It'll help me sleep. And I might as well tell you, I plan to do a little morning wake-up when we go dry feet in Maine."

"I'm not your mama." Biano got comfortable in his seat, checked the gauges and tapped the fuel indicators.

Jesse drank his beer and became mesmerized by the faint horizon of flat ocean that reached in all directions. He bunched his jacket against the window, rested his head on it and tried to sleep.

Biano tapped him on the shoulder. He could have sworn it was ten minutes later, but it was time to refuel. Biano went aft.

With difficulty, Jesse shook the dust and fog from his brain and monitored the flight, on course and still fifty feet up. He fortified himself with a couple of snorts and was fumbling with the charts when Biano came forward and took the charts from shaking hands, and didn't looked pleased. Biano pointed out a location at the mouth of the Gulf of Maine. "I'm going to need you for this approach. Only you and Santee have seen the runway, if you can call it that. This plane needs at least three hands to fly. From the looks of yours, we'll barely fill the order."

They flew on in silence. Jesse poured and drank some coffee.

Biano took some too and offered some advice. "It's going to get harder in the end, even assuming all goes well. The fuel and weather look good, but the approach will be a bitch. We'll need to watch each other. I'll fly the plane, you work the gear and the flaps and monitor the approach. There'll be a tendency to fixate on an instrument, settle for lower standards, react slowly, and fall into some bad decisions that could put us into the trees. You've got to watch me."

Biano consulted the charts and told Jesse the rocks of coastal Maine were just over the horizon. They should go dry feet in ten minutes.

Jesse sat up straighter and rubbed his face. His hands shook, but not too badly. He thought of Claire. He felt a bubble burst inside his breastbone, which he hoped was excited anticipation.

Biano climbed to 500 feet. It was too dark to see the coast clearly. He flew well east of Acadia National Park, over the shoreline and the southern reaches of Washington County, then north with the desolate forests of Downeast Maine sliding underneath.

The drop was west of Oxbow. Even for a Fourth of July weekend, it was far enough north in Aroostook

County for there to be no witnesses. That was the plan, anyway.

The traffic on I-95 was modest, mostly big rigs hauling goods north and south. The Mitsubishi crossed the highway at 400 feet and pulled westward off course to avoid overflying a truck. Then Biano brought her back, centered the needle, then looked over at Jesse. "We fly over the strip, then bank to port and go outbound to set up a straight-in approach. By the time we're established inbound, Flagler and Claire should have the flares lit. We'll bring her in low and slow."

Jesse nodded and prayed that all the phantom way-points were true. Soon enough, they'd find out.

Biano flew solely by instrument. When the Loran clicked the distance down to zero, he banked thirty degrees to the left and slowly brought her around southbound. Jesse tried to see the runway, but it was pitch black. He brought his head back into the airplane and got ready to lower the gear and flaps.

The turboprop came to the final-approach course at a forty-five-degree angle. Biano banked left again and centered the needles. He retarded the throttles, slowed the aircraft and bled off altitude.

"You see any fucking flares? We can't fly around all night, even if we had the fuel."

Jesse strained his eyes, looking deep into the darkness, searching for some illumination. He thought he saw a spark, then another. They were straight ahead, but seemed strangely high. Then there were more, two lines running parallel and away from them, lit one by one down the strip. Jesse said, with obvious relief, "This just might work."

Biano barked, "Flaps to ten degrees." Jesse dropped the flaps and the sleek plane pitched forward. Biano pulled back the yoke, confirmed on course, needles centered. "Gear." Jesse lowered the landing gear. With a whir of electric motors running hydraulic pumps and rushing resistance in the air, the wheels clunked down and locked in place.

Jesse confirmed, "Three green, gear down."

"Twenty degrees of flaps. Be ready for forty."

"Flaps at twenty."

Nose up, high angle of attack, steeper descent, decaying airspeed, just above a stall, they floated down toward the runway.

Biano flew visually. Jesse knew he had to take his clues from the flares, and something looked wrong. The angle of the flares was not changing. Too much sink rate. Jesse looked at the glide path indicator and called, "More power. We're too low."

Biano reacted wordlessly. He'd obviously come to the same conclusion. He increased thrust, arresting their descent into the trees, and climbed to the proper glide path.

The flares were lit and the runway looked way too

short. But Biano was committed. He made small aileron adjustments and called for full flaps.

Jesse dropped the flaps to forty degrees.

The landing light lit treetops. They came in close, brushing the top of an oak. Biano pulled back and floated her above the grass.

They ate up the runway. Trees loomed in the windshield. Biano settled the plane, waited a few seconds for wheels to take the weight, then stood on the brakes.

Jesse braced for impact, hands on the instrument panel.

The MU-2 stopped just short of the stand of trees, a big trunk filling the windshield. Biano locked the left brake, applied power to the starboard engine, spun the plane around and taxied up to Flagler and Claire.

Jesse looked at his watch—3:22 am. Biano killed the engines. They unbuckled seatbelts and headed aft to unload the plane.

Flagler pulled on the refueling lines, then hooked them to the fueling port underneath the wing. Claire was in the cab of the truck, looking back over her shoulder, waiting for Flagler's signal to engage the pump. He gave it and she started the fuel flowing.

Jesse dismantled the pails and hoses and tossed them out the door. Claire and Flagler popped the tops and stacked the pails. Biano brought two of the twenty duffle bags of cocaine to the door and Jesse carried them to the truck.

Flagler shut down the refueling and spooled up the hose. Claire ran like an elf along the line of flares, entering the glow, extinguishing it, slipping it in her bag, and on to the next. Her hair streamed out behind her as she ran.

"Cold fucking bitch."

Jesse, surprised, turned to see Flagler. He had finished his job and had nothing better to do than be ugly. He wore a red bandana around his neck and Jesse wanted to choke him with it.

He walked up to Flagler and said in a low tone, barely audible, so that Flagler had to lean in a little, "You don't have anything good to say, keep your mouth shut."

Jesse leaned in a little closer, for emphasis, staring into the eyes filled with hate. Flagler moved back and spat on the ground. He reached into his breast pocket, pulled out a Pall Mall and lit it.

Jesse watched him closely. Flagler backed up some more, then turned and said something about loading the pails and the duffel bags.

Jesse lit a smoke of his own, watching Claire pick up the last of her flares. She left the final two, so Biano could judge his way out.

Jesse had to piss. He walked to the edge of the clearing, appreciating the smell of the pine forest. It was good to be back in Maine.

Biano came over and unzipped. He looked over, "Got a good grip on yourself?"

Jesse looked down. "You seen your father since he went bald?"

Biano looked over at Jesse. "He start smoking early, stunt his growth?"

Jesse smiled. "Fuck you." Then, "You going to be all right flying all the way to Lancaster today?"

"I'm okay. Flagler could keep the dead awake. And he knows enough to monitor the autopilot if I want to nod off. He even speaks to air-traffic control, believe it or not."

Biano hunched over, tucked in and zipped. He turned face to face. "She's all loaded and ready to go. How are you? Don't tangle with anyone who wants to take my paycheck. Mama would be real mad."

"I'll be fine. Just a couple of tourists heading home. I'm going to sleep for the first couple of weeks."

"Couple weeks? You might as well not bother to wake up. And I'll let you in on a little more advice. Claire looks pretty and all, but you can rely on her if you get in trouble. In fact, follow her lead. Thank God she's on your side." Biano looked at his watch. "You're running late. Get out of here, so we can leave."

Claire came striding up. She put a hand on each of them, then kissed Biano on the cheek. "Thank you for trading Jesse for Emmett. And don't you worry. I'll keep him safe."

Biano and Jesse shook hands.

CHAPTER 21

CLAIRE SLID INTO the driver's side and with a wave, they were off.

The access road was canopied with tree branches and a bit uneven. The camper swayed. Claire took her time, concentrating on the dirt road.

She'd tied her hair back in a ponytail and looked like a teenager, stunning in the dashboard light.

Jesse locked his passenger door and leaned against it. He was supposed to keep a sharp eye out for police. He closed his eyes. He could look tomorrow.

The lack of sound and motion woke him up. They were parked on a dirt shoulder at dawn. The cab was empty.

He felt someone open the rear door of the camper. He hoped they were in Knowles Corner, close to the landfill where they were ditching the refueling pails. He leaned forward and felt under the seat for the machine pistol. There was no gun. He found it behind the seat. Stupid place.

He looked in his side mirror and saw a pail sail through the air. He got out, waited for Claire to toss another before he stepped in the way.

"Hi, sleepy head," she said as he rounded the corner.

"Good morning, sweetheart. Do you require any assistance?" Jesse looked around. "Where's the landfill?"

"We passed it several miles back, but it was getting too light. I drove to this side road to have more privacy."

"You know you are really pissing off the Sierra Club." Jesse flung a stack of pails into the swale.

"Fuck them," she replied.

It took all of four minutes and they were back on Route 11 headed south. Ten minutes later they were doing sixty-five on the highway. Jesse pulled a pack of Camels from his shirt pocket and motioned to Claire did she want one. She nodded. He lit two in his mouth with Santee's gold lighter and handed one to her. It was sort of like kissing her. He put the lighter away quickly; he didn't like Santee intruding. Claire noticed.

The cab filled with smoke. They cracked windows. He took some tobacco off his tongue.

It was early Tuesday morning, July Fourth. The sun was rising bright on their left, heralding a glorious summer day in Maine.

Claire spoke up, breaking the spell. "This is your

backyard, huh? Bring up any memories? Interesting stories?"

Jesse sipped thermos coffee from the plastic top. "The chance of being recognized is minuscule, but there's always a chance. Once we get out of Maine, we can relax. How far do you want to drive?"

"I thought we'd stop around Portland today, hole up in a campground, then make the rest of the trip tomorrow. We don't have to rush. The meet is at the Holiday Inn in Hicksville at three p.m. on Wednesday. *No problema*. Okay?"

"Sounds good to me, but I meant how far do you want to drive right now?"

"Getting a little fidgety, are we?"

"I make a lousy passenger. I need to be in control. So anytime you want to hand it over..."

"You need to relax and enjoy the scenery, Jesse. Life isn't accomplished, it's savored and enjoyed."

"Yeah, yeah. When can I drive?"

Claire laughed heartily at the road and leaned in toward Jesse. "You can have her anytime you want, Jess."

Jesse leaned into her, close enough to smell her perfume, feel the warmth emanating from her bare neck.

Before he could kiss her, she sat up straight and said, "We'll switch at the next rest area or fast-food joint. Didn't you say it was foolish to stop on the highway?"

"Something like that." Jesse straightened himself up, feeling slightly put out.

"Where did you live, exactly?" Claire asked.

"Don't you mean, 'Where *do* I live'?"

Claire looked over and studied Jesse. She looked back to the road, thinking. She drove with both hands on the steering wheel. "You still think this is a part-time job, don't you?"

"Well, no." He started slowly, looking ahead, "Yes… Truthfully? I guess I do. Santee needs me to establish this Maine thing, help out on the big picture. Then I'm coming home. I miss my kids."

"That's nice, Jesse. It reminds me of a fairy tale." Anger crept into her voice. "We're riding on half a ton of cocaine worth twenty-five million dollars. People would kill for this camper alone, for Christ's sake!" She took a breath. "And let's say someone runs into us. Or maybe the deal goes sour in Hicksville. You think we're such good buddies with Santee he's going to give us some constructive criticism and let us try again?"

They were going too fast and Jesse pointed at the speedometer. Claire shot back a steely glance, but took her foot off the accelerator. "How the hell did we get here, Jesse?"

"I think you're being too pessimistic."

She looked over. "I don't. Santee has all of us off in some podunk backwater in bumfuck South America, ruling the world. And he really believes it. He keeps it mostly secret, but he's put a ton of money down in

Guyana. He gets up and paces, talks plans, he's out of his mind. It gets real scary."

She looked back to the road. "What he wants includes you. You're going to have to do some fancy high-wire act to shake this off."

Claire reached over and put her hand on Jesse's knee. "You're a nice guy, but you're out of your league. Maybe God protects people like you. Me? I'm on the down elevator." She looked suddenly older, sadder. They drove on in silence, yellow dawn catching in her hair and illuminating her profile.

The rest area south of Millinocket was deserted. Claire pulled up beside the restrooms. While she scoped out the entire parking area and surrounding woods, she warned, "Be careful how you look around. There is a class of people that look around—police, intelligence operatives and criminals. And the police take interest in anyone who looks like they might be casing a place. A tourist couple with Dade plates might be Miami-careful, but they'd check us out anyway." She slid her seat back, checked the Walther in her purse and went to the ladies room.

Jesse got out and stretched. He walked around the hood.

He took his turn when Claire returned.

She was brushing her hair in the passenger seat when he climbed into the cab. He said, "Thanks for the advice." He adjusted both mirrors and backed out. Jesse settled at cruising speed and asked, "You think we ought to act more like a married couple?"

Claire leaned. "Maybe we aren't getting along. The optimist and the pessimist." Her tone was playful.

"What if we *are* getting along, friendly, arm in arm, for cover?"

Claire chuckled. "Where do you think arm in arm's going to lead, Jesse? You know what I'm talking about. Trouble is, Santee does too. I think that's why he teamed us up together—to see how far we'll go."

Jesse looked into Claire's eyes. "So what's your answer?" After a brief pause, they both laughed.

As they got closer to Bangor and into familiar territory, Jesse grew more and more uncomfortable. He was thirty minutes from his past, from his children. Also from years of drifting, hurt and pointlessness. But what was he doing now, and what was he getting in trade? The sense of belonging and usefulness he'd found these last few months had come at a price that was yet to be determined, but had to be paid eventually.

Jesse was shocked at how little he'd thought of his children in the time he'd been away. Now they were within arm's reach. It was the Fourth of July. He imagined a picnic, cold beer, beach fire, lobster, corn, sparklers and fireworks across the water. Were they happy? Did they miss him?

They passed the Hermon/Hampden exit. Jesse stared into space and realized that even if he could pull away now and head for Belfast, even if Santee wouldn't sic Flagler on him, he couldn't turn off. He had to finish this. He'd come too far.

At a truck stop down the road, two big-gutted truckers held the glass doors as Claire came out with the thermos and a big brown bag of food. She smiled sweetly at each and they beamed, then they looked mildly disappointed when she climbed into the camper with the tanned guy. "I just love truck stops. Don't you?"

"They're okay if you like greasy food and fat truck drivers." He liked those things.

"Aren't we ugly this morning!" She took a long look at Jesse. "Here are our souvenirs." She pulled two ceramic Dysart mugs from her bag. "For as long as we live, whenever we have coffee in these mugs, we'll remember this morning, this trip." She pulled out two fried-egg sandwiches in wax paper, set them on the seat, and poured coffee.

They started to eat. Egg yolk oozed onto Jesse's shirt. He swore and smudged it in, then swore some more. Claire laughed and leaned forward, careful with her egg. She wiped her mouth and said, "I love egg sandwiches with tomato and mayo. How come you pronounce it wrong?"

"You pronounce it wrong. It's supposed to sound like the Spanish month of May—my-oh, so you get my-oh-naise. So you don't go into shock, I also say to-mah-to. 'May I please have a hamburger with to-mah-to and my-own-naise?"

Claire laughed. "Where'd you learn to talk so funny?" She washed down a bite with coffee.

"Major English blood, don't you know." He was enjoying the little world they'd created in the intimacy of the cab of the truck. "My mother told me that mayonnaise was invented by a French chef on the Spanish island of Majorca, thus the pronunciation. Made sense to me. It's what I've heard all my life, father and mother both."

"You'd actually go in there, sit at the counter in front of all those white-collar types and ask for a sandwich like that?"

Jesse smiled. "Sometimes I ask for sliced tomaytos with mayo. It sounds almost poetic." He trailed his words.

Claire slapped him with a folded map.

They hit the road. At Augusta it was ten o'clock and hot. Jesse was having a hard time staying awake.

"Claire, you feel like pressing on? Driving to Portland? I'm beat."

"Sandman visited me half an hour ago. What say we pull over and have a nap?"

Jesse looked over with raised eyebrows. "Euphemism?"

Claire didn't take the bait. "Separate bunks."

Jesse shrugged. He needed a shave, shower and clean clothes.

He pulled off the highway into a mall and parked in the Sears section with all the other cars. They put the handguns in Claire's purse, locked the doors and climbed into the camper.

It was a nice one, small kitchen, dining area, the long seat over the stashed coke making out into a bed. Claire took the Berretta from her purse and handed it to Jesse. She kept the Walther. She opened the windows. The breeze puffed the gingham curtains.

"Did you order up the curtains special? Make sure it looked like a love nest?"

"Attention to detail."

Jesse took two Coronas from the refrigerator, gave one to Claire, and sat down on the bench behind the dining table, his bed. He pulled the Berretta slide back, confirmed the cartridge in the chamber. He dropped the magazine into his left hand, nodded at the sixteen rounds. He drove the mag home and slipped the pistol beneath his pillow.

Claire took her bag from the closet and pulled out a long pink T-shirt. She turned her back and switched shirts, undid and pulled off her jeans, held them to her side, arm bent and hips cocked, and said, "Ta da."

"Never make it as a stripper."

"You might be surprised," she said.

"No, I'm perpetually confused."

Claire produced toothbrush and paste. She foamed her mouth facing Jesse with her butt on the edge of the sink. Through froth she mumbled she wanted it to be like bedtime. She leaned over the sink and took with tilted head water directly from the tap. Jesse admired her calf muscles as she stood tippy-toe. It was all so domestic. He wanted to protect this woman.

She climbed discreetly into her bunk and put head to pillow, brought the sheet to chin, and watched Jesse. "Your turn."

He finished his beer and tossed the bottle in the trash can. "We boys don't have fancy undressing tricks." He pulled his shirt over his head. From the closet he pulled out a flannel blanket and tossed it on the bench. He patted his pillow. Toe to heel of sneaker, he slipped off one, then the other. He turned away and dropped his jeans.

"Nice buns, but how come no plaid boxers?"

"Haven't worn them since the fourth grade. Seemed like a stupid piece of clothing, until I caught my foreskin in the zipper a couple of times.

"That must have hurt." Claire did a mock cringe.

"I like the button fronts now." Jesse crawled into his bed, pulled the covers up, rolled over and smiled up at Claire.

The sound of highway traffic lulled him to sleep before he had time to get into any more trouble.

CHAPTER 22

JESSE WOKE FIRST and was surprised by the light. Of course it was light; it was still daytime. He looked at his watch: four-thirty. He stretched like a dog, one way, then the other, then swung his legs to the floor. The slight sound made Claire stir and roll away from the wall. He watched as she put on clean underpants and khaki shorts under the night shirt. She turned away to put on a loose yellow tank top.

He wondered how any waist could be so small. Her back climbed to strong shoulders and tight arms. She pulled aside the curtains and brushed her hair, looking out.

Jesse was sitting, pulling on his jeans, private behind the table. "Too bad we can't run away." Claire turned.

"Nice dream." Her smile was like sunshine.

Jesse brushed his teeth and washed his face with very hot water. Claire watched as he shaved by feel without a mirror. He unlocked the door and they stepped into the warm early evening. Southbound traffic was heavier. Jesse said, "Let's push on. New York is only eight hours. We'll be there by midnight, one o'clock, if all goes well." He took her hand. "We can sleep in tomorrow morning. " He squeezed her fingers. She squeezed back.

He took the thermos from the cab, walked into the mall and found the food court. He got a refill of coffee and took out a couple of deluxe cheeseburgers. Up the road was a Maine State Liquor store where he bought a fifth of Wild Turkey.

On the road again, the Willie Nelson tune in the back of his mind. He felt like an old person, driving the speed limit, everyone else going so fast. He reached under the seat and brought out the Wild Turkey. "Will you pour some into my coffee?"

"You think it's such a good idea?"

"Just to take the edge off. Just a little."

Claire poured the bourbon into the Dysart mug, topped it off with coffee from the thermos, took a sip and shuddered. She handed it to Jesse.

They followed 495 south toward the Mass. Turnpike, passing the turnoff to Groton. Jesse said, "I used to take that exit to boarding school. All boys."

"A different world, huh? Sounds so myownnaise and tomahtos." Claire laughed with her head back. "Tell me about it."

"We wore coat and tie, had classes on Saturday mornings. The teachers all had a PhD and we called them masters. Some of them gay, you can imagine. They called me Mr. Langdon." He smiled. "For being in the lap of luxury, we sure were isolated from the world. We used to go to chapel every morning, boys dressed up, shoulder to shoulder looking up at our headmaster, saying a prayer. Can't remember it now. Something about go out and save culture for all of mankind."

Conversation lagged. They drove.

Claire took Jesse's hand. "I'd tell you to close your eyes, but that wouldn't be prudent under the circumstances. Keep your eyes on the road and tell me what I'm spelling." With her fingernail, she scribed a letter onto Jesse's palm. The sensation sent shivers down his back. It was first an A, then a B, then C.

"The alphabet."

"Right so far. Now what animal?" She drew an E, an L, an E.

"Elephant."

"You're so good." She squeezed his hand.

Jesse was wrapped in the intimacy as they played the game through animals and minerals and flowers. Then she said, "This is the last one. It's a four-word sentence. You may not ask me about it. You'll drive on, while I sleep. Agreed?"

"Whatever you say, Claire."

Jesse was about to guess "flag" until Claire tacked

on the L. The game was over and this was serious. Part of Jesse wanted to pull his hand away. By the first letter of the last word, Jesse had figured out the message. "Flagler knows about Reefer."

Jesse glanced at Claire, who still held his hand. She brought it to her mouth and blew *sshhh* across his fingers. Without a word, she settled across the seat, put her head in his lap, and closed her eyes. He stroked her hair, full of thought.

The truck was handling well, powerful and tight. On Route 91 out of Hartford, Jesse brought the speed up a bit. The safest drivers always went five to ten miles above the speed limit. That way *you* were coming up on the other cars, instead of being overtaken.

He felt lightheaded as he took another drag off his Camel. He resolved to deal with Flagler when they got back. It did no good to speculate, except it took real effort to think of something else.

Jesse drove into the night and the pace of traffic eased. It had been a good idea to drive south late on the Fourth, blending with the holiday crowds returning to their work-a-day world. The sip from his mug went down hard; he'd mixed a strong drink. The aroma of coffee dominated by bourbon swirled around his head as he exhaled. Claire slept soundly on his thigh.

The truck came up swiftly on a slower car plodding along in the left lane. In a fluid motion, Jesse checked the side mirror and pulled right to pass. As he sped past, he was pleased by the implied curse, you dumb shit, get over where you belong. He pulled back into the left lane, cutting a little too close to the slower car with the trailer. It made him feel good. He pushed the pedal and went faster. His mind fumbled a bit with the spectacle of red taillights and approaching white headlights on the other side of the highway. Good thing most all the coffee was gone. Maybe he'd take a slug from the bottle.

Jesse looked in his mirror and noticed a set of headlights rapidly approaching. He pulled over to the right to let it pass. It too pulled over to the right. Some asshole. Jesse sped up to put some distance between them, but the car kept coming. At the same moment Jesse thought "police," blue lights came alive and the vehicle behind took on the quality of a spaceship. *Fuck!*

Careening down the highway with a ton of coke, speeding, drinking, playing chicken, no regard for danger, no sense of priority or responsibility. Now it was the end. Drunk driving, drug trafficking, caught with Claire. John Settlemire would have his hands full. And what would Emma and the kids think?

Jesse maneuvered the liquor bottle to the floor and shoved it under the seat with his boot. He manage to find the mug and set it at his heels. Maybe the cop wouldn't smell the bourbon.

Risking a twenty-five-million dollar load for want of a little liquor and excessive speed. He thought, I'm one dumb asshole. He'd tried to believe there was dignity in running drugs well, but there was none in being this stupid.

He thought about Santee. Forget respect, that would be gone. Retribution. Once out on bail, Jesse would probably be invited along on a little fishing trip of his own.

His mind raced and stumbled as he slowed and pulled over. He rolled down the window to air out the cab. Claire, stirred by the rushing wind, pushed herself up. Jesse pointed to the mirror. She seemed calm enough. How could she be? He was near panic!

He prolonged the inevitable by slowing down over a great length of highway. He needed to think, but everything was coming too fast. The shoulder was gravel and he heard the crunch as he pulled to a stop. Cars whizzed by. He wanted to be in one.

He looked in the mirror. The police spotlight came alive and nearly blinded him. The blue lights twirled and spun and made him dizzy. He felt Claire's hand on his. He looked over. She lowered the Walther between the seat and the door, and said, "It'll be all right. Be cool. They don't know anything."

Right. Just fine.

Jesse reached for the handle and opened his door. It was always better to deal with the police on the neutral ground between the cars.

That plan was brought to an abrupt halt. *"Get back in your car! I don't know you!"*

Jesse shut the door. The policeman approached the window, hand on his gun, and held back, shining the focused flashlight. Jesse took a deep breath. This was it.

Crisp blue uniform filled the window as the cop bent down and shined the light in Jesse's face. "Driver's license and registration." Jesse slowly pulled out his wallet and produced his license. Claire handed him the registration from the glove box and remained silent. The state trooper turned the light on her and studied.

He took the papers and returned his attention to Jesse. "How much have you had to drink?" His eyes were blue and searching. He was patient. He stared directly into Jesse.

"Just one bourbon, officer." Jesse didn't dare say more. His words were tumbling out and his legs were shaking. He had to smell like a distillery.

The trooper straightened and studied the papers. Jesse felt Claire's hand on his thigh, but didn't look over. The policeman filled the window again. "Now you can get out of the car." He stood back.

Jesse prayed he could stand straight. He opened the door and stepped onto the gravel. Air, pushed by the passing cars, ruffled his T-shirt. Their headlights streamed past and he knew what they were thinking. *Better him than me.* They didn't know the half of it.

The cop backed away toward the hood of the

truck, into the headlights. "Mr. Langdon, please walk toward me." He had the light trained on Jesse. Jesse was well aware of the drill. He took five deliberate steps and stopped in front of the trooper.

The cop studied his eyes. He was perfect for the part, trim and full of authority, except he looked too young. "How much have you been drinking?"

"I had one bourbon with supper." It was hard to answer with the light in his face. Jesse was pleased that he was standing firm on that line of reasoning that had come to him so suddenly. Admit to the obvious. He felt cold in the warm Connecticut evening air. His ass and the backs of his thighs were shaking as he stood facing the cop. He willed himself to relax.

The policeman reached forward and felt Jesse's jean pockets. "Do you have any weapons?"

Jesse almost laughed out loud. He ran through an inventory of all the weapons, while hoping Claire wouldn't do anything drastic. In the meantime, by instinct alone, he said no, while scaling the mental mountain of other infractions and violations: open bottle of Wild Turkey under the seat, marijuana in his duffle, oh, and a thousand pounds of coke in the camper. Not a bad evening's work for this young lawman. Make his career.

"How many drinks?"

"One with supper."

"Where did you eat?"

Jesse's mind went blank. Where were they now? How far had they come? He blurted out an answer that sounded drunk. "At the Muddy…the Muddy Rudder or something." Fuck, that was up near Portland. They were south of Hartford. He recovered, and added, "I don't quite remember the name, but it was close to Vernon."

"What did you have to eat?"

"Nachos." The lie came out good.

"Who is the woman in the truck?"

"My girlfriend."

"Where are you going?"

"Philadelphia, to visit family."

"Where are you coming from?"

"Up north, you know, sightseeing." Jesse was attempting to be friendly now. He wished he'd thought more about a situation like this, what to say. He still couldn't control the shake in his legs. The cop didn't seem to notice.

"I don't know. Answer the question. Where are you coming from?"

"Portland."

"Please spit your gum out and place your hat on the hood of the truck."

Jesse took the gum from his mouth and flicked it into the darkness. He carefully took off his cap and rested it on the truck. He turned again to the cop, who now held a pen in his right hand.

Reaction test. Better than a Breathalyzer, but once he failed this, that was sure to follow.

"I want you to look at the top of this pen. Keep your head still. Follow the top of the pen with your eyes as I move it around. Do you understand me?"

"Yes, sir."

Jesse concentrated mightily on the pen. It was a Cross. He took a deep breath and folded his hands together behind his back. He tried to relax. One thing at a time. The pen.

The policeman moved the pen to Jesse's left. Jesse watched the top of the pen.

The policeman said, "You're moving your head. Keep it still."

"Sorry." Jesse threw in an ingratiating smile. The pen came back to center and moved left again, slowly. The cop was looking into his eyes, and he wondered what would give him away, what he had to do to pass the test. He didn't feel drunk, but he knew there was no way he could pass a breath test.

After moving the pen several more times, the policeman said, "You can put your hat back on, Mr. Langdon, and get in the truck."

Jesse gathered his cap, then walked on weak knees to the driver door and slid in. The policeman returned to his cruiser and turned on the dome light. Jesse looked through the mirror and saw the cop talking on the radio. Backup.

With her singsong voice, Claire said, "Your ass was shaking like a leaf. I can't believe he didn't notice. Other than that, how'd you do?"

"Shit, Claire, how do I know? I think we're fucked." He was beyond mortified, getting pulled over on the highway in front of her.

They sat in silence and waited.

Finally, the policeman got out of his cruiser and came to the window. He handed the registration and license to Jesse, then another piece of paper. "This is a warning. It is illegal to pass on the right in this state. You were also exceeding the speed limit." Good evening, Mr. Langdon. Ma'am." He touched the brim of his cap as he nodded to Claire. "Obey the law and drive carefully."

Jesse mumbled that yes, he would, and thank you. The cop returned to his car. Jesse, in a state of disbelief, started the truck, put on his signal, waited to pull into a gap, then sped up to fifty-five miles per hour.

He checked the mirror. The cop was behind him. After a mile, the cruiser pulled into the median and went in the opposite direction.

He reached for the bottle. "A fucking miracle. What a fucking miracle." He drank deep before Claire took the bottle from him. Tipping her head back to drink too, she said, "He'll never know how close he came to making the last decision of his life."

CHAPTER 23

THEY WERE JUST a couple hours out of Long Island and Jesse was still wondering if somehow Santee's protection could have spread so far afield. To the Connecticut State Police? Was it that, or had he just been incredibly lucky?

Claire was asleep again, this time propped up against her door. Jesse had refused her offer to drive. He was tired, but his mind was sharp and finely focused. He couldn't help wondering what would have happened if the policeman had tried to arrest them. He didn't ask Claire. He was afraid of the answer.

It wouldn't have made sense to kill the cop, but sense might not matter to Claire. He wondered about her depths. For all his attraction to the woman, he knew very little about her. She might be afraid of capture, for a number of reasons. He tried not to think about it. It was over.

By the time they crossed the Throgs Neck Bridge,

it was one a.m. Wednesday morning. Fourteen hours until the meet, but how many since leaving Medellín? At the apex of the bridge, Jesse looked right out on the dazzle of Manhattan. It seemed like all the lights were on. He took the Cross Island Parkway, then went east on the Long Island Expressway. There were still a fair number of travelers at this hour.

At the Hicksville exit, Jesse took a right and cruised down North Broadway. Claire opened her eyes and said, "Well, this is much better than the last time I woke up. She stretched and showed belly skin. "We want a well-lit parking lot with a space beneath a lamp post. The criminal element will stay away and the cops will serve and protect."

They moved slowly along the wide and nearly empty street. The Sears lot on the left had all the elements. Jesse pulled up beside a flatbed trailer and attached Kenworth tractor. The streetlight made it seem like day. They surveyed the lot, checked their weapons, locked the cab and climbed into the camper. Claire pulled all the curtains tight to fight the brightness.

They bedded down without the titillation of the afternoon. It was business now. Jesse drank a beer lying in the semi-darkness. He wondered about the meet. He'd been more or less a bystander at these affairs with Biano, but now he was stepping center stage. Sleep came only fitfully.

It was a warm sunny morning with breeze clearing

away the humidity. Jesse woke up in a foul mood. He wasn't hung over exactly, but felt slow and stupid. His head was foggy.

Claire was still in bed, but awake and studying something from her purse, which lay open beside her on the bed. She looked down and said, "You want to know the details?"

Jesse put his head back down on his pillow and looked at his watch. Ten forty-five. "Before coffee and a smoke?" He fumbled for the cigarettes in his shirt on the floor. The first puff was definitely worth waking up for. "Go ahead." He flicked an ash on the floor.

"We pick a restaurant. That's where I meet the courier and sample his cash. If it's okay, I call his tester and send him over to you. I'll call you on the cellular, so you'll recognize him. He checks it out, you call me, and the deal is done. You bring him to the restaurant and we switch vehicles. After dinner and a movie, we drop the money in the city, catch a plane to Miami. Home for a nightcap with the boss."

"Dinner and a movie?"

"Kidding. Just seeing if you're paying attention." But Jesse was also confused by the car swap and the flight to Miami. "When did the plans change?"

"They never changed. You never knew them. Just thought you did."

"Jesus Christ."

"Oh, don't get all moody. It's need-to-know. You

don't expect Santee to trust you with *all* the details on your first big score." She swung naked legs over the side and slipped out of the bunk in panties and a short T-shirt. "I need to freshen up. Then let's get some brunch."

Jesse got out of his bunk naked and pulled on his pants and shirt. Claire was watching in the mirror. He was in a foul mood and wanted to scowl at her, but her wide eyes, in mock surprise, made him laugh.

Claire took forever in the small shower, and Jesse wondered if there would be any hot water left. He lay on his bed and fretted about the afternoon. He didn't like the plan. He'd be alone. Claire would be alone. Any number of things could go wrong, even with the buyers knowing neither of the locations.

She came out in a rush of steam. Her hair was wet and brushed straight back. She had on a sleeveless cotton blouse and a denim skirt cut above her knee. She held white sandals in her left hand.

Jesse showered and shaved and felt better by the time he was dressed. They climbed in the cab and drove around, looking for a meeting place for Claire and a parking lot for Jesse.

Claire settled for a diner on the corner of Broadway and Bethpage. They parked in front and sat in the smoking section by the window so they could watch the camper, though after eating with Biano in dark corners for so long, Jesse felt utterly exposed.

Jesse ordered a double Bloody Mary and Claire had orange juice. It was a nice place, bright, open and shiny. The booths were magenta Naugahyde, had a personal jukebox. Art deco neon, polished aluminum, cut glass, green tinted windows to dampen the summer sun and heat.

Jesse ate a pastrami omelet, Claire a cantaloupe with chicken salad and bacon. Jesse remembered a toothpick in his pocket and gave it to Claire for the lettuce in her teeth. He pointed to his left upper row, she found it and smiled wide for inspection.

"You do this often, Claire? You don't seem nervous."

"This isn't my thing, though I've accompanied Santee on drops. I don't like anything that depends on faith and honor. Foolish, if you ask me. But we depend on each other, and more often than not, it works."

"I don't like your choice of words, Claire. More often than not?"

"Christ, Jesse, at this level there's enough coke and money to be worth any risk." Claire got up. "I'm going to call them now." She left the table for the payphones between the double front-entrance doors. It was two-thirty p.m.

By the time she returned, Jesse had paid the bill. She said, "Let's go."

They went back to the camper until a little before three p.m. When it was time, Claire rested a hand on

Jesse's arm and said, "Good luck. If all goes well, we'll be back here in an hour. If not, use everything Coley taught you. You should be all right." She stretched up on tiptoes and kissed his lips. Jesse felt her warm breath.

Claire walked back into the diner. Jesse drove to the mall and parked behind Sterns. He locked the cab and walked to the payphone outside the Michelin Tire Center and got the number. He got back in the camper and looked beyond the curtains at the phone. He waited for the call from Claire.

At 3:14 the cellular phone rang. "It looks good on this end. It's real and weighs right. I will call your friend and send him over." Claire described him, then hung up. Jesse sat back and watched the phone booth.

A brown sedan pulled up and parked beside the phone. A guy got out the driver's door, a Latin male about five-ten, 150 pounds, dressed natty in pressed trousers, fancy leather thin-soled shoes and a light sports jacket, cream color. He didn't appear to be looking at anyone. That was good. He leaned on the hood of his car and lit a cigarette.

Jesse waited a little longer, looking around for anything suspicious. It looked clear, so he dialed the payphone. The guy was real cool. He went in slowly, taking his time, no rush. He answered with an accent. "Jes?"

Jesse said, "Look across toward the big store. See a

red Ford truck with a camper? I'm in the camper. Drive over and knock. I'm watching."

"No problem."

He hung up the receiver, got in his car, drove over. He didn't look suspicious or nervous. Jesse wished he felt as calm. He was keyed up, condition yellow, bouncing his knee. He didn't know if he should get out his gun. The guy didn't have his out. No shit.

With the knock, Jesse unlocked the door. The tester came in and Jesse held out his hand to shake. The guy looked confused, but timidly took Jesse's hand and shook loose and limp, no eye contact. Jesse shut the door.

The guy turned, not leaving his back open. He turned some more as Jesse went over to the bench and lifted the cushion. Jesse pulled the Leatherman off his belt, cut the seal and lifted the top of the compartment off. The guy looked over his shoulder and whistled. Jesse got out of his way. The guy struggled with the first duffel and managed to get it up on the table. He took a switchblade and cut through the plastic wrap into a kilo package. He spread the wound.

From inside his coat he took the test kit and put a bit of coke in the tube, shook it, looking at the color. "Nice color, real pure." He wet his finger and stuck it in the wound, put it in his mouth, brushed his gums. "Nice, real nice."

Jesse came over and took a little for himself. Gums went numb. He returned to his spot by the door.

As the tester reached into his inside breast pocket to put the kit away, the camper swayed from the weight of a foot on the stoop. The door opened. A huge black man, gun in hand, shouldered inside and shut the door. "Stay calm," he said.

The tester froze, hand half in his coat. Jesse was standing close to the intruder. The gun was a stainless steel revolver, very big bore filled with large-caliber hollow points. The black guy, looking around, eyed the duffel on the table and the open compartment, and said, "Well, well, looks like a big-time score." With wide eyes, he looked at the buyer and said, "Hand out of your coat, man, real slow." He waved his pistol up and down.

From yellow to livid red. Jesse had come all this way and now this fucking asshole was fucking up *the whole fucking thing*! He was flexing his fists. His mind was blank, empty. Time stretched, elongated into slow motion.

The tester at the table said, "Wait a minute," and the black man looked over. Jesse took the opportunity to allow his fury to overflow and he struck out with his left hand at the gun arm, then jammed his right fingers into the neck. The guy had frozen for that split second, as if he was startled that anyone could be so fucking stupid. Jesse's fingers wrapped around the throat, the gun clattered to the floor, and both the guy's hands went up to cover the pain. He went down on his knees. Jesse took the heel of his hand and slammed it into the left temple. The man went down hard and semiconscious.

Jesse got the gun, amazed it hadn't fired. He pointed it, shaking, at the buyer, who said, "Now wait a minute. He isn't with me." He held up both hands.

Jesse had no idea what was happening, what to do next, who to trust. He decided to tie both men up, stabilize the situation until he could call Claire.

The man on the floor groaned and Jesse kicked him in the head, holding the gun on the tester. He took out a roll of duct tape from the closet. "Sit down! In that chair," pointing with the gun. "Put your arms on the arm rests. *Now!*" He tossed the tape to the guy. "Tape your right hand to the chair. Do it!"

The guy did as he was told, but didn't like it. "You got this all wrong. I don't know this *cabrón*. Just bad luck, man, he stumbles on the buy looking for small change." He finished with his taping job.

Jesse made sure the man on the floor was out, then went over and taped the other arm. He took a small automatic from the tester's shoulder holster and flung it up on the top bunk, mumbling to himself, "Fuck shit fuck shit fuck shit." Jesse went over to the other guy, pulled his arms together and taped the wrists. Then he did the same with his feet, taping at the ankles. It looked like he wore a size eighteen shoe. Finally, he took a turn around his head, taping his mouth shut. Didn't want any yelling. He put the gun on the far end of the table, dragged the man to the open compartment and managed to get him up on it, sort of sitting.

Panic had given way to just being fully pissed off. Why the hell couldn't this go fucking right?

A darkness descended, containing all his confusions about the past and all his terror about the present web he'd wrapped around himself. It gushed from his soul and came in a flash flood.

He poured some water from the tap into a cup and splashed it on the black man. He filled it again and took a sip, spilling some over his shaking hands.

The black man was opening his big watery eyes. They immediately filled with fear and he tried to get up, but fell back to squirm and struggled against the tape around his wrists and ankles, until he gave up. Then he, along with the tester, looked at him, waiting for his move.

Jesse couldn't get a straight thought to make its way through his brain. On the surface, this was almost certainly a setup. How likely was it that some random robber stumbles on a deal like this? He had to go with the surface indications, assume a setup and try to prove otherwise.

The tester said, "Look, man, we got a little complication is all. All you have to do is call your people.

They'll tell you it's a clean deal. No harm done here.
You wrapped him up good, so we take care of the rest.
We just do the buy like planned. You get your money,
we get our stuff." Jesse looked at his watch. It was 3:37.
Claire was waiting for his call. He leaned against the
counter and dialed.

"Yeah?"

"Hi." Jesse didn't know what to say next.

"You don't sound so good. You all right?"

"No. It's all fucked up." Jesse's voice was uneasy.

"What are you talking about?"

"There are too many people over here." Jesse waved
the pistol back and forth between the two men. Their
eyes followed the barrel.

"You're not making sense. Start from the
beginning."

"Okay." Jesse took a deep breath, but he still felt
like boiling water. "The buyer fits your description
comes over and is testing the stuff. He likes it. Then
all of a sudden this huge black guy comes in with a big
fucking gun. I got both guys taped up. What the hell
do I do now?"

"You what? How could he have just walked in?
How the hell did you get them taped up?" Claire wasn't
pleased.

"Goddamn it, I forgot to lock the fucking door!
That's how! What do I do now, for Christ's sake? I'm
thinking these guys are together." Jesse was shouting.

"Quiet down. You don't want to attract attention. Let me think."

Jesse's palms were sweating, the pistol getting slippery. He looked at the black man and said, "You got any more friends out there?" With that, he remembered the door and went to lock it. He looked out the small window. Nothing but shoppers. Then he stood there and shook, waiting for Claire to figure something out.

She said, "The money man here says he doesn't know anything about it, says they never work with anybody but Colombians. That should tell you right off. It makes sense to me."

Jesse felt a tight pressure in his chest. His heart wanted to beat its way out. He mumbled into the phone, "Teach this dipshit fuckhead to fuck with me."

On the other end, "What are you going to do?"

Jesse was in a world far off. The voice in the phone sounded as if it came through water. He said, "Figure out what's going on here." He put the phone down beside the black man.

Furious. Man of action. James Fucking Bond. He reached over and grabbed the man's index finger and twisted until it snapped. He savored the sweet release, the succulent sound like dogs eating chicken gristle, *pop*. The black man tried to shout, but the tape across his mouth held fast.

Jesse looked over at the guy sitting in the chair, looking for a reaction. Pissed his compatriot was hurt?

Hatred for Jesse screwing up the scam? But all the guy looked was nervous, thinking his finger was next.

Jesse went back for more, on a roll. It was good the man was coming around, could feel this next one. A nerve worm gripped Jesse's scalp, then let go. He took the middle finger, looked directly into the black man's frightened eyes, and started bending it backwards, back, back, until it broke. The snap was delicious to hear and feel, like a twig. The black man fainted and slumped over onto the duffels of coke.

Jesse checked the reaction of the tester. He still showed self-interested fear, but now there was also a fascination, a morbid magnetism, as if he were witnessing a plane crash into a building, or a train plunging off a trestle into a raging river. Jesse trusted his instincts. There was no camaraderie here. He was satisfied they weren't working together.

He took a deep breath and rinsed the sweat off his face in the sink. He picked up the phone, said, "It's okay now. They aren't together."

"What was that sound? What are you doing?"

"I'm telling you, it's okay now. No big deal."

Claire didn't respond. Jesse filled in the silence. "I guess we go along with the switch. I'll drive over and we swap the vehicles. Black man's tied up good. These guys get him in the bargain. They can deal with him. "

"Then get over here and let's finish this." Claire hung up.

Jesse went over to the buyer, took out his Leatherman and brought the blade up. He reached down and cut the tape off each arm. "You heard what I said. We got a deal. You take care of that." Jesse nodded toward the unconscious man.

"You crazy, man." The buyer was rubbing his wrists, shaking his head. Wary, looking at Jesse as if for permission, he reached up and got his gun from the bunk, put it in his shoulder holster.

Jesse took the big pistol and put it in the front of his pants, pulled his shirt out and let it hang loose. He took the car keys from the peg and looked over at the black man.

Jesse pulled in to the diner parking lot beside a white Econoline van with no windows and plenty of dents. Fine fucking trade. He waited. Claire and the courier walked out of the diner's back door, came over and got in the camper.

The courier, acting like the boss, said, "What happened? You got some company the lady tells me." He went over and nudged the black man, looking him over, noticing the twisted fingers. He looked up and addressed Jesse. "You one mean motherfucker." He looked over to the tester, "Remind me not to piss off this gringo." He tossed off a laugh.

Claire looked at the black man, then squinted at Jesse. "I see you made your point."

The tester said, "Man's fuckin' loco. Give him the

keys and let's get out of here." The courier started to hand the van keys to Jesse, but Claire said, "I'll take those."

Jesse looked around, checking for personal items. He got his satchel, Claire's bag, the two Dysart mugs from the drying rack, and smiled weakly at Claire. She followed him out of the camper and they walked away. Claire was all business. "We go into the city and drop this stuff before anything else can go wrong. I'm driving and I don't want to hear any shit. You're in no shape."

They drove in silence to the diamond district, 47th Street and 6th Avenue. Claire double parked, went to the door of a closed shop and knocked. A woman opened the door. They talked and Claire came back.

The corrugated metal door to the right of the shop began to roll up. Claire pulled across the street and drove into the opening. It was just big enough for the van. The door closed.

Inside, it opened up and was well lit. The woman, with puffy brushed-back hair, black eye makeup and painted brows, came through a door with a pudgy man. He was about thirty-five, dark hair styled back curly to his shoulders.

Heeling beside him was a massive German shepherd. When the man stopped to shake hands, the dog sat and watched. The man introduced himself as Steve, his wife as Donna, and the dog as Snort. Steve chuckled and it struck Jesse as funny too. Claire seemed to have lost all her sense of humor. Donna was serious too.

Claire led them to the back of the van and opened the doors. Snort jumped in and started to sniff at the boxes. He passed over the first, second and third but got excited about the fourth and fifth. Steve called him out and he sat at his side. Donna slid the boxes out and Jesse and Steve carried them to the table along the left wall. The fourth and fifth were put off to the side. Steve patted Snort and said, "Those we have to launder. I like the pun. But really, we have to get any coke residue off the cash, so the feds don't get all excited."

There was a waist-high scale beside the table. Donna came over and weighed herself, a flattering weight. She and Steve weighed each box, then opened them. She took a random sampling and made sure it wasn't counterfeit. Donna nodded her approval.

She said, "We'll deposit this in the appropriate accounts specified by Mr. Santee over the next few days. It takes time to count this much cash." She extended her hand and they all shook. Jesse and Claire had been dismissed.

They got their luggage from the van and caught a cab to LaGuardia. By seven-thirty, they were on Flight 643 to Miami.

PART V

CHAPTER 24

THE SEATS IN first class were roomy, comfortable and too far apart. Jesse wanted to be closer to Claire, and he leaned in. She leaned more toward her window.

They ordered drinks as soon as the stewardess came by. Jesse's double went down before Claire had taken the second sip of her martini. After the Scotch, Jesse was inclined to talk, but Claire wasn't. He ordered and drank more Scotch, but it wasn't affecting him like he wanted. He wanted to blanket himself with the liquor, to feel the heavy weight press down and take away the need to address a newness in himself.

His mind, lubricated by the booze, told him his actions had been correct. Logic and common sense insisted that the ends justified the means, especially with so much at stake. What were a couple of fingers in the great scheme of things? But what were the depths he could plumb? Was it bottomless? He didn't see a lot of future in the present scheme of things.

"You remember when you thought the world was safe?"

Jesse opened his eyes and rolled his head toward her.

She looked directly into his soul. "Safe and benevolent? Calm? And then some senseless violence reacquaints you with the darkness, the darkness that's so close." She took a sip of her drink and said, "I'm there now." She paused. "Are you?"

Jesse closed his eyes, wanting it all to go away, and wanting it not to. "Yes."

"It feels like I'm transitioning," she said. "Like maybe I'm starting to want something different. I saw the fingers on that man. Am I getting squeamish now, after all I've done?"

Now Jesse looked back into her soul. "Are you?"

She said quickly, "What do you think is happening to that guy, like maybe right this minute?"

He wanted nothing more than to unburden himself of the pain of his own realization, the same as she was doing now. But it was too immediate, too raw, for him to process out loud. He clenched his jaw and said, "None of our business, Claire. None of our business."

She said, "Isn't it? I think it is."

"Why?"

"Because I think it's most dangerous when you

straddle. That way, you aren't either place, so you don't know which set of rules applies. I think we're both straddling."

"It's over, Claire. Done and gone. Not our problem."

"Wrong. It's not over. It's just beginning."

Jesse closed his eyes and finally fell asleep.

Pasque met them at the airport and drove them back to La Primavera with the glass partition shut tight. For all the hard and dangerous work, there was no champion's reception. It was late and the house was quiet. Claire and Jesse said goodnight at the head of the stairs and went to their separate rooms.

Carla knocked at seven and woke Jesse. He rolled over and tried to ignore her, but she came in and pulled the curtains open, explaining that Santee wanted to see him in an hour.

Even with a shower, first hot, then cold, and several healthy snorts from the full coke bowl, Jesse couldn't shake the drowsiness, the torpor and depression. He was the last to arrive at breakfast. Nobody got up except Santee, who rose and came to shake his hand.

"Congratulations, Jesse, on a job well done. My people in New York report very good things. Please, sit and let us celebrate." Santee ushered Jesse to the seat on his right, opposite Claire.

Coley sat to Jesse's right, Biano opposite him

beside Claire. Flagler was on the other side of Coley, a Pall Mall smoking in the ashtray at his side. Santee sat after Jesse, then clapped his hands to signal Carla and Mrs. Sanchez.

From the pantry came the women with trays of food that they put on the sideboard and uncovered. Santee nodded to Coley, who uncorked two bottles of Dom Perignon, poured and passed. Jesse reached across and filled Claire's flute, then Santee's. He filled his own glass and waited; Santee seemed ready to say something, to give a toast.

"I believe we are truly on our way. I declare that the Fourth of July is now the holiday to celebrate the dawning of a truly global organization—the United Narcotics Organization, or UNO, for the number one." He raised his glass and everyone followed. The champagne was ice cold and perfect. Jesse took another big sip and wished for an accelerant shot of Wild Turkey to fill the little empty shot glass that sat lonely beside his orange juice. Carla came around with the very thing, and poured some in each of their glasses.

"Now we chase it with the Wild one." Santee smiled to Jesse. "It is Mr. Langdon the Third's favorite drink. To Jesse, who is now truly *uno*, or one of us." Santee raised the neat bourbon and they all drank it down.

Jesse felt the warm rush dive to his belly, where

it glowed. He thought of the drive in the camper and glanced over at Claire, who wore a pained expression.

Jesse smiled around the table. He felt better now, and he was greeted with warm faces, all except Flagler's, who was looking at him with steely eyes.

Santee urged Carla to pour more champagne, which she did, then served scrambled eggs with green chilies, medallions of smoked ham and hot tortillas. For the moment, the food took center stage, but Jesse knew he was on display. He didn't know to what extent until Santee produced five sheets of paper, each with a copy of a small newspaper article in the middle. He passed them out and said, "In today's *New York Post*, on page twenty-seven, is testimony to the fine work that Jesse is capable of doing. Read, and then I will explain. I think Jesse here is too modest."

The table was silent as everyone read the small article, about the unidentified body of an African American male shot once in the back of the head, execution style. A police spokesman stated that two fingers had been broken prior to death, which suggested that the torture and killing were related to an escalating turf war on Long Island over drug territory. Santee looked around at the reaction. The glow in Jesse's belly turned into a swimming dread that spread up and into his throat and got stuck.

Flagler took the bottle of Wild Turkey and filled Jesse's shot glass. Jesse smiled his appreciation until he looked at Flagler's face. His smile drained away. Flagler was doing no favors.

Jesse drank the bourbon, then regretted it. It wanted to come right back up. He wanted to be in bed with the covers pulled over his head. He let Santee's words wash over him.

"What an unfortunate thug. Wrong place, wrong time. Jesse can lay no claims to the bullet, but it appears that the finger business was his inspiration. Is that not so, Claire?"

Claire shifted in her seat and looked at Jesse. "I wasn't there."

"Not for the finger business, but you know about it. Surely you can explain it to us."

"As I understand it, the man intruded as the buyer was testing the coke. Jesse subdued him and bound both men, unsure of the allegiances. He broke the fingers to determine that the buyer and the man were not in collusion. I guess this article is proof of that."

"Coley," Santee said, "You have tutored Jesse well. He is a quick study. This intruder was well armed and substantially larger than Jesse, yet Jesse protected the shipment and the deal. Well done, Coley, Jesse." He beamed at both. "There is a minor point that eludes me, however. Exactly how did you determine the two men were not in cahoots? You had taped the black man's mouth shut, had you not?"

All eyes shifted to Jesse. He wanted to hide. The pit of hungry fear in his stomach grew like a watermelon.

Flagler filled his shot glass again, but Jesse didn't touch it. He'd had enough of everything. He could feel Santee looking at him. Jesse raised his head and looked defiantly back into those black eyes. "I was mad. If they were together and I was hurting one of them, I knew I'd see sympathy in the other's face. Yes, the black man was gagged. And I saw no sympathy from the buyer. I knew then they weren't together."

"And why the second finger, Jesse?" Santee was baiting.

Jesse felt the power. He sat up straight. He recalled the sensation, the bones of the finger finally giving way. He was looking at Santee and remembering.

Santee reached for his champagne glass. Jesse's hand came out and grasped Santee's wrist. Santee raised his eyes to Jesse's. Jesse said, "The second one was for me. I knew after the first they weren't partners. The second finger was just for me. And Sheldrick?" It was the first time Jesse had ever called the boss by his first name, and he said it softly. "I liked it. When the bones broke, it was delicious. That's what you want to know, isn't it? You want to know if I enjoyed someone else's pain. Well, I did. Maybe you and I are more alike than either of us want."

Jesse let Santee's hand go.

"Well, well." Santee was momentarily shaken, and

though he tried to disguise it, it escaped no one. He took a swallow of champagne and regained his composure. "You are now in, all the way, my friend. You are an accessory to murder. The copy of the article is for your scrapbook. May it end up full. A toast." He raised his flute and the others followed.

Jesse took the Wild Turkey and drank it down.

"Now let us eat. We will need our strength for all that lies ahead. I would like a celebration, massive festivities, many important guests, to show our appreciation for all that we have. The party will be a week from Friday."

"Excuse me, but I'm afraid I've lost my appetite." Jesse rose from the table. He put his napkin down and walked out. He ran up to his room and got to the toilet just in time. On his knees with a circular embrace, he threw up into the bowl again and again. The dry heaves were endless and welcome. His eyes watered. His nose stung. Jesse returned to bed and fell asleep under the covers with all his clothes, even his shoes.

Jesse dreamed of Flagler. He was pouring endless shots of poison that Jesse couldn't help but drink. They seemed to have some sort of lethal pact.

Reefer was there, too. They were all skipping across steppingstones that became land mines, some defused, some not. Jesse followed Reefer. They were prodded by Flagler, who was dressed all in red. Each stone stood like a single star in a galaxy of endless darkness. Jesse's survival depended on stopping Flagler. He must eliminate danger points, one at a time. There was a writhing and a lashing out, flailing.

Jesse woke, twisted in the covers. His clothes were bunched in knots. He knew he had to immobilize Flagler. But that was only to get his shot at Santee. As Claire said, it was only the beginning.

CHAPTER 25

JESSE DROVE OUT to Surfside and lay down on his back on a huge beach towel.

Blazing sand, sun baking and burning, etching golden domes behind the eyelids. The sound of surf and the smell of tanning oil on nearby naked skin. Jesse drifted and floated, in and out.

The dream held the seed of truth. Flagler was merely the mask, the twisted face of the malignant tumor that had burrowed its way into Jesse. He needed to take the scalpel soon, cut deeply and swiftly, rid his life of this cancer. But first, he needed what Flagler knew about Reefer. Flagler was close now, already, to making his own play, to acting on his jealousy and rage and hate. All Jesse had to do was wait him out and be ready.

The trampoline operation on the Mexican border was the most vulnerable. A few fuckups would stand out. The operation had been so smooth since Jesse had eliminated the Louisiana cover and devoted all south-western resources to the trampoline. It represented a third of overall revenue. If he could toss a wrench into the system there, it would throw Santee off balance and have the added benefit of tarnishing Flagler. It could be the first step on the path out, however that would unfold. But it was also like playing with dynamite, and could set the two unstable players into unpredictable and probably lethal directions.

Santee, Flagler and Jesse knew the schedules. Coley knew too, because he was involved with the security. But it was Flagler's territory. He would take the fall.

Jesse checked the schedule in the morning. He called the Texas Rangers from a payphone just before the tanker truck was to cross the border. Cowboy cops would grab the truck and the headlines. He didn't think they'd scope out the entire operation, but it was a risk he was willing to take. The transfer points and the rest of the smuggling effort should remain intact.

But the loss would hurt. Plant a little seed in Santee's head, and watch it grow.

The news came swiftly. Jesse, Coley and Flagler were summoned in the afternoon. Santee was hopping mad. He commanded them all to sit while he paced back and forth.

"Something the fuck is going on here. I just got a call from a DEA guy in Texas, says one of the tankers got stopped and the cops got the driver and the customs man we got on the payroll. What is the damage, Coley?"

Flagler was relieved the first focus had not been on him. He looked over at Coley as if he were interested in the answer, watching Coley's skin fry instead of his own.

Before Coley could answer, Santee turned on Flagler and said, "This is your operation. You are ultimately responsible. Only the four of us in this room know the details of the trampoline operation. If there is a leak, you will find it. You understand me? Because if you do not, you will be wearing a tag on your toe before the week is out.

"Coley?"

Coley never wilted under pressure. He probably didn't know what the word stress meant. He answered matter-of-factly. "The driver gets his instructions once he's crossed the border. We move the transfer stations periodically, but it wouldn't matter, because this driver is new. He wouldn't know any details. Even if we lost him and the transfer station, there is containment there, and no links to anywhere else.

"We were lucky that only the local cops got involved. The DEA might have tagged the shipment and watched. We'd have lost a great deal more if that had happened.

"The loss of the customs agent is more of a problem. Nothing will lead here, of course, but corruption revealed usually leads to some public outcry and a whip-saw reaction. It only lasts a short time, but it's inconvenient. They'll suspect that there are more officials on the take, and that the corruption is wider spread. I think we're plenty deep in that regard, but it might cost us a little more money in the short term. The heat will be turned up.

"As long as this is an isolated incident, I would label it as inconvenient."

Santee turned on Flagler. "Have you got anything to contribute? Do you know anything at all?"

"No sir, Mr. Santee. I agree with everything Coley said. It's not much of a deal if it's only this one time."

Santee said, "I don't care if it is only one. I want to know what went wrong. You get out there and find the fuck out. *Now!* I want answers."

Flagler looked confused, as if he didn't know what *now* meant, exactly.

Santee shouted, "*NOW!*" again, and Flagler rose and left the room, bound for Texas.

Santee turned to Jesse. "What about you?"

Jesse was worried and hoped it looked like concern for the shipment. He couldn't think how it could go wrong, but if it did, he'd have the toe tag.

"One shipment is a substantial loss, but in the big picture, it's only a dent to UNO. Any more losses mean something else, perhaps a temporary shutdown of that territory. We would then have to plug the leak before we continued. That would impact an operation that represents a third of our overall revenues. The effect would be to delay the timetable for revenue accumulation, and perhaps the plans to move offshore."

Jesse knew Santee wouldn't like the news.

"That is unacceptable. Absolutely unacceptable. We better hope this is the end of it. There will be hell to pay if it is not."

Jesse went into town and revisited the second floor of the *Miami Herald*. It was a long shot, and all he had was the possibility that Flagler and Reefer were connected in some way. If the two were not acquainted, and Flagler only had news secondhand, the link would never surface in the papers.

He concentrated on the larger picture. If Reefer was smuggling dope in Maine and wanted to go bigger time, what ladder would he climb? What outfit was running Maine?

One article described the effect of the tighter enforcement in Florida. Besides the obvious—more drug busts—the operations were branching out to less patrolled locations. The northeast coastline was increasingly plagued by the criminal element. The Colombian cartels were enlisting the help of newly formed Mexican organizations to transport contraband across the southern U.S. border. Two outfits had established dominance in adjacent territories, but there was tremendous violence between the rival factions to consolidate control.

As Jesse read on, he recalled Santee's trip to Monterey. They'd gone from there to a smaller town.

Then it was right in front of him. Guadalupe. Details of the massacre were more graphic than Coley or Santee had related. There was a picture of the smoking remains of the building and two rows of bodies lined up in the dirt. Apparently, several men had been allowed to live, presumably to tell the tale and relay the message.

The facilities were believed to be part of the Espinoza cartel's operation, a growing menace in that part of Mexico and tightly tied to the Cali cartel. The paper speculated that even with the destruction of this major facility, the overall amount of drugs flowing across the border would barely be affected.

Another article related the struggle between the Cali and Medellín cartels for control of the drug trade. The results were predictably gruesome.

Nowhere was there mention of any link to Maine. It was almost certainly too small-time to register. Jesse left the building trying to sort out the possibilities. It looked like Santee's new UNO was in a life-or-death struggle with the forces from Cali. At the moment, his team was winning.

CHAPTER 26

LA PRIMAVERA WAS bustling for tomorrow evening's party. Claire directed the florists and the caterers, showing them around, pointing out where the three bars would be situated and how she wanted the floral arrangements placed.

Coley was busy with security arrangements. He'd expressed his concern to Jesse in the gym last evening. All he needed was a high-profile party with multiple connected guests, especially when the Mexican connection might be unraveling. Coley was clearly worried. Coley was briefing the guards and the watchmen.

With all the commotion, it was an ideal time to skip away. Jesse took the small BMW and drove to Miami Beach and found a payphone. He made a call to the bank in the Caymans and instructed them to wire funds from his account to several shell accounts, then into Flagler's account. Jesse didn't know exactly how this was going to play out, but it could never hurt if

Flagler had some unexplainable cash. There was no way the transfer would be traced back to Jesse.

He drove aimlessly around, checking for a tail. He didn't see anyone following, but he decided to go shopping for cover, just in case. He was home in time for evening cocktails, sporting a new silk shirt.

Claire was explaining to Santee about the party plans, and he looked bored. Coley had a pad in his lap and was writing and figuring. Jesse poured Wild Turkey and sat down in his now-customary chair beside Santee's desk. He lit a smoke and listened to Claire.

"The guest list is up to 300. The bigwigs from Mexico City are flying in tomorrow afternoon. Sam is getting ready for all the planes. We should give an award for the farthest traveler. I've got RSVPs from Washington, Los Angeles and Houston. The word is out, and everyone wants to attend." Claire smiled at Santee. He was preoccupied. "We're using the usual caterer, the one Coley checked out. They still come with your recommendation?"

Coley looked up from his notes and leaned toward Claire, who sat on the other end of the sofa. "Yes. They're run by the sister of one of our best local buyers. It's a great cover and they do fine food."

The phone rang. Santee picked it up and listened. He turned a shade of red but remained silent and still. At the end he said he understood and hung up.

It was deadly quiet. Santee let out a breath and looked around, calculated calm.

"It seems we have stirred the hornet's nest. The Cali people are overreacting." Santee spoke so low that Jesse had to strain to catch the words.

Santee stood and took Claire's hand and pulled her from the sofa.

All through the next day, the caterers arrived in vans full of men and women dressed in black and white. They unloaded platters and cooking trays and cooler after cooler. Under the watchful eye of guards, they set up in the kitchen on folding tables.

Carla and Mrs. Sanchez hovered in the beginning, but quickly realized the scope of the party far outdistanced them. They retreated to the peace of their rooms.

Claire helped place the people into convenient stations. Outside the garage door near the kitchen, they set up the enormous barbecue grills heaped with still-unlit natural charcoal. The grilled lamb and swordfish would come from there, hot hors d'oeuvres from the kitchen ovens.

Jesse resisted the urge to hit the coke and Wild Turkey. He'd be on display this evening. Tonight he'd need to keep his wits. He found himself standing in the kitchen admiring the efficiency of the caterers. They wasted no moves in a complicated dance. The guest list was now up to 500.

A small girl in a white blouse and a short black skirt was rolling strips of smoked Atlantic salmon off a piece of golden cardboard and placing them on a huge platter of capers, lemon wedges and leaf lettuce. "Would you like some?"

"Sure."

She held out a small piece of rolled salmon. He took the orange flesh and laid it in his mouth. All he had to do was crush it. It was too tender to chew. The slightly smoky flavor swirled with the oils of the deep and slid down his throat. He opened his eyes to find the girl smiling at him. She said, "Good, huh?"

She handed him another, and he savored it again. "What exactly is that?" he asked. "Where does it come from?"

She took the package and looked at the fine print. "I know it's Atlantic salmon and that it's smoked, but I don't know where it's made. Let's see." She turned the packaging over and found the label. "It says here that this stuff comes from some place called Ducktrap River Fish Farms, in Belfast, Maine. That's weird. I thought all Maine had was lobster. And I thought Belfast was in Ireland."

Jesse took a swallow from the bottle of Red Hook ale he held in his hand. It seemed that whenever he forgot about his past life, a gust would come and remind him. He thanked the girl and went out the door to his room to dress.

Claire had done a spectacular job. From the window of his room, he looked down on the pool area and dock. An enormous yacht was tied up at the float. The Bertram had been moved to the neighbor's dock. Everything was illuminated with strings of small white lights, even the boats. Crowds of people in clusters chatted around the pool. From the sound of it, the house was filling up too.

Jesse dressed for the occasion in cream colors. He was wearing linen trousers the color of light coffee. His shirt was of fine Hong Kong pale-yellow cotton, open at the neck to reveal his simple gold chains and Claire's Saint Christopher.

In front of the mirror, he noticed how hollow his cheeks were, how drawn his face. He tucked the shirt into his trousers, smoothed the fabric across his flat belly and adjusted his loose belt. From the desk drawer he took the Walther and checked the slide. A gleaming splash of brass reassured him of the round in the chamber. With his thumb he ejected the mag and confirmed six Hi-Shock cartridges. The Walther, with regular ammunition, was a small gun with limited stopping power. But these bad boys, with pellets like shotgun shells that expanded immediately upon impact, gave the .380 the stopping power of a .357 magnum.

He fingered the frame of the photograph of his kids. They were so far away, a world away. He realized he'd been naive to think this would be a fleeting experience. He was in Santee's clutches and the path out, if there was one, was fraught with danger. He popped the cardboard back-plate, removed the picture and placed it in his breast pocket, over his heart. He vowed to keep the picture, and thoughts of his children, close. They represented his future, such as it was.

Jesse slid the pistol into the small belt holster inside his trousers in the small of his back. It seemed silly to go armed to the party. With Coley in charge of security, the place would be more secure than the White House. Nonetheless, he felt better with his weapon. Jesse swung on his brown silk jacket and straightened the lapels in the mirror.

Music from a mariachi band beside the pool wafted through his window with the cooling night breeze. He opened the desk and took a small hit of marching powder for the conversational aspects of the drug. Even though he could drink more while doing coke, he made a mental note to lay off the bourbon and stick to beer or champagne.

Jesse hadn't planned on making an entrance, but as he slowly descended the circular staircase, one pretty face looked up from the crowd and saw him. She smiled bashfully, as if she shouldn't have been so impolite as to look directly at him. Another face followed her gaze, then another, as if they were all looking skyward toward a jumper in the thirtieth-story window. His right hand sliding along the banister, Jesse marveled at the sight of a sea of heads and shoulders filling the foyer. Most had just arrived and were engaged in chatter before they headed toward the bar or groups of more important people they wanted to be seen with.

At the bottom of the stairs, Jesse took two glasses of champagne from a waiter, pretending to have an escort somewhere close for whom he was being gallant. He took a big sip and looked around. People weren't about to risk introducing themselves before they had talked to others about who exactly this tanned white man was. In the crowd he was anonymous again and he eased himself out the front door onto the steps.

It was an orderly and busy scene. Coley was supervising the parking arrangements. Guests were arriving fashionably late in a steady stream. Some drove their own Aston Martins, Ferraris or Rolls Royces, and reluctantly relinquished them to the attendants. Others came in limousines, from which emerged huge bodyguards who opened rear doors for beautiful people. The drive was clear of cars, so that guests could drive up and leave their automobiles for the parking attendants who lined them in neat rows on the grass on either side of the driveway.

Jesse could smell the charcoal grilling meat and fish. He took the final sip from his first glass and deposited it on a post before starting on the second.

A low-slung silver Lamborghini whined up to the door and stopped. A doorman skipped to the passenger door and opened it. Long tanned legs, short silver dress, blonde hair. As best she could, she kept her legs together, but the car wasn't designed for the elegant withdrawal of short skirts. No one watching seemed to mind. Neither did the woman. She stood and smiled demurely at her admiring onlookers and smoothed her dress. A short middle-aged Latin gentleman, impeccably dressed, exited the driver's side and snarled at all the men he could see. He came around and regained possession of his date. He growled at the man about to park his car. "You put as much as a fucking scratch on this baby and I'll have your balls."

Coley came up all dandy in a white silk suit and no tie, but buttoned at the top like he'd seen actors do. "Fucking madhouse. How the hell is anyone supposed to make this secure? Hope no one wants to knock off a business associate." Coley didn't wait for conversation and strolled off toward a group of armed men waiting at the gate.

Jesse finished the second glass of Dom Perignon, put that glass down with the first, and headed around back. The patio was in full swing. On the other side of the pool, the band played and couples danced beside the bar. He plucked another glass of champagne and some smoked mussels, then settled on the railing overlooking the pool. He took his Camels from his coat and lit one, blowing smoke into the overhead lights.

A hand fell lightly on his shoulder and Jesse turned

to find Claire close and smiling. "Are you enjoying the party?" She looked around, taking in the scene. "Think we did a good job?"

Jesse smelled her jasmine perfume. She was wearing her hair up Gibson Girl style, slight wisps escaping and caressing her slender neck. Her low-cut, black-velvet dress ended just above her knee. Her naked brown legs led to bare feet and red toenails. Jesse's attention rose to the freckles on her chest. Between her beauty and his desire, it was hard to find words.

They both looked around. Jesse noticed the sweet marijuana aroma and saw that beside the incline in full light of the dock, two men were sharing a joint. On the dock, two couples were boarding the yacht, probably bound for drugs or sex or both. That prompted him to ask Claire if she wanted a drink, or maybe to dance. She considered the pace of the music and said, "Let's go get a drink and wait for something slower." She took his hand and led him down the right-hand staircase to the pool and the bar.

He ordered her a martini, very dry. He stayed with the champagne. "So who are all these people?"

"They're the usual assortment of unsavory characters—politicians, lawyers, judges, spies, drug dealers and crooks. I don't know most of them. They're either business associates or people he wants to impress. Santee has a message for everyone here, you can be sure of that. Not that he'll talk to everyone, but when they leave, they'll know where they stand."

She drank some of her martini. She looked across the pool to a small gathering of men in concentrated conversation. "If I'm not mistaken, those were not invited." Claire motioned with her head toward the group. "The small one talking is Iker Espinoza, once a small-time drug runner from Matamoros. I've heard Santee mention him. It seems he has powerful friends high in the Mexican government, an up-and-comer. Santee doesn't like him. Iker is not happy. Seems a warehouse and a bunch of his people near Monterrey were taken out recently."

The band switched songs. Claire took his drink, placed it on the rail and led him to dance. It was the first time he'd held her. He was keen to the wrap of her right arm on his shoulder, her hand in his. He breathed in the smell of her hair as he led and Claire followed. The song ended and they returned to their drinks. Jesse lit a smoke. "Thank you, Claire."

She kissed him lightly.

The music struck up again. They both looked to the house. It was beautiful. Jesse looked to his window and saw a silhouette. The stance, the posture, the hands on the hips. Santee was looking down on his party.

He would know that Jesse and Claire had danced.

Claire had noticed Santee too. She raised her hand and waved. Neither could see his face. He showed no reaction. He turned and walked out of the room, trailing a shadow across the ceiling.

It was sobering. Claire said she had to check on the kitchen and Jesse said he'd better mingle. He watched her go, stepping lightly up the staircase, not looking back like he wanted but didn't expect. She was swallowed by the crowd.

Jesse smoked and watched until he saw through the window that Santee was holding court in the living room. It was time. He put down his drink and strolled to the house with his hands in his pockets.

Santee looked sharp enough to cut yourself and not notice until later. His hair was slicked back. His clothes fit like skin, sleek shimmering black-and-brown silk. Two huge diamond rings sparkled on his fingers. Jesse had never seen Santee wear big rings. Santee turned as Jesse entered the living room as if his appearance was timed and expected.

Santee swept his arm in Jesse's direction. "I would like to introduce my key logistics man, Mr. Jesse Langdon the Third. My people tell me you can find him in the social register. We have blue blood amongst the rabble rousers. This organization does not discriminate. We are an equal opportunity employer."

Santee laughed, as did the others, politely.

Jesse came up to the group. Santee put his arm on Jesse's right shoulder. "These gentlemen are from our good neighbor to the south. In the years to come, we will be working closely with each other." Santee introduced the first man standing to Jesse's left as Hector Gallo Rivera, a first cousin to the president of Mexico. He took Jesse's hand and shook it firmly, saying, "*Mucho gusto.*" Jesse answered, "My pleasure," and listened to Santee list Rivera's vast real estate holdings in central and northern Mexico. Senor Rivera looked humble. He was several inches shorter than Jesse, ten years older and balding. He wore a finely tailored dark suit. His stare was steely and direct.

The next man was huge, standing at least six-four and weighing well over 250. The massiveness was concentrated in his head, neck and shoulders. He had a crushing handshake, a penetrating glare and strong Aztec features. His name was Julio Santa Payan.

Santee continued, "Julio is head of Mexico's intelligence operations, the Distrito Federal de Seguridad, the DFS. It is much like our Central Intelligence Agency, and in fact they often work closely together. They know many things.

"Will you excuse me a moment, gentlemen? I need to retrieve an item. Please remain here, for I have an announcement to make." Santee made a little bow and walked away toward the foyer.

Jesse looked back to the two Mexicans, who were staring at him. Mr. Payan said, "I understand you are having some trouble at the border. Perhaps I could take a personal interest and be of some assistance. There is a certain swiftness in Mexican justice that is not found in the American courts."

Jesse replied, "I'm sure Senor Santee would be very grateful for any help you could give us. I believe the situation has been stabilized, but if not, we would welcome your involvement."

Mr. Rivera touched Jesse's left arm. "Certainly, we cannot afford any more interceptions."

It dawned on Jesse that these men were partners and had a stake in the operation, something to lose.

A waiter went by and Jesse detained him. "Gentlemen, may I offer you a drink of some sort?"

They opted for dark rum. Jesse wanted a Wild Turkey, rocks. While they waited, he offered each a Camel, which they took. He lit the three smokes all around. The drinks came promptly and Mr. Payan raised his glass in a toast. "To your good health and long life, Mr. Langdon."

The Mexican guests were joined by their female escorts. The girls were half the men's ages, obviously not wives. They said hello and kissed cheeks.

Claire came up. The men fawned over her hand and said it was so good to see her again. There was an awkward moment, until Santee joined them with boisterous energy, probably freshly coked up. Santee wrapped his arm around Claire's waist and it made Jesse jealous. He stood back.

Santee raised his voice and announced to the

room, "Ladies and gentlemen, may I have your attention, please." The room went quiet when people realized it was their host who was speaking. The music stopped and people on the patio crowded at the room's openings to watch and listen.

"I would like to present a gift to someone who has come farthest to join the festivities." The crowd immediately did mental calculations and most discounted themselves. "He is a man of honor, of breeding, one on whom you can place your faith and trust. And because he resides in Oaxaca, Senor Hector Rivera receives the prize."

Mr. Rivera seemed genuinely surprised and embarrassed, but he smiled graciously. The room waited in silence for the revelation of the gift. No one expected anything small. All eyes were on Santee.

Santee raised his hands. He removed each ring. "I present to Senor Rivera my two rings. They are matching diamonds from South Africa, ringed with seven Colombian emeralds." Santee handed the first to Mr. Rivera. There was hushed appreciation. "This ring is for friendship that we have today and will have tomorrow." Everyone clapped, then were silent for the second presentation. "And this second ring represents loyalty. Among friends, loyalty is the most important consideration. It is what ensures the successes of the future." Santee placed the second ring in Mr. Rivera's right hand. The room erupted in cheers and applause.

Santee raised his hands. The crowd quieted. Santee got the first word out, but was interrupted. Eyes turned toward the booming voice. The crowd parted as the speaker came forward to center stage. It was Iker Espinoza.

"Senor Santee is a most generous and gracious host. We all owe allegiance to this marvelous man."

Santee looked mildly amused and tolerant, as if waiting for Iker to dig a grave.

Iker said, "I too would like to present a gift to Senor Rivera, a valued business associate." He unbuttoned several buttons of his shirt and revealed a dazzling display of wealth and pretension. Around his neck hung pearls and globes of gold, ending in the middle with emeralds and a straight string of diamonds, a golden straw. "This is no small gift." He bowed his head, removed the necklace and walked over to the circle of guests. He handed the present to the cousin of the President of Mexico.

Mr. Rivera did not look well. His golden complexion had turned sallow. He had no desire to be between these two warring egos.

Iker addressed Santee directly. "My gift represents the prosperity that comes with proper associations. One must choose carefully in these times."

Santee had been upstaged. Jesse could feel the tension coming from his boss. The room was deathly still.

Santee said through thin lips, looking deeply into

Iker's eyes, "You would do well to examine your own choices, Mr. Espinoza. Your failures in the Northeast and then in Florida have only led to disaster in Mexico. You skim the surface of the lagoon like a seabird, oblivious to the dangers of the deep. Beware the mouth that rises in your path." Then he reached into his pocket and pulled out a set of keys, still looking into Iker's eyes. He said, "I present to Mr. Rivera a symbol of God's speed. Perhaps it is you, Senor Espinoza, who could benefit most from such a gift, however..."

Santee turned to the small man who was the unwilling focus of this competing largess. "These are the keys to the Ferrari that is parked in my garage. May the winds whisk you from the clutches of poor choices and unwise friends. May God's speed be with you." Santee placed the keys in Mr. Rivera's hand, on top of the necklace.

It was a tension buster. The crowd broke into wild applause. Santee raised both arms again and when the uproar died down, wished everyone an enjoyable evening as Iker Espinoza was storming from the room.

The two Mexicans went to the patio for drinks. Santee turned to Jesse and Claire and said, "The nerve of that little shit. He's fucking lucky I had those keys. I would have had to castrate him right here, and that would have ruined the party." He chuckled, still regaining his composure.

Santee said they needed air and went outside with

Claire. Jesse took a bourbon off the tray and stood in the middle of the room. The confrontation between Iker Espinoza and Santee, it seemed, had given the guests a reason to *really* party, indulge in a no-holds-barred frenzy. The music was louder and faster, the dancing wilder and the temptations greater. No one resisted. Liquor flowed, joints smoked, lines snorted, and the earth spun.

Jesse headed for the bathroom. The door wasn't locked.

He opened it and was halfway in when he saw the naked ass of a fat man, woman's legs wrapped around his waist. He was pumping away, oblivious to the intrusion. She was sitting on the vanity and her right hand was mussing up the pile of cocaine at her side. Her face came around the side of his body and smiled apologetically as she was rocked violently back and forth to the rhythmic grunts of her partner. Jesse closed the door. He needed fresh air and walked out the front door to stroll amongst the lavish automobiles. He saw Coley, but didn't want to talk. The guards, on high alert, knew him and nodded.

A car came through the gate, up the drive, and passed him. The brake lights went on and it stopped. White reverse lights came on and it backed up until the driver's window was beside Jesse.

Flagler's head came out. He looked angry and tired and crazy. He tossed his half-smoked Pall Mall onto the grass and got out of the car. Jesse backed up. Flagler spoke. "Follow me, cunt head. I'm going to tell you what they'll be saying at your funeral."

Flagler strolled confidently off to the right of the house and into the shadows. Jesse followed. He needed to know what was giving Flagler so much confidence.

They stopped in the shade of the house. Music came curling around from the back. The parked cars reflected the lights from the front.

Flagler was a spool of nervous energy. He came in close to Jesse's face, vibrating in anger. "I had an interesting trip to Texas. Learned some things you might want to hear before I tell Santee and he fries your little white candy ass. I got friends in the phone company down there. They told me that the call that tipped the cops to the shipment came from a payphone around here."

He looked triumphant. "Well, I asked myself, who from around here would want to tip off the cops?"

"You could have made the call, Flagler."

Flagler was rocking on the tips of his toes, bouncing up and down. "The way I figure it, you made the call."

"Why on earth would I do that?"

"Because of Reefer, or if you don't know shit about that, then for the same reason I'd've done it to you if I'd thought of it first. I'd like to see you dead."

The little bubbles inside Jesse were becoming

bigger bubbles, beginning to boil, fueled by hatred for Flagler. "You're going to tell me what happened to Reefer, whether you want to or not."

Flagler laughed. "Dream on. After I beat the living shit out of you, we'll go to Santee, and he can have the pleasure of finishing you off."

"Who do you think he's going to believe, Flagler? He already has a death warrant out for you."

Flagler was purple with anger, humming, vibrating. He came hard and fast. Jesse couldn't get out of the way of the first punch. It caught him on the left side of his face and knocked him onto the grass.

The fear in his gut transformed itself into a slow-motion white rage. He gathered the available light from his surroundings and the world became clear and focused. He felt mastery over the dark forces within. For the first time in his life, he felt he could draw power, rather than fear, from his waking nightmares.

He jumped up and lunged at Flagler, driving his head into his stomach. Flagler was surprised at the ferocity of the counterattack and he went down hard with Jesse on top, the breath driven out of him.

Jesse straddled Flagler and drove the heel of his hand into his upper lip and nose. The nose collapsed as his arm followed through. There was just enough light to see Flagler's wide surprised eyes as the bone splinters rammed into the soft tissue of his lower brain.

Flagler's body went slack and Jesse rolled off, as if

death were contagious. He crab-crawled a yard away, breathing heavily. Flagler refused defeat and tried with his last strength to get up, but collapsed in a heap, reaching toward Jesse, trying and failing to say a last word. Life's last tendrils twitched like dog dreams in Flagler's death throes.

CHAPTER 27

O N HIS KNEES, Jesse gathered his breath and
stared at Flagler, who even in death, held the
secrets surrounding Reefer. The Bermuda grass was cool
and bristly on the palms of his hands. The music coming
from the back was obscenely joyful. He looked around
front. The cars sat there shining. Jesse wondered about
the cameras. He looked up and saw only stars.

Jesse wondered if he should throw up, break down
in tears or shake uncontrollably. He felt nothing like
that. Rather, he felt detached and removed, but triumphant. The night seemed clearer. Jesse's relief at winning
the battle turned to pride. He was the one alive.

The elation quickly gave way to more practical
matters. It wouldn't bode well for the party to have a
dead body discovered. He rose, grabbed Flagler by both
wrists, dragged him toward the house and left him under
a bush. After brushing himself off and straightening his

clothes, Jesse walked to the front lawn and looked for Coley.

Coley stood beside Flagler's dirty station wagon, clearly annoyed that it had been left in the driveway.

Jesse walked up and said, "It's Flagler's, and he's dead."

To Coley, the words didn't seem to go together with his duties, the parking, or the party. He turned to Jesse with a confused look on his face. "Could you say that again?"

"Flagler just got back from Texas. And I just killed him over there." Jesse pointed to the side of the house.

Coley's gaze followed Jesse's arm. He said, "Show me."

They walked across the lawn, Coley staring at Jesse's silhouette, to the shadows of the house, and looked down on Flagler's body. Coley knelt down and felt for a pulse. He rose and rubbed his chin, as if he was wondering how to change a flat tire.

"Never liked the bastard, never understood why Santee kept him around. Maybe his ruthlessness struck a chord. He sure could put the fear of God in people. I can say that much." Coley looked to Jesse, thought, said, "Guess you did us all a favor, the Mexican thing and all. You sure are a quick study. Flagler was a tough old bird, not easy to take out." He thought some more. "Back the car over here. We'll put him inside and cover him up. Then see what Santee wants to do."

They curled the body into the back of the wagon. Jesse parked in the middle bay, lay a tarp over him and locked the car, checking each door individually. Together, they went to find Santee.

They found him entertaining beside the pool, talking and waving and making them all laugh. From up beside the house, Coley caught his eye and motioned with a minuscule head movement. Jesse watched Santee excuse himself and climb the stairs. Without words, the three went to the third floor. Coley closed the door.

"I take it this is important." Santee sat down and lit a smoke. A fly buzzed past his head.

Jesse didn't know what to do. This was the moment it all might come undone. He took out a smoke and lit it, and now his hands were shaking. Santee eyed him curiously.

"Well?" Santee waved his hand at the fly.

Coley spoke. "Flagler is back. Seems he attacked Jesse beside the house and now he's dead and in the back of the locked station wagon in the garage."

Santee let it settle. He looked back and forth from Jesse to Coley. He said to Jesse, "And not a mark on you except a bruise on the side of your head. Must not have been much of a fight." He reached for the phone and punched the intercom button.

While he waited, he looked searchingly into Jesse's eyes, assessing, wondering. Into the receiver, he asked for a bottle of brandy and three glasses. He hung up and told them to sit down. They did. Then, "What about it, Jesse?"

He cleared his throat and hoped his words wouldn't stutter. "Flagler drove in and saw me. He said he was going to kill me." Jesse lightly fingered the swelling on his face. "I went down. I guess I got angry. I got up and tackled him and rammed his nose. It was over. I did what I had to do."

Santee laughed. "You got angry? You fucking just got angry? You ever heard anything like that, Coley? Life and death, and Jesse gets angry!"

Jesse was made nervous by the mocking tone. There was a knock on the door and Carla came in with a bottle and glasses on a tray. She put it on the desk, bowed to the three men, then left.

Santee poured generous portions and they each took theirs. Santee raised his glass. "For the nerves. This should take your shakes away, Jesse."

The brandy slid down smooth and fiery. It did, as predicted, absorb the tension. Santee refilled the glasses and sat back in his swivel chair.

"Why did he come back?" Santee asked Jesse.

"Stupidity."

"Stupidity? For all Flagler was, he was not stupid."

"Maybe he figured your reach was too great."

"Pretty slick ending for him, wouldn't you say?"

"I got lucky."

"Guess we won't be having any more problems in Mexico, will we, Jesse?"

"That should be it."

Santee turned to Blades. "We have a disposal problem. What do you suggest, Coley?"

"Alligators off Route 41. We dump the body into the swamp."

Santee thought about it, sipping the brandy. "I need you here tomorrow." He turned to Jesse. "I want you and Biano to do it. Make arrangements. Take the wagon. Strip him. Dump him good and don't get caught. Take his gold teeth if you want." Santee laughed at that.

The fly landed on the desk. Quick as a mongoose, Santee's hand came down and squashed it. He examined the remains. He looked up at Jesse and said, "Someday we will all look like that."

Santee rose and said, "I have a party to host. No more interruptions, please." He walked out.

Jesse was smoking a Camel and sipping hot coffee on the front stoop when Biano arrived early the next morning. Jesse motioned for him to park alongside the garage.

Biano got out. "The master beckons, the servant shows. What's happening?"

Jesse was at the garage door opener. He pushed the button and over the sound of the motor said, "It was quite a party last night. You missed an interesting time.

There was a disturbed guest and he's feeling terrible this morning."

Biano followed Jesse to the rear of the car and stood out of the way as Jesse unlocked the tailgate and swung it down. They both looked into the rear.

Biano knew it wasn't anything good, but he was shocked when Jesse pulled away the corner of the tarp to show Flagler's unkempt hair and yellowish face with the pushed-in nose. "What happened?"

"He attacked me last night and I killed him in self-defense. Santee wants us to dump him in the Everglades this morning. We have to strip him first." Jesse grimaced at the thought.

Biano stood back, considering. "Santee must not think much of us. He want us to get caught? It's the fucking weekend. There's all kinds of people out there, farting around, just waiting to watch two stupid fuck-heads dump a dead body."

The thought had occurred to Jesse. "We just have to be careful. We might as well strip him here." Jesse went to the side, turned on the lights, closed the garage door, and locked the side door. They tugged on Flagler until he was resting on the tailgate. He was stiff, curled up. They cut off his clothes.

Flagler had pale skin and surprisingly little body hair. His legs were scrawny, his toenails long. Small dick, big talk. Biano gagged when some gas escaped.

They spun him back into the car and covered him.

Biano closed the tailgate and looked almost as pale as Flagler. Jesse said, "Let's get it over with." He put the clothes in a garbage bag.

As Jesse drove out the gate, he turned serious and asked, "Biano, I have to ask you something. I know you told me to leave the search for Reefer alone, and I did, until Flagler mentioned him before he died. Also, last night, there was an incident with Iker Espinoza. Santee insulted him in some subtle way. He mentioned failures in the Northeast. Seems like there might be some connection there."

Biano looked into Jesse's eyes, then spoke reluctantly. "Espinoza is part of the Cali effort to expand their operations in the U.S. They tried to run drugs into Maine, but it didn't work out. Don't ask me why; I don't know. Too remote. Too big. Too white. Where the hell you think Santee got the idea? Without you, who knows if we'd be up there? Anyway, Cali concentrated in Florida. When it got too hot here, they took their assets to Mexico. I believe that Santee is trying to convince Espinoza that it was a big mistake." Then Biano changed the subject. "We have to go by Mama's first. I told her I'd bring her some donuts. I've got to wash my hands."

Biano directed Jesse to an address in an affluent Latin suburb of Miami. Jesse drove very carefully. He pulled into the driveway behind a brand new Ford Taurus wagon. The dirty business had rattled Biano and Jesse wasn't invited inside. He got out, sat on the curb and looked at Flagler's old station wagon, grease and grime coating the sides and windows.

Children playing on the other side of the street took an interest and came over, asked him if they could write stuff in the dusty windows of his car. Jesse said sure.

There were three of them. Two little brown boys in clean white shirts, dark shorts and new sneakers. The girl was older, maybe eleven, yellow dress, white lace socks and patent-leather shoes. They took turns writing on the back window. "Wash me." All three let out little peals of delighted laughter.

Jesse watched them. He patted the photo in the breast pocket of his shirt and thought of his children, how he was missing these precious moments in their lives, and how he was shirking his parental responsibilities.

He marveled at these children's carefree sweetness. All the world, all the future, lay ahead for them. He smiled at the innocent childlike faith in the future, full of glee. Not so long ago he'd felt like that—far removed from the chill of these darker depths.

Now he was a death driver.

The pretty little girl drew a question mark on the side window. The little boys copied her.

Jesse lit a smoke.

What was he doing? Jesse realized the decision had been a long time coming. It was time to go home.

PART VI

CHAPTER 28

I T WAS A week since the party. Santee was pacing feverishly around the library, excited about something. It was their weekly strategy meeting, a formality suggested by Jesse to make the organization more efficient. Coley, Biano and Claire were there. Jesse looked at Claire, who sat staring into the unlit fireplace. He hadn't seen her for a few days; Coley said she'd been in New York, shopping.

"I told him he would need God's speed. I guess God worked fast on the little bastard. Teach Iker Espinoza to mess with me!" Santee turned and studied Claire. "Why so moody? You did fine work, Claire, fine work and after all, you ought to be used to it by now. It's beautiful, really. Men are always the most vulnerable when sound asleep after a little loving. You have earned your keep again, Claire. You should be proud."

A lump in Jesse's throat fell heavily into his stomach and anchored him to the chair. It dawned on him what Santee was talking about. Had Claire seduced Iker? Had Iker taken his revenge by fucking Santee's woman? Then did she kill him in his sleep?

Jesse felt repulsed and protective at the same time. How dare Santee put her on the spot in front of them, parade her business like a cheap whore? He might as well have asked her to strip naked and demonstrate how she did it. Jesse had an urge to leap up and push Santee's nose through his face. He let it pass.

"*Dios mio*, I do love to squash those little shoots, pull them up by the roots and shake them dead. I'd grind them up and eat them if I could. I should pick someone out once a week; do the deed, kind of like a New Year's resolution. It must be good for me, rejuvenating. What's the matter, baby. Didn't you enjoy it as much as usual? At least you haven't lost your touch." He laughed.

Claire got up from her chair, shot a sharp glare at Santee, and left the room.

As she walked out, Santee said, "Well, well, aren't we sensitive tonight? She must have the curse. Bloodletting after bloodletting." He chuckled at his joke. No one else laughed.

Santee switched the focus of his excitement to the next Maine run, scheduled for the second week of August. The plans were pretty much the same, except they'd land on a strip in the far western part of the state, with Pasque arriving with Claire in the camper.

Except for Santee, the mood was somber and reflective. They covered each sector, went over details, discussed weak points and solutions, planned for contingencies. The meeting lasted an hour and a half. Santee dismissed all but Jesse. He went to the bar and poured two drinks, brought them to the desk and placed Jesse's Wild Turkey on the coaster in front of him. From the desk, he removed a pack of Garams and offered Jesse one. He sat down and swiveled back, looking at Jesse.

They stared at each other. Jesse took a sip. He took a drag and savored the sweet clove taste. "You have something to say, Santee?"

"I admire you, Jesse. You are ruthless. That trait has come out of you, swollen from the depths. I didn't think you had it in you, but you do. You're my kind of man."

"What are you talking about?"

"I suspected all along. You don't get as far as I have without instincts. But I was not sure until I watched the tapes."

"Tapes?"

"You and Flagler. You might call it his last chapter. You set him up. It was you who tipped the cops to the shipment. You even transferred some of your money into Flagler's accounts. You did all that for no personal gain. A loss actually. All to set Flagler up and get rid of him. You must have wanted his territory very badly.

That, and you probably thought he was a threat to you and your position. So, you got rid of him."

Santee removed his revolver from the desk drawer and lined up a row of bullets.

"You need not be modest. It was a good plan. As I say, I admire your drive. You did well in the last scene, too. Flagler could have killed you. He had much more experience than you. At least he thought so. But you surprised him. Hand to hand, no gunfire to disrupt the party. It was clean and neat, and even in self-defense. You must have a clear conscience."

There was nothing for Jesse to say. He watched Santee load the cylinders. He let Santee continue.

"I am proud of you. Your cunning is more valuable to me than Flagler's loyalty. I admit for a time I was not sure if you and I would make it. I did not know if you had the right stuff. But now I know my plans are good, and you will help me achieve them, because it means unlimited power and wealth. We make a good team."

Santee spun the cylinders and pointed the gun at Jesse. "But don't let this go to your head." He paused, then lowered the gun. "Never forget who I am and what I can do. From now on, there will be no straying from the fold, no acting on your own initiative.

"Tomorrow we will meet on the third floor. From there we will make our Guyana paradise a reality. Drink up, my friend. To a successful partnership and long future together."

It was very early in the morning and still dark. Jesse couldn't sleep. The alarm clock said three-twenty a.m. He was hungry. He put on a robe and went down the dimly lit back stairs to the kitchen.

A sliver of light came from under the pantry door. He swung it open to find Claire sitting at the stainless steel table with both hands wrapped around a steaming cup. She looked up and smiled weakly. "Hot chocolate, of all things. You want some?"

"Sure." Jesse pulled up a chair. She put milk in a pan and turned on the burner. She got a cup from the cabinet and spooned in Ovaltine, turned toward Jesse and leaned against the counter. She was lovely in the long cotton nightgown. Her sadness made Jesse want to hold and comfort her, but he waited for her to speak.

She said, "I couldn't sleep."

"Me either."

She looked at him, hard. "I'm done, Jesse. I've had enough, more than enough. But I don't know what to do, where to turn. My mind races through plans and scenarios, but there's no giving notice, no severance pay, no farewell watch. Only a bullet."

Jesse glanced around, worried.

Claire laughed. She said, "Santee is sound asleep. I just left him. For someone so paranoid, he sure is a heavy sleeper. And as for bugs, I know he isn't interested in kitchen conspiracies. He doesn't think of Carla or Mrs. Sanchez as a threat, though the way he treats them, sometimes I wonder why they don't poison him. Poison us all."

He had to wonder. He'd learned new things about Claire. Was she telling the truth? He thought back on their trip to New York, on the feeling of her waist as they danced at the party, on the look she gave Santee as she walked from the library. Or was she spying and setting him up?

Claire watched him think. She waited for his decision.

He said, "You can come with me."

"Do you trust me, now that you know?"

Jesse leaned back. "The milk is about to boil over." Claire took the pan and poured the steaming milk into the cup and stirred it with a spoon. She set it down in front of Jesse. She topped off her cup and sat down beside him.

He answered, looking into the cocoa, letting it cool. "I guess it's just time to trust something. I need to have faith in you. I don't think either one of us can do this alone. We need each other."

"We may not make it, you know." He knew she was trying to meet his eyes, but Jesse didn't look up. "And if we do, he can always find us."

"That may be true. I don't have it all worked out, but there must be a way.

"Jesse, you need to see the whole picture. He has

friends everywhere, at all levels, on both sides. There's so much at stake here for so many. Even if *he* goes down, *they'll* never let us get out alive."

"Maybe we can turn state's evidence. Testify. Go into the witness protection program. Or just disappear, take our money and go."

"What about your family? What do you think he'll do to them when he can't find us? You think they'll be safe?"

How could he have been so stupid? Now that Claire had said the words, it became crystal clear to Jesse. There was no way he could shield them from his choices, not involve them in his life. Of course Santee would use them against him, pull them into the cold shadows until he exacted his revenge.

The elation Jesse had felt about escaping Santee's infinite web, especially with Claire, was now replaced with horror—the web was too intricate, too sticky, and upon the faintest wiggle, Santee would pounce from the side in a rush and spin him into a straitjacket cocoon of strangling silk.

Claire touched his cheek and said, "I'm sorry for extinguishing the flame of hope. But there's no room for dreaming, for unreasonable expectations. Santee is too cunning and powerful. If we can get out at all, it'll be because we're smarter. Smarter and luckier." She took her hand away. "We have time to think about it, Jesse. There may be a way after all."

"But we can't linger. Too much can go wrong. We can be buried too deep, if we're not already. We have to leave before the next shipment to Maine. That gives us two-and-a-half weeks. Even if it's not perfect, we have to get out now. There may not be another chance." After a thoughtful pause, he added, "That should help us sleep." He smiled at Claire and she smiled back. They finished their cocoa and went to bed.

CHAPTER 29

JESSE HAD NEVER known how to juggle, and now he could truly appreciate just how difficult it could be, especially keeping emotions, lies and schemes in the air. He had a running chainsaw, a razor-sharp machete and a ripping mongoose going all at once.

For the moment, he had to continue in Santee's good graces. Everything depended on their escape being a complete surprise. If they had any chance, they'd need a sizable head start.

With Iker Espinoza out of the way and the Mexican cartels fighting amongst themselves, Jesse was beginning to focus on Santee's dream of controlling Guyana, owning an entire country and expanding his operation without restraint.

It was Wednesday July 26. It had been three days since he'd talked with Claire in the kitchen. The Maine flight was scheduled for Saturday August 12. There was no plausible reason to put it off. Jesse had already made all the arrangements.

The sun was setting in the west. Amber light came through the open window and caught the mixture of dust motes and smoke from their cigarettes. Jesse sat at the broad table in the middle of the electronic extravaganza on the forbidden third floor. He and Santee were brainstorming the future. They each had pads and pencils spread out before them. Jesse looked at his figures and said, "We're going to need more money. It's going to cost a hell of a lot more than we have coming in now."

Santee said, "I've spent so much already. I must own half the government. But if we need it, force is cheaper and it makes a stronger point." Santee watched the smoke gather at the ceiling.

"How so?"

"An assassination here, an exile there, violent demonstrations, insurgents in the mountains threatening the capital—we are talking about South America, Jesse, passionate but easily manipulated and stampeded. I've moved in slowly, with money and influence, buying up the jobs and the people. It's only a matter of time before I install my puppets and pull all the strings. The foreign aid from the U.S. alone will be in the billions— every year!"

"But we need more cash flow." Jesse tossed his pencil on the table and leaned back, took the last puff from his smoke, and watched Santee. "The contras alone are costing us a million a month."

Santee walked around the crowded room, deep in daydreams, probably wondering how long it would take, not wanting to wait, but trying to listen to reason. He said, "If you say so, tell me where the money will come from."

Jesse creaked forward in the swivel chair and snubbed out his smoke. "We keep running the weapons to the contras. That gives us the insulation we need. Then we expand into the retail markets across the country. We'll have to ally ourselves with the Jamaicans or the Cubans. It's going to piss off the Colombians.

"Our move to paste will really tick them off. We go directly to the source, buy from the number-one family in Peru. We fly it to Mexico and refine it ourselves. Rivera and Payan should be good partners. It means a lot more for them.

"While we're at it, we should expand our European markets. We can flood the countries with high-grade low-cost coke until they get used to it, then we raise prices. We can work with the Sicilians and help them with the Burmese heroin. A rising tide lifts all boats.

"That should bring us enough profits to buy up the rest of Guyana. No one will care where the money came from. You'll have free rein to run the business from there."

As Jesse talked, Santee became more and more

animated. He raised a fist into the air. "I will have my own army, my own air force, with jet fighters, the whole works. I will have my own currency. Foreign aid from ten countries. Eleven-digit credit line from the IMF. Half the infrastructure on sale to the Chinese. Best of all, I'll be legitimate."

Of course, none of it was possible, and Jesse couldn't help wondering if the CIA might be setting Santee up to take a great fall. He wouldn't be the first would-be self-proclaimed king to find himself a marionette—at the end of a noose.

But now it was time for the last flash. If Jesse played it right, the illumination might be bright enough to blind Santee momentarily. He and Claire might just slip away. Jesse said, "You know, I was thinking. You're the power behind the rulers of Guyana, the man with the money and the vision who engineered a brilliant coup without bloodshed, offering economic opportunity and development. You'll be famous." He paused for a dramatic three-count. "Why not have someone write your biography?"

Santee stopped in his tracks. He said, rubbing his chin, looking at Jesse , "You think anyone would want to read it?"

"Of course they would. Think about it. There'll be something mysterious about you. People will be curious, they'll want to know. Everyone admires success.

You're a self-made man, Santee, an example for people. It'll be a bestseller."

Santee was in Neverland. He sat down heavily and stared into the empty space, totally consumed. "You know, I think you are right. Who would write it?" He turned to Jesse.

Jesse leaned in. "Hell, some Harvard professor! Yale. Princeton. Stanford. Take your pick. Even the biggest biographers in the book business would jump at the chance to write a guaranteed bestseller. All you have to do is dangle the carrot: master criminal turns master philanthropist." Jesse was having too much fun, spinning this fantasy.

"What about implicating myself in crimes, incriminating myself?"

"You'll be beyond reach. Who can extradite you from your own country? It's perfect."

Santee smiled. "I can see it, Jesse. I can see two books, maybe three." He leaned in, conspiring. "You know, I've documented details. I have kept a scrapbook—the arms deals, the drug runs, the payoffs, the contacts. I never thought it would come out, but of course it must. I have all the material for the greatest story ever told!"

Santee stood up. He slapped Jesse on the back. "By God, Jesse, we are going to be fucking famous. I will be immortal."

CHAPTER 30

"YESTERDAY SANTEE MENTIONED a scrapbook, details about the operations, some history. Has he mentioned anything like that to you?" They were sitting at the stainless steel table again, three in the morning. It was the safest place in the mansion.

Claire sipped her herbal tea and wondered. "I don't remember anything specific. Sometimes he gets on a roll, his ego going so fast I can't keep up. I do have the impression that he's always wanted to be known, to have a wider sphere of influence and admiration. How would this fit into anything?"

"That first week in Maine, he brought up the idea of a biography, to glorify and immortalize himself. When I reminded him of it yesterday, he said he could release the whole history to a writer, after the move to Guyana."

Claire rubbed her cheeks with both hands. "It's so scary. I'm beginning to think anything is possible. If we wanted to go along with Santee, all this dreaming might end up reality. Can you see him as ruler of an entire country, the subject of a tell-all book?"

"I wasn't thinking about that. What if he really does have evidence that ties him into the arms, the drugs, the protectors? It could be our ticket out, Claire. All we have to do is get it and get out of here without getting killed. It would be a standoff. If anything happens to us, the information goes public before he can establish safe harbor in Guyana. Just think how many people would go down."

She held his hand. "He might kill us for spite, regardless of the consequences."

Jesse tried to sound reassuring. "That's why we have to get far enough away, initially, so that when he knows the score, he has time to think, to reason." He tried not to think about Ashley and Ike. "We've got a couple of weeks to get away clean. I've been formulating the plan. It involves the Santee scrapbook, my airplane and a safe place not too far from here."

"Santee's just going to let us waltz away in your plane? And how the hell are you going to find the scrapbook, if it even exists?"

Jesse was uncomfortable talking about the details of the plan under Santee's roof. It was a clear death sentence if a whisper was heard. "Listen, Claire. This is what I'm good at. Remember? And you once told me that it's better not to know too much, in case we're passing each other on that dead-end street. We might not make it. But we have to try."

"Okay, but one more question. What about the money, Jesse? The Caymans will be out of reach. If we try to cash in, it will alert Santee. And he sure won't let us touch it after we go."

"Don't worry about money. I've got money. Enough to start from here and plenty if we make it out."

The days passed slowly. He pretended to be genuine and conscientious, while he planned betrayal. There was little going on before the Colombia/Maine trip. He and Coley worked out in the gym and spent time at the firing range. Jesse was becoming proficient with his handguns and was accurate with the Uzi. He planned to take it with him.

Before he called John Settlemire with instructions, he had to get the Lake away from the hangar. And before he could secure the scrapbook, he had to find the damn thing, if it existed at all. It all seemed so insurmountable. But he plodded along, going through the motions, like a death-row inmate filing last-minute appeals.

It being so slow, he planned to ask Santee if he could take a little time to go bone fishing in the Keys. The Lake was perfect for that. Before heading for the Keys, he'd search the Glades for a spot beside an access road where he could hide the plane. He could hitch-hike back, or take a cab, and claim engine trouble that meant he had to leave his plane.

It was easy to make excuses to be on the third floor, the one place Santee would keep a memoir. It was the nerve center of La Primavera, filled with electronic monitors and computers. A large rectangular room with a peaked roof, two windows looked toward the channel, two toward the front gate. File cabinets lined the back wall and a conference table with streamlined swivel chairs dominated the remaining space. Half the table was cluttered with surveillance monitors and listening devices. This was where he'd replayed the final moments of Flagler's life.

Jesse had his papers spread out on the conference table. There were piles of notes on Guyana—geographical, economic, political, infrastructural, the soft points that Santee could exploit. He had information about real estate, even plans for the mansion.

He was putting together the logistics of setting up refining labs in Mexico for the Peruvian paste. He'd located sources for the chemicals and organized untraceable routes from Europe to South America and on to Mexico. He also had feelers out in various European countries regarding supply and demand for cocaine, heroin and marijuana. Some information was official, some from the drug suppliers. There was indeed huge potential to expand the market.

He'd tried looking for a physical scrapbook to no avail, and had narrowed it down to his last option, the computer. He had permission to use it. It was his only shot.

Jesse explored the Microsoft Windows domain, looking for any program he might not understand; anywhere the information might be hidden. Anything that looked strange, he brought up with a mouse click. All proved to be false trails, and he was getting discouraged.

Then he noticed that the computer had a relatively large capacity hard drive and a small amount of free space. It didn't make sense. Something was using up a lot of disk space. He got behind Windows with the MSDOS prompt and brought up the directory of the hard drive. No names made sense, so Jesse started at the top and worked down, accessing each.

Toward the middle, he hit a wall. The customary change-directory command brought up an "invalid" response. It was a large file, recently updated, that Santee had hidden behind a password. And his chances of coming up with that by accident were exactly nil. He didn't have the luxury of time to bumble through his guesses. He shut down the computer and leaned back with his eyes closed.

The escape plans stretched like elastic in his brain. At first, they'd seemed plausible and relatively easy. Then they grew to test the limits of credulity. Then it all seemed possible again. And here he was again, back to hopelessness. It was the story of his days. He was walking in the fog.

Life with Santee was figuratively over. It was only a matter of time till it ended for real. Either he and Claire escaped and by some miracle were safe from Santee the rest of their lives, or they'd die trying.

Life expectancy is a topic for the actuaries, a thought most people postpone until lying on their death bed. Jesse was no different. Now, however, he knew himself to be a very bad life-insurance risk. He had a terminal disease: exposure to Santee. Realistically, his life expectancy could be measured in weeks, maybe days.

Being with Santee had, in a strange way, given him the life he'd been losing by slow degrees in Belfast. Today, he felt more alive, more capable, more in tune with himself and life around him. It wasn't the drugs or the criminal world or the money. He felt like he knew himself more completely, trusted his instincts and his capabilities and was more in control of his destiny. These benefits had been slow in coming and only now, after he'd made his decision to leave, did they bloom.

In finding new life, ironically, he had put it into jeopardy. And it wasn't only his. Ashley, Ike and Emma came into the equation.

It was sobering to think of his slim chances and he

resisted the urge to drown his fear in alcohol and coke. Their success depended on clear thinking.

Now more than ever he needed Claire. On his own he could never unlock the file. He had absolutely no idea what the password might be. Claire was his only hope.

CHAPTER 31

Miami Herald, July 28

William von Raab, the exiting commissioner of the U.S. Customs Service, blasted the government's drug war effort, saying that it was mired in complacency.

COLEY WAS ON the West Coast, obtaining C4 explosives. They were running low. Biano had dropped Santee in Mexico and returned. Santee was Senor Payan's guest, shooting game in the northern mountains. Biano was scheduled to take the Lear and retrieve Santee on Friday August 4. Today was Tuesday the first.

Biano had invited Jesse to his mother's house for a meal, but he'd declined. He had too much on his mind. And he was already too close to Biano.

Claire was at La Primavera, but they kept their distance. Jesse was aware of all the monitoring devices.

The data went into a sealed vault. For all Jesse knew, Santee could remotely access it from Mexico.

Now wasn't the time to take chances. If Santee was suspicious, the setup was perfect. Leave the co-conspirators together, alone, and watch them plot and plan their own way to hell. It was the way Santee thought, the game he played, the entertainment he relished.

So they were rarely together. Carla wanted to prepare meals and sit them down, but either Claire was out or Jesse was busy. The only time they were side by side was by the pool, center stage for Santee's cameras.

Jesse worked on preparation papers in the hot sun. Sweat ran down his chest, but immersed in his work, he didn't notice. His face was hidden in the shadows of his cap and mirror sunglasses. When he looked up, his view was Claire in a skimpy bikini, lying on her stomach on the chaise. Jesse admired her form, the rise from her waist to the tight seams of her bathing suit. It made his heart race.

He returned to his work, writing a letter to John Settlemire. His back was to the known cameras, shielding the paper. It was an open-in-the-event-of-my-death letter, postmortem instructions for John and a love letter to Ashley and Ike. Brief, it explained only that in his heart, he hadn't abandoned them, and that he would always be with them in spirit.

Jesse wrote *PASSWORD?* on the bottom of a page, ripped it off and crumpled it in his hand. "Jesus, it's hot!" He laid the paperwork face down on the side table, stood and stretched. He took off cap and glasses and squinted at Claire. "You coming in?"

She rolled onto her side and behind her own glasses said, "Maybe a little later. Let's see how well you enjoy it."

Jesse dove into the deep end, then swam back to the near edge. "This spot is particularly nice." Before he got out, he opened his hand and let the piece of paper float beneath the edge's lip.

He settled on his reclining chair. "I highly recommend a dip."

Claire dove in and breast-stroked around. She was about to swim toward the steps. Jesse said, "This spot, right here, is the best. It's cooler for some reason."

Claire was puzzled, but she swam over to test it. She made no visible sign that she'd found the slip of paper. She pulled herself out with open palms. Jesse was disappointed she'd missed the clues.

She took her towel but didn't dry herself. "I'm going to change in the bath house, then go shopping. It's the only thing that works on my depression when Santee's away." She strolled off.

She came out moments later with combed wet hair, in a yellow sun dress and flat sandals. She tossed her towel at Jesse. "You won't mind taking this up when you go, will you, flyboy?"

"Sure thing," he replied, annoyed. She laughed, turned, took the stairs three at a time.

Jesse put the towel down beside the chaise and, as he leaned to get his paper, he noticed a corner of white peeking from the sea of blue towel. He dropped his cap, got two fingers around the paper, retrieved the hat, and settled back to finish his project.

The note said, *You don't have to look so disappointed. I put the note in my bathing suit. I came up with things he mumbles in his sleep—destiny, maximum, mama, nemesis. Best I could do. Good luck.*

Even though Jesse wanted to race up to the computer, he lingered by the pool for another hour. He finished his instructions for John Settlemire and drew little pictures on the letter to his children. It was strange to work on details that would only come alive once he was dead, but he felt refreshed, as if he had put his own death behind him.

Carla fixed him a sandwich. He took it and a Kaliber to the third floor. He sat down and stared at the surveillance equipment. He wondered if there was information as to the location of homing transmitters that must adorn both his car and the Lake. He would have to remove them, but it would be easier if he knew where to look.

First things first.

He turned on the computer as he munched his sandwich. When he got to the DOS prompt, he typed in *DIR I MORE* and brought up the hard drive directory. He moved the cursor down the list until he came to the wall he'd hit before—Windows Bat. He typed *cd windows bat*. He pressed Enter. The "invalid" response came up again.

He had to first get past this firewall. He picked the first double meaning that came to mind. He typed "cripple." He paused and took a deep breath, then pressed enter.

The computer hesitated and Jesse was sure he'd failed again. Then the screen came back with *password*.

Jesse typed *mama*, then enter. Invalid.

Maximum. Invalid.

Destiny. Invalid.

Nemesis.

Jesse held his breath as the screen filled with a table of contents that listed a series of years starting twenty years ago. He moved down to the current year and pressed enter. The text came up, everything Jesse wanted. Santee had documented detail after detail. Who told whom to do what. Who was protecting the operations. Who was receiving the weapons. How much it cost to pay off law enforcement, judges, politicians. Jesse recognized a few names on the national level. Santee, bless his megalomaniacal heart, had indeed kept his own scrapbook.

He saw his own file. He saw all the sources of Santee's confidential information.

The extent of the information chilled his blood. Santee's reach was further than Jesse had ever imagined. And not one person in any of the files could afford to have it go public. It would send them all away forever. It would shake the faith citizens had in their government, their law enforcement institutions, and in their courts.

Jesse clicked the page-down key. It was amazing enough that Santee had amassed so much information, but to save it all? To do the opposite of erasing his tracks? To fully document and centralize this kind of information, Santee must feel, and have felt for decades, that he was totally beyond reach, too big and powerful to fall. No wonder the idea of a biography excited him. This information was Santee's paradise. And it was Jesse's salvation.

The word "Emerald" caught his attention, Coley Blade beside it. Jesse stopped the scrolling screen and read the entry. It was the story of the killings at the emerald mine owner's ranch outside of Bogotá. All the men were murdered in front of their wives and lovers, even the cooks and musicians. The story alone, the cold brutality, sent shivers down his back. But it was only a ripple. The big wave crashed over Jesse as he read the rest.

The mine owner had been a conduit for arms delivery to the contras in Nicaragua. In return, he was given carte blanche to smuggle cocaine into the

United States, via a single wholesaler in Los Angeles who turned it into crack and distributed it throughout the ghettoes of South Central L.A. and beyond to Texas, Missouri, Ohio and New York. But he'd crossed the CIA. He'd gone rogue and funneled arms to the Shining Path guerrillas in Peru. Santee had received a directive from a named person in the CIA to terminate the situation, at his discretion.

Santee had sent Coley to Colombia. He'd gathered Los Palestinos, and they'd clearly gone overboard with the job.

CHAPTER 32

JESSE SPENT THE morning at the firing range.
His motions were mechanical. He hit the target
accurately. Each shot was a dull thud in his protected
ears. He took deep breaths of wasted gunpowder. Brass
casings ejected from the Beretta and danced on the
floor. Shooting had become like meditation for him.

If Santee had booby trapped the computer file,
Jesse was as good as dead. But Claire would be safe;
she wouldn't be implicated until the very last. And if he
were killed, Emma, Ashley and Ike would be safe.

If he stayed alive for the next week, either Santee
was playing with him, letting out the rope, or he knew
nothing of the breach of security. Could Santee be so
lax, or trusting, or convinced of his own invincibility
as to leave all the incriminating information so vulnerable? Or maybe, like most people, he placed his trust in
a simple password.

Jesse thought not. If any of the people in the file

knew about the file, they themselves would kill Santee for sheer stupidity.

If he didn't rig the file itself, he'd probably rigged a trip wire on any attempt to copy it. Jesse would do it at the last moment. He made a mental note to pick up floppy disks.

Jesse reloaded his magazines. The tips of his fingers felt raw. He was half into the third box of ammunition. He needed to convince Santee to let him go bone fishing. And then he needed to return without the plane, unsuspected.

Jesse tried some rapid fire. He emptied the magazine and brought the target forward on the wire. He didn't bother to remove the hearing protectors. All sixteen of the bullets found the target, most within the inner three circles.

From the small of his back, he drew the Walther and fired three series of double taps at a closer target off to his right. Jesse walked over and retrieved that target. All had fallen in a dinner-plate area. Coley would have patterned them inside a salad plate.

Folded in the front pocket of his shirt was the letter to John Settlemire. He had to mail it, call John, and arrange for the car and a motel room in Alabama.

All of it had to be finished before Friday the tenth. Once he and Claire were away, out over the Gulf, Coley and Santee would have a hard time finding them. Unless, of course, he didn't find all the bugs in the car and plane, or Santee had people in the AWACS. Anything was possible.

Jesse took off the ear pads and rubbed the sides of his head. He scooped up the casings and dropped them into the bucket.

All the while he'd have to act normally around Santee. The charade would continue. He cleaned his pistols.

The mall was lively for a Thursday afternoon. School was out. Attractive teenage girls in short skirts and tanned legs walked by whispering and conspiring.

The phone rang for the sixth time and Jesse wondered if he had the right number. Then a male voice answered. "Hazard, Settlemire and Boguslaw, attorneys at your service." He sounded so serious.

"John, you must not have any real clients. At least no one you want to impress." said Jesse.

"Jesse, Jesse, you da *man*, baby. Wonderful to hear your voice. I know *you're* impressed. You're still on the line."

"I don't have much time, John. You'll be receiving a letter with certain instructions. It's imperative, for the safety of the children, that you follow them precisely. I know I can trust you to do that. Beyond that, I'm counting on you. Heavily."

"*Jefe*, you are my maximum leader. Your wish is golden with me. When are you coming home?"

"That's the second part. These requests are going to sound a little strange. I'm telling you they're not only real, but critical. I need a car parked at the Fairhope airport, east of Mobile. That's Alabama. Park it close to the ramp, clear it with the FBO, no questions asked. I also need a reservation for a motel room in Fairhope. The motel is just up the road on Alternate Route 98. It's the first one on the right, coming from the south, with a lighted sign hanging over the curb. Make reservations for Mr. and Mrs. Bigbee Stevens. I need this done by late evening of the tenth. If all goes well, we'll be there on the eleventh. Make the reservations for a week starting on the night of the tenth.

"None of this can be traced. I don't want cops questioning the car. It needs to be legal and discreet— really discreet."

"Yeah, yeah... Hold on, I'm still writing this down. Secret, discreet, legal... I *am* a lawyer, you know. I do legal stuff. Is this going to get me in trouble?"

"John, the only one out on a limb is me."

"And this Mrs. Stevens. What about her?"

"I can't go into that. I hope to be able to explain this to you over cocktails by the end of August. I'd like to chat, John, but there's not much time. Hope to see you soon. And thanks, for everything." Jesse didn't let John say anything more before he hung up.

La Primavera came alive, as it always did, upon Santee's return. He'd bagged a trophy sheep and had secured the cooperation of Senor Payan. They now had Mexican protection at the highest levels. Mr. Rivera was already onboard. Once the paste was sent from Peru and Bolivia, the labs would be refining the highest-quality coke on the planet.

They all sat in the library with drinks and smokes. Santee was telling them about his cunning and marksmanship. They watched their boss. His pleasure was real, and everyone was entertained by the stories about the head of the Mexican intelligence agency and the *campesinos* hired to carry the provisions.

Everyone but Jesse. He was reserved. He wasn't draining his glass as usual. He was watching Santee for any sign of worry, of predation.

Santee noticed and said, "Jesse, you are so quiet tonight. You do not laugh as hard as Coley or Biano or even Claire at my stories. Perhaps they do not amuse you?"

"It isn't that. I guess I'm just a little...preoccupied with planning our trip to Bolivia. It's a tough country."

"Business, business. There is more to life than business. We will save business for later, after the weekend. The weekend is to celebrate. Jesse, you work too hard. You should relax more."

Jesse seized the opportunity. "You know, you're right. With all the high flying we've been doing, I thought it might be good for me to get away."

Santee retrieved the bourbon bottle and topped

off Jesse's drink. He did the same for Coley and Biano. Claire was sharing a bottle of Dom Perignon with Santee. He stared at Jesse, hard. "Nobody gets away, Jesse. It is a rule of the organization. You know that."

Jesse tried not to flinch, and resisted a powerful urge to glance at Claire.

Then Santee burst out laughing.

It wasn't funny to Jesse. He couldn't avoid Claire's eyes, but they gave away nothing. She was as cool as stone, and even managed to look amused at Jesse's expense.

He managed to smile. "I just meant for an afternoon, take my plane and head to the Keys for some bone fishing. I haven't been in the Lake since I got here. And I noticed you got the proper rigs on the Bertram. I could spot them from the air, cut the engine, land downwind. I hear they're fun to catch."

Santee considered the proposal. "That is a splendid idea, Jesse. I wholeheartedly approve. Why don't you take Biano and Coley along? They have done it before."

Jesse's heart sank. He couldn't refuse, and was about to reluctantly accept the offer and dash his plans when Claire spoke up.

"Shell, perhaps Jesse should go alone. He's lost his enthusiasm. Look at the long face. Maybe some time to contemplate his good fortune, how much you've made possible for him, how really good life is here. It would do him good to be alone to think."

Santee looked toward Claire, frowned, looked back at Jesse. Risky of Claire. Santee thought, then smiled and said fine. He knew he could trace the plane. "That is why Claire is such a trusted adviser. She senses and sees things that elude me."

Jesse didn't know whether to rejoice or feel like a cornered mouse.

August third. The first step toward going home. He'd been away from his plane for too long. It was good to pat her bow.

Sam was anxious to have him test the new equipment and babbled on about the intricacies of the Loran and the extended fuel capacity as Jesse loaded in the fishing gear, his knapsack and his lunch. He paid special attention to the drain plugs during the preflight. He'd be leaving the Lake in the brackish waters of the Everglades for two nights. All would be lost if she sank or was too heavy to fly.

If Santee was consistent, someone had placed a homing device underneath the instrument panel, just as one had been placed in the Mitsubishi. That was where Jesse found it.

He climbed onto the port wing and opened the engine nacelle to check the engine oil. It was on the mark. He unscrewed the hydraulic dipstick. As he started to refasten the access panel, his eye caught a small protrusion that was out of place. He reached it and pulled. It was a second transmitter. Jesse's heart raced. Luck had brought him to the second bug. But it meant there might be others.

He got clearance to depart south into the clear blue sky. The Keys stretched out into the Gulf of Mexico. He flew over the Everglades and did some preliminary scouting, looking for the ideal place to hide the plane. He saw no obvious locations.

He had to play out the ruse. His heart was far from fishing, but he had to pretend. He angled west and searched for a school of fish. He found them, swimming leisurely in the shallows. They were fascinating in their languorous movements and Jesse felt godlike, spying down from the heavens into their lives. He circled to the left, descended, and touched down lightly into the small ripples of the sea. It was a perfect day.

In fact, he got lost in the fishing. Claire had been right. With all the tension and turmoil brewing on the horizon like thunder clouds, the focused attention, hooking and fighting a bone fish, was so absorbing that all else fell away forgotten.

He drifted with the breeze, standing high enough on the wing to see the fish swim toward him. He cast the lure way out and slowly reeled it in. He caught and released three fish. He set the gear aside, sat leaning against the fuselage, smoked a Camel and drank a soda. Out here the peace was extreme. The blue-green color of the shallow water spread out in all directions. The small islands of the Keys dotted the southern horizon. A few boats steamed toward unknown destinations, trailing white wake. The sunlight was heavy, but not oppressive. Jesse rocked in the gentle swells. This was the only world. He didn't want to leave.

He stowed the pole and tackle box on the rear seat and started the engine. He closed the window and latched it tight. He advanced the throttle and she came quickly onto the step. He skimmed the sea and with a touch of back pressure was airborne. Jesse turned to starboard and flew toward Key West.

Jesse landed and followed a man waving a flag from an old jeep with its windshield laid flat. He parked where he was told, and said he was just here for the early afternoon, a sightseer.

The coffee was strong. Jesse sat in the small restaurant overlooking the field, searching for a stationary target for the homing transmitters. He needed to be sure that at least for the next several days, they wouldn't move away from the field. He picked an engineless Cessna 172 tied down in the last row. The installation of the overhauled engine would take three days, even if they started this evening. It was a safe target.

Jesse preflighted the Lake and removed the two transmitters. He put them in his pocket. He wanted to leave as soon as he'd replaced the bugs, so he opened the bow compartment and checked the anchor and tie-off lines. Magnetized to the side of the compartment, behind the plates of ballast, was a third transmitter. It qualified as an infestation and almost a guarantee that Santee knew his scrapbook had been violated. Still, he continued going through the motions, sneaking all three bugs inside the cowling of the 172. He departed the airspace and prayed that to Santee, he was still stuck on the ground at the end of the Keys.

He flew to the Everglades. The reflection of the western sun gleamed into his eyes as he searched for the right spot. First and foremost was access by road. It took almost an hour of following dirt roads off the pavement to wet spots long and straight enough to handle both today's landing and the getaway takeoff.

He found the spot, but it was occupied by people in boats. Although he'd refueled in Key West, Jesse was wasting range he might need later on. He had no choice but to climb, circle to the west and wait until they were gone. It took another hour for them to pack it in. Jesse kept waiting until they were way down the channel.

He couldn't see others, but he decided on a low-power approach. It was imperative that the plane's location remain a secret to all but him. He had to take his chances. He brought her in high and picked a piece of swamp grass for the touchdown. He held her off and she plopped into the murky water and settled quickly. Jesse spun her around and risked a little power so he could taxi over to a place beneath the trees.

He shut down and opened the hatch. It only occurred to him now that he was on the water that there could be snakes and alligators in it. He shuddered, death at every glance.

The trees were on solid ground, but he'd have to wade through a canal to get to the dirt road. He tied the bow and stern to the small trees, took the camp saw and cut branches and placed them over the bright white fuselage. The concealment took over an hour, and by the time it was done, Jesse was dripping in sweat and scratching his insect bites. There'd been no sign of lizards or snakes.

He left the plane unlocked and slid the ignition key underneath the seat cushion. It was all so obvious, but if the plane was discovered, the game would already be up. The canal was waist deep. He tossed the knapsack onto the high ground, splashed muddy water over his head and cleaned away most of the dirt. He undressed and took from his sack a change of clothes. He hid the soiled garments under a flap of sod.

A small amount of plane was showing, though not enough to catch an innocent eye. Jesse made note of the two huge trees on the left, dripping with Spanish moss. He'd need a landmark to find this place again.

His cigarettes were damp in the pack, but his smoke lit. He started his walk out. The paved road was about a mile away. He hoped he wasn't so grungy or dangerous looking he'd have to walk the whole way back to La Primavera.

If there was suspicion, it didn't show.

Biano and Coley were away. Santee, Claire and he were eating at the small table in the corner of the dining room. Jesse poured what was left of the bottle of merlot into Claire's glass. Santee rang the bell and asked Carla to bring another bottle. He was being exceptionally polite this evening. Jesse was tuned to anything unusual.

He'd returned without fanfare. The ride in the pickup had dropped him off at a market; from there he'd called a cab. Jesse had the cabbie drop him off at the airport's FBO. He walked over to the InterRegional hangar. Sam had been very concerned about the Lake. He couldn't imagine that it was a mechanical problem. He took it personally and wanted to ask Mr. Santee if Biano would fly him down to Key West so he could fix it.

Jesse assured him it was something small and they could pick it up after the flight to Maine.

Santee had known the plane was in Key West before Jesse mentioned it. He chastised Jesse for not calling Biano to fetch him. After all, he was a very important person. Santee told him to start thinking like one. Jesse assured him that he would have called if he hadn't been fortunate to hitch a ride on an empty return charter.

They ate with prolonged periods of silence. The roast chicken and rice were delicious enough to take words away, but it was more than that. Jesse was wary of Santee's slipping mood. As he speared a last slice of dark meat with his fork, he asked, "Santee, what will you do when you're set up in Guyana?"

Before answering, Santee washed down his last bite with the wine, pushed his plate away and rang the bell. Claire was still eating, but Santee didn't notice. He replied, "Jesus, Jesse, I guess more of the same."

Carla came in and removed their plates, but didn't hover over Claire. She said she'd bring coffee.

"No, I mean, how will you treat the people, the Guyanese?" Jesse asked. This caught Claire's attention and she looked up.

"They will love me, of course. And if they do not, I will beat them until their mood improves." He chuckled. Jesse did too, but without much mirth. It was all too true.

Santee sensed the reservation in Jesse, and tried to explain. "I will bring so many good things to the people. The children will have opportunities I never had. They will be sheltered, fed, and have good schools to go to. Their parents will have jobs. Not just jobs with us, but in industries, in the military, with the police. There will be no crime in the streets. We will see to that. Any criminal behavior will be punished severely and justice will be swift, no appeal. The people will be safe and comfortable behind the doors of their houses. Be sure, Jesse, the people will love us. There are less than a million of them, as you know. Not so many to look after."

Santee sat back and savored the vision. "Coley will head the security police, of course. We will need to be very careful. We will have many enemies, and not only governments, but jealous competitors who will wish they had thought of this idea on their own."

Jesse spoke. "You will be the beneficent ruler then, rare for Latin America."

"Ah, you make a good point, Jesse. Yes, most Central and South American dictators had only narrow vision. I will not need to hold my people down like they did. No. I will be able to lavish wealth and opportunity upon them. I will give them what they need."

"What if they want something other than what you want for them?"

"Then they will die."

The finality of that statement brought an end to the conversation. No one had the will or energy to revive it. Jesse declined coffee and retired to his room, depressed. It seemed hope had drained from his veins like an endless blood donation, until he was empty.

He lay down on the bed with all his clothes on and wanted to melt into the mattress.

He knew he should be planning, or worried, or

nervous, but all he felt was tired. Powerful forces would be unleashed soon and only God could see over the horizon. He was praying, humbly, as he fell asleep and didn't wake until morning.

He came fully awake with a sense of urgency, a need to do something. He took several breaths, trying to calm down and think. It was Thursday. They would escape tomorrow. He needed to rendezvous with Claire, but that could be arranged. The plane was stashed and if it was in trouble, he wouldn't know until it was too late. It was all in place, but there was a nagging tug that was making his heart leap.

He stared at the ceiling. It started to recede. The corners of the room seemed far away. His peripheral vision encompassed the two posts on the footboard of his bed. They seemed miles away. He was slipping again into the crease between this world and beyond. He started to fight it, but he knew it was futile. It would have to pass on its own. He needed faith to let it go. He was small in the face of the huge, but this time, he felt connected to the powers that would free him; it was different, reassuring. His self-assessment was calming. The spell gradually lifted the weight that had pinned him to the bed. The world came forward and took its rightful dimension. The clarity was like a cold front coming through, pushing the haze out to sea. Jesse dared move a hand, then an arm. He stretched.

His only remaining task was to copy the files off

Santee's computer. He'd planned to do it at the very last minute, in case Santee had booby trapped the copy command. Now it seemed imperative to copy the file as soon as possible. If he let it go too long, the opportunity might be lost.

He went downstairs and saw Santee and Claire were walking out the door, headed for the docks. Santee said, "We're going across the channel to the marina. I'm going to need a bigger ship if I'm going to be a magnificent leader. You want to come and lend your advice?"

"Thank you, but no. With the trip to Colombia looming, I think I'll take it easy and rest up. But you guys go and pick out a good one. Get me something in the hundred-foot range." He smiled and they all were merry. "What time do you think you'll be back?"

"Early afternoon, but we will not see you. I want you to check the plane today. The cases that you will deliver arrived in the night. You can never be too careful, and who knows what tomorrow will bring?" Santee's smile was more like a leer. "Claire wants to go shopping this afternoon. We can all meet here for drinks at six."

He watched them descend the incline and board the Scarab. Claire took a bandana and tied it around her hair. The sky was darkening and the winds were picking up. It would have been a fun ride across the channel.

Jesse had coffee with Carla and Mrs. Sanchez in the kitchen. Jesse wanted to thank them, tell them that they'd been right all along, that it was not his way. He was extra polite and the two women noticed. They each kissed him on the cheek when he rose to leave. They told him he was a good boy and he should be careful. Amen to that, he thought, walking away, a little sad.

He took the blank disks from his satchel, went through the metal door, and climbed the stairs to the command room. He half-expected the combination to have been changed, but all was normal, so he sat down. The chair creaked as if to give him away. Jesse scrolled through the directories until he reached the file. Bracing for the worst, he typed the commands. *Cripple* worked. *Nemesis* worked, too. He was in.

He inserted the first floppy and the little disk made a slippery sound as it spun. He typed the *xcopy* command and the files started their transfer. Jesse watched the monitor, wondering when it would crash. Would a hidden file destroy the copy when he shut down? He'd find out, one way or the other.

The computer asked for another disk in the drive. Jesse complied.

Santee had been thorough. The entire file took three and a half floppies. He gingerly backed his way out, as if he might trip an alarm. When the computer was off, he sat back and stared at the empty screen. It had been too easy. Santee had surely set some trap.

Jesse got the car out of the garage. It was a bad day, nasty weather for Florida in August. Good thing they weren't leaving until the system pushed off.

At a stoplight, Jesse touched the envelope with the disks in the side pocket of his silk sports coat. He wasn't going to leave them anywhere. They were as precious as life itself. After putting in his appearance at the hangar, he'd stop at the office supply store, seal them in a manila envelope, and mail them to John Settlemire.

PART VII

CHAPTER 33

Miami Herald, August 4

The first federal report on the corporate structure of the illegal drug trade has identified 43 major groups, from operatives of the Colombian cartels to onetime moonshiners of the "Dixie Mafia."

8/5 William Bennett promised that within a month, his department will produce a comprehensive national policy to combat drug abuse.

JESSE BACKED THE BMW between Biano's Mercedes and Sam's brand new Suburban with its mysterious tinted windows.

The hangar was deserted. Four wooden crates sat next to the scale beside the Mitsubishi. Jesse glanced through the picture window into the lounge and saw Sam and Biano standing at the desk, looking down at the phone. They looked up at him when he came through the door.

The brightness of Jesse's greeting faded when he saw the concerned look on their faces and heard Santee's voice on the answering machine. The message finished and went dead. Biano pushed the rewind button.

Sam took several steps backwards and brought a hand to his mouth.

Santee's voice filled the room. "Sam, I want you to detain Jesse when he comes in to check the plane. Do not alarm him. Make some excuse, but be sure that he remains at the hangar. I am sending Pasque and another man. Make sure he stays put."

The machine said the message came in at 3:42 pm.

Jesse looked at his watch. It was quarter after four. La Primavera was forty-five minutes away. Pasque was ten minutes out, maybe less.

He looked up into the hollow end of a muzzle from a pistol in Sam's hand. Sam said, "I have to follow the instructions or else I'll pay, too. You understand, don't you, Mr. Langdon?" Sam's voice was shaky and the gun was wavering. "Nothing personal."

Jesse looked at Biano. Time stood still. Nobody moved or said a thing. Then Biano looked over at Sam and took control with a strong voice. "Oh, Jesus Christ, Sam, put the gun down. What are you doing? Santee will never know if we got the message or not. It's best if we leave it all alone." He grabbed the gun as Sam lowered it, then turned to Jesse and handed it to him. "You don't have much time." Biano walked to the closet and

pulled out a Mossberg twelve-gauge and a box of shells.
"You might need this, Jesse. Sam and I are going to get
real scarce. Your car is bugged. So is mine. Take Sam's
Suburban."

They looked over at Sam. "Go ahead, I guess. The
keys are in it. It's brand new, you know. Please don't
hurt it, okay?"

"I'll do my best, Sam. Thanks. And thank you,
Biano. It was fun knowing and flying with you." There
was no time for this. Jesse backed out of the office.

Tires screeched just as he shut the Suburban's
door. Jesse fumbled with the box of shells and spilled
the ammunition on the passenger seat. He turned the
shotgun over and loaded five shells through the breech.
It took all his concentration to control his hands.
He looked up to see Santee's big BMW careen into
the parking lot and come to a sliding halt beside the
Suburban. The doors flew open and the two Cubans
jumped out, pistols drawn, each threaded with a
suppressor.

Jesse did his first stupid thing. He started the car.

Pasque looked over and hesitated, apparently confused by the tinted glass. Jesse realized he couldn't see
who was driving. It gave him the tiniest advantage. In
the time it took Pasque to decide to shoot whoever it
was, Jesse brought the Mossberg to the window and
pulled the trigger.

The blast blew out the driver's window, lifted

Pasque off the ground, and tossed him backwards through the air. In the second of confusion the other Cuban froze. Jesse pumped another round into the chamber, stuck the shotgun out through the shattered remains of the window, and shot him in the chest.

All of Jesse's world was smoke and roar. He couldn't hear the engine running, but he put the Suburban in gear and ripped out of the parking lot. He didn't want to go fast, but he couldn't help himself. The tires spun, gravel flew, and the Suburban fishtailed onto the access road that led out to 137th Street.

He forced himself to slow down as he came to the light. The traffic was heavy and the left-turn lane was full. The green arrow was lit and it looked like he was going to make it. Then it turned yellow. Just then, across the street, two cars turned into the airport. Jesse recognized both. The second was Santee's Ferrari. He caught Santee's astonished look. He gunned the Suburban through the now-red arrow and watched in his rearview mirror as both cars turned.

The opposing traffic surged and Santee had to stop. Jesse's last glimpse of Santee was of him smiling calmly, confident.

Jesse pushed out the remaining pieces of window with his elbow. He had the smallest of head starts.

He fished out his cell phone and dialed Claire's number. It rang once. She said hello. Jesse said, "He knows, Claire! I've got Sam's car and I'm a couple of blocks ahead of him. Where're you? I've got to pick you up. Where are you now?"

She didn't answer.

After a pause that was too long, she told him that after returning from yacht shopping, Santee had gone to the third floor, then peeled out fast. She'd also left in a hurry and was in Coral Gables, waiting.

"I can be at the corner of Bird and 40th in ten minutes. Be at the light. Be there." Jesse tossed the phone on top of the shotgun shells.

Claire stood at the light in a short blue dress and white sandals. Jesse pulled over and stopped. He swept the seat clean and she climbed in.

The entire world poked along in slow motion, while Jesse hurtled through space at Mach 5. Every driver conspired to get in his way. It took all his effort to keep his hand off the horn and his foot off the accelerator.

Claire pushed the lock down on her door, pulled the seatbelt around her, turned to Jesse and asked, "What happened?"

Jesse checked the rearview mirror for the thousandth time and took a deep breath. "You know when you get running too fast down a hill, and your upper body gets too far ahead of your feet? There's a section of time between when you know for sure you're going to fall, and there's nothing you can do about it, and you know it's going to be bad? My day has gotten ahead of me and I can't catch up."

"Jesse, what happened with Santee? How'd he find out? You're driving too fast."

Jesse looked again in the mirror and didn't see anyone chasing them. He slowed down. The road signs promised adventures in the Everglades. He hoped it wasn't true. "I got to the airport to check the plane and the crates of guns, as instructed. Biano and Sam were in the office, standing over the phone. Santee's voice was on the answering machine telling Sam to keep me there until Pasque came and got me."

"Why did you think it was bad? He could have meant anything."

"Claire! He said to detain me and not to alarm me! Sam drawing down on me didn't help."

"How'd you get away?"

"Biano convinced Sam to lower the gun, that there was no way for Santee to know they got the message. Then Biano gave me the shotgun." He nodded toward the floor.

Claire picked up the Mossberg, checked the chamber and added two shells. She looked in her side mirror. "I wonder why they're so lackadaisical."

Jesse pulled onto the Florida Turnpike and headed south. "Probably because Santee thinks he's got everything pegged, bugs everywhere, can track us wherever we go. He can sit back and take his sweet time." The thought was sobering. "He couldn't have figured I'd take Sam's car. Now he's in the dark. I can't see how he can find us. We could spend the night in Florida City, leave tomorrow." Jesse squinted into the overcast to the west, brightened by the setting sun.

They both thought about that. Claire spoke first. "I suggest we don't underestimate Santee. How do you know he doesn't have Sam's car bugged? I think we should put distance between us and him as soon as we can. You get the stuff out of the computer?"

"Yeah, I got it. That's what must have tipped him off. I didn't have time to send it to my lawyer. All the post offices are closed. We have to get away clean to protect them." Jesse transferred the disks to his breast pocket, next to Ashley and Ike, and buttoned it down.

They took the Florida City exit. Jesse estimated the ceiling at 700 to 1,000 feet, clouds hauling ass over the treetops. It was breaking up to the west, bright flashes of sunlight turning the foliage an evening yellow. The conditions were less than ideal for a flight across the Gulf to Alabama. If they were going to bed down, it would have to be around here. Accommodations were scarce in the Everglades.

The light at an intersection turned yellow to match the holes in the sky, and Jesse had to slam on the brake. He and Claire leaned forward in unison. The tension was dissipating, at least a little, now that they were away. It was a typical four corners—a Texaco station, a Burger King... and Santee's BMW. Parked beside it were Coley and Santee in the Ferrari. Only Santee was smiling.

The light turned green and the driver behind Jesse honked his horn. Jesse accelerated slowly and watched the BMW pull out to follow. Santee was holding back; he probably didn't want to get his hands dirty.

Jesse looked toward Claire, whose skin was white. He was staring at his own death reflected in her sweet face. The inevitable violence, the horrible end—nothing to do but pass through. There must be an afterlife, peace and well-being at the end of the inevitable pain.

"*Hit it!*" Claire was dumping the shotgun shells in her lap.

Jesse floored the Suburban, but the overdrive took its time kicking in. It was a double yellow line and they were cresting a little hill, but Jesse passed a wizened old lady who could hardly see over the hood. The BMW was back, picking up speed, not on his tail. He swerved in, just avoiding a Winnebago with full horn, shiny grill and a red-faced driver. They were doing seventy, approaching eighty. "What's the use?" Jesse was ready to give up. "Like you said, they have this thing bugged too. They can follow us anywhere."

"So now what? We just pull over and say it's been a terrible mistake? You're out of your mind if you think I'm not going to take as many of them with me as I can."

Her tone stung. He wanted to tell her how slim their chances were, how they needed a good lead if they were to have time to get away in the plane, how the shotgun was useless in a gunfight. Well, fuck her too! Jesse let the whole thing out, all four-fucking-hundred horsepower. He couldn't look over at her, but he could smile when she said that was more like it.

Jesse tried to picture the approach road, the left turn onto dirt where he'd hidden the Lake. They wouldn't be expecting that, but Santee wouldn't let them get too far out front, not knowing what they had planned. He might have suspected they had the Lake, or he might be putting it together right now. Jesse chanced a look behind. The BMW was coming up fast, a guy hanging out the window, an H&K in his hand, smoke coming out of it.

The automatic-weapon fire sounded like hail. Jesse and Claire ducked low, then Claire spun and fired through the rear window. It came apart in a burst of glass, which he saw more than heard; the first had taken all Jesse's hearing.

The chase car swerved and slowed.

Claire jacked another round in the chamber and fired again. This one was different, a dull thud against his head. Claire smiled at him and shouted something, which he couldn't make out. He looked over and couldn't believe his eyes. She was smiling, having fun.

What the hell! He was doing a little over a hundred now.

The BMW was closing. The turn was coming up. Jesse braked hard and nearly lost her coming around the corner onto the dirt. He yelled to Claire. "Get ready to bail out! Put the ammo in the backpack! We need the backpack!" He sounded very strange to himself, as if his ears were plugged.

He accelerated and the tires spewed gravel as the Suburban had a hard time gaining traction. So did the BMW. Claire fumbled with the shells that were floating across the seat. She got most in the bag. She reloaded the gun.

Ahead, the road, full of setting sun, rose over a canal. They were almost at the plane.

It was not so much of a plan as a realization. The Suburban came light on its springs as she came up over the rise. The setting sun took full center in the windshield, but Jesse didn't need to see. He stood on the brakes and spun the steering wheel to the left. She went into a drift, fishtailed across the small road and came to a halt.

They leapt from the car and dove into the right-hand swale. The BMW came over the rise and into the light. If there were brakes, Jesse couldn't hear any, nor did he sense any panic as the shiny black car came down heavy and plowed broadside into the Suburban.

Jesse could feel the concussion, then a blankness

in the air. Metal fell back to earth, gasoline flowed, and with a *whumph* the car caught in a sunset burst of orange flames.

There would be no screaming. Death was coming to the unconscious.

Jesse grabbed Claire's hand and pulled her out of the ditch and along the road. They'd bought some time. It might be enough.

It was a good two-hundred yards to the telltale trees. They were light and it was a fast sprint. They weren't looking back, but about three-quarters of the way there, projectiles started whipping by their heads. Claire pulled him down flat.

Jesse grabbed the Mossberg, brought it up, and aimed. Coley and Santee were kneeling behind the Ferrari and shooting at them through the crash, which blocked the road. Santee was taking his time, believing he had them cornered. Coley was walking his machine gun from left to right, but seemed to be shooting high.

Santee fired, and a plume of dirt leapt to their right, sending stinging gravel into their skin. Jesse aimed at Santee and pulled the trigger. The shot hit just to his right, lodged in the headlamp, and gave him a pause. Jesse looked at Claire, who circled her thumb and forefinger and shouted, "Slugs!" That explained it.

Coley's spray was mowing into the foliage above their heads as they ran crouched and thrashing through the underbrush along the rise that paralleled the road.

Claire had lost her sandals and her feet were bleeding. But she was ahead, pulling Jesse along. He looked back, swinging the Mossberg, pulling the trigger, gun leaping against his wrist. He couldn't see Santee, but he knew they were coming.

Through breathless lips Claire yelled, "Where the hell are we going? Why am I leading? You find the fucking plane!"

It was beyond dusk, the trees beginning to blend into a solid mass of impenetrable gloom. He pulled them up short and tried to get his bearings. "They have no idea we have the plane. That must be why they aren't in a hurry. Santee knows this is a dead-end. Probably thinks the alligators and snakes will get us." They looked at each other, then surveyed the muddy bottom.

Jesse led them farther into the swamp along the only high ground. The road was now out of sight, but a burst of automatic fire came through the trees and they both hit the ground again. Jesse knew they were making too much noise, revealing their general location. They were trapped on this little rise. It must be what Santee was thinking.

A voice came from the road. "You two are finished! Night is falling, the animals are coming out! All you've got is water behind you, Jesse! What are you going to do, have Claire swim for it?" Santee laughed, a hollow sound.

Jesse's head was still ringing from the shotgun blasts in the car, the crash, and the rounds traded, but he heard when Santee spoke again, more normally. "Don't feel conversational? Well then, I'll tell you a little something. You are going to end up just like that precious brother-in-law of yours. I might as well solve that mystery for you. When you asked about him, I put my people on it. I found out early on that Reefer had moved up in Espinoza's operation. Big mistake! He was in Guadalupe when we took them down. Reefer ran out the front. They were all lying in the dirt. Flagler picked out the only gringo, went over, said his name. Reefer looked up, surprised. Flagler checked with me and I nodded. He shot your brother-in-law right between the eyes. Face it, Jesse! The women in your wife's family marry losers!" He laughed.

"Now Coley and I are going to stay right here until the animals flush you out. Curious what it comes down to, isn't it? I sincerely thought we could make it. We had good dreams, a good future together. The world was ours to take. And I believe you came to know your true self, Jesse."

"You're right, Santee. I did come to know myself. And my choice is the opposite of yours. It's the way it has to be." Jesse's voice penetrated the coming darkness.

"Yes, the way it has to be. I liked you, Jesse. I still do. I don't want to kill you, but you've left me no choice."

"We'll see," It was all Jesse could muster. He whispered to Claire. "I think the plane is over there, through those trees. If we find it now, we might have enough light to take off."

Jesse followed her, looking back along the muzzle of the Mossberg. They cracked a branch and drew some fire. Jesse replied with two blasts from the shotgun. He wondered how many shells were left in the gun.

The plane loomed up so suddenly that they almost ran into it. Jesse withdrew his Leatherman and sliced through the line holding the tail. He waded to the front and cut the bowline. The sloshing sounds attracted no bullets, but he decided to let the camouflage rip away as the plane surged from beneath the overhanging trees. The odds against them getting away were high. Even with the small element of surprise and the growing cover of darkness, Santee and Coley would open fire. The Lake presented a big target. A lucky shot could kill an engine or him. Or they could plow into unseen obstructions while attempting the takeoff. Jesse tried to picture the surrounding canal and its trees, but couldn't.

Claire stood thigh deep in the muddy water beside the pilot's window. Jesse leaned in and whispered. "Everything we do, until I start the engine, has to be really quiet. Our only chance is to take off before they can shoot us down. Get in and pray."

Jesse turned the latch of his window and lifted the

hatch. It sounded like dolphins frolicking in the surf as Claire unsucked her legs from the muck and climbed into the plane. He followed her in, a muddy mess across the leather seats.

She settled into the right seat. He eased himself down and took the penlight from the side pocket beside his knee.

Santee's voice distracted him. It sounded so close. "You can't get away, Jesse. Claire, talk some sense into him. Tell him to come on out, and it will be swift."

There was no time to check the circuit breakers or the hydraulic pressure. An act of faith. Jesse illuminated the fuel selector and turned the valve on. Overhead, he felt for the throttle and opened it a tad. He pushed the prop governor full forward, moving the mixture to full rich.

The silent part was done. He rehearsed the next moves. No matter what happened, he had to follow the sequence.

Jesse took a deep breath and looked through the gloom to the silhouette of Claire's face. "Here we go. God bless us." He handed the flashlight to Claire and looked out at what little of the canal he could see. The surface just off to the right was shimmering with light and dark grays. The rest had faded black.

With his right hand up holding the overhead throttle lever, he pushed the electric fuel-pump switch with his left and started to count the five seconds it took to prime the engine, a riot of whining and whirling, too loud and metallic to be confused with glade life.

One one thousand, two one thousand, three one tho…

It took that long for Santee to put it all together. Jesse heard the cry, "Son of a bitch!" over the engine noise, followed by two separate bursts of machine gun fire.

Five one thousand!

Jesse turned the ignition switch and the propeller blade made a laboriously slow rotation, then another, and another. The engine coughed and the prop took another rotation. The engine caught with a deep roar.

Jesse had forgotten to close the canopy. He reached up, took hold of the latch and brought the hatch down. A bullet pierced the Plexiglas and sent shards into Jesse's forearm. He had only enough time to register the stinging and the blood. His right hand pushed the throttle full forward.

The 250-horsepower turbo-charged engine surged and the plane leapt from under the trees, the prop slashing through the foliage. Jesse yelled for Claire to latch his window. She reached across and twisted the handle into place. A bullet came through the window behind Jesse's head and through the cabin and exited where Claire's head had been.

The Lake picked up speed and the rudder became

effective. Jesse pushed the right pedal and the plane came out into the canal. He straightened out, at least he thought he did. The banks were black. His only reference was the slightly gray sky up and forward. He steered for it.

Over the roar of the engine, Jesse shouted for Claire to illuminate the instrument panel. He kept his eyes focused on the lighter part of the sky. "Read out my airspeed! I can't look down!"

Claire leaned over and watched as the little needle started to nudge into the green arc. Then it started a steady progress, thirty knots, thirty-five, forty.

Jesse pushed the control wheel forward and the Lake came up on the step. She accelerated smartly now. Claire called, "Forty-five! Fifty!"

The starboard sponson tank caught something and the plane swerved to the right. Jesse stomped on the left rudder and the plane straightened out.

"Fifty-five! Sixty!"

Jesse applied some back pressure and the nose came up.

She seemed heavy. Jesse remembered the flaps. He felt for the lever and pushed it down to twenty degrees. The small motor turned the gears and spun the connectors and the flaps came down. The Lake became lighter and lighter. But the faint gray that constituted Jesse's whole hope seemed to be getting darker. The Lake surged through the darkness and broke the suction of the swamp.

He fought the urge to pull up. He needed more airspeed. They'd be dead whether they hit a cluster of trees or stalled and spun into the murky waters and drowned.

"Seventy! Seventy-five! Eighty!"

Jesse pulled back on the yoke and started to climb. He reached down and flicked on the instrument lights. "I can see now. Thanks, Claire." He concentrated on the panel. Airspeed at best rate, flaps up, rudder in.

Jesse scanned the panel, checking his attitude and airspeed, trimmed the plane. He brought the throttle back to twenty-five inches and the propeller back to 2,500 rpm. He leaned the mixture.

The plane climbed through 500 feet and Jesse made a gradual turn to the right. The compass started to swing to the north.

Jesse busied himself with all the small tasks of staying airborne. It kept thoughts of death at bay. The wind rushed through the hole in his side window. His forearm was starting to throb. Blood from the fiberglass embedded in it dripped onto his left thigh, which was wet and sticky.

"After I get her established and secure, Claire, could you look at my arm? In the back, behind your seat, is a survival pack with bandages and gauze and tape. We also need the survival blanket to stuff in this window."

He turned on the radios one at a time, careful not to activate the transponder and become a blip on Miami Approach Control screens. He tuned in the Automatic Terminal Information System for Miami International and a soothing voice filled the cockpit. It ran through the information needed for a landing at Miami. Jesse listened for the winds and the barometric pressure; his hearing was steadily improving, though he knew it would take a while to return to normal.

He dialed the right pressure into the altimeter and the altitude hands moved to their true height above the water. Then he set the throttle and prop for cruise and leaned the mixture. He descended to 300 feet, quite sure he was beyond any obstructions, and finally looked over at Claire.

She was fidgeting. There was mud on her face. She said, "What can I do? There's nobody to shoot at." She laughed.

He joined in, and said, "That was close, in every respect."

"I know."

He put his palm on her thigh. "You can keep an eye on these engine instruments." Jesse tapped each one. "Oil pressure. Cylinder head temperature. Hydraulic pressure. Especially the oil pressure. I want to head straight across the Gulf to Mobile, but we can't do that if all the shooting damaged the engine. It all looks good now and the flight controls feel normal. But if there's a problem, it'll show up soon."

She nodded, eyes fixed on the oil pressure reading.

Jesse navigated and adjusted the various radios. He told Claire exactly what he was doing. "I'm tuning in the Miami navigational aid and turning this dial so that when we cross this airway," he pointed on the chart, "the needle will center. Once we're past there, we'll be able to go even lower. We need to be below radar. By the time we get to the airway, we should know if the old bird is going to hold together.

"The winds are pretty strong from the west and it'll be choppy down next to the water, but we don't have a choice. No one can know where we are. Santee may have a man in Miami Center. Once we secure our information and he has a chance to relax, see some reason, we'll be safe."

"Such a nice word, 'safe.' Are you sure you got all the bugs off the airplane? If not, we'll have a reception committee waiting in Alabama."

"Won't happen. Santee was surprised we had the airplane."

"Then how about a drink, to celebrate?"

"I'd kill for one."

"Nice choice of words. How about a smoke?"

"I think the swamp got them."

Jesse dialed the Mobile longitude and latitude into

the Loran and watched the needle center. All he had to do was keep her right in the middle. He adjusted his heading a bit to port—320 degrees—so he could track a 312-degree path across the Gulf.

"We're over 500 miles from Mobile, almost four and a half hours away." He tried to sound matter of fact, no great shakes. They had the fuel.

He looked at the gauges. The flight from Key West had used most of the fuel from the new extended-range pods. The Lake had five other fuel tanks, but only the main tank in the fuselage and the two wing tanks had gauges. The small tanks in the sponsons each held seven gallons and had to be electrically pumped into the wing tanks before the fuel was available.

As a precaution, Jesse brought the power back to maximum-endurance cruise and retrimmed the plane. As much as he wanted to scurry across the water, they were in no real hurry. Having gotten this far, ditching in the ocean because of fuel starvation would be a shame, literally.

Claire broke the train of his worries. "I don't generally do this flying part. It isn't my deal, Jess. Just how far out to sea are we going to be?" There was a whole lot to worry about. Jesse was glad he wasn't the only one doing it.

"Too far," he replied. That struck them both as funny, gallows humor to take the edge off, the razor's edge they were riding. The laughter made his arm hurt, and he brought it across his body so Claire could take a look.

He turned on the overhead light and it shined down on a pulpy mess. Several splinters had lodged in the muscle of his forearm, blood seeping down the elbow onto his trousers.

"You want me to pull these out?"

"I don't think so. Might make it bleed more."

"Well, it looks like the bleeding has almost stopped, but I hate the idea of putting the bandage over all this stuff."

That was funny, too, and when they stopped laughing again, Jesse's arm was really throbbing. He said, "You've got to stop making me laugh." Which made them laugh yet again.

Then she got serious, and while he watched the navigational needle start to swing, she gently rolled pieces of gauze around the shards of Plexiglas, wrapping the bandage around and around his arm. Her touch was tender. When she was finished, she asked, "Well, how far out are we going to be?"

"I didn't distract you enough. Looks like everything is in the green." He pointed to the engine instruments. "We'll go down on the deck in a few minutes and head to Mobile. Most of the time, we'll be about fifty miles out. At the farthest point, we'll be a hundred miles from shore."

"It doesn't matter anyway, does it? Five, ten, a hundred. It's all too far to swim, right?"

"Claire, we're in a flying boat. We can ditch in the water and float."

"Yeah, right. This puny little plane is going to take a whole lot of waves?"

Jesse was offended, though they both knew Claire was right. "You don't have to insult my plane. It's bad luck. No sense worrying about a midnight swim."

Jesse descended to 200 feet and remembered flying with Biano up from Colombia. His missed his copilot, sharing the load in the twin. The full weight was on his shoulders this evening. Biano had also saved his life.

The weather was worsening, about an 800-foot ceiling, winds out of the west at fifteen, gusting to twenty, and at least four more hours of moderate turbulence.

He could let his mind run with all the reasons they wouldn't make it, but better to focus on the positive. After all, they'd already done the improbable. They were alive and mostly unhurt, and if their luck held true a little longer, they'd be safe in the small motel in Fairhope, Alabama.

Jesse turned on the heater. The outside temperature was high, but they were wet and the rigors of the night had left them feeling depleted and vulnerable.

They settled into the flight. It would have been nice to be better prepared. Jesse was hungry and couldn't remember when he'd eaten last. They had no food, no clothing, nothing to drink. The thought of a cold beer at the end of their escape brought Jesse a flood of saliva.

Claire wrapped herself in the second survival blanket and leaned against her window. After a few minutes, she appeared to be asleep. Jesse was feeling drowsy himself. It would be so easy to nod off, fly and fly and never wake up.

His whole plan hinged on the prospect of Santee recognizing their respective positions. Mutually assured destruction was in no one's favor. He and Claire were betting their lives on Santee letting them go, out of respect for the danger of having the evidence released, knowing what effect it would have on his future plans and how all his "partners" would feel about their faces smeared across the front pages of the *Miami Herald* and *USA Today*. Jesse unconsciously touched the disks in the buttoned pocket of his shirt, nestled next to the picture of his children.

In the short term, he might play along. But Santee was a man who, ultimately, would take any risk to taste the sweet nectar of revenge.

The yoke was heavy on the left and Jesse had to keep constant pressure on the right to keep the plane level. Something was becoming unbalanced. It could only be improper fuel burn, but both wing tanks registered half full. Maybe the problem was farther out-board in the sponson tanks.

Jesse activated the fuel pump to drain the out-board tanks. It took about twenty minutes. And when the tanks were empty and the plane was flying level, Jesse knew the answer. And it wasn't good.

They'd lost fuel from the starboard sponson tank, probably due to a bullet hole. That was seven gallons less. Jesse took out the handheld flight computer and did the calculations. It put them over the coast with breaths of fuel, and that assumed the winds didn't freshen.

Jesse engaged the autopilot and dialed in the Mobile navigational radio. The Loran already had the relevant data—210 nautical miles, 1.75 hours until arrival. They should land just after two in the morning. The VOR was land-based, and when the needle started to come to life, it would mean they were close.

The cockpit was now warm and dimly lit by the instrument panel, shedding eerie light off the white gauze bandages that covered his left arm. Like a wel-coming warm pool, sleep invited him to start the slip-pery slide.

Jesse listened to the engine, smooth and gentle, the monotonous drone sucking him farther and farther away from what was the past and toward what might be the future.

A strong body shudder broke the serenity, a jolt

that presaged sleep. Jesse came fully awake, grateful for the adrenaline rush and pounding heart. The engine sounded louder and more like the grinding explosions that propelled them along. He listened carefully. It was all in his mind.

The night took on a haunting quality. He glanced to his left, imagining a figure of death smiling from the port wing. He saw a woman in flowing gray robes outlined in black, but she disappeared just as he began to focus on her smile, her teeth, on the passage down her throat.

Jesse rubbed his face with both hands. He slapped his cheeks. He moved around in his seat. His ass hurt. He started to hate the plane, the confinement, the fact they were just feet from the cold ocean, way out to sea, under a solid gray overcast. He was losing the will to fight. It would be so easy to just nose her down and scatter the plane across the wild surface of the sea, sink with Claire into the dark oblivion. Now he wondered if he had the energy to resist the temptation. He was tired of this game and wanted to turn it off.

But he owed more to Ed Fischer. And to Biano. He could never see them quit. He could plow into the ocean, and nobody would ever know the story. But they had taught him to persevere, to take care of himself, even in the face of great danger, for the love of family, for the love of life. He couldn't let them down.

They slipped across the Gulf.

They were fifty miles out, thirty-five minutes. Jesse tuned in Pensacola ATIS, wanting a voice to break the spell. Silence. The silence of sleep.

Ed Fischer shouting at him. "Cabin fire! Cabin fire! Cabin fire!"

Silence. The silence of death.

Jesse closed his eyes. His jaw went slack.

It came faintly and with static, but he heard it and it was real. He emerged into consciousness and was aware of droning through the night toward the Alabama coast, with the automated terminal information beginning to come in clear.

The winds had diminished, blowing more from the south, pushing them along. Jesse adjusted the barometric pressure and corrected their altitude. He watched the numbers on the Loran click down and down as they closed in on the Fairhope airport.

He woke Claire.

PART VIII

CHAPTER 34

JESSE MADE A reasonable approach, but botched the night landing. The plane hit hard and porpoised. He advanced the throttle, stabilized the plane in ground effect and eased her back onto the tarmac. His leg was jumping as he braked for the next taxiway.

Claire touched his knee. "You arrange that thrill ride for my entertainment?"

"I wish."

He taxied up to the small operation shack and shut her down. Only one light shone from the deserted ramp.

And one car was parked in the lot behind the chain-link fence.

They stumbled out into the evening quiet and stretched. Jesse went to the car. The key was on top of the left front tire. Claire followed with the backpack and shotgun.

They followed the directions on the passenger seat

to a motel in town. There were two cars in the parking lot and the lobby was empty. They rang the bell that woke the skinny teenager who checked them in.

Jesse started to explain that they were arriving a day early, but the boy was so sleepy, and maybe still stoned, that he didn't seem to notice Jesse's arm was wrapped in a bloody bandage, Claire was dressed only in a short light jumper, they didn't have any luggage, and they both were filthy. He just wanted to collect the money, hand them a key, and get back to sleep.

They found the room, pulled the covers down, stripped naked, and fell asleep in the warmth of each other's arms.

Jesse dreamed of the Everglades and mud making his running interminably slow, almost motionless, the threat massive and coming quickly closer. Yet he wasn't afraid. He waited for it calmly, ready to welcome whatever it brought.

Jesse woke spooned to Claire's back, baking in the heat of skin that smelled like sweet swamp. She was asleep on his good arm, all tingling pins and needles. His wounded arm was sore, but he hugged her closer with it. His nose was in the nook of her neck. The faintest scent of perfume mingled with the rich marsh smell.

He let the day seep in. He felt whole, a clinging completeness, a peace of connectedness. There was much to do, but Jesse felt no hurry or panic.

Claire stirred and rolled onto her back. She looked up and Jesse stared into her aquamarine eyes that looked so innocent this morning.

She asked, "What time is it?"

Jesse unwrapped his arm from around her stomach and consulted his watch. "Almost ten-thirty."

She asked, "Do you want to make love to me?"

He put his head on her shoulder and she cradled it in her arm. He thought about it as she hugged him to her. "It would break the spell, wouldn't it?"

They lay there in the silence, cocooned together against the day and all the frayed ends that needed braiding and tending.

Jesse took her hand. "What I want is to lie here beside you, breathe you in, take life from your skin, give you mine."

"Sounds like sex to me—and then we'll be doing it sure as hell." She laughed and squeezed Jesse. He squeezed her back.

They separated and talked about the day. They needed food and clothes, to do something about the plane. Bullet holes in strange planes tend to bring unwanted attention. Jesse had to send the disks to John. They should call Santee.

"I need a long hot bath, which I'll take while you buy me a toothbrush, a hairbrush and a size-six gingham dress down at the hardware store." Claire slid out of bed. "Sure you don't want me?" She smiled and cocked a hip.

Jesse considered her. "Maybe after your bath."

She threw her dirty dress at him, swayed her way to the bathroom and shut the door.

All the scummy weather had blown east, and the day was warm and still and bright.

Fairhope was small, but had a clothing store. He bought himself work boots and wool socks, a blue-jean shirt, some thick brown canvas trousers. The lady sales clerk with a thick southern accent helped him select underwear and a short blue-checkered dress for Claire.

At the drugstore next door, Jesse bought toiletries.

The clerk at the post office was friendly. He sold Jesse an envelope, postage, and insurance, and said the package would get there on Monday, at the latest. He wished Jesse a good day.

A payphone caught Jesse's attention as he drove toward the fast-food restaurant along the main drag. It was car-window height. Jesse pulled up, leaned out, and took the receiver. He used his calling card number to dial La Primavera.

On the fourth ring, his call was answered. It was Santee. He sounded distressed and was talking to himself. "Where the fuck is everybody, yeah, hello, what do you want?"

"Santee, it's me."

There was a long pause as Santee pulled himself

together. Jesse could almost hear the gathering in, the tucking of shirttails, the ordering of thought.

"Where are you?"

"Kind of an obvious question, isn't it? I'm just calling to tell you I sent the disks to a person with the usual instructions, you know the ones. 'In the event of my death, please release these tapes to the *New York Times.*"

Santee started a small chuckle that grew into a roaring laugh. Jesse could picture his dark face, his fathomless black eyes. He sounded sincerely amused, and the flippant tone gave Jesse a chill.

"Oh, Jesse. You are such an asshole. What the fuck do you do now? Did you see what you copied, Mr. Langdon the Third? Don't you realize that I can never be touched?"

There was a rattle in Jesse's voice, not so confident now. "If your story comes out, Santee, at least one of your high-up friends will be extremely displeased. Maybe more. You know these people don't tolerate mistakes. You can't afford to have that happen. Not if you want to retire to Guyana. So you'll leave Claire and me and our families alone. It's going to be a truce."

"What fantasy land do you live in, Jesse? One with white hats and good guys? None of this is ever coming out. This kind of truth never does. The big guys won't fall. They never do. "

It dawned on Jesse that Santee might be right, that

the levels of corruption went so deep, all faith would be lost if the truth were known. Still, he had to keep playing his trumps. "Sure, but don't they always have a fall guy in place? A scapegoat that the government commission insists acted alone? You'd certainly fill that bill—if the big guys are as big as you say."

"All I say is you are a dead man, and Claire is your dead woman. Maybe not today, but certainly tomorrow." He paused, distracted by a noise. "It was good to know you, Jesse, and hunting and killing you both will be fun while it lasts, but—"

Santee's sentence was interrupted by a ripping sound and the line went dead. Fucking payphones. Still, obviously, the conversation was over. Jesse had played his cards, but Santee was holding the deck. He slowly hung up the phone and stared out the windshield. The day no longer seemed so sunny.

A television talk-show host was entertaining Claire as she sat wrapped in a towel on the small desk chair. She had another towel turban-style around her hair. A look of concern replaced her smile when she watched Jesse come into the room, carrying the clothing bags and their takeout breakfast. He sat on the bed and told her.

The room seemed to get smaller and smaller, until it was the size of a prison cell, as they contemplated their failure. She took her new clothes into the bathroom, modest now, and got dressed. She looked country splendid when she came out.

Jesse said, "Nice, Claire. I like the new you."

"It sure looks too bright to wear to a funeral. Well, we can always eat. Maybe things will look better on a full stomach."

Jesse laid the Styrofoam plates on the tiny circular table and brought the two chairs in close. A Southern breakfast feast—scrambled eggs, sausage, grits, toast, orange juice and steaming black coffee. They devoured the entire lot without any talk. It was a relief to be immersed in something as basic as eating.

Jesse leaned back from the litter and took out a Camel. Claire pointed to one, for one. He lit two smokes and handed her one. They sat smoking and drinking their coffee in silence.

The knock on the door was small, tentative. A soft voice said, "Maid service."

Jesse cracked the door and saw a tiny Mexican woman surrounded by three large men in charcoal suits, white shirts and differently colored ties.

Jesse stared at the men, who stared back.

The smallest of them, still taller than Jesse, thanked the woman, and she exited to the right out of sight. He pushed Jesse back with a soft hand on the chest and his two companions followed him in. One of them shut the door. They stood at attention like bookends, their hands clasped in front of their groins, feet spread shoulder width apart.

The smaller man addressed Jesse by name, asked him to sit down, and began to speak. It was a high-pitched voice, but the words were well chosen, delivered with strength. His face was remarkable too. He had a shiny head and close-cropped blond hair that stood straight up. He was about forty, impeccably groomed and totally in charge.

Jesse sat on the foot of the unmade bed, smoke rising from his untended Camel. He looked at Claire, who was coiled. Her hands under the table. Steam came from the coffee cup amongst the breakfast mess.

"So that there will be no accidents, Miss Seekins, please put your gun on the table and keep your hands in plain sight."

Eyes went to Claire. Hands hovered around waists as she brought the Mossberg slowly out from under the table, laid it across the plastic dishes, and took her coffee with both hands, as if to warm them.

"Thank you."

Jesse spoke the obvious. "Who are you? How do you know our names?"

"None of that is important, Mr. Langdon. What is important is that you listen to what I have to say. If at the end you do not understand then, by all means, ask a question. Perhaps we will be able to answer one."

He stood straight and looked to Jesse, then to

Claire, and back again. "What I have to say is brief and to the point. It's time for you both to go home. You will be safe. Mr. Santee no longer poses any threat to either of you. He has been dealt with.

"What you have are memories, no more than memories. Nothing will come of the recent past. You will *not* reveal any information regarding Mr. Santee or his activities. All evidence is locked up, suppressed, classified or destroyed. There is no corroborating information." He reached into his breast pocket, removed the disks Jesse had mailed thirty minutes earlier, then returned them to his pocket. "It would be the height of foolishness and conceit to stir this stew. Deniability is one-hundred percent."

"Who are you?"

"It doesn't matter who we are or how we found you. All that matters is that you are now free to return to your lives. It is over and you're safe." He was finished. "Good day to you both."

The man closest to the knob opened the door and stood aside while his boss swept out into the Friday afternoon, then he followed. The other one covered Jesse and Claire, then shut the door behind him.

CHAPTER 35

"YOU THINK IT'S true, what they said?" Jesse was still sitting on the bed amongst the rumpled blanket and sheet. He leaned to the table to flick an ash into Styrofoam.

"We could call someone, see what happened. Maybe Biano knows what's going on." Claire was brushing her hair, quite unconcerned.

Jesse put out his smoke, moved to the bedside table and picked up the phone. From memory, Claire recited Biano's mother's number. He dialed and waited.

Biano's mother, in broken English, said he was outside and to hold on while she got him. Jesse stared absently into Claire's eyes as he waited. Biano came on the line, sounding excited.

"So, *mi amigo*, you're alive. Good. Very good. And Claire is safe too? Yes?"

"Slow down, Biano. We're fine. What's going on?

We just had a strange visit. Men dressed and acting like federal agents. Tell me what's happening."

Biano was breathless. "La Primavera exploded a little before noon this morning and burned to the ground. Carla and Mrs. Sanchez had been called away. They are blessed, those women. The only one in the house was Santee. He was found dead in the wreckage."

"How do you know this?"

"Hell, man, it's all over the news. A Miami mansion blowing up? A rich guy's body being removed? Live cameras on the scene."

Jesse did the calculation. He must have been the last one to hear Santee alive. The explosion itself probably ended their conversation.

Biano continued, "They're saying it was a gas leak. Everything is gone. The business is finished. Sam called to tell me cops seized the InterRegional hangar. No flight tomorrow, obviously."

"What about Coley?"

"I don't know. He doesn't exactly report to me." Biano laughed. "He was back from his trip to the coast. Santee, he and I all ate supper at La Primavera last night. I came home to Mama and he remained. That's the last I saw of either of them."

"Did you check on the accounts?" Jesse caught Claire's eye and they both raised their eyebrows.

"That's the best part! My account was still there. I moved my money this morning. I assume yours is accessible, and I suggest you don't let it grow any moss. Gas leak, my ass. They're on top of us. We've been shut down hard. Curious that it happened so soon after you and Claire took off..."

Jesse let that pass. "What are you going to do, Biano?"

"Lay so low I'm flat. Me and Mama are headed somewhere far south, take a vacation the rest of our lives. How about you and Claire? What are you going to do?"

"We haven't discussed that. Biano, you saved my life. I will never forget. Thank you. And if you do talk to Coley, will you thank him for shooting high? He'll know what I mean. And good luck." Fuckin' fantastic. Teared up, even!

"Sure I will. And you're welcome. I'm sure you would've done the same for me. *Vaya con Dios, amigo, y buena suerte.*" Biano hung up.

Jesse cradled the phone. "It really is over. Santee blew up in La Primavera this morning. Everyone else is okay. The money is still in the Caymans. Coley is gone."

Claire let out a little laugh. "What a morning! From alive to dead to alive, all in the course of a couple hours."

Jesse rose. "All this is going to take some settling. I feel like the world is spinning around and I'm getting dizzy watching."

"You should go out to the airport. The drive and communing with the plane will do you good. When you come back, we can discuss what to do."

"You don't want to join me?"

"Nah. That's flyboy stuff. You don't need me hanging over your shoulder. You'll be back in a jiffy. Then we can go for a walk, figure things out." She got up and started on the breakfast mess.

"Okay." Jesse was too disoriented to do anything but take her direction. He got the keys and walked to the door.

Claire came up and took his head in her hands. "You'll be all right, Jesse. You did good. You saved us. And it looks like you set much bigger plans in motion. You're a good man. Just don't get lost." She laughed and kissed him sweetly on the lips.

Jesse drove to the airport. Thoughts swirled about his millions, about Claire in the motel, about his wife and children in Maine. The plane had been moved into the flight line and was attracting no interest. The right sponson tank had a bullet hole in it.

When he returned, the room was clean. And empty. There was little sign anyone had been there— except for the note on the bed. *We were told to return to our lives. Yours is in Maine. God speed, Jesse. I love you too. Claire.*

Jesse sat down heavily on the freshly made bed and tears came to his eyes.

When he paid the bill, the clerk, an older man and probably the teenager's father, added the charges for two long-distance calls made from the room.

Jesse asked, "Two?"

"Yes sir. One earlier this morning, the other about an hour ago."

Jesse would think later about that first call, the one he didn't make, the one Claire made while he was out shopping, and wonder who she'd spoken to and what was said. Who had she really been working for? But for now, he unconsciously toyed with the Saint Christopher around his neck as he thought about calling flight service and filing a flight plan for home.

Miami Herald, August 13

A classified section of a soon-to-be released national drug strategy calls for expansion of U.S. military training for local forces in three South American countries and allocates $300 million for anti-drug efforts.

8/15 William Bennett says that the drug crisis is the number-one problem and that Americans are in a "wartime mode." He says that the narcotics war can be waged without any new taxes.

The End

I hope you enjoyed this story. I would greatly appreciate you taking a moment to write a review for Amazon. And if you thirst for more, my novel about Maine and lobstermen, *Vacationland*, is available at your local bookstore or from all the usual ebook retailers. Again, thank you for your interest in my work.

Nathaniel Bowditch Goodale comes from a deep seafaring heritage. He is licensed to captain a 100 ton vessel, pilot a single engine flying-boat in instrument conditions, and drive a big rig on the Interstate Highway System. He was a 40 year resident of Waldo County, Maine,  where this story begins. He now resides in Cuenca Ecuador, where he is writing his third novel. He is married and has four children. For more information, you are invited to visit him at www.natgoodale.com.

Thanks - Over and out.